Practical Rules for Cursed Witches

Practical Rules for Cursed Witches

Kayla Cottingham

DELACORTE PRESS

This book contains references to physical and verbal child abuse, along with depictions of parental abandonment, PTSD, minors consuming alcohol, memory loss, and brief gore and violence that may be triggering to some readers.

Text copyright © 2024 by Kayla Cottingham
Jacket art copyright © 2024 by Dani Pendergast
Map art copyright © 2024 by Virginia Allyn
Interior mushroom art and textured background used under license by stock.adobe.com

Visit us on the Web! GetUnderlined.com

Educators and librarians, for a variety of teaching tools, visit us at RHTeachersLibrarians.com

Library of Congress Cataloging-in-Publication Data is available upon request.
ISBN 978-0-593-81397-3 (hardcover) — ISBN 978-0-593-81399-7 (ebook)

The text of this book is set in 11.3-point Adobe Garamond Pro.

Editor: Hannah Hill
Cover designer: Ray Shappell
Interior designer: Cathy Bobak
Copy editor: Colleen Fellingham
Managing editor: Tamar Schwartz
Production editor: Tracy Heydweiller

Printed in the United States of America
10 9 8 7 6 5 4 3 2 1
First Edition

Random House Children's Books supports the First Amendment and celebrates the right to read.

To anyone working to break the cycle of generational trauma: you're stronger than you know.

And to Forrest and Jesaia, the first family I ever found.

PROLOGUE

The sleepy town of Kitfield was the perfect reprieve before an adventure.

Someone else's adventure, anyway.

Kitfield sat in a gentle cradle of land between mountain and sea. It was the sort of place where travelers and witches stayed overnight on their way into the city or the dark shadow of the woods, depending on where their journeys took them. In that sense, Kitfield was a place where one could meet a hundred new people in a week yet remain quite lonely, as any new friend would stay only until the sun rose and the road opened up in front of them.

For the town's residents, this meant a lifetime of fleeting smiles, stories, and goodbyes. No attachments, no strings.

That last bit was how Delilah Bea came to, well, be.

It started one stormy night in Kitfield when a man—the townspeople had yet to discover whether he was a simple traveler or a witch—entered the Sunflower Bakery on Wisteria Street after it had closed. The bell above the door rang, cutting through the tinny buzz of jazz playing softly on the radio on the wooden countertop. Only then did the woman inside realize she'd forgotten to lock up at nine, as she had every other day for five years.

Many would later say this forgetful moment was, in fact, the hand of fate.

Charlotte Bea—a waifish, bright-eyed little thing with a chain of flowers woven into her hair—was boxing up a cake to take home when the bell rang. She spun to discover a man in ragged clothes braced against the doorframe, gasping for breath. Rainwater pooled in the entryway below him, stained pink.

Here the townspeople diverge in their storytelling. Some say the man collapsed in a heap and Charlotte somehow summoned an incredible burst of strength that allowed her to drag him into the bakery. Others say he came in of his own accord and tipped his hat to her quite pleasantly, considering the stab wound in his abdomen.

One way or another, with a bleeding man on her doorstep, Charlotte Bea did the only thing she could think to do: she brought him to the back of the bakery, turned on the lights, and went to work stitching up the wound.

The man was lucky he'd stumbled into the Sunflower Bakery. It was only a part-time gig of Charlotte's while she studied medicine with the local doctor. It wasn't the fancy sort of schooling one might expect, with a university and a degree, but Kitfield wasn't the sort of place where anyone cared about the bells and whistles. Charlotte closed his wound, sanitized it, and tempted him back to the world of the living with some day-old pastries, all in less than an hour.

"I'm surprised to find you toiling away in a place like this," he told her as he munched on one of her lemon bars. She'd been told she made them too sour, but he didn't seem to mind. "It's not often you stumble upon a baker who can stitch up wounds so skillfully. Much less one with a smile as beautiful as yours."

"It's only for a bit longer," she said, blushing at his compliment. "I'll be a doctor soon."

"No, no," he argued. "Not this place. *This* place." He gestured to the town at large. "Kitfield. This can't be all there is for you."

Charlotte had never considered that anything else might be for her. Kitfield was her home, her mother's home—everyone in her matrilineal history had lived here.

She said as much to the strange man. She'd been forced—certainly forced, as she was a lady, after all—to remove his shirt to reach the wound, and he'd yet to slip it back on as he lingered at a café table. The rain had dried from his bare torso save for a few tiny droplets that had fallen from his curly brown hair onto his shoulders. They shone in the low light like a tiny constellation dotted across his skin.

"But the whole world needs doctors. You could go anywhere."

"*Kitfield* needs a doctor." She handed him another lemon bar, which he gratefully accepted, nearly shoving the entire thing in his mouth at once. Charlotte giggled.

She went on: "And I'm happy here. I don't need the thrill of the city or some grand adventure out in the woods or at sea. Some lives are meant to be quiet."

He reached out, gently stroking the curve of her cheek. "Not yours."

At this point in the story, ladies in hat shops whispering the tale would begin to giggle, while men at the local pub would bump elbows and waggle their brows. They didn't mean to shame Charlotte—she was an adult, of course, capable of making her own decisions—but no gossip was more fun to whisper about in a town like Kitfield than a one-night affair with a witch.

At the time, Charlotte didn't know he was a witch. She certainly didn't know he was a famous one with a bounty on his head. It wasn't a particularly pressing issue at the moment, or so she would say.

Regardless, like all the others before him, the strange man left the next morning. Charlotte made him coffee, filled a basket with lemon bars, and bid him farewell. He disappeared down the road toward the train station, nothing but a small dot on the horizon. Barely a whisper of a memory.

However, it became apparent soon after that something strange was happening to Charlotte. After a lesson at the doctor's office, Charlotte stood to discover tiny pink asters had sprouted beneath her feet. She had to start closing her window at night because birds kept flying in and nestling into her blankets with her. People at the farmers market spilled their deepest secrets to her, unprompted, while she was considering tomatoes.

"I can't imagine what's going on," she told the doctor one morning. "It's not like a normal person can become a witch overnight."

"Certainly not," the doctor agreed. She shot a glance at Charlotte. "Tell me, dear, have you been feeling ill recently?"

"A bit sick," Charlotte admitted. "In the mornings."

The doctor nodded. As she stood to retrieve her tools, she patted Charlotte's shoulder and gave her a warm smile. "Congratulations," she said. "It's a witch."

CHAPTER ONE

Rule #12: Even magical secrets are no match for small-town gossip.

"When you channel your magic," Ruby Flick, the Kitfield village witch, explained, "it's not about force. It's allowing raw magic to flow into whatever medium you're working with—be that packing a tea bag or performing a piece of music. Slow but sure."

Delilah Bea, whose face was scrunched up as she drew magic from her chest and out through her fingers, exhaled and dropped her hands. She glared up at the ceiling. "I know, I just . . ."

"Lack patience?" Ruby guessed.

Delilah took on a look of melodramatic betrayal. "Me? *No.*"

"Check it out," said Clarissa, Ruby's fifteen-year-old daughter. Delilah paused in her attempt to shove tea leaves into a little gossamer bag and found that Clarissa had already tied off her own tea bag and placed it in water. As the tea steeped, curls of red from the hibiscus she'd added darkened the liquid to almost the color of blood. The steam rising from it curled into little heart shapes before fading into the air.

"Always the theatrics with you," Delilah said, chuckling. She'd known Clarissa most of her life. While they were friends, their two-year age gap had always made Delilah view her more as a little sibling than a peer.

"Let's test it," Ruby said. She reached for her daughter's teacup and took a careful sip. She paused, tasting. "You were going for a spell that mimics the feeling of romantic love?"

Clarissa nodded, eyes bright. She looked exactly like her mother, save the crow's-feet and smile lines. They shared the same long blond hair and green eyes, and the faint smell of rosemary Clarissa gave off when she practiced her magic was almost identical to her mother's trademark scent.

Ruby inhaled, closed her eyes, then exhaled. "This is closer to upliftment. But"—she pushed the cup back toward her daughter—"still lovely work."

Clarissa's face fell a bit. Delilah quickly said, "Hey, don't worry about it. It's hard to channel an emotion-based spell if you've never felt the thing you're trying to channel."

Clarissa's cheeks reddened. "I know what romantic love feels like."

Delilah and Ruby both raised their eyebrows and said, "Oh?"

Clarissa's eyes widened, and her blush only grew.

Delilah bit back a smile. *Puppy love—how cute.* "And who exactly are you in love with? Don't tell me it's Annamarie's daughter—she may have great arms from kneading dough at the bakery, but she *always* smells like yeast."

"I shouldn't have said anything," Clarissa muttered.

Before Delilah could press her more, a knock sounded on the door.

A voice called, "Hello? It's Charlotte." The door pushed open the next moment, the little bell attached to it jingling.

Delilah's mother stuck her head in. "Am I early?"

"No, we were just wrapping up," Ruby said, collecting the piles of different leaves and buds the three witches had been using to concoct spelled teas. "Come on in."

Charlotte Bea stepped inside. She wore her slightly graying sandy hair up in a bun with a few pieces loose. The gray eyes she shared with Delilah were hidden behind round glasses that she'd only started needing in the last couple years. She tucked her hands into the pockets of her loose canvas pants—the ones she usually wore for her shifts at the clinic—and leaned against the wall with a small smile.

Ruby lived in a cottage at the edge of the woods outside Kitfield. For generations, it had been the home of the village witch, whose title had been passed down from parent to child, just as Ruby would pass it to Clarissa someday. Thorny vines and twining flowers cloaked the old bungalow in a blanket of green and pink and white as soon as spring came. At the moment, just the four women were inside; but often on days like this, multiple townsfolk would have crossed the lake that divided the cottage from the edge of town to ask Ruby for custom spelled teas and brews.

Delilah began packing her things into her shoulder bag and told Clarissa, "You know, if you're looking for a chance to ask someone out, you could always do it at my birthday party this evening. I'll be your wingwoman."

Clarissa muttered something under her breath that Delilah couldn't hear and punctuated it with a sigh.

"This is a bit bittersweet," Ruby said as Delilah rose out of her chair and shouldered her bag of magic tools—chalk for drawing runes, a wooden spoon for spelled baking, herbs and ingredients for teas or simmer pots, and parchment for notes.

"Last magic lesson before you leave on your Calling," Charlotte agreed, smile not quite meeting her eyes.

"I'm going to miss our lessons together," Clarissa added. "You'll have to send me plenty of letters about your Calling so I know what to expect when I go on mine."

Ruby asked, "How do you feel about it, Delilah?"

"Honestly? Overwhelmed," Delilah said, rubbing the back of her neck. "I'm trying to think more about this evening and less about the fact that the Council is about to show up. You're both coming tonight, right?"

Ruby nodded. "It would be wrong to send you out into the world without a proper goodbye." She came to Delilah's side and took her hand, holding it between her palms. "You're going to do great things out there, Delilah. So long as you're patient with yourself."

Delilah sputtered a laugh. "Because I'm famously good at that." She shook her head. "But thank you. I appreciate it."

The mothers and daughters quickly said their goodbyes. Delilah and Charlotte headed out the door to where the lake lapped at the shore not far from the Flicks' cottage. Charlotte had pulled their canoe onto the grass. She sat in the front while Delilah pushed them off from the back, then jumped in, her collection of magic-casting objects clanging around in her shoulder bag.

"If I were the village witch," Delilah said as she gave the canoe one final push away from the shore with her oar, "I'd build a road."

"But think of how much mother-daughter bonding time we'd miss if we didn't do this," Charlotte said with a laugh.

"We could bond in a car," Delilah pointed out.

"*Cars,*" Charlotte spat. She shook her head, blond hair springing loose from her bun. Delilah had inherited very few of her mother's features, a fact that made her increasingly bitter with every passing year. Her mother was small and slim with the face of a pixie, whereas Delilah had inherited her father's height, thick frame, dark, curly hair, and obtrusively large nose. Every time she saw him grinning at her from the front page of the newspaper, she silently cursed his weirdly strong genetics.

"We don't need that kind of thing," Charlotte added. "No point."

"But a car would mean we could leave Kitfield," Delilah pointed out. "We could go anywhere! Maybe as far as Gellingham—you could finally take those medical classes at the university we always hear about on the radio. Get a legitimate medical license so you could practice in the city."

After a brief pause, Charlotte mused, "Your father's in Gellingham."

Silence overtook them. The sounds of the oars parting the water and the crows shrieking in the pine trees that surrounded

Silverside Lake weren't enough to drown out the rush of thoughts that echoed in Delilah's head.

Before she could start off on her usual tangent about how much she hated her father, her mother said, "I'm sorry, again, that you've never been able to meet him. That he never got to teach you magic." Her eyes dropped, mouth curving into a small frown. Her rowing became weaker. "I'm sorry I could never teach you magic."

Delilah stopped rowing, and her fist tightened around the top of the oar. They were in the middle of the lake now, a breeze lightly dimpling the glittering water. Her mother stared forward over the bow of the boat, hiding her face.

"That's not your fault," Delilah reminded her. "He's the one with the gall to totally ignore my existence for all these years."

"I just . . ." Charlotte exhaled. "If I were a witch, I wouldn't have to ask Ruby to teach you. It feels like having to ask someone else to give my child the birds-and-bees talk."

Delilah choked on a laugh. "*Mom,* it's not like that at all—"

"I'm serious," Charlotte said. She shook her head. "I know she's taking a risk teaching you. I know that in a town like Kitfield, having another witch could put Clarissa's future in jeopardy. But I still asked her, despite that, to teach you. And now if you want to practice magic, you'll have to leave."

Silence overtook them again. The birds sang and the water lapped at the side of the canoe.

It was true, but they'd never acknowledged it out loud. Since Clarissa was considered Ruby's official apprentice, Delilah would never be Kitfield's witch. Not unless the public's opinion of witches—tainted by years of unrestricted witchcraft and inter-coven conflict that had resulted in its fair share of collateral damage—improved and groups of witches stopped making them ill at ease. Or if Delilah challenged Clarissa to an old-fashioned magical duel and beat her, effectively evicting her from the town. While it was entirely possible she could beat the younger witch, it would be a massive betrayal of trust to both Ruby and Clarissa. They'd made the unspoken promise long ago that once Delilah's training was over, she'd either become the village witch of another town or stay in Kitfield and not practice.

Or go to the big city. There the public attitude toward witches was more trusting, and casual magic and enchantments were considered the norm. There any witch with a license could practice magic for money.

Delilah bit her lip. "I . . . could always stay here. And try something else. Maybe get a job at the Sunflower Bakery and make normal pastries."

Her mother didn't hesitate before she said, "You'd never be happy doing that."

Again, she was right. Magic was Delilah's passion. It always had been, from the time she was a toddler inadvertently casting joy spells through her crayon drawings. She loved being a witch.

But she also loved her mother and Kitfield. And recently it had become more and more apparent that she couldn't have both.

"I feel terrible leaving," Delilah said. "Not just because I'll miss you, but because of our . . ."

She didn't finish the sentence. She didn't need to. What she was referring to was something all the Bea women, for generations and generations, had lingering in the back of their minds all the time. That hollow feeling every time someone shot them a smile or casually touched their arm during a conversation.

Every time someone like Clarissa mentioned falling in love.

Charlotte was silent. She gripped her oar and dipped it into the water, exhaling through her nose. "Let's save this conversation for another time, hmm? It's your birthday, after all." She looked over her shoulder and offered her daughter a watery smile. "We can worry about the future another day."

Delilah hesitated, but said, "Yeah. All right." She jutted her chin toward the basket in the center of the canoe. "You think we should make a dark chocolate torte to go with the raspberries you picked?"

Joy sparked in Charlotte's eyes. "Oh, *absolutely.*"

They rowed the canoe the rest of the way across the lake, turning off onto a lily pad–speckled waterway. They beached the canoe on the grass and dragged it onto the shore together— Delilah doing most of the lifting, as she was a fair amount bigger and stronger than her mother.

"I'll put this away," Delilah called to her mother. "Would you mind preheating the oven for me in the meantime?"

Charlotte took the basket and nodded. The edge of the lake was about forty feet from the small cottage the two of them shared. Ivy encased it, trimmed back only at the windows and doors. The open shutters were painted light blue with little yellow flower de-tails Delilah had added when she was younger. Facing the outer ring of Kitfield, the street beyond it recently becoming more filled with cars than ever before, the cottage felt like a barrier between the small-town bustle and the magic on the other side of the lake.

"See you inside!" Charlotte called.

Delilah waved to her, then grabbed the canoe's pull rope, dragging it toward the shed—careful to avoid flattening her mother's flower garden. She made it just a few steps before the wind suddenly changed.

A smell hit her. Within seconds she was gagging, covering her mouth and nose with her hand.

It was like nothing she'd ever smelled before: a bizarre mix of decaying flesh, peat, and earthy rot. Her eyes watered. She forced herself to push the canoe into the shed before closing the doors and using both hands to block her nose and mouth. After a second, she recognized the scent.

A curse, and a deadly one at that.

She cast a quick look around, at the edge of the lake where the lily pads floated lazily, the yard dotted with flowers, the woods—

For the briefest second, Delilah saw a flash of movement. She turned in time to see a figure vanish into the trees.

As it disappeared, the stench began to fade.

Delilah, shoulders tensed and nostrils flaring, backed her way to the cottage door and slipped inside.

"Everything okay?" her mother asked as Delilah came into the kitchen.

She absently touched her nose. "Yeah. It's . . . nothing, I'm sure."

Something told her that wasn't true.

That night, after Delilah had baked a lovely torte, changed into a long, belted skirt, and tucked a button-down shirt into it, she left with her mother for the Landsmeet Pub. Just off Kitfield's central square, the pub boasted rooms for travelers on the upper level and a bar down below. It was a stone structure, but the windows and doors were made of hawthorn wood—a holdover from the old days, when people feared witches enough to decorate their homes with one of the few materials that could block their magic. Most of the houses in Kitfield had it built into them somehow. Delilah remembered what a massive pain it had been for Charlotte to tear out the hawthorn parts of their cottage when Delilah was little so she could practice her magic at home.

The pub's windows revealed people already at tables, swigging beer and laughing. Golden ale sloshed to the floor in bubbling clusters like sea foam. A wall of sound hit Delilah as she opened the doors, everyone inside shouting her name and wishing her a happy birthday.

A smile crept across Delilah's face. The pub was packed with family friends and people from school—an uncommon sight for the Landsmeet, which mostly catered to travelers. Most people were drinking merrily while others danced to the music from the band playing in the corner. The bar was decorated with summer blooms; the walls featured images of Kitfield locals over the years, including pictures of Charlotte as a child with her mother and grandmother. A few mounted deer heads had been fitted with flower crowns for the occasion, and green swaths of fabric hung in waves from the ceiling.

"Do you like it?" Charlotte asked.

Delilah hugged her. "You've outdone yourself."

"Well, you only turn seventeen once," Charlotte said.

Delilah squeezed her mother tighter. This time she caught the scent rolling off her skin—the one she'd known her whole life. It was old and musty, like a room locked up and untouched for decades, filled with aging, brittle paper and old leather. It might be unpleasant to another person, but Delilah had learned to find comfort in the smell.

Even if, ultimately, it was evidence of something that had haunted the Bea family for years.

"Darling," Charlotte said, "let's get you some ale."

Delilah grinned. The drinking age in Celdwyn was seventeen. "Get me something that doesn't taste like piss."

"All ale tastes like piss. But this one is raspberry piss."

"Perfect."

Charlotte came back with a pint for each of them, and they knocked their glasses together before taking hearty swigs. The tart raspberry flavor masked the fermentation enough that Delilah went back for a second taste. Her mother looped her arm through hers and led her to seats in front of the band. Ruby and Clarissa were already at the table, Ruby drinking from a stein full of ale while Clarissa enjoyed an elderflower soda.

"Thanks for saving us seats," Charlotte said.

Delilah and Ruby clicked their glasses together while Ruby laughed. "Like I said, we need a proper goodbye."

Clarissa frowned as she took a sip from her drink. She stared at her thumb as she rubbed a circle onto the glass's side. "I'm going to miss you."

Delilah chuckled and punched her friend's shoulder lightly. "Come on, Clary. Don't be a sap."

"Ow!" Clarissa shook her head, rolling her eyes. Under her breath, she added, "Why are you like this?"

Onstage, the squeal of a fiddle mixed with the tin whistle and bagpipe. It was a traditional dance tune, the kind that had people rising out of their seats. Delilah stood while everyone else at the table stayed seated.

Delilah held her hand out to Clarissa. "Dance with me?"

Clarissa's cheeks turned pink. "M-me?"

"Why not?" Delilah asked, hauling her out of her seat. "Come on—looks like plenty of people from school are here." She narrowed her eyes and shot Clarissa a sideways grin, waggling her eyebrows. If there was one thing Delilah enjoyed, it was playing matchmaker for her fellow townsfolk. "I can help you cut in with your crush. Do you see them?"

"Um—well—yes—"

"Perfect." Delilah grinned. "Let's go get 'em."

Clarissa didn't have time to argue before Delilah pulled her onto the floor. A few people from school called Delilah's name and waved as she shot them a smile. She spun and put one hand on Clarissa's waist and intertwined their fingers with the other. When Delilah met her gaze to say something, Clarissa's face was deep pink, lips pursed and eyes wide as if she were holding her breath.

Delilah tilted her head to the side. *Does she have a fever or something? I've never seen her get this pink.* "You okay?"

Clarissa nodded furiously. "Fine! Fine. I'm fine."

"All right." Delilah chuckled and spun her around, making Clarissa yelp. Delilah caught her, side-smiled, and whispered, "If you say so."

The music sped up, mixing with the sound of feet stomping against the hardwood. People twirled across the dance floor, some better than others but all well-versed in this particular traditional dance. Delilah and Clarissa moved to the center of the floor, Delilah swinging her partner around faster than before. Her heart soared. She loved this place, these people—she couldn't ask for a better way to celebrate. Even with Clarissa clumsily stepping on her feet and cursing to herself, all Delilah could think about was how much she was going to miss Kitfield.

She'd always dreamed of seeing the world, but that didn't stop her from preemptively missing home.

The fiddle music picked up in double time, and Clarissa's skirt twirled and bloomed like a white rose around her legs. Delilah's hand held tight to her waist, never threatening to come loose. After a minute, the music slowed, and Delilah met Clarissa face to face again. Clarissa was breathless, forehead slick with sweat.

Don't think about the future, Delilah reminded herself. *You're here now. Enjoy it while it lasts.*

Hoping to distract herself, she asked Clarissa, "So, have you spotted your crush yet?"

Clarissa blinked and looked away. "Well—yes."

"Oh, great!" Delilah glanced over her shoulder. "Where are they? I figure we can slide in next to them real smooth, strike up a little conversation, then you can ask them to dance—"

"You!" Clarissa suddenly burst out. Delilah's eyes snapped back to her as she managed to turn even redder than before. "It's you. I'm in love with *you*, Delilah."

Suddenly, Delilah felt as if the two of them were in a bubble, blocking out the sound of the band and the people dancing around them. Delilah's hands loosened, her smile slowly shrinking. Clarissa's words felt like an icicle that had been stabbed into Delilah's heart, cold radiating through her with each pump of blood. Her shoulders wilted.

Of course this is how I close out my last night here.

"Delilah?" Clarissa said. Her face paled. "Wh-what's wrong?"

Delilah's hands dropped. "I'm . . . so sorry, Clarissa. But you're not."

Clarissa blinked. "What?"

"You're not in love with me." Delilah didn't say it with any malice—it was purely factual. She sighed. "That's why you couldn't make that romantic love spell today. Whatever it is you feel about me, it's not love." She shrugged. "It's all right. It's not your fault."

Clarissa's face was totally blank. "Wait . . . *what?* That doesn't make any sense."

"It's a complicated issue—"

"Are you saying there's something wrong with me?"

"No! Of course not." Delilah rubbed the back of her neck. "It's just that I'm . . ."

"You're what?" Clarissa shook her head. "Do you only like boys?"

Delilah blushed, looking away with a laugh. "Oh—no—gender isn't a factor—"

"Then *what?*"

"Well—" Delilah choked on the words as Clarissa's eyes welled with tears. She'd known Clarissa for years, but even after all their time doing magic lessons together, Delilah had still never told her friend everything about herself. Some secrets were just too taboo, too heavy, to casually mention unless she absolutely had to.

But seeing the sadness and confusion in Clarissa's eyes, something in Delilah broke.

"Because," she admitted, "I'm cursed."

Clarissa's eyes widened. "*Cursed?* You mean the rumors about your family are true?"

"Rumors?" Delilah repeated. "What rumors?"

"That if you fall in love with a Bea woman, you die?"

A few people dancing around them turned and stared. Delilah quickly faked a laugh to throw them off, doing her best to look as if Clarissa had told a spectacular joke. The dancers paused but kept moving while Clarissa stood with her jaw hanging.

Damn it, Delilah thought, faking a broad smile. *Of course there's no such thing as a secret in Kitfield.*

She still vividly remembered the day her mother sat her down and explained the Bea family curse to her. It had all started with Delilah's great-great-great-grandmother, who had a passionate affair with a traveling witch; when he returned months later to propose to her, he discovered that she was already married to another man and had a baby on the way. The witch had been so furious that he cursed the Bea women so no one could ever fall in love with them—at least, not without tragic consequences. Since then, each generation of Bea women had remained unmarried, though they always seemed to wind up with a single daughter from some loveless fling. Delilah just so happened to be the most recent in a long line of mothers and daughters incapable of being truly loved.

Delilah lowered her voice. "People don't *die* if they fall in love with us—that would be a little extreme, don't you think? It's more that they . . . well . . . forget us."

"But I haven't forgotten you," Clarissa pointed out. "A-and there was that boy—"

That boy. Delilah did her best not to wince at the mention of *that boy.*

Theo Fletcher. Big brown eyes, tight curls shaved on the sides and woven into dreads up top, and rich, dark brown skin—he'd been the handsomest boy Delilah had ever seen when he arrived in Kitfield for his Calling. Her heart ached as he flickered through her memory, and she nearly winced as she forced the image of him from her mind.

Delilah put a finger to Clarissa's lips to quiet her. She whispered, "If you had truly fallen in love with me, I would have vanished from your memory the second you realized it. I'd be a stranger to you now."

Just like I was to him.

Before Clarissa could voice her next thought, something caught Delilah's attention. The smell of magic had suddenly hit her. Three different kinds: one earthy, with notes of macadamia nuts, one fresh like honeydew, a third sweet and floral, like violet syrup.

"Delilah Bea?" a woman asked.

Delilah turned to find three witches standing behind her. Her heart hammered. She'd rarely been in the presence of more than two other witches at once, save for when traveling covens passed through Kitfield, usually on their way to larger towns on Celdwyn's southern coast. That sort of thing was always the source of local gossip for days afterward, given the general unease outside witches caused. They hadn't earned the town's trust as Ruby and Clarissa had, and they didn't come from well-loved family lines like Delilah's.

This coven was made up of a man and two women, all dressed in traditional witches' traveling cloaks with matching gold clasps at their throats. Each clasp was shaped like a twin moon and sun—the moon being symbolic of witches and the sun of non-magic folk, representing the era of peace that the Witches' Council and its rules had created.

Delilah choked back an anxious laugh. The vintage cloaks looked, admittedly, a little funny compared with everyone else's modern skirts and slacks—as if the witches were dressing up for Kitfield's autumn equinox costume contest.

"That's, uh"—Delilah forced a smile—"that's me."

"We're here on state business," the man said. Nearly everything about him struck Delilah as square—he may well have been the squarest man she'd ever seen, with pale skin, a sharp, stubbly chin, and a body hinged on right angles. He wore a suit under his cloak, and his hair was slicked back, accenting the squareness of his head. She was, to some degree, impressed. *It's as if someone put a curse on a milk crate and now it has to wear silly capes and pay taxes.*

"We're here to present you with your Calling," the woman on his left said. She had the floral magic, and the rich brown skin beside her eyes and mouth was crinkled with smile lines. "You're to arrive at the central square tomorrow at a quarter to noon. You'll be given a chance to present your own task, or you'll be assigned one by us. Do you understand?"

Delilah nodded, trying not to let the spike of adrenaline that instantly hit her bloodstream show on her face. *Tomorrow?* Ruby had said they'd arrive on her birthday, but given that Kitfield was so far from their headquarters in Gellingham, she'd hoped she would have a little more time. "Yes, ma'am."

"Have your things packed," the woman said. "There's no guarantee where your Calling will take you."

Delilah nodded again. "U-understood."

The third person, a small, pixie-like woman with short black hair and gold-toned light skin, patted Delilah's shoulder apologetically. "Sorry to interrupt your party, dear. It's just procedure."

Delilah didn't know what to say, so she just shrugged and muttered something along the lines of *c'est la vie*. She glanced around the room—most people had stopped to stare. Charlotte had risen from her chair. Ruby, meanwhile, offered Delilah a sympathetic look. Clarissa was still a little teary, mouth closed tightly and eyes pinned on Delilah.

Delilah cleared her throat and told the witches in front of her, "I'm, uh, I'm gonna go take a walk. Get some air. I guess I'll see you in the morning."

The witches didn't say anything, but as Delilah made her way to the door, her mother called, "Delilah! Hold on—"

Delilah didn't stop, just walked until the sound of the pub and the smell of everyone's magic faded behind her.

She kept walking aimlessly into the night.

CHAPTER TWO

Rule #14: A good witch always has something
up their (tasseled) sleeve.

When Charlotte returned home from the pub, Delilah was curled up on the floor eating raspberry torte directly from the serving dish with a spoon.

"Oh, dear," Charlotte whispered.

Delilah pointed to the cake and wiggled her fingers. "Want some? I cast a spell through it. It's supposed to trigger pleasant nostalgia."

Charlotte paused for a moment before walking to the kitchen, grabbing a fork, and joining her daughter on the floor. She stabbed into a raspberry and a sliver of cake, popping it in her mouth and nodding. "Ooh, that *is* pleasant. You've outdone yourself."

"Sorry I left the party," Delilah said, wiping chocolate off her face with her fist. "I just . . . got really overwhelmed."

"What happened with Clarissa?"

"Said she's in love with me."

Charlotte's eyes widened. *"Oh."*

"Right? Big fucking *oh*." Delilah took another bite. It tasted like a summer day a year ago when she and her mother took the canoe out to a swim dock in the middle of Silverside Lake and had a picnic with wildflower-honey buns and sparkling cider before swimming until the sun turned their skin pink.

It almost made her feel less like screaming.

"And you told her about the curse?"

"I did. Apparently, the villagers think people who fall in love with us die."

Charlotte nearly spit out the cake. "They *what?* Goodness, that's worse than the last rumor. Back when I was pregnant with you, people were saying my curse had turned your father into a beetle."

Delilah scoffed. "If only."

"I guess it's probably for the best she knows. Maybe next time the rumors about us will actually be true." Charlotte took another bite, making an exaggerated *mmm* sound behind her closed lips. "Delilah, this torte is incredible. When you become the village witch of another town, they're going to be lining up outside your door to get your enchanted cakes. Ruby was right to let you train as a kitchen witch."

Delilah's mouth quirked into a small smile. "Maybe I'll open a magic bakery as soon as I'm done with my Calling."

"Speaking of, I meant to ask: do you think you'll propose your own task?"

"Yeah. I . . ." Delilah paused. She wasn't sure if she was ready to tell her mother yet. "I do."

Charlotte didn't push. "Do you feel ready?"

"For my Calling? The six-month-long test seventy percent of witches fail and wind up losing their magic over?" Delilah spun her spoon around with a flourish before winking and pointing it at her mom. *"Nope."*

Charlotte chuckled. "I know you hate when I say this, but you really remind me of your father sometimes."

Delilah scoffed. "Mom, you were with him for, like, *eight hours.* And you were sleeping for at least some of it."

Charlotte poorly withheld a laugh, wiggling her eyebrows. "Not much."

Delilah stuck the spoon in her mouth and pantomimed gagging.

"It's a compliment," Charlotte justified. "Your father has a way with people, just like you. He's broken more curses than any other witch in Celdwyn's history. And, most important, you have all his gifts."

Delilah let out a heavy sigh.

Charlotte set her fork down and scooted over to her daughter's side, wrapping her arms around her. "I know it's a lot of pressure, but you're a talented witch, Delilah. And I believe in you."

Delilah hugged her mom back. "I'm gonna miss you."

"Yeah." Charlotte leaned her head into her daughter's shoulder. "I'm gonna miss you too, kid."

That night, the two Bea women fell asleep on the couch, empty torte tray abandoned in the middle of the floor.

The next morning, the rising sun lent a sparkle to Silverside Lake and a vibrant green blush to the early summer leaves. The clock tower in the central square ticked down the minutes until noon, and people began to gather one by one in front of a small stage that had been set up overnight. It was a tradition that a witch's Calling was a public event, especially in small towns, where there might be only one or two in any given generation. It had been established back when the Witches' Council took power a century ago, the hope being that the public setting would help prove to the town a witch intended to serve that they were trustworthy. In Delilah's case, that didn't exactly apply, but it didn't stop the crowds from flocking to get a glimpse of the Council in action.

The Beas left their house at a quarter to noon. Aeroships floated across the cloudless sky, flapping their mechanical wings in a languid wave. Cars puttered around cobblestone street corners, their canvas tops lowered to let the air in. Flowers in the neighbors' planter boxes had grown lush and colorful, and tricolored Celdwynian flags rippled in the breeze atop the buildings, with their green oxidized-copper roofs and balconies.

The shops along Kitfield's main street were open but appeared empty. Most had their doors flung open to let in the breeze and any travelers, though Delilah suspected that most wouldn't be looking to buy knickknacks while the day's grand event was still to come.

As the Beas neared the central square, the crowd began to thicken. People slowly stepped aside as whispers of the women's arrival swept through the square. A path cleared before them, and soon Delilah was staring up at the stage where the square man and the two ladies from the night before waited.

Charlotte took her arm and walked her to the front step. She stopped, then went onto her tiptoes to kiss her daughter's cheek. "Good luck."

Delilah whispered her thanks, stomach flipping.

At that moment, two things happened: the clock struck noon, letting out a thrumming note, and the breeze changed direction. Loose pieces of Delilah's braid ruffled in the wind, and a familiar scent hit her nose. She nearly retched. It was the scent of death and decay and peaty magic that lingered behind their house yesterday.

The smell of a powerful curse.

"Delilah Bea," the square man said, interrupting her gagging. "Step forward."

Delilah cast a final look at her mother before stepping onto the stage. Her heartbeat sped up. The scent of the curse was so close it felt as if the figure she'd seen in the woods must be breathing down her neck. Her gaze swept across the crowd, searching for the source, but she came up empty.

"Are you all right?" the woman with the bright smile from the night before asked. "You look pale."

"Too much ale last night?" the other, stern-faced, guessed.

"N-no, sorry." Delilah steadied herself, breathing through her mouth. She tasted the curse on the air, which made it even worse.

"Then we'll begin," the square man said. He stepped forward, toward the audience, and pressed a finger against his throat. As he did, his eyes began to glow faintly—an easy way to tell when a witch summoned their magic. When he spoke, his voice boomed loudly enough to reach even those at the very back of the crowd.

"Welcome, residents and travelers, to the Calling of Delilah

Bea. My name is Garmond Fetz, and assisting me are Athena Green and Melrose Vince."

"It is a tradition among witches," the kinder-looking of the two women—Athena—continued, speaking at the same volume, "that when a witch reaches seventeen, we must test them before allowing them to practice their magic at large. If a witch finishes their Calling within six months, they'll become a recognized member of our society and be eligible for state sponsorship. If they fail, and prove to be unequipped to handle life as a witch, their magic will be taken away."

"Delilah," Garmond said, staring her down with dagger-like eyes. "Do you accept these terms?"

She swallowed, once again tasting the curse; she could barely focus, it was so strong. When she did manage to speak, it was at the same volume as the others. "Yes. I accept."

"Do you have a proposal for your task?" Athena asked.

Delilah looked out at the crowd. She'd known what her Calling task would be for as long as she'd known she was cursed.

Time to confirm the rumors once and for all.

"I propose a cursebreaking," Delilah said. Her eyes fell to Charlotte, and she took another breath, managing not to choke on the lingering scent. "I intend to break the curse on my family that makes anyone who falls in love with a Bea woman lose their memories of her."

A ripple went through the crowd, and Charlotte sucked in a sharp breath.

The other witches lowered their voices to discuss among themselves. They seemed to be consulting Melrose, who stepped close to Delilah and inhaled deeply. After a moment, Melrose cleared her throat and addressed the crowd.

"The girl is correct," she said. "I can smell a curse on her. Because of this, we verify the merit of her task. If Delilah Bea can break her family curse, she will be welcomed into our ranks."

"If any soul objects to the terms of this Calling," Garmond said, "please speak now."

Delilah's breath caught in her throat.

Then a voice from the crowd announced, "I have an objection."

The crowd roared with surprise. Delilah's eyes rounded as the townsfolk's gazes flitted about, searching for the owner of the voice. It had been clear, loud—as if from the heavens themselves.

No, no, no.

This can't be happening.

"Who speaks?" Garmond's gaze slimmed. "Step forward and make yourself known."

The crowd parted, and a blond boy around Delilah's age stepped forward. Delilah's heart dropped into her stomach.

Suddenly, she knew exactly who the curse she'd smelled yesterday belonged to.

The boy's curls were pulled back into a ponytail, leaving high, delicate cheekbones exposed. He had alabaster skin, as if he hadn't seen the sun in years. His eyes were sunken, shadowed around the edges as if bruised. One was brown, but the other— the left—was a startling, ghostly shade of blue. His clothes looked gaudy and expensive; when Delilah squinted, she noticed *tassels* on his sleeves.

"I invoke the Rite of Mortality," he said. "And I conscript Delilah Bea to perform her Calling by breaking my family curse."

Delilah couldn't stop herself: "I'm sorry, you want me to do *what?*"

"You can't do that!" someone in the crowd called. Others shouted the same thing, slinging doubt and displeasure in the boy's direction. He didn't waver, though.

"Hear me, Councilors," he said. "It's my right."

Delilah spun, expecting to find them ready to shoo him away. But instead, they were exchanging hushed words.

"No." Delilah shook her head, taking a few steps back from the boy. "No! I refuse. I've already decided I'm breaking *my* curse, thank you very—"

"Unfortunately," Melrose cut in, "the Rite of Mortality allows any person suffering from a deadly curse to ask a witch for their assistance in breaking that curse. It's considered the most hallowed type of Calling for any witch to perform."

"And I can't say no?" Delilah's mouth fell open as she shook her head. "That's ridiculous. I shouldn't have to work for this knockoff Lord Tackycoat just because he's cursed!"

Delilah wasn't sure, but she thought she saw the boy blush and mouth, *Tacky . . . coat?*

"You will if you want to keep your magic," Garmond said, crossing his arms across his broad chest. He looked at his fellow Councilors, then at the boy, and asked, "Who invokes this rite?"

"Kieran Pelumbra," he responded.

All three of the Council members went silent. Murmurs of

recognition went through the crowd, as well as doubtful whispers. Delilah narrowed her eyes at him.

"Pelumbra?" she repeated. "Why does that sound familiar?"

"Because the Pelumbras are one of the most prominent families in Celdwyn," Garmond said, stroking his salt-and-pepper chin whiskers. "Wealthy witches with a lot of sway in our government. But I've never heard of a Pelumbra curse."

"I encourage you to spread the word," Kieran said brightly. "My family would *hate* that."

"I can smell it," Melrose said, wrinkling her nose. "He's telling the truth—at least about being cursed. In all my experiences with the Pelumbras, they've never mentioned a Kieran."

"Considering how disgusted you both look, smelling the curse on me," Kieran said, his smile faltering as his eyes darted between Delilah and Melrose, "you can probably guess why."

Delilah righted her face, blushing. Few witches had a nose for magic—it was a rare skill that ran in certain families—but hers had always been particularly acute, occasionally to her detriment.

"But you're the daughter of the greatest cursebreaker in Celdwyn's history," Kieran continued, meeting Delilah's gaze. "It should be easy for you to find a solution."

"Easier said than done," Delilah grumbled. She turned back to Garmond. "So you really mean that? Either I help this guy or I get my magic taken away forever?"

The Councilors exchanged looks. Finally, Garmond said, "Indeed. Those are the terms. Do you accept?"

Delilah let out a deep sigh as the weight of the situation

pressed down on her. She looked at Charlotte, who'd gone as pale as a ghost and likely would have toppled over if nudged. Nothing in her face offered a clear answer.

"Damn it," Delilah hissed through her teeth. Finally, she turned back to the Councilors and said, "You know what? Fine. I'll help Prince Broodyface with his family curse." She curtseyed and cut Kieran a sideways look. "You have my word."

"A decision has been made," Garmond proclaimed as he held his arms out, gesturing to the crowd. "Delilah Bea is hereby tasked with breaking the curse placed upon Kieran Pelumbra and his family. She has a period of six months to complete the Calling. Should the curse go unbroken, or if Kieran should die before its resolution, Delilah will have failed, as is the nature of the Rite of Mortality."

"Oh, great," Delilah muttered under her breath. "Let's not forget that part."

"With this, we conclude our meeting," Melrose said. "Adjourned."

As people shouted their frustrations at the Council witches, who were preparing to take their leave, Delilah and Charlotte slipped away from the town square, fighting their way through the crowd back to their cottage. As soon as Charlotte shut the door behind them, the phone in their kitchen began to ring, and she ran to disconnect it. Even if the caller meant well, she knew that Delilah wouldn't want to speak to anyone.

Charlotte pressed her back to the door, exhaling a breath, while Delilah went to the couch and flopped down on it in a heap.

Charlotte whispered, "This is my fault."

"What do you mean? Did you recruit that guy to hijack my Calling?"

Charlotte shook her head. "No, I . . . I shouldn't have been public about who your father is. I knew his status would impact you eventually. I just didn't think word would ever get out of Kitfield."

"It was bound to happen somehow. Better to be honest about it." Delilah grabbed a pillow and shoved her face into it, moaning.

Charlotte observed her daughter for a moment before saying, "I'll make tea."

Delilah closed her eyes and tried to focus on her breathing while Charlotte set their copper kettle over a flame. She willed herself to wake up from this nightmare and go back to the real world, where she was done with her uninterrupted Calling ceremony and ready to start figuring out how to break her own curse.

She was supposed to break the Bea curse to become a full-fledged witch, not get recruited by some stranger to break a curse she'd never heard of.

And lose her magic forever if she didn't.

By the time Charlotte returned with the tea and sat down on the couch beside her daughter, Delilah had brought her heart rate back to normal, even if her mind was still racing. Charlotte placed a mug in front of her daughter and took a sip from her own.

Delilah gathered the mug in her hands, pressing her palms against the sides. "I'm so sorry I told everyone about our curse,

Mom. All I wanted was a chance to break it, but now everyone knows the truth and it's not even my Calling."

Charlotte exhaled, pinching the skin between her brows. "You have nothing to be sorry for. People will gossip for a day or two and get over it. It's not like we're Gellingham nobles or anything."

"That's true. But—I'm still going to break it," Delilah said. She began to undo her braid to keep her hands busy. "My official Calling might be this other nonsense, but that isn't going to stop me."

"Sweetheart, it's okay." Charlotte put a hand on her daughter's knee and met her eyes. "Focus on your Calling. Our curse has been around for hundreds of years. You have the rest of your life to break it—and plenty more resources if you pass your Calling."

Delilah nodded to herself. It was a good point: once she was able to practice magic as an official, state-approved witch, she'd be able to access resources—things like restricted archives, spell-casting materials provided by the Council, state-funded travel—that would make it much easier to break a curse. Still, she didn't appreciate having to wait.

She muttered, "You're right, I suppose."

"Plus, if this boy is telling the truth and he is a Pelumbra . . . well, they're one of the wealthiest families in Celdwyn." Charlotte winked at her daughter. "Might make a rich friend in the process. I bet he'll pay you *handsomely* if everything goes well."

Delilah's eyes lit up. "Ooh, you're right. Maybe I can buy us a *car*."

Charlotte groaned melodramatically. "What is it with you and cars?"

The two of them managed a laugh just as a knock sounded at the door.

Charlotte shouted, "We're not home!"

"It's Kieran," a voice said. "Can I please speak to Delilah?"

"She's fled the country," Charlotte shouted back as Delilah got up to get the door. "Left you here. Gone abroad to sell magic sweets."

"Mom," Delilah reprimanded, but she was smiling. She shook her head while her mother held up her hands and made a faux guilty face.

Delilah smelled the curse before she even opened the door, but it flooded in as soon as she did. She gagged outright, unable to hold it in.

Kieran raised an eyebrow that was a few shades darker than his sandy-blond hair. "Well, all right, then. Hello again to you too."

"Come in," Delilah managed, voice thick as she tried not to retch. When Kieran just stood there staring at her, she added, "Look, I'm sorry, but you have the worst-smelling curse in history. It's nothing personal."

Kieran paused for a moment before cautiously sniffing his underarm. "Is it that bad?"

"She's the only one who can smell it, dear," Charlotte said, going to the door and closing it before the townspeople lingering outside could peek their heads in. "Delilah, honey, go to my room and open the side pocket on my medical bag. There's some menthol rub in a tube you can dab under your nose to block the smell of the curse out."

While Kieran took a seat on the couch, Delilah excused herself from the room to do so. She caught the tail end of her mother telling Kieran, "I'm one of two doctors in town, so I wind up doing my fair share of autopsies. Menthol blocks out the smell."

Kieran's voice rose nearly an octave: "Well, goodness, isn't that something?"

Delilah found the tube and applied a liberal amount under her nose. Its smell was strong enough to almost entirely mask the other, even if it made her eyes water a bit. Then she quickly opened all the windows in the cottage. She was sure the curse scent would cut through the menthol if she didn't get a breeze flowing through the main room.

"Sorry," Delilah said, taking a seat on the couch. She met Kieran's gaze, studying his strange blue eye. "I know you can't help it."

It was odd. Delilah had expected to feel angry the moment Kieran showed up after the stunt at her ceremony. But looking at him now, it was hard to muster anything other than . . . well, pity. His eyes were huge and round; his mouth was set in a tight frown as he wrinkled his forehead, clearly self-conscious about his curse smell. He reminded her a bit of a kicked puppy. Or a baby bird that had fallen out of its nest before it could fly.

And despite the devil-may-care approach she took to most things, Delilah knew exactly how painful it was to live with a curse.

"By the way"—she held out a hand—"I'm Delilah. This is my mom, Charlotte. I figure we should probably have a less dramatic introduction after all that."

He took her hand, not offering much in terms of a grip.

"Kieran Pelumbra." He rubbed the back of his neck, a little sheepish. "I'm . . . sorry about the smell. That might complicate our traveling together."

"Traveling together?" Delilah had never heard of a witch going on their Calling with another person. "What do you mean? I figured this was going to be a solo adventure."

"Well—I have some leads I want to investigate, and since I know the most about the curse, it makes sense for us to just . . . go together." When Delilah shot him a look with one eyebrow raised, he added, "I understand that's a bit uncomfortable—traveling with a strange man you've never met—"

"'Man,'" Charlotte repeated with a small chuckle. She gestured to his lean frame and whispered to Delilah, "Bit willowy for that, don't you think? You could snap him in half."

"Mom," Delilah said, trying not to laugh. Kieran *was* a beanpole. "Be nice."

"How old are you anyway?" Charlotte asked him.

A bit of a blush came into Kieran's cheeks. "Oh—well. I'm nearly eighteen. Just . . . eight more months."

"Generous use of *nearly.*"

"Mom!" Delilah smacked her mother's knee with the back of her hand, which only made Charlotte giggle. To Kieran, she said, "Sorry. Listen, why don't you tell me what you know about the curse, and then we can decide on the best plan of action? The sooner I can get this over with, the sooner I can work on my own curse."

"Right." Kieran bit his lip. Delilah noticed him looking at Charlotte out of the corner of his eye.

Delilah said, "Mom, can you give us a minute? Curses are . . ."

"A touchy subject. I know." She stood, cutting Kieran a look. "What you did at the Calling? Very bold. I hope you know what you've gotten her into."

Kieran went red again. It seemed he might have a bit of a blushing problem. "I—I thought . . . I didn't know Delilah was going to propose her own task."

Charlotte and Delilah's expressions both softened.

"I'm sorry about that," he added. "I wouldn't have done it if I'd had any other option. I've done a lot of traveling and researching and . . . you're kind of my last hope."

At the shine of tears in his eyes, the last of any niggling frustration in Delilah's head dissolved.

"Well, then, I'll give you both some privacy," said Charlotte as she grabbed her keys from a small bowl by the doorway. "I'm going to go talk to everyone. I'm sure Ruby and Clarissa will have plenty to say about this. I'll be back in an hour."

"We'll be here," Delilah promised, despite Kieran's opening and then closing his mouth before he could interject. He stayed quiet, and with that, Charlotte slipped outside. The door squealed to a close, and the lock clicked into place behind her.

"Sorry, she can be a little intense," Delilah said, standing and brushing off her skirt. "You want tea? The water is still hot."

"Oh—sure."

Once Delilah had made him a cup and brought out a few biscuits, she settled into the couch and crossed her legs. Kieran looked grateful for the snack—considering how quickly he downed the biscuits, he must not have eaten before the Calling ceremony. Then again, Delilah had been so nervous beforehand that she hadn't eaten much either.

"So," Delilah said, cutting through the silence, "you're dying."

Kieran choked a bit on his last biscuit and quickly drank some tea to wash it down. He met her gaze and said, "Well. Yes."

"You said it's a family curse, so is that all it does?" She cocked an eyebrow. "Kill you slowly?"

"Erm—no, not just that." He wrung his hands. Delilah noticed his fingers, slim and long, pale like the rest of him and probably cold from the look of them. "I have . . . half the curse. My twin sister has the other."

"Is she also dying?"

"I'm not sure." He shrugged. "We've never met."

Delilah steepled her fingers. Despite herself, her heart had begun to beat a bit faster.

Curses were a unique form of magic. While most witches could channel whatever spells they wanted to cast through their preferred artistic or crafting method, curses worked best when written. The only kind of magic that shared writing as its main method of casting was blessings, but they were infinitely less interesting to Delilah. She had seen only a few written curses in her life, but she found them endlessly fascinating. Most curses were nothing but overcomplicated riddles.

Delilah *loved* riddles.

"A family curse on one of Celdwyn's most prominent families, divided between twins who have never met each other." Delilah smiled, flexing her eyebrows. "Go on."

"You've got a bit of a . . . wicked smile, you know."

"One of my more charming features." She ran her fingers back through her hair and shook it out, dark curls pooling on her shoulder. "Now. Curse. Explain."

"Well—a lot of it is foggy. We've never been able to find the exact wording—"

A flicker of a memory struck Delilah. "Did you try the Library of Curses?"

"The what?"

"In Gellingham," Delilah said. "It's the only professionally curated collection of curses in Celdwyn. The only way to make a true curse is to put it down in writing, but for it to stay powerful, whatever it's written on needs to be preserved. If taken care of properly, curses can last for eons. Considering how powerful yours is, the Library of Curses seems like a good place to check."

Kieran blinked in disbelief. "I'm . . . impressed you know so much about this."

Delilah shrugged. She'd always had an interest in curses, ever since she learned about her own, but it had been Theo who'd taught her most of what she knew about them. They'd spent hours flipping through library books together and listening to radio broadcasts about the latest cursebreaking gossip straight from Gellingham. But as with everything that had to do with Theo, Delilah did her best not to linger too long on the memory.

Once I'm done with my Calling, he'd told her as he pressed a kiss to her cheek, *we'll go to the Library of Curses together to find yours. I promise.*

"We'll add it to the list," Kieran said, snapping Delilah out of her own head. "After we find my sister, that is. From what I *do* know about the curse, she's the key to breaking it."

"Is that so?"

Kieran nodded. "Every generation in my family, a set of twin witches are born. In the beginning, our abilities are perfectly matched, but over time, the magic of one begins to siphon from the other. Once the last of the one twin's magic is drained, that twin dies and the other . . ."

"Is really powerful?" Delilah guessed.

Kieran shook his head. "Something else. Everyone in my family was always vague about it. Just that it's terrible. Something about the power becoming overwhelming and hurting the bearer somehow."

Delilah drummed together the tips of her fingers. "Oh, that's good."

"*Good?*"

"Er—terrible. Very terrible. It's awful that you're dying because your magic is being sucked out by your sister." She shrugged. "Listen, to be good at breaking curses, you have to understand curses. And leaving the terrible conclusion to a curse vague and threatening is a great trick. Makes it much harder to crack."

"Oh." Kieran nodded as if he knew what she was talking about. "Well. That's the gist of it. Trouble is, it seems like my sister's going to suck out the last of my powers . . . sooner rather than later. So I'm a bit desperate. Hence the . . ."

"Calling hijacking?" Delilah offered.

Kieran winced. "Right. I *am* sorry about that. I just . . . I thought my best chance at living would be to ask you. Knowing your father and everything."

"Bastard," Delilah grumbled.

"He's broken thousands of curses!"

"Still a bastard. Trust me." Delilah stood. "So, to summarize: we need to find your sister, who's sucking out your magic, because something about her is the key to breaking your curse? Is it safe for you two to be near each other? Could that . . . inadvertently expedite the process?"

"That's what my mother thought," Kieran admitted. "It's why she sent Briar—that's my sister—away. But my father admitted to me before I left that it isn't true. So I want to find her."

"You think she wants to be found?" Delilah asked. "Briar, that is. Good you know her name, at least."

"I don't know." He shrugged. "It's a very lonely curse on your own. I'd expect she'd at least want to talk."

"Compare notes," Delilah agreed. "Doesn't seem like a bad place to start. Any idea where she is?"

"I paid an information broker, who told me to try Port Lorring. There are rumors of a shopkeeper there with a single blue eye like mine."

"Port Lorring is a week's walk from here on foot." Delilah sighed. She looked at her heeled boots in the entryway, considering whether or not they could hold up for that long of a journey. She groaned. "*Miles* and *miles* away . . ."

"No need." Kieran stood, straightening his fancy duster. "I have an aeroship. It will get us there in two days at most."

"An aeroship?" Delilah's eyebrows shot up.

"Plenty of room for both of us to have our own space. The crew is small—"

"*Crew?* How big is it?"

"Just three decks," he replied defensively. "Practically a poor man's ship."

"A poor man's ship would be his legs."

"I can't imagine an aeroship is that expensive." Kieran reached up and adjusted his blond curls so the top layer was up in a small bun at the back of his head while the rest hung above his shoulders. "Well, then. It would likely be best if we set out now so we can reach the ship before dark. I left it in the airfield outside town."

"You don't want to wait until tomorrow? It's been quite a day already." Delilah put on her best wide-eyed pout. "Plus, my mother *will* kill you if you take me away without my saying goodbye."

"I don't want to keep the crew waiting any longer. And we're on something of a tight deadline here." Kieran bit the inside of his cheek, then sighed. "But we can certainly wait until your mother comes back."

"Ah—fair enough, then. I'll get packed in the meantime." Delilah patted his shoulder as she walked by. "We'll be off before you know it."

CHAPTER THREE

Rule #7: If you don't know what you're doing, square your shoulders, lift your chin, and pretend you do.

Charlotte sobbed openly as she said goodbye to her daughter, and Delilah didn't hold it together much better. Kieran stood by, checking a silver watch on his wrist. Delilah was grateful he didn't say anything.

"You'll do great," Charlotte said into her daughter's hair as she clung to her. "Blow your father out of the water."

"Screw that guy," Delilah sobbed.

"I'm so proud of you." Charlotte gave her a final squeeze and pulled away, holding her hands. "Get out there and break some curses."

"I'll do my best." Delilah dabbed her tears dry with her sleeve, then kissed her mother's cheek. "I love you."

"Love you more." Charlotte shot Kieran another glare. "If anything happens to her, I'll make you regret the day you were born."

Kieran held up a hand. "Lovely meeting you as well, Mrs. Bea."

"That's *Miss* Bea." Charlotte hugged Delilah once more. "Bye, darling."

"Bye, Mom."

With a final wave, Kieran and Delilah set out down the path away from Kitfield while Charlotte stood watching them go. Delilah kept her chin up until she lost sight of Charlotte. She'd known this day would come. She'd told herself she'd be ready for it. But something about walking away from her mother, from Kitfield—it felt unreal. As if any second Kieran would admit that this was all a joke and she could return to her normal life.

Maybe that life didn't exist anymore. Maybe it never would again.

Thinking of her mother's eyes, framed by thin crow's-feet, as she smiled and waved goodbye, Delilah let herself cry.

"You really love her, don't you?" Kieran whispered.

"She's my mother," Delilah replied, wiping away tears.

"Must be nice to be close to your family," Kieran said wistfully. He gestured ahead. "Come on. We're getting close."

The aeroship was parked in a clearing a mile or two outside town. It was huge, with the frame of a sailing ship. Two large red balloons were attached to the top, held in place by thickly woven netting; a crow's nest stuck up between the balloons, tall enough to look out over the trees for miles. There were three tiers of windows, one for each deck, and metal wings hung in waiting at the craft's sides.

At the far end of the ship, a door opened and a gangway slid out. Kieran gestured for Delilah to follow, which she did after a few more moments of gawking.

"Practically a poor man's ship," she muttered to herself. *Sure.*

At the top of the gangway, a young woman—she was probably in her early twenties, Delilah guessed—greeted them with a weak smile. Her extremely pale skin and white-blond hair contrasted sharply with eyes that were such a deep brown they seemed almost black. She had a straight, small nose, and her legs and arms were long and thin, not unlike Kieran's.

Kieran held out a hand to her. "Delilah, this is Adelaide. She used to be a maid for my parents before she decided to come with me. She tries harder to keep the ship in good shape than the rest of us do, but we do our best to share cleaning duties."

Adelaide looked Delilah over quickly and then glanced back at Kieran, flashing her eyebrows.

"Yes—she's the witch I mentioned," he told her. "She's going to help me break the curse."

"Nice to meet you, Adelaide," Delilah said, trying to catch her breath. Kieran was a very fast walker, and she was winded from trying to keep up with him.

Adelaide stepped forward a bit, and Delilah's nose instantly wrinkled. Adelaide smelled . . . well, *ancient.* Like the decaying foundation of an old manor left in disrepair, with water-stained, curling wallpaper and creaky old floors. Under that was a familiar earthy smell.

Before Delilah could say it, Kieran clarified: "Adelaide is cursed as well. She's unable to communicate with anyone—not by speaking or writing or using sign language. We've tried just about everything, but . . ."

Adelaide opened her mouth as if to say something, and her jaw instantly slammed shut. The muscles in her cheeks stretched as she tried to open her teeth once more, but nothing happened, even as her eyes squeezed closed and she fought to speak. For a moment, Delilah stared in horror, then Adelaide's face settled and she smiled sadly in Delilah's direction.

"Goodness," Delilah breathed.

Kieran exhaled a sigh, then said to Adelaide, "That was a bit much, don't you think?"

The woman stifled a silent chuckle, and Kieran added, "Yes, I get it, you're making a point, but still." Then: "Adelaide, would you be willing to take Delilah's bag up to her room while I show her around the ship?"

"I'm perfectly capable of carrying my own bag—" Delilah began.

Before she could finish, Adelaide's eyes glowed ember red. She unwound three different-colored strings that had been wrapped around her wrist and threaded them around her fingers. With speed Delilah had never seen before, Adelaide wove the strings into a complex braid, then looped them around the handle of the bag. She tied the ends together, and the woven circle suddenly lifted into the air, carrying the bag with it.

"Oh—you're a witch," Delilah breathed, mouth hanging open as she met Adelaide's eyes. Their glow faded as she stopped channeling magic. The bag and its enchanted handle floated beside Adelaide, ready to follow wherever she commanded.

Kieran said, "She's very good at sewing- and weaving-based magic, clearly. She'd probably offer you some pointers if you're interested."

"That would be amazing," Delilah replied, eyes brightening.

Adelaide smiled once more before flicking her hand so the bag followed her inside, leaving the others alone.

Kieran took Delilah around the ship, showing her the dining room, kitchen, engine room, crew cabins, and a small study with a sitting area. Everything was decorated with hardwoods, plush creamy yellow cushions, and various knickknacks. Along the hallway walls hung landscape paintings as well as oil portraits of what appeared to be Kieran's Pelumbra ancestors, based on their resemblance to him.

"And over here," Kieran said, opening a door on the bow, "is the control room."

The door popped open to reveal a messy scene. Books, clothes, and coffee mugs were strewn around the room. Pulleys hung from the ceiling, some tangled together. A control panel with levers sat before the front windows, along with a wheel where a few undershirts were hanging, seemingly drying after being laundered.

Standing in front of the control panel was a tall man with tan skin, a slim but muscular frame, and a coiffed undercut. At first glance, he appeared to just be leaning over the controls.

Until Delilah spotted a person pinned under him with their back pressed into the panel.

Delilah's eyebrows shot up. "Oh—excuse me—"

"Has the reading changed yet?" the person beneath the man asked. Delilah realized now that they were in the midst of holding one of the ceiling pulleys in one hand and turning something on the wall with a wrench in the other.

"Not yet. You'd think they'd put this pressure gauge somewhere a bit more convenient," the tall man said. He had an accent—Delilah guessed from Esperona, Celdwyn's neighboring country to the southwest. He tapped the gauge on the control panel over the other person's head, then paused to glance down at them. His shoulders slumped, suddenly sounding as if he hadn't slept in days as he added, "Ariel, did you cut your own hair again? It looks *mangled.*"

Kieran cleared his throat, not looking perturbed. "Santiago? Ariel?"

"Not right now, Kieran," the person under the man said, tongue between their teeth. They turned the valve on the wall again. "Very . . . delicate . . ."

The valve let out a hiss, and the tall man said, "Pressure levels are dropping—it's at one-oh-two-point-two."

"One-oh-two-point-two? Perfect," the other person replied, then let go of the pulley and patted the man's arm. "You can move now. Before I hit you with the wrench."

"Sometimes I don't know if you or your ship is more temperamental," the man replied, chuckling. He straightened, ran a hand through his hair, and said, "Ah, look. He's back. And—"

He trailed off when he saw Delilah. "Well, well—you made a friend."

"Delilah, this is Santiago Luna," Kieran said, pointing to the man. "He's a professional chef who used to cook for my family but has since left their employment."

"Look at this—he's picked up another one for us to babysit," Santiago stage-whispered to the other person as they straightened and tossed the wrench into a box full of other tools. Now that she could see his face, Delilah guessed Santiago was probably in his mid-twenties.

Ignoring this statement, Kieran added, "And this is Ariel Zhang. They're our pilot."

Ariel came around from Santiago's side and saluted them with two fingers. They wore a loose pair of white pants and a rumpled vest over an oil-stained undershirt. They had light golden-hued skin and a round face—Delilah guessed they were probably in their mid-twenties as well but could have been younger, considering their baby face.

They rested their hands on their hips, arms akimbo. "You must be the witch with the famous dad that Kieran was talking about. Nice to meet you."

"Likewise." Delilah's eyes wandered around the room. "Do you . . . live in here?"

"Yeah, sort of." Ariel glanced over their shoulder. "I should probably straighten up."

"Probably," Kieran agreed.

"My, you're one to talk," Santiago scoffed. "We've seen Adelaide's face when she passes by your room."

Ariel chuckled and held out a hand, which Santiago regarded for a beat before slapping it.

Kieran's face turned pink.

"That aside, good to meet you, Delilah," Santiago said. He hooked a thumb toward the control panel. "Pardon our appearance. The meter Ariel needed to read to make sure the repair was working just so happened to be under them, so I stepped in to help."

"Plus, he's ruggedly handsome and smells like pastry," Ariel said with a wink. "So. Win-win. But sorry for freaking you out."

"Oh, don't worry about it." Delilah stepped forward, coming to the front window. She placed her hands on an empty part of the control panel and leaned forward to peer out. The scenery was nothing but trees at the moment, but she could imagine how sweeping it would be once they took off. "Must be a nice view from here."

"Best seat in the house," Ariel said. "Want to see what it looks like when we take off?"

"Like, right now?"

Ariel glanced over their shoulder at Santiago. "Are we good to go?"

He shrugged. "Should be."

"We might want to—" Kieran started to say.

Before he could finish, Ariel had reached up to one of the pulleys on the ceiling and yanked it. A low rumble started under their feet. Out of the corner of her eye, Delilah spotted the wings beginning to flap, slowly at first. Then, with a powerful push, the ship rose into the air.

"Take a seat, Delilah," Ariel said, gesturing to the copilot's chair. Santiago went to their other side, holding on to Ariel's chair for support.

"Where am I supposed to sit?" Kieran called, desperately

holding on to the wall as the aeroship lurched upward again with another sharp flap of its wings.

"That's *your* problem, my friend," Ariel replied, pushing another lever forward. "Away we go."

Delilah took a seat just in time before the ship blasted forward into the clouds, leaving the forest behind them. Kieran yelped and fell into the door, which opened and sent him tumbling down the hall with a shout. Ariel and Santiago chuckled while Delilah tried not to laugh.

"You know the point of this whole ordeal is to keep me alive, right?" Kieran shouted indignantly from the hallway.

"Noted," Ariel called back.

The ship lifted the rest of the way into the sky, hovering above the first layer of clouds. They created a wispy frame for the land below, with its rolling hills, forest, and, to the east, sparkling blue sea. Ariel directed the aeroship to hug the coastline, pointing them northeast toward Port Lorring.

Delilah saw Kitfield for a few brief seconds before they glided on, and something heavy settled in her chest. She'd never viewed it from this vantage point before—never seen the strange layout of Kitfield's cobblestone streets or the way the green copper roofs looked with the sun beating down directly on top of them. She recognized the town square, where the farmers market was held each Wednesday, and the dress shop where her mother took her before the first day of school each year. Even the meadow outside town by the edge of Silverside Lake—the one with the massive willow trees that looked hundreds of years old. She'd spent days and days lounging under them, first as a daydreaming child, then when she got older and wanted privacy with Theo before . . . well, before everything happened. Odd to see it all now looking foreign for the first time.

Kieran righted himself and walked to the front to rejoin them. He stood by Delilah's other side, crossing his arms and tilting his head. Out of the corner of her eye, Delilah observed him surveying the landscape. For a minute, they watched in silence.

"It's beautiful up here," Delilah said to Ariel as their fingers drummed lazily atop the controls. "Is it hard to pilot?"

"Not particularly. One of these days I can show you how."

Delilah smiled. "I'd like that."

Kieran tapped Delilah's shoulder. "Would you like to see the upper deck? Your room is there."

"Right, yeah." She stood. "Nice meeting you both."

"Feel free to stop in next time you've got a minute," Ariel said. "It's been a while since I spoke to a witch."

"*I'm* a witch," Kieran pointed out.

"Perhaps they mean a witch who does magic without risking their well-being," Santiago guessed.

"Fair point," Kieran conceded. He held out a hand. "Delilah?"

Delilah paused, staring at his hand with its long, skinny fingers. He had nicely trimmed nails, not broken and ragged like so many she saw in Kitfield. Not callused from work or chapped from harsh conditions. Just soft, gentle hands.

Delilah wasn't sure exactly why, but she found the sight of them comforting.

She took his hand. He helped her up and gestured for her to follow him.

❦

The top deck of the aeroship was a half-enclosed space, which consisted of three bedrooms, and half open deck, with some seating and access to the crow's nest. Delilah was given the aft cabin, down the hall from Kieran's and an empty room he informed her he intended to offer to his sister once they found her. Much like the rest of the ship, Delilah's room was decorated with mahogany furnishings and art on the walls. It also had a compact feather bed, onto which she collapsed as soon as she saw it. Kieran excused himself, leaving her to collect herself.

As the curtain of night drew across the sky after dinner, Delilah found herself unable to sleep. Thoughts of Kitfield, her curse, Kieran, Clarissa, Theo—it was all too much. How was she supposed to save someone's *life*? She'd spent years mentally preparing to break her own curse. At the thought of having more than just the fate of her family's romantic relationships in her hands, a cold sweat broke out on the back of her neck. The whirring of the ship's engine and the metallic wingbeats didn't help either.

With a huff, Delilah rolled out of bed, pulled on a sweater, and went out onto the deck to get some air.

The night was cool but sticky with humidity, the smell of varnish fresh on the boards at her feet. Above her, the clouds had cleared, leaving a perfect view of the massive, starry sky. She went to the foredeck, rested her arms on the railing, and sighed, craning her neck. She wished Charlotte was there, and her heart ached.

"I take it you couldn't sleep either?"

Kieran came to stand beside her. His hair hung around his

face, half tucked behind his ears. He had on a loose sapphire-colored shirt with silvery embroidered details and matching pants.

"Yeah. Today was . . . a lot." Delilah paused, biting back a laugh. "Are those silk pajamas?"

Kieran looked down at himself. "Well—yes. Is there a problem with that?"

"I've never even seen silk in real life before," Delilah chuckled. "It just seems a bit"—Delilah waved her hands in a flourish, wincing slightly as she finished—"garish."

Kieran's mouth twitched toward a frown. He had thin lips with a strong cupid's bow. "I— Sorry. They're not unusual where I come from." When Delilah didn't immediately respond, he blurted out, "My family, um . . . has money."

Delilah feigned surprise. "*No. Do tell!*"

Kieran pressed his palms into his eyes, groaning. "Sorry. I've spent my entire life on my family's estate. This is the first time I've really interacted with people who aren't Pelumbras or our employees. Sometimes it's hard for me to gauge when I'm being an ass."

"If you've been on your family's estate for so long"—Delilah bit her lip, considering how to ask what she had on her mind— "how did you decide you were going to find me, of all people?"

"Oh, right. Well . . ." He sucked a breath in through his teeth. "I'd heard of your father—hard not to, with all the news about him breaking curses all the time—and I paid an information broker to tip me off on his location. I found him at a bar in Gellingham, and he said he couldn't help me but maybe . . . you could."

Delilah's jaw dropped. "*Klaus Hammond* sent you to *me*?"

Kieran nodded. "He told me about the Rite of Mortality. Seems like he has a lot of faith in you."

"He's never even *met* me," Delilah said, heat flooding her chest as her teeth locked together. Her fists tightened at her sides. "Maybe if he had fallen in love with my mom and forgotten her because of the curse, I'd understand, but he doesn't even have that excuse! She was just another inconsequential fling to him. So how, pray tell, can he pretend to know anything about me, much less if I could break a massively powerful family curse?"

"He did seem a bit . . . self-involved. And he was quite drunk." He bit the inside of his cheek. "I just hope he didn't tell my family that I spoke to him. Or where I was going."

Delilah studied him with a sideways glance. "Your family is kind of famous too, right?"

Kieran *mm-hmm*ed in the back of his throat. "If you go anywhere up north, the Pelumbras are all you'll ever hear about. That's why they kept me on the estate my whole life—if word got out that the Pelumbras have been cursed for generations, it would ruin the perfect reputation they've constructed. According to official records, Briar and I were never even born."

"Is that why you're not doing your Calling right now?" Delilah guessed.

He nodded. "Since Briar and I were born in secret, we were never marked down as witches. You can't send people on their Calling or take away their magic if they don't exist."

Kieran turned so his back leaned against the railing. He tipped his head back, staring at the sky. In the darkness, Delilah could make out the faint glow of his blue eye.

He seemed to notice her staring at it. "The eye doesn't do anything special, in case you were wondering. Sometimes it glows brighter when I'm about to have an attack, but beyond that, it's just . . ." He shrugged. "Spooky. I suppose."

"An attack?" Delilah's brows furrowed. "What do you mean?"

"It happens whenever Briar is siphoning my magic," he explained. His fingers tapped the wooden railing, skating over it as he spoke. "It happens in bursts. It used to be only once or twice a year, but now it's almost every other week. I don't think she can control it."

"What happens to you?" Delilah asked. Kieran winced a bit at the question, and she added, "If . . . you're okay with talking about it."

"It's perfectly fine—most people just don't like to hear about it." He closed his eyes for a moment. "First the eye glows. Then my heart speeds up. I get this . . . tugging sensation between my eyes. Then I usually faint, and I'm gone for a bit. Then I wake up an hour later feeling . . . hollower. The emptiness never really goes away."

"Oof," Delilah said. "That's . . . awful."

"Yeah, it is." He aimed a small smile in her direction. "But now I have you. So hopefully it won't happen too many more times."

Delilah straightened and turned so she leaned against the railing as well. This close she could see she was a bit taller than Kieran—which wasn't unusual, seeing as Delilah was around six feet tall—and probably had about fifty pounds on him. She wondered if he'd be less willowy without the curse that was slowly hollowing him out from the inside.

She really was the only thing standing between Kieran and a slow, withering death. The thought immediately made her stomach twist into a knot, and bile threatened to crawl up her throat.

"I'm gonna give it my best shot," Delilah said, half trying to convince herself. If she repeated it enough times, maybe it would sink in. "For your sake and mine."

"Thanks for that." He tucked loose strands of hair behind his ear, and his voice got a little quieter. "And for listening. I know it's a lot to hear about the attacks and all that. My mother always said telling people would make them uncomfortable, so I don't bring it up often." When Delilah shot him a pressing look, he added, "She's . . . very protective."

"If she's so protective of you," Delilah said, worried she might be overstepping, "why did she let you do all this? Get an aeroship, travel the country with a bunch of your family's former employees, tell everyone in Kitfield about your family curse—that doesn't sound like something a smothering parent would allow."

Kieran pursed his lips in an attempt to stop a smile, but it didn't work. He started to chuckle, and soon he was all-out laughing, one hand pushing his hair back while the other supported him against the rail. His shoulders shook, and he tossed his head back. Delilah just looked at him, worried she might have broken him.

"She'd never allow it," he finally said, wiping away a tear. "Never in a million years."

Delilah stared at him.

"I suppose I forgot to mention one thing," he said. His eyes brightened, scintillating and uncontainable. He gestured at the ship, grinning: "I stole this."

❦

"He did," Ariel said the next morning, laughing around a bite of eggs, "but it's not nearly as exciting as it sounds. The ship was his father's. The heist was just Kieran grabbing me, Santi, and Adelaide and flying away."

Delilah blinked in disbelief. "Still impressive that Kieran stole a whole ship, if you ask me."

Delilah sat with Ariel and Adelaide at the dining table, sunlight streaming in through the ship's massive windows. She had finally managed to fall asleep after her talk with Kieran, and she'd slept until her room was bright with the midmorning glow. She'd rolled out of bed only after Kieran shouted through the door that breakfast was ready.

The table was decorated with an impressive spread of food, including a pile of fluffy scrambled eggs, strips of crispy bacon, and waffles topped with melted chocolate, strawberries, and whipped crème fraîche. Beside those was a plate of still-warm buttery croissants that made Delilah desperate to ask Santiago for his recipe. Her croissants never had that kind of lamination.

"I'm just hoping Kieran's old man doesn't hire someone to chase us," Ariel added, slathering a bagel with more cream cheese than Delilah had ever seen a person eat in one sitting. They took a bite and, cream cheese smudged around the corner of their mouth, added, "We spent the first few nights in the air taking shifts to keep an eye out for following ships."

"Would he do that?" Delilah asked. "Kieran's dad, I mean."

Adelaide's face crumpled into a frown, and Ariel nodded as if agreeing with her. "Oh, absolutely. If Kieran could prove he was a Pelumbra and expose them as being cursed? The social fallout would be *spectacular.*"

Delilah blinked. "But—he announced he was a Pelumbra back in Kitfield. All those people know he's cursed."

Ariel sucked in air through their teeth. "If he could expose them beyond your little town, I mean. No offense. Gossip out of a small town in the south isn't likely to make much of an impact among the northern gentry."

"Much to my chagrin." Kieran stepped into the dining room wearing high-waisted pants, a button-down shirt, and a blue-and-silver duster with frilled sleeves. He set a pile of papers down beside the spread of food.

Before he could say anything, Ariel raised an eyebrow at his ensemble. "I wasn't informed of a costume ball."

He glanced down at the getup. "It's not a costume. I bought it in Kitfield. The locals dress like this."

Adelaide reached out and gently touched the sleeve, shoulders shaking in a small, silent laugh. When Kieran raised an eyebrow at her, she patted the sleeve and smiled at him.

"Thank you," Kieran said to her. To the others, he added, "See? Adelaide likes it."

"That's traditionally a woman's duster," Delilah pointed out. Kieran blushed and she added, "Not that it matters. It suits you."

He lifted one of the flowing sleeves. "Maybe it is a bit much."

Santiago appeared behind him and clapped him on the shoulder before placing a carafe of coffee on the table and sitting down. "So are you. Wear it with pride."

Kieran considered the sleeves for another moment before shrugging. "I suppose you're right. Anyway"—he looked at Delilah, then gestured to the papers—"I have a little gift for you."

"Paperwork?" Delilah guessed. "I thought agreeing to break your curse at the Calling ceremony was enough of a contract."

"Oh—goodness no," Kieran interrupted as he realized what she meant. "It's all the information on my sister's recent whereabouts that I was able to buy from an information broker. I figured there might be some useful stuff in there that can help you plan out the next steps for breaking the curse once we find her."

Delilah paused. "Help *me* plan . . . ?" She trailed off, however, as soon as she noticed everyone's eyes on her. Of course they expected her to take the lead. This was her Calling, after all, and she was the daughter of the most famous cursebreaker in Celdwyn. She was supposed to know all the next steps, to have a plan, to fix the problem as if it were nothing. It was the whole reason Kieran had come looking for her. It didn't matter that she'd never actually broken a curse before, much less one that had poisoned one of Celdwyn's most powerful families for generations.

The eggs in her stomach suddenly threatened to reverse course.

Delilah quickly took a gulp of water and cleared her throat. "Right. Of course. The—next steps. Which I'm definitely planning. It'll . . . definitely help with that." When everyone simply stared at her, she squared her shoulders. *Fake it till you make it, Delilah.*

Pointing at the papers, she asked, "So what all is in here? Give me a summary."

Kieran didn't miss a beat, to his credit: "Pictures, some

employment information, a long list of pseudonyms—stuff like that. There's even a performance review from her boss at her current job. Apparently, she reads too much on the job."

"Why would she use pseudonyms?" Delilah asked. She shuffled a few of the papers and pulled up a hotel log, where the name ROSE ALBRIGHT had been circled in red.

"My aunt Wrenlin volunteered to raise Briar after my mother decided we shouldn't be around each other," Kieran explained. He snagged one of the croissants and took a bite. Swallowing, he went on, "But Briar ran away about six months ago. My father has tried to track her down, but none of the people he's sent after her have come back."

Delilah gasped with glee. "Did she kill them? Is she an assassin? A *lady* assassin?"

Kieran furrowed his brows. "Why do you sound excited about that?"

Delilah realized everyone was still staring at her, and she quickly cleared her throat. "Oh, um, excited? No, that was— horror. I'm horrified. Please. Go on."

Kieran paused for a second to eye her before restarting: "We don't know their whereabouts, so it could be a lot of things. Regardless, we'll need to approach the situation carefully."

Kieran picked up a photograph and held it up. It showed a girl with a shaved head, large, catlike eyes, and thick lips, with a prominent cupid's bow like her twin's. She had his pointed chin too, and her nose was on the smaller side, rounded at the tip.

Kieran said, "This is Briar."

Delilah studied the photo. Briar had a brown left eye and a

blue right eye—the opposite placement of her twin. Under the left eye was an inky-purple bruise, and she had a bloodied lip. A small but defined scar sliced through one of her thick eyebrows, and her unbruised eye was rimmed with kohl. If Delilah had seen her cold glare on the street, she likely would have crossed to the other side.

"This looks like a mug shot," Santiago said, leaning his hip against the table as he munched a pastry. He gestured to Kieran with it. "Are we bringing a delinquent on board?"

Kieran's voice cracked as he explained: "Well—this was public intoxication. But she got out the next day!"

Santiago hummed a soft note to himself. "Ariel, darling, may I borrow one of your locks? I need to secure my liquor cabinet." When Kieran shot him a look, he added, "I've spent too long collecting vintage reds to have them stolen by a teenager."

"In any case, we'll be arriving in Port Lorring later today. Briar works at a witch-supply shop called the Lavender Establishment, and we can try to speak to her there." Kieran looked at Delilah. "I was thinking you and I could do it. I'll appeal to her as her twin, and you can explain that you intend to break the curse."

Delilah shrugged. "Seems easy enough."

"Good." Kieran put his hands on his hips. "Ariel, when do you expect us to arrive?"

"Probably two hours." Ariel finished loading their plate with seconds and saluted Delilah, Adelaide, and Santiago. "Which reminds me, I should get back to the controls. Santi, I'll leave that lock in the pantry for you."

"Bless you," Santiago said, pressing his hands together as if in prayer.

"We can meet back here once we land," Kieran said to Delilah. "Sound good?"

"Sounds good."

He pushed the papers across the table to Delilah and turned to go, a small photo slipping out of the stack and landing on the table in front of Adelaide as he did. Softly, she picked it up with two fingers, flipped it over, and set it back on the table. It was an image of Briar when she was younger, probably seven or eight. Back then, she had long red hair and rounded cheeks.

Instead of the sharp gaze in her mug shot, though, in this photo her eyes were rimmed with red—huge and empty. Her thick lips were curved into a tiny frown—the kind of aching, quiet expression that rested on a face that knew no better.

At her side was a woman standing a healthy distance away—enough to signify they were related somehow but didn't seem to share any pleasant feelings. She looked young to be raising a child, with her jaw tight and arms tense. An expensive-looking red gown adorned her very slim frame, though the dress looked frayed at the ends.

Delilah heard a sniffle. Only then did she realize that Adelaide had a single tear sliding down her cheek. Very carefully, Adelaide reached out, long white fingers tracing the side of the younger Briar's face.

"Adelaide?" Delilah asked.

Adelaide squeezed her eyes closed and quickly wiped the tear away. She took a deep breath to steady herself and passed the photo to Delilah, then quickly squared her shoulders as if nothing had happened and took a bite of bacon.

Delilah pursed her lips, then went back to examining the photo.

Something told her she had a lot to learn about Briar Pelumbra.

CHAPTER FOUR

Rule #21: There's nothing wrong with a little
subterfuge for the greater good.

The ship landed in the humble fishing town of Port Lorring as the
sun dipped into the sea. Most of the buildings were small, with
gray-shingled walls and colorful planter boxes in the windows. A
network of sun-bleached docks hosted a fleet of fishing vessels and
houseboats that bobbed up and down in the sapphire surf. Most
fishermen were pulling in their hauls for the day, the smells of sea
spray and fish heavy in the late-spring air.

Once the aeroship was safely on the ground, Kieran and Delilah had no trouble finding the Lavender Establishment, only a few
short blocks from the docks. Vines bursting with purple moon-
flowers crept up the shop's whitewashed exterior, the facade decorated with faded stenciled shells. A hand-carved wooden sign with
the shop's name in curling script hung from an iron rod above the
door. An orange cat slept in the front window.

Outside, Kieran paused, spinning to Delilah. He straightened his frilled sleeves. "Do I look okay? I feel like I'm on fire."

"A bit sweaty but passable," Delilah said with a shrug. She cocked an eyebrow. "Anxious?"

"Painfully." He ran a hand through his hair. "What if she doesn't believe I'm her twin? Or she doesn't trust us? Or she doesn't like me?"

"Does it matter if she likes you as long as she agrees to help us break the curse?"

"Delilah." He put his hands on her shoulders and met her eyes. "I need *everyone* to like me."

Delilah couldn't help herself—she laughed in his face. She reached up and removed his hands, chuckling, "That sounds exhausting." She patted his warm cheek with an open palm. "You'll be fine. Come on."

She took another step toward the door, but Kieran didn't move. He whispered, "I don't know what to say."

"Then let me do the talking. Don't worry—I've got a foolproof plan." Delilah pointed her thumbs back at herself. "Plus, I've got a way with people. Trust me."

Before he could respond, Delilah was pushing open the door, a silver bell ringing overhead.

At first glance, the shop appeared empty, but Delilah's nose told her that wasn't the case. She had to withhold a gag. Even with the menthol under her nose, she scented a curse in the air, stinking of rotting undergrowth and coppery blood.

The orange cat watched them through lidded eyes as they entered. The floor was hardwood with eyelike knots in the pale boards that creaked when Delilah and Kieran stepped on them. The window display showed various brewers' supplies for witches who channeled their magic through ale-making—a common way for witches to cast spells in small towns along Celdwyn's coast, since most of the grains and other ingredients grew in this region. The ceiling was covered in hanging herbs midway through drying, probably meant for teas like the ones Ruby and Clarissa made back in Kitfield.

A number of silk-covered tables contained baskets full of art supplies, including one table with a variety of different-colored inks that claimed to conduct magic for witches who wrote spells. A small card sat beside each item, detailing, in neat calligraphy, which kind of witch it was best for, be it painter, cook, writer, or brewer. There was even a corner boasting specialized shoes for performing ledrith, the ancient Celdwynian art of combat dance. While ledrith had mostly been popular before magic was regulated by the Council and turf wars were common among covens, some still practiced—though under quite a bit of scrutiny from people who wondered why magic needed to be used for combat at all.

At the cash register was a line of pre-enchanted wares. A mini bouquet of dried pink flowers that could be pinned to one's lapel to ward off negative emotions. A vial full of a shimmering liquid that, when added drop by drop into water, could warm the body without a coat. A pair of boots crafted to eliminate the sound of one's steps.

Perfect, Delilah thought. *If they've got these, my plan might actually work.*

Delilah hit a little call bell on the counter. "Hello?"

Kieran, meanwhile, busied himself frantically looking through a basket of yarn.

After a beat of silence, the cat behind Delilah mewed loud enough to make Kieran jump.

"I know, I know," came a voice from the back. A short, slim girl came out of a swinging door, not looking at Delilah. She said, as if to an invisible coworker, "I heard her. You don't have to yell at me."

The cat narrowed its eyes at her before lying back down in the sun, looking like an orange bread loaf.

"Sorry about Cinnabar," the girl said. She had a fairly deep voice, rough around the edges. It reminded Delilah of cinnamon whiskey somehow. The girl finally looked up, meeting Delilah's gaze, and added, "He's an asshole."

Instantly, Delilah recognized her. Unlike in either photo she'd seen, Briar had long blond hair that fell nearly to her elbows and a face decorated with red lips, swooping eyeliner, and doll-like blush across her pale cheeks. An eye patch covered her right eye. Delilah might have thought she was pretty if it weren't for the ugly scowl carved into her face.

Briar demanded, "So? What do you want?"

Delilah's eyebrows shot up. She hadn't really been anticipating this level of sharpness so soon.

"Well—um. I-I'm a witch," Delilah started.

"A *witch*?" Briar repeated with mock surprise. "Here? No kidding." She palmed her cheek. Delilah was startled by the state of her hands. She had long, thin fingers like her brother's, but the nails were bitten down to jagged stubs, and the skin beside them was scabbed from torn hangnails. Hairline scars cut across the bruised knuckles and down her palms. Some of the scrapes still looked red and fresh, as if she'd been in an unfortunate tangle with a rosebush.

Briar added, "Who'd've thought."

Delilah bit her tongue. She couldn't tell if this girl was just impolite or . . . well, trying to mess with her in the playfully rude way that some people thought constituted flirting. Considering the tense line of her lips, Delilah assumed she was being an ass.

"A pleasant surprise, I know." Delilah swung around her shoulder bag and set it down on the counter between them. "I came to see if you'd be willing to sell some of my pastries here. I'm a kitchen witch."

"The owner is out right now," Briar said, examining Delilah's face as if trying to analyze the manufactured smile that had settled on her lips. She narrowed her eyes. "I can't promise she'll be interested. But I'll pass your inquiry on . . . assuming you have a sample. And it seems worth selling. We only have so much counter space for pre-made enchantments."

"Of course." Delilah held the smile—which was becoming difficult as she attempted to avoid choking on the curse stink. She reached into her bag and pulled out a biscuit wrapped in cheesecloth. She'd whipped them up shortly before getting off the ship, so they were still warm. "Here. Give it a try."

Briar didn't move to touch it. "What's it supposed to do?"

Before she could answer, Briar suddenly reached out and took her hand. Delilah jumped, moving to pull away, but Briar's grip tightened. "And don't lie. The ring I'm wearing has a single-use enchantment—if it's touching you and you lie, it'll break in half."

Delilah stared at her, wide-eyed.

"Basic precaution," Briar explained. "Everyone who works here wears them. Safety and all that."

Delilah took a breath. *Not a problem. I planned for something like this.* "It's pretty simple—just a relaxation spell. Something to take the edge off when you're anxious, et cetera."

A beat passed. The ring, which was carved out of wood—interesting, Delilah hadn't met a woodcarver witch before—had intricate glyphs scratched into it.

It stayed in one piece.

Briar let go of Delilah's hand. "I see."

Briar unwrapped the cloth and took a pinch of the crumbling biscuit between her fingers. She offered Delilah another narrow-eyed look before popping it in her mouth. Delilah tried not to sweat.

If she only ate that much, the spell might not work.

Briar's eyebrows shot up. "Oh—*mm*. That's really good."

She took a full bite.

Delilah nearly sighed with relief. "There's garlic and sharp cheddar in the dough. Pretty simple but delicious."

"The magic is subtle too," Briar mused. Her shoulders relaxed. "Not too heavy, but it works. Well done. I'll let the owner know."

Delilah beamed.

"Do you have a phone number I can give her? And a name?" Briar asked.

"The name's Delilah Bea," she said, dimpling. "But—real quick—I did have a question for you."

Briar raised a thick eyebrow, though her expression didn't seem nearly as sharp as before. *Good. It's working.* "For me?"

Delilah nodded. "Do you recognize the name Pelumbra?"

Kieran froze where he still was pawing, elbow deep, through the yarn.

Briar didn't react. "Sure. They're those witches who live up north and run most of Celdwyn's government. You'd have to be stupid not to know them."

"I guess I'm not being specific enough." Delilah kept a close eye on Briar's posture. Her muscles were relaxed, and she'd started slouching. *Perfect.* "Do you know Kieran Pelumbra?"

Briar's shoulders slumped, and she shook her head. "There are a ton of Pelumbras . . . how am I supposed to . . ." She shook her head as if to clear it and met Delilah's eyes. "What . . . did you do to me?"

Her body slouched sideways, and Delilah was just fast enough to catch her before she fell off the stool. Briar glared up at Delilah from where she hung limp in her arms, cursing. Delilah carefully propped her up against the counter. Briar weakly lifted an arm, fist clenched, but it fell before she could swing it.

Kieran straightened. "What in— *Delilah!*"

"All according to plan," Delilah interrupted him. His jaw fell slack, and she said, "What? Did you not hear your own story? You said she killed all the people your dad sent after her! I'm not looking to die today!"

"They disappeared—that doesn't mean she killed them!" Kieran shot back.

"You're acting like I did something wrong!"

"You *drugged* her!"

"No, I didn't," Delilah huffed. She crossed her arms. "I cast a spell on the biscuits that would relax her muscles so much she . . .

can't move for a little while. It won't last too long. Fifteen minutes or so."

"Who the hell are you?" Briar asked, voice slurred from barely being able to move her jaw. She managed to crease her eyebrows using sheer force of will. Even with her movements dulled, rage was burning through her visible eye. "And what . . . the *fuck* do you want? I . . . I'll kill you."

"This is not how I wanted this to go," Kieran moaned.

"I think you're both overreacting," Delilah said. She held a hand out to Kieran. "Briar—yes, don't look at me like that, I do know your real name—this is Kieran Pelumbra. He's your twin."

"I am so sorry," Kieran said to Briar. "I really—I've wanted to know you for as long as I've known you existed." It was only then that Delilah realized he'd tangled his hands up in the yarn and appeared to have knotted his fingers and wrists together.

Delilah sighed. *It's a good thing he's pretty.*

Kieran went on: "But—it's true. I'm Kieran." He held up his bound hands as if to wave. "I'm your brother."

"You've got to be kidding me," Briar growled.

"And I'm Delilah, like I said. I'm a witch"—she gestured to the biscuit crumbs that had fallen to the floor—"as you know. But I'm also on my Calling, and I'm going to break your family curse. Trouble is, we need you to break it." She put on a smile. "So here we are."

"Is that so?" Briar asked. Delilah was surprised at the ease with which she said it. The spell was supposed to be stronger than that.

Delilah met Briar's gaze, only to discover a hint of glowing blue light leaking from beneath her eye patch.

"Um." Delilah blinked. "You okay?"

Briar said, "Cinnabar, help."

"What's that supposed to—?"

Something struck the side of Delilah's head as if she'd been punched. Starbursts of light ruptured across her eyes. She reeled, catching herself on the counter just as Kieran shouted her name. Her head swam, but she glimpsed an orange ball of light touching down on the counter she was grasping. In a flash, the glowing fireball turned into a cat once more.

It hissed at her, eyes flaring blue.

Delilah realized aloud, "This thing's your *familiar*—?!"

The cat sprang. Delilah swatted at it as it yowled and landed on her shoulder, claws sinking into her skin. She cursed, shrieking.

"Delilah!" Kieran called. He pulled the yarn tighter, desperately trying to free his fingers. "I-I'm gonna help, I swear—"

Briar struggled to her feet, ripping off the blond wig and the eye patch. She threw them in Delilah's face with surprising dexterity, revealing a glowing blue eye and a reddish buzz cut.

"Bad news: you didn't make your spell strong enough for a witch like me," she said with a wicked grin. "Great biscuit, though."

With that, Briar turned and ran for the door, shoving her brother into the yarn basket on her way out. He yelped and fell as the cat on Delilah's shoulder suddenly vanished. It whizzed away in light-ball form after Briar.

"No you don't!" Delilah growled. She took off sprinting, also shoving Kieran out of her way as he tried to get up.

Just as Briar went to shove open the door, Delilah tackled her from behind and they toppled into the street. A group of men passing by had to jump out of the way to avoid them. The girls rolled over each other in the dirt, screaming curses and clawing at each other.

They halted, Delilah on top, pinning down Briar's limbs. Delilah felt a swooping sensation in her stomach, and her heart raced in her ears. Staring down at Briar like this, she realized the size advantage she had. Briar was small and slim, whereas Delilah was six feet tall with a sturdy build. Even fighting with all her might, Briar couldn't so much as make her budge.

"What are you?" Briar spat in Delilah's face. Their noses were inches apart, nearly touching. Delilah's heart hammered in her chest while Briar bared her teeth, newly split lip leaking blood. "A fucking giantess?"

"Among other things," Delilah replied, a pointed smile cutting across her face. Her cheeks warmed. She leaned in closer, lips tickling Briar's ear as she whispered, "Ask nicely and maybe I'll let you go."

The door behind them flew open. Kieran stumbled out, rubbing his arm where he'd fallen over. His hair hung around his face, a few pieces of yarn still caught in his curls.

He cried, "Delilah! Are you okay?"

"Peachy," she said through her teeth. To Briar, she snapped, "You know we came here to help you, right? Typically, witches don't hurl their magic cats at people with good intentions."

"Why the hell would I trust you?" Briar snapped back. "You cast a spell on me, attacked me, and now you're cutting off the circulation to my limbs!" She jerked her chin in Kieran's direction.

"And I'm sure he's got some deal with his awful family to bring me to them. Anyone with the name Pelumbra is a monster."

"Briar," Kieran said, gently holding out his hands. "I know our family has been nothing but horrible to you. They haven't exactly made my life easier either. But it's not about them—it's *us*. This curse is killing me and hurting you too. We should at least work together to stop that."

For a moment, something in Briar's expression softened in surprise. "Hurting me?"

Kieran's eyebrows rose. "Well—I don't know exactly what it does to you. No one at home ever spoke about it."

Instead of offering an explanation, she just whispered, "Huh."

Despite the look Delilah shot him, Kieran didn't question it. "Briar, I know you don't trust us, but I swear we're here to help. I didn't hire Delilah to break the curse—it's her Calling. If she can't break it, she'll lose her magic."

"And Kieran says we can't break it without you," Delilah added, staring into Briar's eyes. Her right one glowed blue, alive with a ghostly light. "We all have a stake in this. Which means this can go one of two ways: either you willingly come with us and help me break the curse, or you and Kieran succumb to it and I lose my magic. Is that really what you want?"

"If you're just doing your Calling," Briar asked, "how is an amateur like you supposed to break a curse that goes back generations?"

"Because I'm Klaus Hammond's daughter," Delilah shot back before she could think better of it.

Briar stared at her for a long moment. "Klaus . . . *the* Klaus Hammond?"

"That's why I asked her," Kieran said. He bit his lip. "Or—well, more like conscripted. I invoked the Rite of Morality."

"That's bold," Briar grumbled.

"So." Delilah applied more pressure to Briar's wrists. "Can you agree to at least hear us out? Without trying to run? Or summoning your familiar to attack us?"

"Fine." Her hands curled into fists. "I'll hear you out. Just *get the hell off me.*"

Delilah let go of Briar's wrists. "As you wish."

"Let's get out of here," Kieran said. "We can talk on the ship."

"Ship?"

Delilah climbed off Briar and gestured for her to follow.

"You'll see."

🌱

Later that evening, when the sun had sunk into the sea and dragged the twilight with it, Kieran, Briar, and Delilah sat at the ship's dining table. Kieran and Delilah were at one end, watching as Briar tore through a hunk of bread with her teeth like a wolf with a fawn carcass. Delilah watched with her nose wrinkled.

Kieran, meanwhile, seemed unbothered. "Can I just say—that was really incredible what you did with your familiar back there. I've never met a witch our age who had one."

Mouth still full, Briar said, "Oh, Cinnabar? Yeah, I've been able to summon him for a while." She pointed a finger at the floor, and a small ball of light popped into existence, morphing and shifting until it turned into the little orange cat from the shop.

Delilah kept her mouth shut. She didn't want to admit it, but being able to summon a familiar was an extremely advanced skill. Familiars were assistants to powerful witches—manifestations of their magic that could exist outside their bodies. Typically, witches could only ever cast through specific mediums, like baking or playing an instrument, so to summon magic directly into a physical form was way out of Delilah's league. The few witches with familiars she'd met as they were passing through Kitfield had been able to summon them for only a few minutes at a time.

She'd certainly never met someone whose familiar was more like a glorified pet.

Cinnabar narrowed his eyes at Delilah and mewed before hopping onto the table beside Briar and curling up next to her plate of food.

Briar swallowed a hunk of cheese, barely chewing it, eyes falling on Delilah. "So? What's your genius plan to break the Pelumbra curse?"

Delilah pressed her lips together, narrowing her eyes in Briar's direction. Briar glared back at her, unwavering. What was this girl's problem anyway? Every time she set eyes on her, Delilah's cheeks flared with warmth and her heart started to pound—how did Kieran's sister manage to be so infuriating just by sitting there?

Delilah bit her tongue. *Just be civil.*

"Well, bear with me, because I've only known about it for two days." Delilah sighed. She put her hands flat on the table. "I think our best bet is to find the written form of the curse. The Library of Curses in Gellingham has the largest collection in Celdwyn, and it seems smart to start there."

"You do know that the library is closed to everyone but

witches who have passed their Calling, right?" Briar crossed her arms tightly over her chest. "Unless you've got some special plan to break in."

Delilah had to breathe deeply for a moment to stop her eye from twitching. The worst part was, Briar had a point: the library *was* closed to the public. She remembered Theo telling her that, saying that once he passed his Calling, he'd go on Delilah's behalf to look for her curse. Of course, that had been before.

And frankly, Delilah had hoped Briar was as ignorant of that fact as Kieran had been. She'd wanted to buy herself more time to come up with a real plan.

"Well," she replied, "I'll just have to do a little more research to see if they have any exceptions to that rule. I'll remind you I've known about this curse for two days."

"You have no backup plan?" Briar asked, voice scornfully dry.

Delilah rolled her eyes. "I'm a balls-to-the-wall sort of person."

"We have plenty of time to float ideas," Kieran cut in before Briar could grind her teeth so hard they cracked.

"Here's my idea." Briar kicked her feet up on the table beside Cinnabar. Kieran started to say something, but the withering look she shot him stopped him in his tracks. She looked Delilah in the eye and said, "We split up. You two can mess around on this ship, and I can keep searching on my own. How does that sound?"

"You might be onto something," Delilah muttered.

"Most of what we know about the curse," Kieran explained, "revolves around your being the key to breaking it, so we should stick together." Briar, meanwhile, stared daggers at Delilah, who in turn wrinkled her nose and stuck her tongue out at Briar.

He sighed. "Can you two please relax?"

"I will if she pulls that thorny stick out of her ass," Delilah said.

"You're an idiot," Briar growled.

"Yeah?" Delilah raised an eyebrow, crossing her arms over her chest. "What of it?"

"Please." Kieran buried his face in his hands. "I'm *literally* dying here."

He'd mostly said it in jest, but the weight of it seemed to give Briar pause. She looked at him—really looked at him—for the first time. Delilah watched her study him, taking in the hollows under his eyes and the pallor of his skin. Delilah had shied away from doing that, because there was a certain wrongness to those features—a warning that something was seriously off.

"Okay, fine. I'll play." Briar gestured around the ship. "Where am I supposed to sleep? Plus, are you willing to deal with all the fools the Pelumbras have been sending after me since I ran away? Can you handle—" She cut herself off before she could finish, then amended, "Can you *leave me alone*?"

"With your sunny disposition, I can't imagine being able to stay away," Delilah grumbled, mostly to Kieran.

"If it keeps you here," Kieran said, "yes. And I'd be happy to show you the room I saved for you."

For a millisecond, a flicker of surprise flashed across Briar's face, replacing her perpetual scowl. Her thick brows knitted together. "You saved a room for me?"

"Ariel asked for it, but I wanted to make sure you had your own space once we found you." He stood up. "Come on. I'll show you."

Delilah recalled there being a third bedroom on the upper deck where her room and Kieran's were—the one directly across from Delilah's. She tried not to let her annoyance at the idea of running into Briar in the hallway cross her face.

Then again, if she stayed on the ship, they'd be running into each other *all the time.*

Delilah seethed.

Kieran took the two of them to the upper deck, across the open section, Cinnabar trotting beside Briar with his tail bobbing in the air. From up here, they could see over the treetops to Port Lorring, where people had returned to their homes for the night, either at the edges of town or on houseboats. Yellow lights danced across the shadowy sea, swaying in time with the tide.

Inside Kieran opened the door to the room across from Delilah's. Instantly, she was struck with a pang of envy. Her own cabin was double the size of her bedroom at home, but Briar's was even larger. The bed looked as if it could fit four people, and an enormous wardrobe was open to a set of new clothes. Another door led to a bathroom, and craning her neck to see, Delilah noted a clawfoot bathtub.

She scowled. *Her* room didn't have a bathtub.

Briar, standing in the middle of the room, surveyed it like someone considering buying their first home. She seemed to be mentally noting every detail of the wallpaper, the scratches and scuffs on the hardwood floor, the state of the huge windows. Cinnabar sniffed around the bed, pawing at the floor with his ears flat against his head.

"How high is the ceiling?" Briar asked, looking over her shoulder.

Delilah and Kieran exchanged a look. Kieran said, "Um . . . maybe nine feet?"

"Hmm." She tapped a finger against her chin. "Are there curtains?"

"I'm sure we could pick some up at the next fuel stop."

"That's not what I asked." She turned the rest of the way around, eyes narrowed. Her blue eye seemed brighter than before, and Delilah remembered what Kieran had said about his glowing brighter when he was about to have an attack. When she glanced at him, though, his eye seemed the same as it had been for the last few days. Briar's seemed to naturally give off more of a ghostly shine, even when she wasn't using magic.

Kieran acquiesced, "Sure. You can have mine."

"Good." Her eyes fell on the door, which was made of heavy oak with an intricate, knotted-loop design carved into it. "One more thing: Is there a lock on the door?"

Kieran nodded. "All the doors have locks."

"What are you planning on doing in here?" Delilah asked, wrinkling her brow. "Cult sacrifices?"

"I've been on the run for six months," Briar snapped back. "It's precautionary."

"What does the ceiling height have to do with that?"

Briar's cheeks were tinged with the faintest touch of pink. "Uh—I'm—claustrophobic."

"And your fear has *specific measurements?*"

"Delilah," Kieran warned, though he kept his voice gentle. "It's not a big deal." To Briar he said, "If there's anything else you need, we can find a way to get it. Money isn't an object."

"For a Pelumbra? I assumed not." Briar went to the bed and pressed a hand down on it. Seemingly finding it soft enough for her liking, Briar nodded. "Not bad." Cinnabar leapt up onto the bed and began kneading at the comforter.

"So?" Kieran pressed his hands together and held them up as if he were praying to her. "Will you come with us?"

Briar exhaled and sank down onto the bed. She ran her hand over the spread. For a second, she paused, then clawed her fingers back gently across it.

"Fair warning," she said, not meeting either of their gazes. "Having me here will complicate things."

"We need you," Kieran insisted. He clasped his hands together, wringing them. "We have plenty of resources to deal with whatever you can throw at us."

Her mouth cut into a humorless smile. "You might regret saying that."

Before Delilah could ask what in the world that meant, steps in the hall alerted them to Adelaide's arrival. Kieran turned and greeted her as she peered around him, a broom in her hand. When she saw Briar, her eyes widened.

The broom fell and clattered to the floor.

Cinnabar hissed, ears flattening against his head, while Briar raised an eyebrow.

"Uh. Hi?" Briar hooked a thumb toward Adelaide, asking Kieran, "Is this another of your weird friends?"

"This is Adelaide," Kieran said. He looked to Adelaide. "Adelaide, this is Briar. She's going to be staying here with us." His eyes wandered back to his twin. "Or—I think she is."

Briar didn't respond, however, as Adelaide slowly approached her. Briar and Cinnabar drew back in tandem, and Adelaide stopped, her eyes shining with . . . unshed tears?

Delilah's eyebrows rose.

"Is she okay?" Briar asked, forehead wrinkled and shoulders bent back as if she could lean her way out of the situation.

"She's cursed too—can't communicate," Kieran explained. "Adelaide—"

Adelaide took one more step forward before halting when Cinnabar let out a low growl in the back of his throat. As if just noticing that everyone could see her, Adelaide looked at Kieran, eyebrows bent upward, breath heavy. Delilah certainly couldn't read her as well as Kieran, but Adelaide definitely looked over-whelmed.

"Yeah—I know. Meeting my sister, it's, um"—Kieran ran his hand back through his hair and met her eyes, addressing Briar with the back half of the statement—"a big moment."

"Seriously?" Briar asked, disbelieving. "Even after everything you've heard about me? Even though I'm k—"—she caught her-self and corrected—"stealing your magic?"

Kieran shrugged. "I know you're not doing it on purpose. And I'm not a huge fan of the Pelumbras these days. They really screwed us over."

Adelaide's neck tensed as if it were stopping her from nodding.

"That's a relief." Briar glanced at Adelaide once more and said, "Well, you all seem deeply strange. But if it gets the curse broken"—she sighed—"then I guess I can stay."

She must have spotted Delilah's eyes rolling all the way to the back of her head, because she added, "As long as it's all right with everyone."

Delilah dragged in a breath. It took all her effort to choke out, "Fine."

Kieran grinned. "Welcome aboard, Briar."

The next morning, Ariel set a course for Gellingham, which they estimated would take about two weeks. As the day turned to afternoon, Delilah wandered the ship before poking her head into the kitchen. It wasn't particularly large, but there was a gas-burning stove and a candy-red icebox full of fresh ingredients. She'd taken stock of the well-filled pantry when she was baking the biscuits she'd used on Briar and had been thinking nonstop about all the other possibilities since then.

From the pantry, she gathered in her arms a jar of peanut butter, a sky-blue tin of powdered sugar, chocolate chips, shortening, and a tiny vial of vanilla extract, then lined them up on the counter. She discovered a turntable tucked back against the stovetop, and when she opened it, there was a record inside—an upbeat Esperonan artist she recognized. She turned the player on, and it let out a low hum before a brassy trumpet melody vibrated through the room.

She cranked up the music, holding a hair tie between her teeth as she pulled her curls into a ponytail. She retrieved a bowl from the cabinets and went to work mixing the peanut butter, vanilla, sugar, and butter from the icebox together with her hands. Her eyes flickered with green light as she drew magic up from the center of her chest and into her fingers, where soft light poured from her fingertips, flowing in like melted chocolate. It vanished as Delilah mixed it in, but it left a tinge of her magic's cinnamon-sugar scent on the air.

She had the music turned up loud enough that she didn't notice when Santiago, followed by Ariel, came into the kitchen. For a minute, Delilah didn't see them as they watched her rolling the dough between her hands and into small balls that she set on a baking sheet, eyes still glowing and magic rolling off her in waves.

"Kieran didn't mention he'd conscripted you to be a pastry chef as well," Santiago finally said.

Delilah yelped and dropped a peanut butter ball back into the bowl. She held up her hands—sticky and sugar-coated—as if he'd caught her doing something illegal. When Santiago and Ariel both started snickering, she lowered her hands, blushing. Santiago reached out and gently turned down the music so it was easier to hear.

"I-I'm so sorry I didn't ask you if I could use the kitchen," Delilah said. Her eyes faded to their normal shade of gray. "I thought—I assumed you were busy—"

"So long as you don't light anything on fire, I see no reason to stop you," Santiago said, flicking a lock of hair out of his eyes. His undercut wasn't doctored the same way it had been for the last few days, so it hung in his face in a mess of waves. He pointed to Delilah's bowl. "What's this?"

Delilah scooped out another small ball of dough and began to shape it. "They're going to be peanut butter balls dipped in chocolate. I just wanted something easy I could put magic into."

"You use baking to channel your magic?" Santiago guessed.

Delilah nodded. "Among other things. But yes."

"I used to put it into my cooking," Santiago mused. A small frown curved the edge of his mouth, but he caught it and forced a smile.

Delilah narrowed her eyes. "But I don't smell any magic on you."

"Here we go," Ariel muttered.

"Well, I was once a witch," Santiago said. He pressed a hand to his heart while he wiggled the fingers on his other hand. "So powerful and incredibly talented. I wowed beautiful people all across Esperona, cooking spells into my food that lasted long after consumption. But for some bureaucratic, horrid, stupid reason—"

"He failed his Calling," Ariel cut in. Santiago shot them a bruised look, and they added, "What? She doesn't have all day."

"I didn't *fail*. I just chose not to pass, thank you," Santiago snapped. He stole a wooden spoon from the counter and lightly smacked Ariel's leg with it. "You *wound* me."

"Oh, do I?" Ariel stuck their leg out and waved it around, grinning. "Hit me again, pretty boy."

Delilah wrinkled her forehead.

"Not in front of the children," Santiago chided. Then he smacked Ariel's thigh once again, sending them into a fit of cackling laughter. He drew back, smiling slightly.

Ariel flicked a hand at him. "Oh, you." Turning their attention back to Delilah, they asked, "So what magic are you putting in there?"

Delilah blinked, having nearly forgotten what she was doing.

"Oh—it's a sort of . . . temperance spell. If you eat one, you'll feel less inclined toward intense emotions."

Santiago asked, "Any reason?"

"Well, it's—" Delilah set her jaw. She frowned as she pressed another peanut butter ball into shape. "I don't want to sound . . . judgmental . . ."

Santiago said to Ariel, "You see? Your nonsense has already made her hate us. She needs magic desserts just to be around us."

"Not you," Delilah clarified. She ground her teeth. "It's— *Briar.*"

They both raised their eyebrows.

"Something about her sets me off," Delilah added, scowling. She picked up the tray of peanut butter balls and moved them to the icebox, letting out a sigh as she closed it. "It's so strange. I've never let a bad first impression get to me, but"—she tightened her fingers into claws in front of her—"even just thinking about her makes me angry. My heart starts beating fast, and I get this head rush that makes me dizzy. It's *bizarre.*"

"She's only been here for a day," Ariel pointed out. "How can you dislike her so much so fast?"

"Talk to her for a minute," Delilah said, rubbing her temples. "You'll get it."

"If you need a break, you're welcome to come to Dothering with me and Ariel tomorrow," Santiago offered. "It's a very cute little mountain town. We're landing the ship there to make a supply run."

Ariel added, "It shouldn't take more than a few hours."

"Oh—sure. I'd love to join," Delilah said, dropping her hands as she brightened at the idea of traveling to a new town. Their trip to Port Lorring had been so brief she hadn't had a chance to explore at all between pep-talking Kieran and wrestling with Briar. "If it's not too much trouble, of course."

"Course not," Ariel said, kicking their legs over the edge of the counter like a child whose feet didn't touch the ground. "Plus, we appreciate the chance to chat with someone new. Before you, Santi and I only had Kieran and Adelaide to talk to. And Adelaide— well, Kieran is a lot better at understanding her than we are. We're still learning how to read her."

"How does Kieran know her so well?" Delilah asked.

"Kieran always clung to her as a child at the estate—his parents were never the nurturing type," Ariel explained.

"When he was a child?" Delilah blinked. "But Adelaide doesn't look that much older than us."

Ariel and Santiago exchanged a look. Santiago asked, "Did Kieran not tell you about the other part of her curse?"

Delilah shook her head.

"Adelaide hasn't aged the entire time we've known her," Ariel explained. When Delilah's eyebrows shot up, they added, "And Kieran never saw her age either, and he's known her his entire life. None of us know how old she really is."

"I didn't know there was magic that could do that," Delilah said. She glanced down at her peanut butter balls. *I'm certainly not going to be baking immortality scones anytime soon.* "Much less a curse."

Ariel nodded. "She's a bit hard to parse. Adelaide's main job at the estate, aside from being Kieran's parents' maid, was teaching the younger Pelumbras magic. Kieran wasn't allowed to learn from her—the thought being that if he used too much magic, it would speed up the curse. But he always found excuses to watch his cousins learn. I think Adelaide took some pity on him and gave him private lessons."

"She has a soft spot for youths," Santiago mused. "Can't imagine why. So loud and demanding." His eyes slowly panned the kitchen and settled on the sink, where a few dishes sat soaking in soapy water. "Including your new nemesis, it seems. I saw Adelaide carrying food to Briar's door earlier. It appears she made it herself."

"But she hates cooking," Ariel said, wrinkling their nose.

"She did seem a bit . . . emotional when she met Briar." Delilah chewed her lip. "Before we went to find her, Adelaide saw me looking through pictures of Briar that Kieran got from an information broker, and she seemed pretty affected by them. As if Adelaide knew Briar somehow. But if Briar grew up away from the estate, I don't know how she would."

Santiago and Ariel exchanged a look, both shrugging.

Ariel said, "Perhaps . . . Adelaide pities her? And wants to be extra hospitable in an effort to keep her around? Kieran did make it sound important that Briar stay with us."

"Strange indeed—but not our problem," Santiago said. He ducked down to one of the cabinets, removed the lock that secured the doors, and opened it. He shifted around glass bottles for a moment before retrieving one. "Now, as lovely as those treats of yours sound, Delilah, would you be interested in a pinot noir?"

She shook her head. "No thanks. I hate the taste of wine."

Santiago used an opener to pop the cork, then poured two glasses, for himself and Ariel. To Ariel, he said, "Children these days—no sophistication." Shifting his gaze to Delilah, he added, "We'll be in the sitting room splitting the rest of the bottle if you change your mind."

The two of them clinked their glasses before leaving Delilah alone with her mixing bowls and her thoughts.

CHAPTER FIVE

Rule #19: While the scent of their magic is far from an indicator of one's character, there's always something suspicious about citrus.

The next day, the ship came to a creaking halt in a public airfield outside Dothering. It seemed the town was a common stop for travelers. Thirty other aeroships of varying sizes were parked around the field, their balloons and flexible metal wings fluttering in the breeze in time with the long green grass.

"Almost ready to go?" Kieran asked Delilah, joining her on the deck outside their bedrooms. She'd invited him to join them for the supply stop. He wore an oversize sweater with ornate patterns woven into it, looping knots that reminded her of the typical garb of the fishing islands off the coast of Kitfield.

Delilah had opted for a floral-patterned yellow A-line dress that fell around her ankles, and black heels with a buckle across the top of her foot. She leaned a hip against the railing, finishing braiding her dark hair and tying it off with an elastic. "Just you, me, Ariel, and Santiago, then?"

In answer to her question, Delilah heard footsteps behind them and looked over her shoulder to find Briar staring at her. She had on a ragged, oversize black coat. Her boots looked big enough to fit a person double her size, swallowing her tiny ankles. An eye patch covered her blue eye.

Delilah averted her gaze, trying not to stare. Her heart squeezed. *She looks ridiculous.*

Briar stared at Delilah for a beat, then turned to look the other way, scowling.

"Briar's coming," Kieran said, all smiles. "She wants to check out the pharmacy."

"Are you sick?" Delilah asked her, frowning.

Briar refused to meet the other girl's eyes. "No. What are we standing around for? Let's move."

Delilah and Kieran exchanged a look, and Kieran shrugged. "Away we go, then."

Santiago was waiting for them downstairs with a shopping list. He greeted the three warmly, hesitating when his eyes fell on Briar. She scowled at him and didn't say anything.

"You know, you're welcome to have breakfast with us one of these mornings," Santiago said, breaking the silence as she glared. "We're not so bad. Usually Ariel chews with their mouth closed."

Instead of responding, Briar started for the door and muttered, "I like to eat alone."

Santiago's smile faltered. He glanced over his shoulder at Ariel, just arrived, who shrugged.

"Don't feel bad," Delilah told Santiago as they followed Briar out. "She's snide to everyone."

He just laughed it off. "And here I thought you were going to be the snippy one."

They all walked to town, Briar ten feet ahead of everyone else. Kieran tried a few times to speed up and speak to her, but she just walked faster as soon as he got close. When it was starting to look as if he was going to run after her, Delilah cleared her throat and waved him back. He gave up, pursing his lips.

Dothering was a rustic village at the base of a small mountain range, with a culture that seemed geared toward outdoor recreation. Most townsfolk wore boots suited for scaling steep traverses, and heavy, layered clothing ready for any weather. There was a fresh alpine chill in the air, a final whisper of winter. Wildflowers in an array of colors burst from the ground, and the smell of them mixed with a hint of tanning leather. The buildings were made largely of pale wood—Delilah suspected it was magic-blocking hawthorn, like they had in Kitfield. *Not fans of witches, I guess.* Most of the windows boasted advertisements for skis and snowshoes despite its being May.

As soon as they reached town, Briar disappeared into a crowd, and they lost sight of her.

Santiago asked, "Should we be worried?"

"No—I could sniff her out from a mile away," Delilah said.

Kieran opened and closed his mouth, still staring off in the direction his sister had gone. His lips pulled into a small frown.

Poor Kieran, Delilah thought. *He really does just want to get to know her. Too bad she has the charisma of a pit viper.*

She looped her arm through Kieran's. "Don't worry about her. Let's go to the market and peruse the wares."

Kieran considered her arm before letting out a sigh and saying, "All right. You lead the way."

🍃

Soon after, Kieran and Delilah split from Santiago and Ariel, who were heading off to get foodstuffs and ship maintenance parts, respectively. Exploring Dothering's farmers market stalls for the next hour, Delilah forcing Kieran to try new foods, and they took turns picking out various hats for each other at the leather-worker's shop. They bought lunch from a stall offering freshly made potatoes with gravy and cheese curds, a local specialty, then took a seat on the grass beneath a massive pine tree after kicking the pinecones away and did their best not to spill gravy on themselves.

"I never got to do stuff like this at home," Kieran said through a mouthful of food. "My parents would never let me go off alone for this long, much less with someone from outside the estate."

"Probably smart considering how much money I just made you spend." Delilah took a bite out of a crisp apple Kieran had bought her, slightly sour and starchy on her tongue. "We outsiders are dangerous."

"It's just—I never knew how good people out here have it." He held his arms out to the world at large. "My whole life, everyone at the estate said the entire world was a horrible, terrifying place where any second someone could sneak up and hurt you. And I believed them." He shot her a small smile. "I thought I'd never be able to make a friend outside the family."

Delilah felt a touch of warmth in her chest as she looked out over the town. *He really is a nice guy. If anyone had to hijack my Calling, I guess it isn't so bad it was him.*

From their spot on the hill, they could see the streets below, mostly quiet, the weekday forcing most people inside for work. Still, parents and small children, people getting lunch, and retired couples brought life onto the cobblestones, faces alight and gazes warm.

"There are plenty of bad people in the world," Delilah admitted, palming her cheek. "But I like to think that, at their core, most people are good. Maybe I'm naive because I've never really been out of Kitfield before this, but back home, I met so many people traveling from so many places. They taught me a lot."

Kieran smiled dreamily. "It makes you want to see more of the world, right?"

"Yes, exactly! I always wanted to, but . . . I didn't feel like I could leave my mom alone, what with our curse and all." Delilah exhaled a breath, letting her eyes wander to the sky. "I've always dreamed of seeing Celdwyn for myself. Y'know, buy a car and take it from city to city, meet new people, maybe even go out of the country. That sort of thing."

His eyes lit up. "That's what I want to do someday too. I want to change my name, start fresh, and see the world. Be someone who isn't just a consequence of where I come from and who my family is."

"That makes it sound like you want to be someone else." Delilah raised her eyebrows. "What's wrong with Kieran Pelumbra?"

"Where do I even start," Kieran muttered, using his fork to turn over potatoes, coating them in the gravy. He popped one in his mouth, then began to gesture with his fork. "The only thing Kieran Pelumbra is meant to do is *die*. My family constructed a whole identity for me—a pure-hearted, kind little martyr—and I believed them. If I can break this curse and make a life for myself, I can prove to them that I'm not just their sweet little boy who's too good for this world. I just"—he held up his hands—"I want to live on my terms, you know?"

Delilah nodded. "It must have been pretty freeing to steal the ship, then, huh?"

Kieran sputtered a laugh. "I was scared beyond belief. Didn't sleep for four days."

"But you did it," Delilah pointed out. "You got out. You've already stuck a knife in the person they thought you were."

"Oh." Kieran blinked, a small smile creeping across his face. "I . . . hadn't thought about that. Maybe you're right."

They went quiet, and Delilah's mind wandered. She'd pictured herself traveling the world with Theo back when they were together. They'd had conversations just like this, but while cuddled beneath the old willows in the meadow near Delilah's cottage. When everything had gone wrong with them, she'd stopped letting herself dream about the future as much.

It was nice to dream again.

She opened her mouth to say something, but a smell hit her that made her choke on her words. She clapped a hand over her nose, gagging.

Kieran raised an eyebrow in question before Delilah started to explain: "I think—Briar's—"

On the street below, they spotted a dark shape weaving through the crowd. The figure was small, agile as she moved through the masses like a fish swimming upstream. Even with her hood drawn up to hide her face, Delilah would know that smell of soggy undergrowth and blood anywhere.

Not far behind her was a man in a trench coat, running after her in a dead sprint.

Delilah's heart began to race.

Kieran's eyes widened. "Is that—? What is she *doing*?"

"That dumbass," Delilah hissed. "I'm going after her."

"You're—?" Kieran stalled while Delilah took off after his sister. He cupped his hands around his mouth. "You can't just leave me— *Delilah!*"

But she was already off, driven by impulse alone. She caught a flash of Briar ducking into an alleyway and followed, her shoes clacking loudly against the cobblestones.

She skirted the side of a ski shop and stopped at the entrance to the narrow alley, shaded by the buildings on either side. There she spotted Briar, tucking herself behind a parked car.

Just as Delilah moved to catch up with her, the sound of pounding feet snapped her to attention. The man who'd been chasing Briar came to stand at Delilah's side. He looked in both directions, teeth clenched. He had close-cropped blond hair, and his eyes glowed yellow-green with magic as his fingers moved to draw a symbol in the air. It had a pungent smell like aftershave, with a distinctly citrusy edge to it.

"Did you see a girl run by here?" he asked Delilah.

"Why should I tell you?" she asked, fighting to keep her

breathing even after sprinting. She narrowed her eyes. "You're not a cop."

"I'm a detective." The man, eyes still magic-bright and glowing, reached into his coat pocket and pulled out an ID badge that read REGEN PELUMBRA, beneath a photo of him. "Now, I need you to tell me if you saw a girl with a buzz cut and a black coat run down this street. She could be putting a lot of people in danger."

Pelumbra.

Delilah's heart shuddered, and her shoulders tensed.

After a moment's pause, she pointed down the alleyway. "She went to the end of the alleyway and turned left, sir."

"Right." He shot Delilah one last, pointed look, seeming to notice she was bit out of breath for the first time. Thankfully, he didn't mention anything about it. "Whatever you do, don't follow her."

He sprinted down the alley and turned left at the end. Delilah checked both ways on the street behind her. The only people nearby were seemingly bewildered townsfolk, shrugging and gesticulating wildly as they chattered.

She ducked into the shadows of the alleyway, out of view, and headed for the car Briar was hidden behind.

Coming around the side of it and kneeling, Delilah started to ask, "What the hell did you d—?"

Before she could finish, something ropelike and thorny launched at her throat and wrapped around it like a noose.

She choked, clawing at it in desperation. Its thorns felt like teeth in her neck. Her fingernails scraped at plant matter—it was a vine.

Briar's eyes widened, burning with blue light. "Oh—it's you. Shit."

Her eyes flickered, and the vine instantly wilted and dropped from Delilah's throat. Delilah gasped, grabbing at her neck. Her other hand landed on the cobblestones to steady her. The thorns had dug into her skin, leaving indents and pinprick wounds that beaded with blood. Her chest heaved as she cursed a blue streak.

"I thought you were that guy with the trench coat," Briar explained nonchalantly. She stood and peered over the side of the car to confirm the alleyway was empty. "I'm glad he decided to piss off."

"What the *hell*?" Delilah gasped, pulling her hand away from her throat to find her palm smeared with blood. "What was that?"

"Ledrith spell," Briar explained. She turned and glanced at Delilah, catching sight of her bleeding throat. She winced, inhaling a hissing breath. "Sorry."

"*Of course* you'd use the only kind of magic meant for fighting people." Delilah suppressed an eye roll and started to ask, "What were you—?"

Her eyes fell on a small messenger bag at Briar's side. It had fallen and spilled its contents onto the cobblestones. Briar noticed it at the same moment Delilah did and immediately turned red.

Tampons. And painkillers.

"Did you *steal* those?" Delilah demanded.

Briar, cheeks burning, gathered them back up into her bag. She shouldered it and snapped, "What of it?"

"That guy was a Pelumbra! And a *detective*!" Delilah snapped. "If he recognized you, we could be in serious trouble!" She peeked over the hood of the car and said, "I sent him the wrong way, but we need to get out of here. Kieran's still up on the hill."

"Why did you follow me in the first place?" Briar demanded. "I would have been fine on my own!"

"Because I—!" Delilah's face warmed, and she frowned. "Because you're not on your own anymore, okay? If we don't look out for each other, we're screwed." She nodded back toward the street. "Now hurry up—we need to get you and Kieran out of here."

Briar blinked and stared for a moment, eyebrows pressed together. Then, after a beat, she set her jaw and followed.

After sneaking around Dothering like fugitives, Delilah and Briar found Kieran wandering near the hill—looking a little more than a bit ruffled as he searched for Delilah and his sister—and ushered him away. Soon after, they managed to track down Ariel and Santiago at the local farmers market. Luckily, the five of them slipped back into the woods without being noticed. Once they were within the safety of the trees, Kieran began asking frantically about the cuts and bruises on Delilah's neck, delicately turning her chin at one point to get a better view of one of the deeper punctures. She pushed his hand away, rolling her eyes and insisting she was fine.

Briar was silent the whole way back, trailing behind the group with a burning glare aimed at no one in particular.

"It's over now," Delilah told Kieran, who was still fretting about the whole incident. "We're okay."

"At least you were kind enough to let me finish my shopping,"

Santiago said. He lifted one of his sizable bags of groceries. "I'm going to make all of you eat something with spice for once instead of that boring Celdwynian food you all seem to like so much."

"And we had time to grab my favorite fruit biscuits," Ariel added. They took a large bite of one they'd pulled from a box and said, mouth full, "Without these, I might mutiny."

"We'll have to keep a close eye out in case we're being followed," Kieran said, glancing over his shoulder. To Ariel, he added, "Keep the ship flying at a higher elevation so we can't be spotted as easily."

Ariel swallowed the biscuit. "Aye, aye, Captain."

They reached the ship a minute later and climbed the gangway while Kieran went on about all the precautions they'd have to take to make sure no one was able to track their path. Ariel waved Kieran away as they headed toward the control room, the box of biscuits held close to their chest. Santiago went to the kitchen to unload the food.

In the study's sitting area, Kieran rubbed his eyes and then reopened them, focusing on Delilah. "At our next stop, we'll have to—"

"Kieran," Delilah interrupted with a gasp. "Your eye!"

He reached up to touch it, seemingly unaware that it was glowing a fierce, fluorescent blue. It cast a spectral glow across his skin, washing away any pink in his cheeks and bringing up the shadows beneath his eyes. His lips parted for a moment before he winced, shoving a knuckle into the space between his eyebrows.

"Delilah," he said through his teeth, "don't panic. I'm about to have an attack."

From behind them, Delilah heard Briar let out a shaking whimper as she entered the room. Delilah took a step closer to her as Briar hugged herself. When she looked up, both eyes shone with blue magic that rose from the edges like water vapor.

Delilah gasped.

"Santiago!" she screamed. Kieran made a faint noise, and Delilah caught his elbow as he began to sway, knees weak. Delilah cried, "Ariel! Adelaide! *Help!*"

Briar muffled a scream with her fist. She ran for the stairs, but a sudden painful spasm hit her, and she slammed into the door-frame on her way out. A portrait on the wall fell and hit the floor.

The glass shattered.

Briar disappeared up the stairs.

"What do I do?" Delilah asked, holding Kieran's arm so tightly her nails dug into his skin. "Kieran, *what do I do?*"

His eyelids fluttered. "Hold on to me."

Delilah did just that when he passed out the next second. Carefully, she lowered him to the floor, cradling his head in her hands. Her fingers sank into his soft curls. Her heart hammered against her ribs.

"Kieran?" She felt the back of her throat tighten. "Can you hear me?"

At that moment, Santiago came running in from the kitchen, swooping down beside them. He went to his knees, shrugging off his coat. "Did he just pass out?"

Delilah nodded, panicked tears pricking in her eyes. "I— I don't—"

"Lift his head," Santiago said, his usual joking expression gone from his face. She'd never heard him sound so serious.

Delilah did as he said, gently tilting his head up as Santiago shoved his coat underneath it, balled into a loose sort of pillow.

"What happened to his sister?" Santiago asked.

Delilah's eyes flitted to the broken portrait on the floor across the room, jagged shards of glass shining in the afternoon light. "I—I don't know—something bad."

"Go check," he said. "I'll stay with Kieran."

Delilah hesitated, hands hovering over him. She was still shaking, mind swimming. Kieran wasn't moving, except for his shallow breathing, as he lay with his head nestled in Santiago's coat. There was a wrongness about that that made it very clear he wasn't just sleeping. It was as if any exhale might be his last.

"It's okay," Santiago said. "I have him. Go check his sister."

Pulling away from him felt like withdrawing her hands from a tangle of thorns. She cast one more wide-eyed look after him before she took off running for the stairs to the upper deck. Briar had tracked in some mud on her boots, and it was easy enough to follow.

Delilah burst onto the open upper deck, eyes scanning. She instantly noticed Briar's coat on the deck in a heap. She picked it up, balling it in her fist.

She shouted, "Briar!"

She took a few more steps, following the mud tracks, until she came across Briar's boots, lying not far from the door leading in from the deck to the sleeping quarters. As Delilah went to examine them, she noticed tiny scarlet droplets on the deck. They painted a small, dappled arc across the wood.

Delilah was positive it was Briar's blood. She'd never thought about where the smell of a curse came from when she caught it on a person, but leaning over the spatter now, she suddenly realized the stink of it must live in the bloodstream. She pressed her hand against her nose, holding in the urge to vomit.

Faintly, Delilah caught the sound of muffled screaming.

That was when she noticed that the door was slightly ajar. Without a second's hesitation, Delilah ran for it, shouting the other girl's name.

Just before she could get there, though, a figure slipped out of the door and slammed it closed. Delilah had to skid to a halt.

Adelaide stared at her with huge, wild eyes. Blond hair floated from the bun at the back of her head, and blood was beginning to seep from a tiny hairline cut on her cheek.

"I have to go check on her," Delilah said. "Please."

For a moment, Adelaide opened her mouth, beginning to form a word, but her teeth snapped shut. She winced, pressing a hand into her jawbone.

Delilah added, "Something weird is going on."

Adelaide reached back, locking a hand around the knob. She met Delilah's eyes, firm, and even if she couldn't say it, her face made it clear enough: *No.*

She had seemed so unassuming when they met. Now the sight of her, with her teeth locked and her eyes bright with a sort of righteous indignation, made Delilah take a step back.

"Adelaide," Delilah whispered, the fight leaving her, "I just want to make sure she's okay."

The woman didn't so much as blink.

"I . . . Fine." Delilah stood, planted, for another beat before backing off. "If you're sure."

She turned and started back to the dining room, where Kieran had gone down.

She didn't realize until she was halfway down the stairs that she was still clinging to Briar's coat, the smell of curse and blood so strong it made her dizzy.

Delilah dropped onto a step, put her face in her hands, and tried not to hyperventilate.

CHAPTER SIX

Rule #9: If kitchen witchcraft is proof of anything,
it's that the fastest way to ensnare a heart
is through the stomach.

When Delilah finally pulled herself together, she came down the stairs to find Kieran sprawled out on one of the couches in the study. Santiago explained that Kieran was sleeping now and would likely wake up in half an hour or so. When Delilah admitted that she hadn't found out what happened to Briar but that Adelaide was handling it, he simply raised an eyebrow.

"But Kieran's okay?" Delilah asked.

Santiago nodded. "He'll be fine. It's only been fourteen days since the last attack, though. Before that, it was twenty, and before that, it was almost two months between attacks."

"That doesn't sound good."

"Certainly not ideal."

Santiago stood, tucking his book under his arm. His usually

coiffed hair was lifeless, and he had shadows under his eyes. Delilah hadn't seen him like this—it seemed particularly stark to see him without a smile on his face. It occurred to her—perhaps for the first time—that he and Ariel were the closest thing they had to parental figures on the ship, despite only being in their mid-twenties. For all his joking around, Santiago had to feel responsible for all of them to some degree.

He took a breath and squared his shoulders, a flimsy smile returning to his face. "But I suppose that's why we have you, right? This will be a thing of the past soon."

Delilah's throat tightened.

"Can you stay here for a bit to keep an eye on him?" Santiago asked. "Ariel wanted to wait to take off until Kieran was stable. I need to tell them—"

"L-let me," Delilah managed. When Santiago raised an eyebrow, she said, "I was going to head that way anyway."

"Of course." His mouth settled into a line. "Are you all right, my friend?"

"I—I'm fine. I'm fine." They held eye contact for a moment, and Delilah became painfully aware that she was mostly trying to convince herself.

Her gaze fell to Kieran again. His eyelids fluttered a bit in his sleep, and his features looked softer. She said to Santiago, "Just call if anything else happens."

While she headed toward the control room, Santiago let out a breath through his nose and whispered, "Of course."

Delilah locked herself in her room for the rest of the night, electing to skip dinner in favor of shoving her face in a pillow and trying to convince her brain to stop panicking. When that didn't work, she started pacing, feeling like she was going to crawl out of her skin. She contemplated punching a pillow to try to work out some of her frustrations, or pulling her hair out, but settled on slumping down in bed and crying.

Kieran's going to die, she thought, *and it'll be all my fault.*

Even with years of private magic tutoring, she'd never expected she'd be trying to break a curse as powerful as the Pelumbras'. She'd been prepared to break her own curse, which, while certainly not pleasant by any means, wasn't going to kill her. The more time she spent on the ship, the more she understood that she had not one but *two* people's lives in her hands. It made her want to scream at the top of her lungs, or maybe run far, far away, go into hiding, and never show her face again.

Not that that was a feasible option, but abandoning society to live as a bog witch wasn't *un*appealing, exactly.

I can't leave Kieran, she decided. *Or Briar. Even if she is a massive pain in my ass.*

Soon, as quiet overtook the ship and the others slunk off to bed, Delilah's growling stomach became too much. Groaning, she hauled herself to the kitchen.

The ship was entirely silent as she snuck through the halls. The floorboards creaked under her bare feet, cold on her toes. She spotted Adelaide through the doors of the study, a broom leaning against the door while she thumbed through a book on the shelf. Delilah stayed quiet, tiptoeing to the kitchen. She flicked the light on to find it immaculate—part of her had been hoping she'd find dinner still sitting on the counter.

No such luck. She didn't find anything in the icebox either. Letting out a sigh, she gathered sharp cheddar cheese, butter, and walnut bread. After digging around for a skillet beside the stove, she found one made of cast iron and put it on the stovetop, cranking up the heat and piling the sandwich inside. While it was warming, she used greens, a chopped apple, ground mint, salt and pepper, and olive oil to make a salad. She shoved bites of it into her mouth while she waited for her grilled cheese to get melty.

She had just flipped it when footsteps caught her attention. "Santiago?"

Instead, Briar stepped inside. She had on a big black sweater and loose canvas pants. She had thumbprint shadows under her eyes, and her shoulders were hunched. She saw Delilah and immediately turned her gaze to the floor, cheeks pink.

Delilah's stomach fluttered. She ground her teeth, turning to stare hard at her grilled cheese. Heat built in her chest as Briar wordlessly went to the pantry. Delilah couldn't even focus on her sandwich—it was as if her ears were tuned exclusively to Briar's movements as she opened the pantry door and started sifting through the contents. Delilah's hand tightened on her spatula, a frown dipping lower on her face.

"Good to see you're okay after everything this afternoon," Delilah said, though her voice came out colder than she'd intended. Part of her wanted to pry into what exactly had happened, but she doubted Briar would tell her anything if she did. She cleared her throat. "What are you doing down here?"

Briar stepped partway out of the pantry with a tin of chocolate chips and a bag of croutons held against her. "Dinner, obviously."

"Chocolate and croutons?"

"You got a problem with that?"

Delilah held up the bag of greens. "Do you at least want a salad to go with it?"

"Gross. I don't eat vegetables."

"At *all*?" Delilah's mouth fell open.

"What are you, the leaf police? Piss off." Briar closed the pantry door with her shoulder and started to leave, snacks in hand. Her face burned sunrise pink, and she couldn't even manage to look at Delilah.

Before she could go, Delilah let out a dramatic breath and snapped, "Do you want a grilled cheese?"

Briar stopped. "What?"

Delilah pointed her spatula into the pan. "If you skipped dinner, you should at least get something warm to eat. This is almost done." Briar looked shifty, and Delilah added, "Seriously. It's fine."

"Did you put magic in it?" Briar asked, lip curling.

Delilah almost scoffed, but stopped herself. "You think I have the energy for that right now? No. It's just bread and cheese and butter. I promise."

Briar bit her lip. Then she exhaled through her nose and put the croutons back in the pantry. She kept the chocolate, though, pulling herself up on the counter on the other side of the stove from where Delilah was working. She took a handful of chocolate chips and chewed them, not looking at Delilah.

Delilah glanced at the chocolate, then pressed her lips together. "Kind of a shitty day, huh?"

Briar chanced a look at her. This close, the smell of her curse was enough to unsettle Delilah's stomach, but it didn't seem quite as strong as earlier. Briar's eyes were catlike but round, equally suspicious and curious.

Delilah's heart sped up. Sweat inexplicably broke out on the back of her neck.

Briar sighed. "Yeah. Not great."

Delilah couldn't stop herself before she asked, "Why did you steal that stuff? You know you could have just asked me if you needed a tampon."

"Oh, because you would have been so thrilled to offer me one?" Briar scowled at her. "Didn't you make special magic peanut butter balls to be less annoyed by me? Because you can't even stand to look at me without getting angry?"

Delilah froze. Her eyes rounded like twin moons, fire in her cheeks. Her stomach flipped.

"I can hear you from my room," Briar explained, pointing to an air vent in the corner of the kitchen. "For future reference."

"I—I—I—" Delilah felt like her entire body was composed of nothing but sweat. She couldn't make herself even look at Briar. Her throat threatened to swell shut and suffocate her.

"I get it," Briar added, stuffing another handful of chocolate in her mouth. She added, "I'm a nightmare. But don't pretend you're any better."

"Oh, come *on*!" Delilah snapped. She slapped her spatula down on the counter and stormed to Briar's side. She looked her dead in the eye—with her seated on the counter, it negated the usual height difference. Without thinking, she leaned in close, so their faces were only a few inches apart. She jabbed a finger into Briar's chest.

"*You* have been nothing but difficult since you got here," Delilah snapped. "And I am *trying* to put up with you, but I—I . . ."

Delilah realized with a start that Briar's scowl had faded away. Now she'd gone pale, aside from a touch of pink in her cheeks and at the tip of her nose. Her body was rigid, which Delilah discovered when she unconsciously pressed a hand down next to Briar's thigh on the counter to prop herself up as she leaned in.

Briar's eyes glowed blue for a brief second. She was also staring, wide-eyed, at Delilah's lips.

And despite herself, Delilah was looking at Briar's.

"Hey. Uh." Briar swallowed thickly, as if her throat had squeezed shut. She whispered, "My sandwich is on fire."

Delilah's mouth went dry. "What is that supposed to mean?"

Briar pointed sideways at the stovetop. "It's, uh, literally on fire."

Delilah blinked and glanced at the stove to discover that strange flames—pink at the edges and blue at the bottom—had suddenly engulfed the grilled cheese. She yelped, grabbing the handle and launching the flaming sandwich into the sink, where it continued to burn. She turned the water on, but the flame only grew larger. Delilah shrieked.

Briar held out her hand, her eyes flaring blue. The fire spit sparks, then began to coil upward, drawn to her hand. Delilah watched with rounded eyes as the snakes of flame wound up onto

Briar's arm, not even singeing her sweater. Briar let out a breath, and her non-cursed eye turned brown.

The flames flickered out.

"Sorry. My magic is hard to control sometimes." She hopped off the counter, grabbing her chocolate. Blushing, she said, "I'm going to bed. Not hungry."

She hurried out the door, leaving Delilah with her heart racing.

Delilah spent the next week of their journey to Gellingham coming up with elaborate excuses for why she couldn't stop thinking about cornering Briar in the kitchen. She'd started with *I only kept staring at her mouth because I wanted to punch it,* followed by *my hands were sweaty because the kitchen is always warmer than the rest of the ship* and *my heart was beating so fast because I was angry.*

Angry. Definitely angry. It was the only logical reason for the whole affair.

She *really* didn't want to consider the alternative.

She did her best to avoid Briar as the days passed in a blur, which was thankfully pretty easy, because Briar refused to leave her room most days. When she did, she hid up in the crow's nest with Cinnabar standing guard in case anyone thought about trying to talk to her.

After the first four days, Delilah began to work out a routine. She woke up in the morning and had breakfast with Kieran, Santiago, Adelaide, and Ariel. Kieran would bring breakfast up to his sister, but based on his disappointment each time he returned to the table, she didn't have much interest in speaking to him. Then Delilah would get dressed in something other than a nightgown, braid her hair, and get to work.

There were numerous books in the study, and a few of them were specifically about hereditary curses. Delilah spent a good amount of the week picking through them, noting passages that sounded relevant to the Pelumbra curse. She kept a journal of notes, updating it as she got more information from the library and from Kieran's answers to questions she asked him.

Unfortunately, Kieran was barely any use at all. He knew practically nothing about the curse, despite having grown up around relatives who seemed to know much more about it than he did.

"That seems odd," Delilah said one day as the two of them sat in the study, both surrounded by piles of books and loose sheets of parchment. Kieran had offered to help her research that morning, which amounted to his staring dreamily out the window while Delilah peered at him over her book. "Why wouldn't your family tell you anything?"

Kieran shrugged, gaze leaving the heavy gray clouds that floated outside. "Dunno. I asked my mom once why they weren't trying to break the curse. She started crying and said looking for help would mean revealing the existence of the curse to people outside the family—it was too much of a risk of jeopardizing the family's success. Part of how we've maintained our fortune is by staying in good social standing with the right people, and she said that if anyone knew about the curse, we'd be cut off."

Delilah blinked. "Your family cares that much about their reputation? Enough to just . . . let you die?"

Kieran's expression darkened. "My mother always said it was an honor. Like my dying was what would ensure that all the other Pelumbras would continue to flourish. My whole childhood, everyone around me said that: *Kieran, you're so selfless, so pure, so kind, such a good person*—stuff like that. I believed, for a long time, that letting myself die was something noble."

"That's awful," Delilah whispered. She thought of her own mother's reluctance to tell anyone about their curse, but that was to shield Delilah from judgment. In Celdwyn, people with curses were seen as ill omens. Some people believed a curse could spread like a plague, while others thought it was proof of a lower moral standing; if you were cursed, some said, it must be because you'd done something wicked. Still, if she had a curse like Kieran's, her mother would have been all over Celdwyn looking for a solution, regardless of stigma. The thought made her chest ache.

Kieran said, "I just wanted my parents to be proud of me. And staying on the estate and letting myself die was how I thought I could do it."

"Maybe it's because I'm not rich," Delilah said, "but I can't even imagine letting my child die for the sake of staying wealthy and socially powerful."

Kieran just shrugged, but Delilah saw a shadow pass over his expression.

"You have to understand—my family is massive. There are at least two hundred of us living in Celdwyn. And of those two hundred people, nearly everyone is a witch. We get private magic tutoring and a great education from the time we can walk. The family connections mean we can get into any trade we want without even trying. Pelumbras get their entire lives handed to them, with butlers and maids and people telling them how special they are every hour of every day. I have cousins who hold lavish balls every night of the week and have attendants just to pour champagne in their mouths."

Delilah stared at him.

"Money like that makes you callous," Kieran said, closing his eyes as he exhaled. "They're so caught up in the fear of losing their privilege that Briar and I are a small sacrifice to them. And with a family as big as ours, it's unlikely the curse will ever die out on its own."

"I'm so sorry, Kieran." Delilah shook her head. "How . . . how exactly did your family become so wealthy?"

"At the very beginning? Mining, I think. I guess we still do that now, but the Pelumbras have been around so long it feels like we've always been rich. Why?" Kieran didn't sound offended, just curious.

Delilah turned her notes around to show him the page she was working on, labeled CAUSE OF CURSE. "Someone put the curse on your family. If we know why and who, we'll have a better shot at knowing how to break it. Usually, family curses are a retribution thing—you hate someone so much you don't just want *them* to suffer, you want their whole family to. So it makes sense that a Pelumbra, at some point, royally pissed someone off. Money like what you're describing tends to be a thing that pisses people off."

"Huh." Kieran reached for the book, and Delilah passed it to him. He studied the notes, eyes darting back and forth as he read. She tried not to use the moment to examine the state of his blue eye—it had been a week since the last attack, and everyone was beginning to feel on edge about when the next one would be.

" 'Jilted lover'?" Kieran read aloud.

Delilah shrugged. "I may be projecting a bit, but—that's what happened to my family. My ancestor pissed off a witch, and now no one can fall in love with us without their memories of us vanishing. Maybe something like that happened to your family."

Kieran bit his lip. "Most upper-class marriages in the north are arranged—not many feelings are involved."

"Messy business anyway." Delilah circled her note. "You know, it might be helpful to get a family tree or some marriage records. See if anyone sticks out. Powerful, jealous witch types."

It began to rain, pounding against the windows in sheets. Delilah stared out at the rivers of droplets weaving in and out of each other on the glass. She tapped the end of her pen against the paper.

Then she spotted something odd: a shadow against the clouds.

"Kieran," Delilah said, rising to her feet. She pointed through the glass. "Do you see that?"

He stood up from the couch, wrapping the blanket that had been on his legs around his head and shoulders like a cape. He came to stand beside her and squinted. "It looks like another aeroship."

"Why is it getting closer like that?"

"I don't—" Kieran cut off. What little color he had suddenly drained from his face. Delilah squinted as a flag atop the ship came into view. It showed a black bird, some sort of raptor, with two heads.

"What is that?" Delilah asked.

"The Pelumbra family crest," Kieran whispered. He spun to her, eyes wide and wild. "We have to tell Ariel."

They took off running, bursting through Ariel's door a few

moments later. The pilot was already in the main seat pulling levers and turning dials. The ship suddenly pitched, throwing Delilah into the doorframe and Kieran to the floor.

"A ship is trying to dock against us," Ariel growled through their teeth. They spun the wheel to the right. "And I can't *see* with all this rain!"

Delilah braced herself as the ship took another sharp turn. The view in front of them was nothing but the downpour, no light to guide them.

Ariel commanded, "One of you, get to one of the side windows and tell me if they're—"

A voice at Delilah's shoulder said, "They're behind us."

The next moment, Briar pushed past, despite Delilah's yelp of protest. She was soaked, her ill-fitting men's button-down shirt sticking to her like a second skin and black pants slick with rain.

She rubbed raindrops out of her eyes as she said, "If we're near where I think we are, there should be a big lake up ahead. If we play it right, we could land there and have them sail right over us."

"You know this area?" Kieran asked.

Briar's jaw set. "You don't remember from all the information you bought about me?" She gestured to the window, eyes narrowed and smoldering. "We're outside Gabriel's Edge."

"Hold on!" Ariel shouted. "We're dropping!"

Indeed, for a brief second, Delilah felt the floor fall out beneath her. She screamed. Her stomach jumped into her throat as weightlessness gripped a hand around her guts. The ship righted itself as Delilah's knees turned to jelly. She had to brace herself against the door so as not to fall.

Ariel started to say, "They should be—"

Something collided with the ship. It jerked sideways, and Delilah toppled to the floor. The control panel whistled, and Ariel shouted, "Shit—they hit one of the balloons!"

"What does that mean?" Kieran asked, pressed against the wall.

"It's about to—"

A tremendous *boom* sounded from above them as a hole ripped open in the balloon. Instantly, the back of the ship sloped down at a fifty-degree angle. Loose objects tumbled backward in a flurry, and Delilah, Briar, and Kieran all hit the wall at once. Kieran and Delilah shrieked, holding on for dear life. The hull let out a low groan.

Delilah feared that the ship was about to snap in half.

Briar clawed her way to the control panel and surveyed the scene below, still clouded by rain. "There," she said, pointing to the left, "that's the edge of the lake!"

"How can you possibly know that?" Ariel demanded, using their full strength to try to stop one of the wings from dipping. "It looks like the canyon, and the river, and most of the damn trees!"

"Just trust me!" Briar snapped back. "I lived here my whole life; I know what I'm talking about!"

"Ariel!" Kieran cried. "They're coming!"

"If you drop now," Briar said, "the fog on the lake will hide us."

"*If* we land in the lake!" Ariel spat. "If I drop us into the woods, the ship will be destroyed!"

"I know it's down there!" Briar shouted, slamming her fist on the controls.

"Ariel," Kieran said, "just listen to her! Put us down."

"Fine," they snarled through their teeth. "But if this is what destroys my ship and gets me killed, it's on you!"

They shoved forward two levers with a groan, and the wings curled in against the hull. The ship shuddered before coasting downward, picking up speed as they dropped through the thick clouds, the Pelumbra ship vanishing above them.

Everyone screamed.

At the last second, Ariel reached up and yanked a pulley on the ceiling. Something deployed at the back of the ship. It caught the wind, and the back of the ship sprang back to where it belonged, sending Kieran and Delilah stumbling.

They had time to take a breath before the ship hit water.

The ship reared forward and back. Delilah hit her elbow against the wall, and pain shot up the bone like an electric shock as water sprayed against the windows. The ship floated to a halt, hissing.

They sat for a moment before the dark shadow of the other Pelumbra ship passed overhead, heavily obscured by the fog. Delilah only hoped it would be enough to hide them, too. She braced for the ship to turn around and land beside them, its occupants forcing their way on board and taking Kieran and Briar away.

But . . . it didn't. It simply flew on, over the trees, into the storm.

"That worked?" Ariel said. They turned around, eyes wide and shining wildly. "It worked!"

"Yeah," Briar growled, hand clawing back across her buzzed hair. "You're welcome."

And for a fleeting moment as the ship bobbed in the water, Delilah stared at Briar and felt something warm prickle in her chest.

Even if they were, quite literally, not out of the woods yet.

CHAPTER SEVEN

Rule #17: Try not to get offended
by your WANTED poster.

Aside from the gaping hole in the rear balloon and some cosmetic damage to the hull, the ship remained largely intact. Ariel beached the ship halfway up the lake's rocky edge; it let out a monstrous groan as it came to a stop. The rain stopped, and soon the sun shone down on them as if the storm had never happened.

Everyone went to the top deck to survey the damage. Ariel let out a genuine whimper, lower lip quivering, as they lifted the edge of the popped balloon. Adelaide, who'd been in her own room during all the hubbub, put a hand on their shoulder and patted it sympathetically.

"Don't worry, my dear," Santiago said as Ariel ran their thumb over the torn canvas. There was a bit of flour in Santiago's hair—he'd been in the middle of whipping up a crust for a pot-pie when the ship started falling and had spent the whole time screaming in the kitchen. "We'll get your ship flying again in no time."

"My ship, technically," Kieran muttered.

"Right," Briar said, picking at her cuticles, "because you did so much to save it, what with all your invaluable shrieking."

Despite herself, Delilah snorted. Kieran shot her a wounded look, and she whispered an apology, trying not to laugh.

"We need to buy a patch for it," Ariel announced, letting the broken balloon canvas flop from their hands back onto the deck. They ran a hand back through their short black hair, frowning. "Which would be much easier if we knew where the nearest town was . . ."

"It's probably an hour's walk from here," Briar said.

"Right—Gabriel's Edge." Kieran surveyed the woods, holding up a hand to shield his eyes from the sun. The leaves were spring-green, still dewy after the rain, and a petrichor smell rose from the soil. "So . . . Aunt Wrenlin lives here."

Briar tensed. Delilah could have sworn she saw the girl's lip quiver for the briefest second.

"You think you can go into town and get us a patch?" Ariel asked Briar.

"I'll go with her," Kieran volunteered before she could argue. He glanced at Delilah. "You want to come?"

She hesitated, glancing at Briar, who wouldn't look at her. Considering how much time had passed since the last attack, Delilah couldn't help but imagine another one hitting the two of them—but this time, in the middle of a town square. They'd be totally helpless.

But also.

Briar.

The kitchen incident was a weird fluke, she reminded herself. *Nothing to worry about in the long run.*

Probably.

After another moment's pause to dash that last thought from her mind, Delilah nodded. "Sure. As long as Briar is okay with being our guide."

Kieran dimpled while Briar's eyebrows shot up. At first, she didn't say anything. But with everyone staring at her, she finally sighed and said, "Sure, fine. I can lead us there."

"Great!" Ariel said. "Adelaide, Santi, and I can start repairing the hull while you're gone." They playfully jabbed an elbow into Santiago's ribs and jeered, "Finally give those muscles of yours a practical use beyond looking nice."

Santiago flexed his arm. "But you admit they look nice."

Adelaide rolled her eyes and waved a hand toward Delilah, Briar, and Kieran, bidding them goodbye.

Ariel added, "You kids have fun. We'll get to work here."

"Perfect," Kieran agreed. He looked to Briar and Delilah. "This is great! We can do some cursebreaker-cursee bonding on the way."

As if it were a venereal disease, Briar spat, *"Bonding?"*

"All right." Delilah sighed. "Let's get moving."

The trip to Gabriel's Edge was uncomplicated, if frustrating. Briar walked a few feet in front of Delilah and Kieran, speaking to them only when she had to give them directions. She summoned Cinnabar to scout ahead, keeping an eye on him rather than on her traveling companions. Kieran tried a few times to strike up a conversation, but Delilah and Briar both refused to engage much beyond a few one-word responses. Eventually, he gave up, letting out a heavy sigh and staring up at the trees.

Once they reached town, Briar dismissed her familiar and led them to a store selling the type of balloon patch Ariel had requested. Briar tensed and stayed in the back corner of the shop while Delilah had a pleasant conversation with the boy at the counter. After discerning that Kieran wasn't her boyfriend, the young man complimented Delilah's boots and said her gray eyes reminded him of the color of the sea in the morning. She giggled and twirled her hair on a finger while Kieran handed over money for the patch and stuffed it into his bag.

Delilah winked at the boy as they turned to go. While she generally wasn't the type to flirt—considering how loaded romantic interactions were with her curse—she did occasionally allow herself a modicum of normalcy when the risk was low. While she'd never admit it, she loved the heart-skipping, warm feeling of flirting with someone.

She scoffed at herself. *I really put the "hopeless" in "hopeless romantic."*

He blew her a kiss in return. Briar's eyes rolled all the way back into her skull.

Just before they left the shop, Kieran paused, staring at a display of pamphlets near the door. He pointed at them and glanced at the shopkeeper over his shoulder. "What are these?"

The boy tore his gaze away from Delilah long enough to tell

Kieran, "Oh, uh—mostly tourist information about Gellingham. We don't get a lot of people passing through Gabriel's Edge, but the ones who do are usually headed for Gellingham. You're welcome to take some if you like—it's mostly maps and ghost tour advertisements."

Kieran's eyes widened. "*Fascinating.* How much?"

The boy raised an eyebrow. "Oh—they're free. Take as many as you like."

Kieran shot Delilah a look like he'd discovered a gold mine, mouthing the word *free* with a glint in his eyes. He grabbed one of each pamphlet, shoving them in his bag with childlike glee. Before he could take the whole display, Delilah grabbed his sleeve and tugged him along after her.

The bell above the door rang and silenced as they left the shop and entered the street. Gabriel's Edge was a small town, smaller than Kitfield, the sort with only a few hundred people. Townsfolk mostly kept inside to avoid what seemed to be ever-present fog and rain, and the only people outside were all pale and gray-skinned.

"Did you get to come into town a lot as a kid?" Kieran asked Briar, whose eyes kept flitting behind them.

"Not often," she said. "Wrenlin didn't like bringing me out in public."

Before Kieran could respond, Delilah heard a commotion in the street. Without thinking, she stepped in front of Kieran and Briar, blocking the view of them as best she could. As they carefully continued, they discovered two uniformed men setting up a blockade. A small crowd of townspeople stood nearby, loudly arguing with a man with close-cropped blond hair wearing a dark coat. On the breast was an emblem: a raptor with two heads.

Delilah smelled the same scent of magic she had back in Dothering—the one like citrus-heavy aftershave.

Her heart stopped.

The blond man glanced their way, and Delilah instantly recognized Regen Pelumbra, the detective. *Must have been his ship that tried to dock beside us,* she realized with a start. She spun around, facing the other direction. She grabbed Kieran and Briar by the wrists and pulled them along with her. A wave of protective fury washed over her, and her heart thrummed in her ears.

"Why are you—?" Briar started, but Delilah hushed her.

"That's the guy who chased you back in Dothering," she said. "The Pelumbra. He must have convinced the city guard to set up a blockade in case we came into town."

Kieran quickly glanced over his shoulder and squeaked a curse. "Oh no—that's our uncle." He looked at Briar. "You didn't tell me *Regen* saw you!"

Briar held up her hands. "I only ever met Wrenlin and our dad! How was I supposed to know who he was?"

"Both of you, shush," Delilah hissed. While her tone was all business, internally, dread crept in like a lit fuse inches from gunpowder. She asked Briar, "Is there another way out of town?"

"We can skirt them if we take one of the side streets to the woods," Briar whispered. She'd gone pale, a waxy sheen of sweat making her look feverish. Her breathing was fast, and Delilah realized with a start that she also looked to be on the verge of panic.

Delilah set her jaw. *I guess I'll have to hold it together for both of us.*

Delilah led them in the direction Briar indicated. They turned onto a side street, Briar still looking like she might vomit. The buildings weren't close together, and the land was fairly flat—easy to see where the town ended and the trees started. No one was outside, so Delilah picked up the pace. Not running but briskly walking toward the woods.

"Hey! Wait up!"

They froze. Delilah and Kieran turned while Briar stayed rooted in place, barely breathing.

The boy from the repair shop, the one Delilah had flirted with, jogged after them. His face was bright with a smile that wrinkled the sides of his eyes.

Glancing over her shoulder, Briar swore.

As he came to stand before them, he said to Delilah, "Sorry— I just—I realized I never got your name before you left. If you're going to be in Gabriel's Edge for a bit before you go to Gellingham, I thought you might want to grab dinner with me." Seeing her expression, and noticing that Kieran and Briar were both sweating as if they'd run miles, he added, "If . . . that's okay?"

"Oh—goodness, that's so sweet of you." Delilah held up her hands. *This is what I get for batting my eyelashes like a schoolgirl. Damn it, damn it, damn it.* "I'd love that, but I'm in a bit of a hurry to get on the road, actually."

"Well, with the police setting up blockades, your best chance is through the woods, but it's really easy to get lost in there. Plus, the police said there's a dangerous witch on the loose. Hold on— they gave me a flyer." He reached into his pocket and drew out a piece of paper with a girl sketched on the front. "See?"

Unfortunately, the boy and Delilah came to the same realization at the same time. While the artist had been somewhat unforgiving with the depth of Briar's facial scars and crooked nose, it was very clearly her, scowling and staring directly into the viewer's eyes. One image was her, bald with her blue eye exposed, while the other was her with a wig and her eye patch.

The one she was currently trying to carefully adjust to cover her eye, to little avail.

"Well," Delilah said, pressing her hands together. She pointed her fingertips toward him. "This is awkward."

Before the boy could open his mouth, Briar twisted her hands in a spell that burst out of her palm like a thrown dagger. It struck the boy in the throat, electric shocks dancing across his skin. His eyes rolled to the back of his head, and he hit the ground, convulsing. Kieran yelped while Delilah moved to help him.

Voice unsteady, Briar insisted, "We have to move."

"Was that necessary? You could have killed him!" Delilah snapped. She pressed her fingers into the boy's neck, determining that his pulse was still healthy, though he was out cold.

"He would have called the police!" Briar hissed back, a furious blush flooding her cheeks. "And you'd agree with me if you weren't so easily distracted by men!"

"Now is not the time—" Kieran started to say.

Sarcastically, Delilah cooed, "Oh, look at you, suddenly Miss Perfect! How nice that you've *never* been sidetracked by attractive men!"

"For once, you're right! I *haven't!*"

"Hey!" a voice called from down the street. A police officer pointed at them. "You three! Don't move!"

"Damn it!" Delilah cursed. "Go, go!"

The policeman cried out, and the three of them sprinted down the street.

They jumped a short fence behind someone's house and finally made it to the woods. Briar gestured for Delilah and Kieran to follow her, and they wove quickly through the undergrowth. Delilah had to help Kieran over a few fallen logs and roots, though Briar seemed at home scrambling through the undergrowth. The soggy soil was slick under their feet.

"Come on," Briar urged. "Come on, come on!"

The three of them ducked behind a massive tree and pressed their backs to it. They waited, chests heaving, trying to quietly catch their breath. At once, all three of them peered around the side of the tree. Delilah narrowed her eyes—one police officer stood about ten feet away with his back to them, while a few others took off to the east.

Kieran started to say, "I think they lost us—"

Briar clapped a hand over his mouth. As he uttered a whimper of surprise, she pulled him back behind the tree, and Delilah followed suit, holding her breath.

They waited a moment before peering out again. The officer who had had his back to them was closer now, scanning the woods. After a moment, he let out a breath and headed east after the other officers, the sound of his footsteps fading into the brush.

Delilah, Briar, and Kieran all exhaled at once, slumping against the tree.

"You're a fool," Briar muttered, more factual than harsh, to her brother.

"I deserve that," he agreed.

"Come on," Delilah said, pointing in the direction of the lake they'd landed in before. "Let's get out of here before they wise up."

❧

They avoided the police as they trekked through the woods. Briar took them on a different, longer path than the one they'd taken into town, hoping to avoid the police. She pointed the way as if she knew every tree and stone by heart. At one point, they stepped into a clearing, only to discover a massive drop down to a ravine, a green-gray river rushing through the base of it.

"The edge of Gabriel's Edge," Briar explained, nodding. "There should be a bridge nearby. This river runs into the lake we landed in, so we can follow it on the other side and be back in an hour."

Kieran adjusted his backpack. "Wonderful! Look at us, evading the law, exchanging banter, making great time." He looked from one girl to the other, smiling. "Bonding!"

Both girls rolled their eyes and kept moving while Kieran paused to frown before jogging to catch up. As they walked, Delilah kept glancing over her shoulder. Every rustle in the undergrowth sent images of potential ambushes to the forefront of her mind. Her nerves felt electric.

A few minutes later, Briar began to say, "And here's the—"

They discovered a bridge. It was weathered with age, completely collapsed in the middle where it hung over the ravine. The boards at the edges looked ready to snap as well. Moss clung to the ropes and ate through the broken edges of the wood.

"Damn it," Briar growled.

"Is there another way over?" Delilah asked.

"No." Briar dug her palms into her eyes. *"Damn it."*

"Let's just take the other way, then," Kieran suggested, pointing to their left. From where they stood, they could make out where the ravine hadn't yet split open, giving them a chance to skirt it. "Come on—it doesn't look too bad."

"I agree," Delilah said. She and Kieran took a few steps forward.

Briar didn't move.

Delilah asked, "What's wrong?"

Briar was quiet. Finally, after a long moment, she breathed, "Wrenlin's house is there."

Kieran and Delilah exchanged a look. While neither of them knew exactly what Briar's relationship with her aunt was, that she'd run away seemed evidence enough not to return. Delilah remembered the picture of them standing next to each other, Briar an empty-eyed child and Wrenlin scowling.

Delilah's expression softened. *Something tells me it wasn't a particularly happy childhood.*

Kieran set his jaw, letting out a low hum as he rubbed his chin. Carefully, he asked, "Tell me if this sounds like a bad idea, but . . . what if we talked to her?"

Delilah and Briar both stared at him, Delilah with her brows up and Briar's eyes round.

Kieran went on: "Listen. Wrenlin knows about the curse! She

might have information we can use, and we're already here, aren't we? There are three of us and one of her—I think we have a solid chance of getting our way."

"She knows what you and I look like," Briar said, squinting at her brother. "She's not going to tell you a damn thing."

Kieran frowned. Delilah got the impression he hadn't heard the word *no* many times in his life. "Why not?"

Briar curled her hands into fists. "I spent sixteen years with that woman, and she refused to tell me anything about the curse. Waltzing in now will just piss her off, and probably land me trapped back there."

"Is Wrenlin a witch?" Delilah asked.

Briar shook her head. "Not anymore. She failed her Calling. But that doesn't mean she can't hold her own—trust me."

"I'm not suggesting we fight her." Delilah pulled her hair back from her face, eyeing the woods at the edge of the ravine. "In fact, here's a thought: What if *I* talk to her? She has no idea who I am— maybe I can level with her."

"Wrenlin isn't the type to *level*," Briar growled.

"You underestimate me," Delilah said, tossing her curls over her shoulder. "You two can hide nearby. If anything happens, we can . . ." Delilah searched for the right words.

"Beat her up?" Kieran suggested.

Briar's mouth went slack.

Delilah shrugged. "Well, I was going to say run, but that's not a bad idea either. I'll go in, see what I can get, and we'll be out long before anyone can get wind of us. We'll be back to the ship in no time."

"This plan is completely unhinged," Briar said frankly. "And if this lands me back in Wrenlin's hands, I'll kill you."

"I like it," Kieran said, swinging his fist up.

Delilah dusted off her shoulders. To Briar, she said, "Watch and learn, ye of little faith. I know what I'm doing."

CHAPTER EIGHT

Rule #22: Sometimes, actually, you *don't* know what
you're doing.

After all the talk Delilah had heard of the Pelumbras' money, she
was stunned to discover that Wrenlin Pelumbra lived in little more
than a glorified shack.

It was a ten-minute walk from the edge of the ravine, in a clearing darkened by thick trees that soared high into the sky, their foliage blotting out what little light snuck through the clouds. Vines
grew up and down the shoebox-shaped house, and an overgrown
garden decorated the front yard. Blue flowers bloomed along the
vines, accented with crimson thorns that Delilah guessed might be
poisonous, considering their vibrancy.

Briar stiffened as soon as the house came into sight. Inexplicably, Delilah felt the sudden urge to wrap her arms around Briar's
shoulders and take her away from this place.

Keep it together, she reminded herself.

"You two can hide in those bushes," Delilah said, pointing to ones near the front of the house. "Come on."

The twins followed behind her, tucking themselves into the overgrown foliage of Wrenlin's yard as Delilah approached the door. She took a few deep breaths, trying to let the earthy smell of the woods calm her.

She steadied herself, squared her shoulders, and knocked on the door.

A few moments later, Wrenlin Pelumbra opened it.

She was a slim, tall woman. Her face was like a bird of prey's, with dark, deep-set eyes and a sharp, straight nose. Her lips were thin, and her long red hair was braided down her back, nearly falling to her tailbone. She wore a shapeless dress that dragged on the floor, the hem mud-stained and torn. Delilah suddenly remembered the picture of her and Briar—she seemed to have aged significantly in the years since then.

"Who are you?" Wrenlin demanded.

"My name is Charlotte," Delilah lied. She let her shoulders fall. "I'm so sorry—I got lost in the woods. I've been trying to get to Gabriel's Edge, but I've been walking for hours now and can't figure out where I am. Is there any chance you'd be so kind as to let me rest here for a few minutes? I'm a witch—I can do any magic you might need."

Wrenlin's mouth curled into a sneer. "It's a mile and a half south. Keep walking."

She went to slam the door, but Delilah caught it. Wrenlin's eyes widened.

Delilah quickly pulled away and started to open her mouth.

Wrenlin cut her off, spitting, "I know your kind. Witches who like to parade around and expect to get everything they want just by wiggling their fingers correctly or singing a magic little song. If you're trying to intimidate me with magic, I can assure you this house is built entirely of hawthorn. You won't be able to summon magic within fifteen feet of this place. Now what do you *really* want from me? No one comes through these woods by choice."

Damn, Delilah thought. *Hadn't considered hawthorn.*

"All right," she said, nodding. *New plan.* "You got me. Let me be completely honest with you, then: I'm here because I'm looking for Briar Pelumbra."

In the bushes nearby where Briar and Kieran were hiding, Delilah caught the sound of a whispered curse.

Wrenlin's face stayed neutral. "Who do you work for?"

"Detective Regen Pelumbra," Delilah lied. "He hired me to check for her here."

"Regen?" Wrenlin's eyes narrowed. "Funny. He called me earlier and said that he suspected Briar might be in the area. He also mentioned she might be traveling with a witch. Tall, curly hair, impressively large nose to stick in places it doesn't belong."

"Hey!" Delilah snapped, touching her nose. She immediately paled as Wrenlin's face twisted into a smirk. "Oh—shit."

"I'll let Regen know you stopped by," Wrenlin sneered with a grin. "Good day."

Before she could slam the door shut, however, Delilah panicked. Unable to summon her magic this close to the hawthorn dwelling, she did the only thing she could think to do.

She punched her.

She aimed for the nose, but Wrenlin dodged. Delilah's wild attack struck Wrenlin's temple instead with impressive strength, jerking her head to the side with a *crack*.

Her eyes fluttered for a moment before she hit the floor, out cold.

"Ow!" Delilah whimpered. She looked down at her hand, realizing the crack had likely come from her thumb, not Wrenlin's skull. She tried to bend it, only to get a hot shock of pain up the tendon. She shook it out, bouncing on her toes and repeating, "Ow, ow, ow!"

Kieran and Briar emerged from the bushes. Kieran stared, mouth agape, while Briar wandered to Delilah's side and whispered, "Did you just *knock her out*?"

"By accident," Delilah said through her teeth. Tears welled in her eyes. "Dammit, I think I broke my thumb."

"You're not supposed to tuck it into your fist when you punch, dumbass," Briar grumbled. She reached out and took Delilah's hand while she continued to whimper. Briar turned it over, frowning. "Yeah—that's broken. Great hit, though."

"Glad to be of service," Delilah sniffled, tears sliding free and dripping down her cheeks.

"Hey, guys?" Kieran crouched beside Wrenlin's unconscious body. "Mind helping me?"

"Help you do what?" Briar asked.

"Well, tie her up," Kieran said like it was obvious. The girls' eyes widened, and Kieran added, "What? We came this far. We might as well get some answers."

Wrenlin awoke bound to a kitchen chair, with Delilah and the twins looming over her.

"Briar," she snarled, eyeing her niece as she blinked herself back into consciousness. A few strands of red hair hung in her eyes but did little to obscure the rage burning in her gaze. "I should have known you were involved."

Wrenlin's stare slid to Kieran, and her eyes widened. "Hold on. . . . You . . . your eye. *Kieran?*"

"In the flesh," he said.

Wrenlin's eyes darted between the twins. "How in the world did you find each other?"

"Dumb luck and money, mostly." Kieran cleared his throat. "It's, ah, good to meet you, Aunt Wrenlin. Perhaps not the circumstances I would have chosen, but what can you do."

"And what are those circumstances?" Wrenlin demanded. She blew a puff of air out to try to get her long, stringy hair out of her eyes. "Come to kill me finally, Briar? Looped in your brother and this hulking excuse for a witch to do the job? Not like you need them for that."

"*Hulking?*" Delilah repeated, unable to hide the newly smarting bruise to her ego. Suddenly, Briar's attitude made a lot more sense. "You're a real piece of work, you know that?"

"We're trying to find a way to break our curse," Kieran cut in. "And we know that you've got more information about it than we do."

Delilah cracked her knuckles on her good hand. "Right— what Kieran said. Tell us everything you know about the curse."

"Or what?" Wrenlin demanded. "You'll break your other thumb punching me?"

Delilah frowned, cradling her throbbing right hand. "Okay, uncalled for."

Briar went to the counter. The kitchen was tiny and open to a small living area. She pulled out a cleaver from a knife block near the sink. Face unchanged, she stood behind Wrenlin and rested the knife on her shoulder.

Delilah expected Wrenlin to call Briar's bluff, but this time, she tensed.

"We don't want to ask again," Briar said. "Talk."

Wrenlin stiffened. Delilah saw her pulse flutter in her throat, the older woman's eyes darting to the cleaver while the rest of her held stock-still. She exhaled through her nose, mouth curved into a tight frown.

"Fine." Wrenlin grit her teeth. "I don't know who cast it or why. I don't know where they keep the written form either."

Briar touched the blade ever so softly to Wrenlin's neck. "You sure?"

Wrenlin inhaled sharply, every muscle going taut at once. Tiny beads of sweat pricked on her forehead, and the color drained from her face. She held her breath as she leaned away from the cleaver's kiss.

Briar followed, refusing to give her even an inch.

"Briar—" Kieran started to say.

Delilah cut him off with a look. He must see that Briar was just pretending.

She had to be, right?

"Yes," Wrenlin said. She'd gone pale, her fingers slippery on the armrests her wrists were tied to, trying to get a grip.

No emotion crossed Briar's face.

"I swear," Wrenlin went on. Her hands had begun to tremble. "I don't know. I was never privy to that information." Turning her head just enough to look at Briar, she added, "How much do they already know?"

Briar's hand tightened on the knife. "That I'm sucking out Kieran's magic and killing him. The same amount I know."

"That's . . . *all* you know?"

Briar pressed the cleaver into her aunt's neck, and a drop of blood slipped down the pale curve of her throat. Another followed, a red rivulet trailing from the cut down Wrenlin's collarbone before it dripped onto the neckline of her dress, staining it.

Delilah realized, skin going cold, *Briar's not bluffing.*

Wrenlin cursed. "Fine—fine! I'll tell you if you get that goddamn knife away from me."

Briar's lip twitched briefly, then she pulled the blade back half an inch.

Wrenlin turned to stare directly at Delilah. She had dark eyes, wild like there were live wires behind them.

"My little brothers had the curse before Briar and Kieran," she explained, jaw clenched. "I watched it kill them. I tried everything to find out how to break it. I searched the whole Pelumbra estate, threatened the head of the family, combed through the entire library—never found a damn thing. The closest I ever got was this: the twin taking the magic is the curse's carrier, so they have to be the one to break it. And the curse is atypical somehow. Standard curses are always negative, but there's something about the Pelumbra curse that benefits the family. That's why they've been letting twins die for all these generations: they're getting something out of it. It's not just because they're scared of the taboo of it."

"How could a curse be beneficial?" Delilah asked, wrinkling her nose. "No one writes a curse because they want to *help* someone."

"That's all I know," Wrenlin said. She glared in Briar's direction. "Now get the hell away from me, you little monster."

Something ignited in Briar's eyes. Her fingers flexed on the knife handle. "Do *not* tell me what to do."

Kieran moved quickly. He grabbed Briar's wrist before she could press the blade any deeper into Wrenlin's throat. The metal winked in the light before the cleaver tumbled out of Briar's fist and hit the floor.

Delilah's gasp caught in her throat in a short, strangled sound.

Briar blinked as if she'd gone momentarily unconscious. Her eyes fell to her hand, where a drop of Wrenlin's blood had slid down the blade, across the handle, and onto her skin. She paled, and for a second, Delilah could have sworn she saw the girl's eyes shine with unshed tears.

Briar pulled away from her twin and rubbed the smear of blood off on her pants, averting her gaze to the floor.

"We should go," Kieran said gently.

Delilah nodded, feeling more than a little sick to her stomach. "Agreed." She stared down at Wrenlin again, narrowing her eyes. "If the curse killed your brothers, why would you volunteer to raise a child with it? Knowing the same thing would happen again?"

"I could have stopped it this time," Wrenlin whispered. Her

gaze swung to Briar. "*She's* the one who refused. She may look harmless, but there's a part of her that enjoys her curse. Don't you?"

"Shut *up*," Briar snarled.

Suddenly, voices floated in through the open window. Delilah and the twins tensed, and when the breeze changed, Delilah smelled the familiar scent of citrus aftershave—Regen.

"Briar, is there a back door?" Delilah demanded. "We have to get out of here."

Briar nodded. She shot a final glare at Wrenlin before telling Kieran and Delilah, "Follow me—I'll get us out of here."

While Kieran and Delilah rushed to follow her, Wrenlin shouted, "She's lying to you!"

Delilah paused for a beat, glancing back over her shoulder.

Wrenlin's hair stuck up at odd angles, framing her snarling face as she spat through her teeth, "Don't believe a word she says. Deep down in that shriveled little heart of hers, she enjoys what she is."

"*What* she is?" Delilah repeated.

Kieran caught her wrist and pulled her along before Wrenlin could say anything else.

They shoved open the back door, and the three of them fled into the trees.

CHAPTER NINE

Rule #6: Drinking games are a long-standing tradition
among alewife covens. Some say they were first used
to ensnare victims into falling in love with the witches
and do their bidding.
Consider that rumor a warning.

As Delilah, Briar, and Kieran snuck away from the cottage, the last
thing they heard was Wrenlin screaming for Regen, demanding he
untie her. It had given them enough of an opening to escape before Regen or the other police caught their trail. After an hour or
so sneaking through the trees and keeping as silent as they could,
the three managed to make it back to the lake.

When they did, though, they paused. At first glance, the lake
appeared completely deserted. Kieran started saying something
about Ariel having perhaps moved the ship, but Delilah cut him
off. She'd caught the faint scent of smoky magic on the air. Following it, she beckoned the twins to join her at the edge of the

lake. As they got closer, a faint iridescent sheen became visible in the air. *Someone must have created a glamour,* Delilah realized—a magic veil to hide the ship. Her suspicion was confirmed when she toed the edge of the shimmer, then stepped through it and found the ship exactly where they'd left it.

Adelaide stood on the other side, her eyes glowing red-orange like twin embers. She had pieces of unwoven rope between her fingers, the braided part lying on the ground. Delilah was stunned into silence at the sight of the woman's hands—she'd never seen someone weave so fast. The glamour rose up from the rope like smoke, creating the illusory veil.

"Damn," Briar breathed as she stepped past the veil. Her eyes followed the length of rope—Adelaide had laid it in a huge circle around the ship. "That's impressive."

"Oh good, you're back!" a voice shouted from the upper deck. The trio spotted Ariel standing at the edge of the ship. "Come up here and bring the patch!"

Over the next hour or so, the trio pitched in to help Ariel and Santiago apply the patch to the balloon. Faster than Delilah had thought possible, Ariel got the ship running, pulled a lever to inflate the patched balloon, and had them in the air headed for Gellingham.

Not until they'd been in the air for a few hours did everyone feel comfortable walking around the ship as usual. It was as if they'd been bracing for another crash landing or Pelumbra raid to happen at any second.

That evening, Delilah went to the kitchen and filled a cheese-cloth pouch with ice. She winced as she pressed it to her throbbing thumb. Briar had been right: it was definitely broken. Not for the first time, Delilah missed living with a doctor who knew what to do about this sort of thing.

She was so lost in thought that she almost ran into Briar as she reached the top of the stairs to the main deck. Briar shot her a poison glare, and Delilah rolled her eyes.

"Sorry," Delilah grumbled, sidestepping to make room for the other girl.

Briar stopped, eyes wandering down to Delilah's hand. She inhaled a hissing breath through her teeth. "You really did break your thumb punching out Wrenlin, huh?"

Delilah frowned, wrinkling her nose. "You're welcome."

Briar pursed her lips like she was thinking of saying something else, but she didn't. She moved to pass Delilah, but at the last moment, Delilah caught her arm with her good hand.

Briar looked up at her as if Delilah had slapped her.

"Listen, um—" Delilah closed her eyes and winced. "I don't know how to mend this kind of thing, and I was wondering if . . . you did."

Briar blinked. Straight-faced, she asked, "Why would I know about that?"

Delilah clenched her teeth and tried not to roll her eyes. "Because you—you clearly know what a broken thumb looks like. I know you were on the run for six months or so, and you don't seem averse to fighting—"

A smirk broke through Briar's blank expression as she tried not to laugh, much to Delilah's surprise.

"I'm messing with you, stupid. If you're asking if I know how to make a splint, the answer is yes." She pointed over to the deck chairs. "Sit down over there and I'll go grab a few things from my room."

Delilah scoffed, "Are you offering to help me?"

"Didn't you just ask for help?"

"I didn't—" Delilah's fingers twitched to curl into a fist and pain immediately shot through her swollen, throbbing thumb. "Ow—damn it. Yes, okay, help would be much appreciated."

While Briar went looking for what she needed, Delilah went to sit at one of the tables on the far end of the deck. She carefully lifted the ice off her thumb and examined it in the light of the sunset. It hadn't bruised yet, but it was definitely a lot more swollen than she would have liked. She sighed, replacing the ice and looking out over the edge of the ship at the pink and orange clouds floating across the darkening sky.

The trip to Wrenlin's had at least given them another lead. Delilah had never heard of a curse that had a benefit to counteract it. A curse that unusual had to have been studied or written about *somewhere,* at the Library of Curses or elsewhere.

The library you still haven't figured out how to get into, a voice in Delilah's head reminded her. *You can't wing it forever.*

Just then, Briar returned with a bone folder, a cloth, and tape. Delilah snapped out of her musing as Briar said, "Okay, let me see it."

"I can't believe you agreed to this," Delilah muttered under her breath as she removed the ice.

"I'm full of surprises."

Briar delicately took Delilah's wrist and turned it to get a better look at the thumb. Instantly, Delilah's pulse betrayed her, speeding up so much she could feel it throbbing even harder in her injured hand. For a moment, she worried that Briar could feel it quicken beneath her fingers. Luckily, if she did, she didn't react.

She's helping you, Delilah reminded herself. *You don't have a reason to be mad at her.*

Overwhelmed by a wave of insecurity, she snapped, "This doesn't mean I like you or anything."

"And you're about to like me even less in a second." Briar placed the bone folder up against Delilah's thumb as she prepared to turn it and the cloth into a makeshift splint. "Because this is going to hurt."

With more force than necessary, Briar pulled the cloth tight around Delilah's thumb. Delilah cursed loudly while Briar tried to hold in a laugh.

"You're such a baby," Briar snickered. She opened her mouth to say something else, then her eyes flickered up over Delilah's shoulders. "Oh. Hi."

Delilah glanced up to find Adelaide watching them with rounded eyes. She had on a long blue dress, her pale hair braided into two parts that hung past her collarbone. She paused before approaching, pulling a third chair up to the table Delilah and Briar were sitting at.

"I broke my thumb," Delilah explained, suddenly feeling strangely exposed out here with Briar still holding her wrist. "Briar's making a splint."

Adelaide beamed at Briar. Delilah's eyebrows rose—Adelaide's look was almost like . . . pride of some sort. Briar averted her gaze and shifted tensely in her seat, clearly not enjoying the attention.

"It's just a splint," she muttered, not meeting Adelaide's eyes. "Don't look at me like I'm curing a terminal illness."

Adelaide soundlessly chuckled—Delilah wasn't sure she'd ever seen her look so carefree. After a moment, Adelaide removed a spool of thread from her dress pocket and gestured for Delilah to let her examine her thumb.

Delilah and Briar exchanged a look. Briar stopped wrapping the fabric, and Delilah held her thumb out to Adelaide.

The pale woman reached out and unwrapped the splint, replacing it with a few twists of thread. After a moment, her eyes began to glow fiery red-orange and bright.

Her fingers suddenly leapt into action, weaving the thread into a complicated pattern around Delilah's thumb. The girls' eyes widened as the swelling began to go down in each area the thread touched. A pleasant warmth flowed up Delilah's arm, tinting her skin pink.

The fire in Adelaide's eyes burned out, replaced by her normal dark brown. Delilah examined her thumb. She gave it an experimental wiggle, only to find that it was completely healed.

"Wow," Briar marveled. "I've never met anyone who could use healing magic before. It's very rare."

Of course, Adelaide couldn't respond, but she did offer a small smile. She stood, gently patting Delilah's healed hand before pocketing her thread.

She gave both girls another pleasant look before heading back across the deck toward the stairs, leaving them in silence.

The next night, just when Delilah thought she could relax, Kieran and Briar had another attack.

This time, though, Delilah kept her head. While Briar vanished to her cabin, Santiago and Delilah took care of Kieran. Delilah helped carry him to the couch, where she had to frantically move the pamphlets and maps he'd taken in Gabriel's Edge out of the way before Santiago set him down. After that, there wasn't much else for them to do but wait until he woke up.

"If nothing else," Delilah told Santiago as she took a seat in an armchair beside Kieran, "I feel less helpless this time."

Santiago stifled a small laugh. "You seem to care about him a lot. It's nice to see."

"Well, sure. He's my friend." She cocked an eyebrow at Santiago. "Why are you looking at me like that? It's not like you don't care about him."

Santiago waved the notion away with a flick of his hand. "Like a younger sibling, yes. I've known him since he was a child. But you—you may well be his first real friend, Delilah. He needs that."

Delilah pulled her gaze away from Kieran, turning to angle herself toward Santiago. "If you don't mind my asking, how exactly did you come to work for the Pelumbras?"

"Well, I'm from Esperona originally, if you couldn't guess from the accent," he said with a wink. "But I wanted a fresh start, so I came to Celdwyn. Simple as that."

"Sure, but you already told me that," Delilah chuckled, rolling her eyes. "I want to know why you left Esperona in the first place.

I mean, come on, the Pelumbras live in Northern Celdwyn, where it goes from nothing but snow in winter to rain all summer. Why willingly sacrifice great food, weather, and beaches for that?"

"And wine," Santiago said mournfully. "Don't forget our incredible wine."

Delilah nodded emphatically to illustrate her point. Esperona was Celdwyn's neighboring country—which, in addition to fantastic cuisine and music, had an even higher population of witches than in Celdwyn. While one out of every one hundred Celdwynians might be a witch, Esperona had three times as many. They had a similar Calling system, but witches had a shorter time to complete their task—only a month, whereas Celdwyn's lasted a half year. Delilah had always wanted to visit, but she and her mother had never had the time or money.

Santiago hummed in the back of his throat. "You're assuming I have a tragic story to tell, hmm?"

Delilah shrugged. "Just curious."

Santiago chuckled. "Well, I had a very serene childhood. My mother is a witch, as are all my sisters. My parents own a restaurant, and my sisters and I worked there. I'm the youngest, so I watched my sisters each take their Callings one after another, just to come home and wind up doing the same tasks as before they left. It seemed profoundly boring."

"Maybe," Delilah said. Her mother's face flashed at the forefront of her brain, and her chest ached. "There's something to be said for home."

He shook his head. "I never understood the appeal of staying in one's hometown. When I got my Calling, I asked for something big and exciting—something in the city. I wound up in Desanero, the capital, and my task was to act as an illusionist making glamours for a wealthy family. Specifically, they needed me to use my magic to disguise their daughter when she went out on the town—make sure she wasn't recognized by people so she didn't besmirch their reputation. All I had to do was keep it up for a month until she got married and I'd pass. Easy."

Delilah scoffed. "Why were they so afraid she was going to ruin their reputation?"

Santiago shrugged. "Adella had a habit of bedding strangers. Often. Not a particularly exciting offense, but the problem was, she was engaged—an arranged affair, of course. If word got out that she was effectively cheating on her fiancé most nights—often with other women—the marriage would be canceled and the scandal would be a huge blow to the family. Esperona hasn't caught up to Celdwyn when it comes to same-gender attraction. It's still frowned upon there, as it used to be here. So I went with her, used magic to make her look like someone else, and everything was fine."

Delilah raised an eyebrow, mostly thinking about what he'd said about same-gender attraction. No one batted an eye in Celdwyn about it—Delilah knew that a few generations back, in her great-grandmother's time, that hadn't been the case, but she couldn't imagine it being a factor now. She was glad she didn't have to deal with that.

Santiago sighed. "And now you're wondering, *But then how did you fail your Calling?*—since Ariel was so kind as to tell you things didn't go well for me. Well, ultimately, I fell in love with

Adella. I came clean about my feelings, and she admitted she felt the same way. I proposed to her, and she broke off the arranged marriage. I failed my Calling as a consequence, but I figured having my magic sealed away didn't matter if I got to spend the rest of my life with a person I loved."

Delilah's eyebrows shot up. She'd never even considered giving up her magic for someone else. It would be like losing a part of herself, an amputation of an intangible limb. It would have to be a truly spectacular love to choose that.

"What happened?"

Santiago's mouth set in a line. He ran a hand back through his hair and sighed. "It's not something I particularly like to talk about, but . . . Adella passed away in an accident. I was a nineteen-year-old widower, and I had no magic to fall back on. Esperona stopped feeling like home. So I decided to come to Celdwyn and get a fresh start."

"I'm so sorry," Delilah said, at a loss for what else she could say. She couldn't even imagine.

Santiago shook his head. "No need to apologize. Of course I miss her, but it's been six years. I like to imagine she'd be proud of how far I've come."

"I think she would," Delilah said gently. "If you don't mind my asking, how did you come to work for the Pelumbras after all that?"

Santiago rolled his eyes. "Kieran's father met me in Esperona. After Adella's death, I went home to work at my family's restaurant. He must have been able to tell I wasn't happy, because as soon as I served him, he offered to pay for me to come work for him in Celdwyn. I was so excited to get out of Esperona I never looked at the fine print. He locked me into a contract that said if I left his employment, I'd lose my Celdwynian visa."

Delilah drew back in shock. "He *what?* Santi, there's got to be something you can do to fight that. That can't be legal."

Santiago let out a bitter chuckle. "*Everything* is legal where the Pelumbras are concerned. With money and influence like that against me, I'd never win. My only choice was to continue working for them or go home. So when Kieran asked me to run away for this, to break the curse and spite his father, I couldn't say no."

"Would it be so bad to go back?" Delilah asked. "To Esperona?"

Santiago set his jaw for a moment. "My parents would accept me back, but I'm not much use in their restaurant without magic. I made enemies with the nobles in the capital because of Adella. And the whole place reminds me of what I've lost." He shrugged. "Celdwyn isn't perfect, but I'd rather be here with people I care about."

"Ariel?" Delilah guessed.

Santiago nodded, exhaling a laugh. "Obnoxious little fiend. You know, when I first met them, I could barely stand them. Always shouting, always making jokes at my expense. But now—I don't know where I'd be without them. They're my best friend."

"Friend?" Delilah repeated, blinking.

"Why the face?" Santiago pressed.

"I just—" Delilah frowned, shaking her head. "I thought you two were a couple."

"Oh, no, no, no," Santiago turned his face the other way, pink tickling his ears. He rubbed the back of his neck, attempting to clear the air with a passive chuckle. "Certainly not. How did you come to that conclusion? Ariel is—"

"You have a crush on them, don't you?"

"I," Santiago said, holding up a finger, "do not, nor have I ever had, a *crush*, thank you very much." Santiago ran his fingers through his hair, smoothing back the long top of his undercut. "I'll take my leave. I'm sure Kieran doesn't need both of us in attendance when he wakes up."

"Don't run away from your feelings, Santi!"

"A second thing I'll never have is the desire to *run*," Santiago corrected as he crossed the threshold.

"You're perfect for each other!" Delilah called after him.

He merely scoffed in response.

Delilah smiled as the sound of Santiago's footsteps disappeared. She glanced down at Kieran, still unconscious. His chest rose and fell softly, but his skin looked even paler than normal. Occasionally, his expression would pull into one of pain, lips pursed and forehead wrinkled, but it would vanish just as fast.

He doesn't deserve this, Delilah mused. Her thoughts wandered to Briar upstairs. Was she in as much pain as he was? Or was it as Wrenlin had said?

Part of her enjoys what she is.

Delilah let out a sigh through her nose. Briar might be a pain in the ass, but Delilah didn't believe anything her toad of an aunt said. Briar wasn't a monster. A bit difficult, sure, but . . . she had a few decent qualities.

Not that Delilah would ever tell her that, of course.

Delilah grabbed one of the pamphlets, unfolding it just so she had something to do with her hands while she considered her situation. It was a map of Gellingham with a list of public events. It was a bit outdated, most of the events having already passed, but as Delilah's eyes scanned the map, they fell on a specific location.

GELLINGHAM LIBRARY, it read. DAWNSUMMER FESTIVAL.

The Gellingham Library—that's the official name of the Library of Curses, Delilah realized with a start.

She'd heard of the Dawnsummer Festival as well, but only in Kitfield's context. There, it was a celebration of the changing seasons in the town square. She'd never heard of how they celebrated the holiday in Gellingham. She set down the map pamphlet and started flipping through the others, looking for any that mentioned the festival, without luck.

Until she got to a thicker booklet—it had a woodcut-print cover featuring the Gellingham skyline, along with the city's name and the year in calligraphy. She flipped it open to find an overview of Gellingham's best events for tourists over the course of the year. She scanned the table of contents and found the Dawnsummer Festival, then flipped to its page.

A celebration of the first day of summer, the Dawnsummer Festival brings with it a host of events throughout the city, the blurb began. Delilah skipped down the lines, eyes scanning desperately. *Nearly all are free and open to the public.*

As she kept scanning, something caught her eye. She let out a gasp.

She shot up from the couch and immediately broke into a

sprint toward the control room. She shouted Ariel's name as her heart raced.

It was a long shot, but that wasn't about to stop Delilah from trying.

🌿

"You expect me to get us to Gellingham in *two days*?" Ariel repeated in horror. "Even going at our current speed, which is faster than I like, we're at four days minimum—"

"Please," Delilah begged, clasping her hands. "This could be our only chance. The Dawnsummer Festival is the only time the Library of Curses is open to the public. I know it's a lot to ask, but if it's possible . . ."

While it took a bit more persuading on Delilah's part, Ariel finally acquiesced. With all systems pushing their limits, the ship barreled toward Celdwyn's capital city at a breakneck pace. The interior heated up to an uncomfortable degree, and the engine was loud at all hours—but, Delilah figured, if this could get them to the library on time, it was worth it.

The next day, as Delilah was standing on the deck trying to let the wind dry the sweat from her brow, Kieran tapped her on the shoulder.

"Cooling off?" he guessed. He'd remained as pale as he'd gone after the last attack, but the heat lent a bit of color to his skin.

Delilah nodded. "Trying to. Maybe we can have dinner outside so we're not sweltering."

"I was actually just going to ask you about that." He beamed.

"I thought, since we're so close to Gellingham and we have a strong lead, maybe we could celebrate up here on the deck this evening. We can have drinks and get out the turntable for music. If Ariel's okay putting the ship on autopilot for an hour, maybe everyone can come."

"Oh—that's a great idea! Can I wear something fancy?" Delilah asked. She swished her skirt around. "Something I can twirl in?"

"It would be a shame if you didn't," Kieran said. "I already talked to Santi, and I think I can convince Briar. I've really started to make some progress with her."

Delilah grinned. Since their trip to Gabriel's Edge, Delilah had begun to feel a lot better about the whole situation on the ship, specifically with Briar. Even if they hadn't exactly shared their most intimate secrets, Delilah felt that she understood the other girl slightly more. She wasn't infuriating on purpose, for example—she'd just been raised that way.

And Delilah did her absolute best not to linger on why the thought of spending an evening with Briar suddenly made her stand a little straighter and her heart beat a little faster.

"I think I have too," Delilah admitted. "She's . . . okay. In small doses. It'll be fun to enjoy some downtime with her."

"Exactly," Kieran said. His mismatched eyes were bright—this time, thankfully, not with a warning of an impending attack but instead with excitement. It was refreshing to see. "The festivities will begin at dinner, then. I'll see if Santiago and Ariel will let us filch a little champagne."

Delilah chuckled. "Looking forward to it."

❧

Briar, despite her best efforts, was no match for her twin's sad-puppy eyes.

Delilah found her by the makeshift dining table Kieran and Adelaide had set up on the deck. They'd even hung string lights to add some ambiance, and Adelaide had woven another spell to help keep the wind at bay. Santiago had made an appetizers-for-dinner meal: lemony mushroom crostini with shallots, salmon rillettes, baked Brie with cranberry sauce, spicy empanadas, and prosciutto-wrapped arugula. The smell of it all instantly made Delilah's mouth water.

Ariel revealed a hidden stash of gin and champagne in the back of the kitchen and mixed them with lemon juice and melted sugar to create a cocktail Delilah had never tried. They were a bit too strong on gin for her taste, but Delilah appreciated the sweetness as it rolled over her tongue.

Briar sat down with some hesitation, sneaking a look at Adelaide, who sipped her drink and ate crostini. Adelaide smiled at her warmly, and Briar quickly averted her eyes.

"The empanadas are just beef and spice," Santiago told Briar, after he'd finished setting dishes on the table. He nodded to Delilah. "She told me you don't eat vegetables."

Briar blushed, glancing at Delilah out of the corner of her eye. She took one, whispering, "Oh—thanks."

"Let's play a game," Ariel said after they'd finished eating, pulling a deck of cards out of their pocket and waving it around. "Any of you ever heard of Curses and Blessings?"

Everyone but Santiago shook their heads. Ariel explained that the game was a race for each player to get rid of their cards; based on the results of the first round, roles were assigned to each player—the highest being High Blessed and the lowest being Low Cursed. Each role came with special advantages or disadvantages.

"The caveat being," Ariel explained, "if you have a bad hand and you want to avoid drawing extra cards on your turn, you can take a drink and wait until next turn."

"Perfect," Briar said, a wicked grin crossing her face. Delilah's heart pounded—*Is she* grinning? *Since when does she grin?*

Briar caught her staring and asked, "What? I love card games." She took a sip of her drink. "And gin."

Delilah cleared her throat and looked away, face turning red. "Y-yeah—let's play."

Adelaide dealt them in. Santiago turned up the volume on the turntable, the music drum-heavy and pounding at the speed of Delilah's heart. Within minutes, the six of them were slamming cards down on the table, shouting with glee and despair as their turns passed. Kieran lost the first round, landing him as Low Cursed, while Briar came out on top, Delilah after her.

"That was amazing," Kieran said as he passed his best cards to Briar to use for the next round. "You're great at this."

"Cards are a great way to make money if you play them right," she explained. "It's how I got my feet under me after I ran away." She shot her brother a look, a smirk creeping up her face. "It's good you have family money or else you'd be screwed."

Everyone froze. While they were used to playfully ribbing Kieran, they'd never heard Briar do it. Kieran too blinked, his eyebrows pressed together. Delilah tensed.

Then he burst out laughing.

"Well, you can be the talented twin," Kieran said. He tucked a lock of blond hair behind his ear, dimpling. "Since I'm clearly the attractive one."

Briar went speechless while everyone else roared with laughter. Ariel grabbed Kieran's shoulders and shook them while Adelaide covered her mouth to hide her grin. Santiago hit his fist against the table. After a minute, the ghost of a smile tugged at a corner of Briar's mouth and she rolled her eyes. She shuffled the cards with ease and passed them out to everyone.

As she spread out her hand, she said, "None of you get to talk until you win a game, all right?" She shot a look at Delilah and added, "You almost put up a fight in that last round."

"Almost?" Delilah repeated, the laughter in her throat dying off.

Briar winked at her. "Almost."

Delilah's skin ignited as Briar passed her a new hand. Her fingers brushed Delilah's.

Both of them tensed.

Briar jerked back, focusing all her attention on passing Kieran his cards. Delilah pressed the hand to her cheek, trying to hide the blood rushing to her face.

She shot Briar a hard sideways look. "You're *dead.*"

For the rest of the round, Delilah took a drink every time her hand started to turn bad. Seeing how much she'd ramped up, Briar began to do the same, until they'd both finished two more drinks, slamming their cards down on the table with twice as much force as anyone else playing.

Soon everyone else stared at them in wonder, having been eliminated. The two went back and forth between throwing down cards and tossing back gin and champagne. Delilah stared down at her hand—she didn't have anything particularly good, but if she didn't put something down, it looked like Briar would be able to take the round. She took another swig of her drink and put down her cards.

Briar cursed, revealing the last of her hand—slightly worse than Delilah's. She said, "You win."

Delilah jumped out of her chair, throwing her hands in the air. Everyone applauded, Delilah bowing and making sweeping hand gestures. Kieran cheered while Briar sat back in her chair, crossing her arms. Delilah's head had begun to feel fuzzy, and she swayed. She caught herself on her chair.

"I'm going to get some water," Delilah said. "You all can start the next round without me."

She tucked in her chair and went to the kitchen, careful to keep her feet steady under. She didn't have a high tolerance for alcohol. If she were Briar's size, she'd be on the floor.

She grabbed an empty jar from the cabinet in the kitchen and filled it with water, leaning against the counter as she chugged it. She had just finished when Briar stepped into the room, stumbling over her feet.

"Put up a fight *that* time, didn't I?" Delilah taunted, watching Briar grab a glass and hold it under the tap. "Bet you didn't expect that."

"If I could handle even an ounce more liquor, I could have won," Briar snapped. She tipped the cup back, then braced herself against the counter. She shot Delilah a sideways look and added, "Are you even drunk?"

Delilah shook her head. "No. Tipsy."

"Shit." Briar rubbed her face. "I am."

Briar finished her water and slumped against the counter, sighing. She ran a hand over her peach-fuzz hair and added, "Sometimes I lose my head when pretty girls look at me for too long."

Delilah chuckled, bemused. "What do you mean?"

"Oh, don't *play* with me." Briar set her glass down hard on the counter, coming to stand in front of Delilah. Her eyes were a little glassy as she stared up at her, squinting as if she were trying to read something far away. "You know I'm attracted to you, and you keep messing with me because you like watching me squirm."

Delilah sputtered a laugh. "You're attracted to me?"

Briar stared at her for a second before bursting out laughing. She pressed a palm into her forehead and shook her head. "Crazy, right? Maybe I'm a masochist. Maybe part of me likes that face you make every time you look at me." Briar pointed between Delilah's eyes. "That one. With the eyebrows and the scowl. You can't stand me."

"Sometimes I fantasize about pinning you against a wall," Delilah admitted, the gin and champagne melting any filter that might have stopped her. As soon as she said it, her face lit up pink. She clarified, "As in—to make you shut up!"

Briar snorted. "Yeah? How does that usually go? In your head, I mean. You know I could take you down even if you are nine inches taller than me."

"No you couldn't," Delilah snapped, rolling her eyes. *Fine. I'll go along if she wants to play this game.* "You're tiny."

Briar glanced over her shoulder, a wicked smile crossing her face. She backed up until her spine was pressed against the wall and crossed her arms, leaning against it. She tapped it twice with her elbow and said, "So funny you should say that when there's a perfectly good wall right here."

"You're awful," Delilah muttered, stomach fluttering. *She's not the only one who can play hardball.* Delilah crossed the room, heart hammering and blood effervescent like soda water. She stood in front of Briar. Her skin felt warm and electric, every nerve ending lit up and crackling.

Briar lifted a hand over her head and pressed it into the wall behind her. "I'll give you a head start."

Delilah locked her hand around it, holding it in place. She felt Briar's pulse thrumming through her wrist, the veins blue-purple like the edges of the twilight sky. Her hand was small; her fingernails were bitten down and the cuticles torn. Scars marred her knuckles. At the sight of them, Delilah wondered how those fingers would feel in her hair.

Suddenly, the joking grin melted off Delilah's face. Heat burned low in her belly, so fierce it nearly sent her reeling. She hadn't felt anything like that since . . .

Oh, *fuck.*

Briar asked, "What usually happens next? In your head?"

Delilah forced herself to look the other girl in the eyes, even as her heart raced as if it were going to shoot out of her throat. Briar's face was flushed from her throat to the tips of her ears, eyes wide. Her smirk was devilish.

Any other time, Delilah would have stepped back. The memories of Theo's blank eyes, the confusion in his voice, would have sunk their claws into her and snapped her out of the moment. But now, with champagne controlling her thoughts and the heat making her sweat, all she could think about was this girl, right now.

And for the first time in years, she broke her own rules.

"This," Delilah whispered.

She bent down and pressed a kiss to Briar's lips. Briar let out a muffled gasp of surprise. Delilah began to pull away, but Briar suddenly used her free hand to grab a fistful of Delilah's dress and yank her closer. Delilah let go of Briar's wrist and let her hands fall to Briar's hips. Briar kissed back hard enough to bruise her lips against her teeth.

The muffled sound of footsteps coming down the hall finally snapped Delilah back to her senses.

She tore away from Briar and took a step back just as Kieran pushed open the doors to the kitchen, shimmying his shoulders back and forth and whistling a tune. He stopped, seeing Delilah and his sister standing a few feet away from each other, and exclaimed, "There you are! Did you hear we're out of gin?"

Delilah and Briar exchanged a look. Briar said, "No?"

"Well, we are." He took a few more steps, then stopped, staring at them. "Are you both okay? You look all . . . red and sweaty."

Briar said, "Never better," at the same time Delilah said, "I have to go to bed. Right now."

She left the kitchen before either twin could speak.

CHAPTER TEN

Rule #24: Know when to improvise.

I am the most hopeless fool alive.

Delilah spent most of her time in the shower the next morning, combing her memory for every interaction she'd ever had with Briar, debating when she'd let things get out of hand. She knew she hadn't exactly been honest with herself about her feelings. From the moment she'd laid eyes on Briar, she'd found her physically attractive, but her personality had quickly squashed the notion there would be anything beyond that. Briar had the charm of a feral coyote. Plus, Delilah hadn't considered whether, in fact, she'd begun to lose her mind and *was* the slightest bit attracted to Briar as a person, or that it might be mutual. She'd certainly never considered acting on it.

Until she did, and woke up feeling like she was living someone else's life. Someone infinitely less practical who had piss-poor impulse control to boot.

When Delilah stepped out of the shower, she pulled her towel off the rack and screamed into it.

This wasn't supposed to happen, she internally moaned. *Not again. Not after Theo.*

She hung the towel back on the rack with a shaky breath. As she got dressed, she tried to think on the bright side: they'd be in Gellingham in a few hours. Then she could get back on track breaking the Pelumbras' curse and stop thinking about Briar. All she had to do was grab breakfast, wait for them to land, and she'd be in the clear.

Or so she thought. Until she opened the door and found Cinnabar standing on the other side, peering through the crack under Delilah's door. The fluffy orange cat let out a startled hiss and jumped back, bristling.

Delilah let out a theatrical sigh and called, "Did you send your magic cat to *spy on me?*"

A beat passed—Delilah standing with her arms crossed— before Briar's door cracked open.

"Perhaps."

Cinnabar's tail flicked back and forth as he stared up at Delilah with innocent eyes. After another beat, Briar came into the hall-way, snapping her fingers so Cinnabar disappeared with a flash.

Briar took his place in front of Delilah. She had shadows under her eyes, and she had on what Delilah was sure was one of Kieran's button-down black shirts. Delilah's chest tightened.

"So, uh," Briar said, digging her hands into her pockets. "Morning."

For a beat, they stood there in silence. Delilah chewed her lip and rubbed the back of her neck with an open hand.

Eyebrows bent as if she were in pain, Briar finally burst out, "Can I talk to you? About last night? The—kissing." She immediately winced and covered her face with her hands. "Ugh, kill me."

Delilah tensed. *Well, there it is.*

"Right . . . well. I was"—Delilah held up her fist and stuck out her pinky and thumb before tilting it back to pantomime drinking—"pretty . . . sloshed."

"You're telling me." Briar bit her lip for a moment before locking eyes with Delilah. "Look, things got out of hand. I was being a drunk idiot. I didn't know what I was saying, and I'd never actually kissed anyone before, and—"

Delilah's eyes widened in alarm. "That was your first kiss?"

Briar managed to get even redder. "I wasn't exactly desperate enough to make out with the trees in Gabriel's Edge, if that's what you're asking."

"Shit—I'm so sorry. I was a total mess last night." Delilah's cheeks burned, and she pressed her fingers into the sides of her head. "It was a mistake."

For a second, a flicker of hurt flashed across Briar's eyes. Still, she quickly crossed her arms and steeled her expression. A prickling feeling dug into Delilah's guts, biting into her like thorns.

"Yeah," Briar said, sniffing. "I figured as much."

"It's not personal," she explained. Her voice got quieter. "Honestly."

Briar laughed, but it was dry.

"Really," Delilah insisted. "I'd say that to *anyone*." When Briar shot her a disbelieving look, Delilah added, "It's because—look, I'm . . ."

Briar waited.

Delilah lowered her voice. Her chest and throat felt tight as she forced the words out. It hadn't hurt to say it out loud like this in a long time. "I'm cursed too, okay?"

"You are?" Briar sounded disbelieving. Her eyes darted up and down Delilah as if searching for some secret flaw that had been lurking in front of her the whole time. "How?"

Delilah winced. Sometimes she wished her curse was something external. At least then she'd never have to have a conversation like this. "A long time ago, a jealous witch cursed my family so no Bea women can find true love. The second someone *does* fall in love with us, they . . . forget. Every happy moment, every passing detail—it all vanishes. We remember it all, but the people who loved us? We become nothing but strangers to them."

She choked up at the end and quietly cursed. She ran a fist across her eyes before the tears welling in them could escape.

"Oh," Briar said softly. She crossed her arms, hugging herself and nodding. "I don't mean to pry but . . . has that happened to you?"

Delilah tried her best to not let the threatening sobs choke her, but the words still caught in her throat. She had to whisper to get them out. "Once. His name was Theo. He was seventeen; I was fifteen. He came to my hometown during his Calling, and we met while he was searching for a rare local plant near my cottage. I was instantly obsessed with him—he grew up in Gellingham and knew tons about curses, and I wanted to know everything about them. I promised to help him find the plant in exchange for teaching me everything he knew about cursebreaking."

"Is that how you learned about the library?" Briar asked.

Delilah sniffled. "Yeah. He dreamed of getting a job there someday. Over the next few months, we spent every day together, and we'd talk about what we'd do when we both became licensed witches. At first, we were just friends, but as time went on . . . I thought it would be harmless to mess around with him a little. I told myself there wouldn't be any feelings involved."

Briar's expression darkened. "I'm guessing that didn't happen?"

Delilah shook her head. "It was fine for a while. Casual kisses here and there, holding hands, stuff like that. But I . . . I couldn't stop myself. Theo was everything I'd ever wanted. Sweet, understanding, smart—he even thought my stupid jokes were funny. I convinced myself that maybe if I loved him enough, it would be different than it had been for all the other Bea women. Somehow, we'd be the exception."

"And . . . you weren't?"

The tears fell harder now. Delilah's mouth curved into a painful frown as she shook her head. "I remember it so clearly, Briar. I showed up at his doorstep after we'd had the most romantic evening on the beach the night before, and he just . . ." Delilah's shoulders began to tremble, and her voice cracked. "He'd forgotten me. After months of telling each other how much we cared, suddenly he meant everything to me but I was *nothing* to him."

As Delilah pressed a fist to her mouth and did her best not to completely break down, Briar stared at her. The other girl's expression had softened. Her fingers twitched at her sides as if she wanted to reach out. After a beat, she moved.

As gently as she could, Briar put a hand on Delilah's arm.

Delilah met her gaze, eyes shining.

"I . . . I understand," Briar said, averting her eyes. "Curses make this kind of thing complicated. So . . . maybe we can pretend last night never happened? Go back to pissing each other off?"

That finally got a laugh out of Delilah. She dabbed at her eyes, shaking her head to try to steady herself. "Sure. But just so you know, I *do* like you. I didn't think I did, but that was probably an excuse to explain away why I wanted to kiss you."

As soon as the words were out of Delilah's mouth, she was blushing, and she did her best not to look directly at Briar. She clarified, "If you feel like you're up to it, I want to be your friend."

Briar blinked. "Are you serious?"

"Why wouldn't I be?"

"I've never really had a friend." Seeing Delilah's expression soften, Briar rolled her eyes. "Don't look at me like that—I was cooped up in the woods for my formative years, all right? I didn't get out much. Not like there was anyone my age to play with wandering around the edge of a deadly ravine."

Delilah coughed out a laugh, wiping away the last of her tears. "If I promise not to fall in a ravine, can I be your friend?"

"*Pfft*—sure." Briar bit back a smile to keep her face even. She started, "So . . . do we shake hands now or—?"

Delilah cut her off, wrapping her arms around her in a hug. Briar sputtered a muffled note of surprise.

"Thanks for listening to my sob story. And sorry I was such an asshole."

"Likewise." Briar went on her tiptoes to hesitantly wrap her arms around the other girl, muttering, "Seriously, how are you so tall?"

"You'd probably be tall too if you ate a vegetable," Delilah said pleasantly.

Without letting go, Briar kicked her in the shin.

"Ow!" Delilah whined. She dropped her arms and smacked Briar's shoulder. "Not nice!"

Briar chuckled, pleased.

"Hey—there you are." The girls glanced sideways to find Kieran jogging up from outside. His hair was ruffled from the wind, curls blown into a wild gold cloud around his smiling face. He hooked a thumb over his shoulder and said, "We're almost there—and the view of Gellingham from the deck is amazing. You should come see it."

Delilah's eyes lit up, and she clapped her hands together. "Oh! This is so exciting." She gestured to both of them to follow her. "Come on, let's go see."

Gellingham was a gilded city.

Surrounded by lush woods and hills on every side, it was stunning from the air. Sparkling white buildings rose out of the trees, flowering vines crawling up the sides. Every detail seemed to be painted in opulent gold. The streets were paved and full of cars—more than Delilah had ever seen in her life. Only a few of Kitfield's richest residents had cars, so to see a whole city crawling with them made her heart hammer and her eyes sparkle.

The airfield was just outside town, and Ariel set them down with the rest of the parked aeroships. Some of the others were polished and detailed, with intricate carvings that made Kieran's stolen vessel look cheap.

"What's the plan?" Kieran asked Delilah as the engine began to quiet, the wings coming to a halt now that the ship had landed in the grass.

Delilah blinked. "What do you mean?"

"Do you know how this whole Dawn . . . whatever . . . Festival works? Do we just walk in?"

Delilah chuckled. "Not exactly. It's the only day of the year the Library of Curses offers guided tours to the public—each one leaves ten minutes after the last. It's basically an olive branch the Witches' Council offers each year to normal folks. Granted, I don't know if it's exactly the kind of thing where you can start thumbing through their collection of curses, but I have a backup plan."

"Which is?" Kieran pressed.

Delilah shrugged. "Sneaking into the curse section?"

"You didn't plan this at all, did you?"

Delilah put a hand to her heart. "Kieran, you wound me. I didn't *not* plan, I just . . . prefer to go with the flow and figure it out once I'm there."

"So . . . winging it?"

"Exactly." Delilah grinned.

Kieran looked a little green as he gulped.

After the ship had settled, Delilah, Kieran, and Briar collected their things and walked to the edge of the airfield, where a trolley station sat tucked into the trees. Kieran and Briar were both wearing disguises—Briar donned a wig and her eye patch, while Kieran wore a comically rumpled set of clothes that would have looked more at home on a newspaper delivery boy. He wore old brown slacks and a slightly stained white button-down shirt and had his hair tucked into a flat cap. Adelaide had also woven him a magic leather-cord bracelet that made his blue eye appear brown. She'd offered one to Briar as well, but the girl had waved her off.

"No Pelumbra would ever be caught in something like this," Kieran had told Delilah with a wink, giving a little spin to show the whole outfit. "They'll never guess it's me."

Briar stifled a laugh with a cough against her fist while Delilah offered him a small nod and a thumbs-up.

Ariel and Santiago had stayed behind to work out business with the airfield's owner, and Adelaide elected to stay on the ship and tidy up. Ariel had explained that if they took the trolley at the edge of the airfield into town, it would drop them off directly in front of the library.

Delilah bopped around the station with bright eyes. She'd never been to a city big enough to have public transportation. Kieran too gawked at the tracks and the wires overhead while Briar sat on a bench and kept a stony expression, save for when she was fighting back a smile at her brother and Delilah gasping at some new, fascinating part of the station.

"Whoa," Delilah said, staring at an advertisement hung on the back wall. "Look at this."

The poster showed a colored-pencil rendering of two young women, one a blond and the other a redhead, both with pinkish fire engulfing their arms. They wore thigh-length dresses and top hats, their hair perfectly coiffed.

At the bottom of the poster, huge red and gold letters read SEE THE FLAMING PELUMBRA SISTERS.

"Oh yeah," Kieran said. He pointed to the blond. "That's Daisy. Her sister's Bella. They're our second cousins. Caused a big uproar at the estate when they started performing—until the family realized how much money they make. Now they're fine with it."

"You weren't kidding about your family being famous," Delilah whispered. Her eyes fell to another poster, this one a more realistic rendering of a man with his dark hair slicked back, eyes stern. Beneath it were the words VOTE AMOS PELUMBRA FOR PARLIAMENT.

"Yeah," Kieran said, eyes widening. "I guess we kind of own this town. And, well, most towns in the north."

"Gross," Briar muttered, rolling her eyes.

A bell rang, and they looked up to find a little green-and-gold trolley pulling into the station. They caught it and took seats toward the back. The breeze blew in through the open windows, fluttering Delilah's long cream-colored skirt. The trolley clicked down the track, ringing a bell every time they came to a stop.

When the city sprang up around them, it felt positively alive.

The streets were packed with people in a way Delilah had never seen, flowing in both directions and stepping around each other like a river around rocks. Every turn seemed to produce a new sound—people laughing, horns honking, music floating from windows, a small dog barking from its spot inside its owner's bicycle basket. Cars puttered down the streets, carrying people with expensive hats and gaudy jewels hanging from their ears and necks. The buildings framed the streets, looming like mountains on either side. Their rounded windows revealed people inside working busily at heavy wooden desks, looking like they were stacked on top of each other.

Delilah stood up and hung out the side of the trolley, holding on to a gold support pole. The sunshine warmed her lightly tanned skin and glinted off the gilded edges of the skyscrapers. The sight of them made her heart soar. She'd spent days as a child looking at books about Gellingham, reading all about the way the city shone in the sunlight, but it was even more incredible in person. Every daydream she'd had of walking the busy streets as a licensed cursebreaker came back to her all at once, and she felt her cheeks begin to ache from the force of her smile.

"Can you believe this?" she called over her shoulder to the twins, the long green ribbon in her hair fluttering in the floral- and exhaust-scented breeze. She felt positively weightless. "This city is amazing!"

Kieran hopped up to join her. He braced himself against the window at Delilah's side, craning his neck to look at the buildings. He gasped. Delilah nodded and said, *"Right?"*

At the same time, Briar begrudgingly stood and went to Delilah's other side. She peered out, cautious, the sun spreading across her face. She squinted her visible eye, the other covered by her patch. Then she looked from the streets to Delilah's face.

A tiny smile tickled the edge of her lips.

"Gellingham Library, next stop!" called the trolley driver.

The trolley chugged a few more streets ahead before pulling to a stop in front of a pointy-topped slate-gray stone tower that reached high into the sky. Rounded windows containing stained-glass images, most of moon phases or constellations, adorned each floor. Ivy crept up the walls, swirling around the tower, which was framed on either side by lush gardens. Outside the arched front doors, a crowd of people waited, many wearing traditional witch's clothes—including capes and pointed hats—as costumes.

Delilah inhaled a gasp, clasping her hands together under her chin. "It's beautiful," she breathed.

Briar let out a low *hmm.* "And it's probably got a fuckton of stairs."

The three got off the trolley and tilted their heads backward to take in the full height of the towering library. The trolley dinged and pulled away, leaving them on the side of the road, cars chugging past as the sun beat down.

"Where do we even start?" Kieran asked, wiping sweat from his brow. He had his long blond curls up in a bun at the back of his head, a few loose ringlets falling around his pallid face.

"Getting in line seems like a fair bet," Briar muttered.

Delilah, standing between them, hooked elbows with both of them, despite Briar's protests. "Let's go."

She pulled the two across the street, dropping their arms only once they'd reached the back of the line, which went halfway down the block. Briar immediately began to shift from foot to foot, and Delilah shot her a look. All they needed to do was play it cool and then—

"I love your bow and your dress," an older, dark-skinned woman in front of them in line said as she glanced back at Delilah and the twins. She gestured to Delilah. "It reminds me of the stuff people used to wear in my hometown. Are you from the south?"

Delilah nodded. "Yeah—Kitfield."

"Kitfield! That's wonderful—I'm from Creckhollow." Something about her slight accent and the way her eyes crinkled instantly reminded Delilah of her mother.

"Impressive you managed to get tickets for a tour today," the woman added, holding up a sepia-colored slip of paper decorated with gold filigree. "I had to fight to get a single one outside of Gellingham—it must have been a huge pain all the way in Kitfield."

Delilah's stomach dropped. "T-ticket?"

"For the tour?" the woman's expression faltered with concern. "Sweetheart, they won't let you in without one. You've got one, right?"

"I—yeah! Yeah, of course I do." Delilah waved a hand nonchalantly, exhaling a *pfft* sound as she rolled her eyes as if it were the most obvious thing in the world. "Definitely. One hundred percent."

The woman laughed her off with a whispered *Oh, good—nice talking to you* before turning back around, clearly having had her fill of Delilah's weirdness.

The second the woman was no longer looking, Delilah leaned toward the twins and hissed, just loudly enough for them to hear, "How the hell are we supposed to get a ticket?"

"I thought you'd know!" Kieran whispered back.

Briar cursed under her breath. "You've got to be kidding me, Delilah."

"Shit," Delilah moaned. Her heart started to race, and the corners of her vision swam. She could barely keep her breath steady. "The pamphlets didn't say anything about needing a ticket! If we don't get in, we won't know if your curse is inside, and if we don't find your curse inside, then Kieran's going to die and I'll lose my magic and it'll be all my fault—"

Delilah cut off only when Briar, out of nowhere, reached out and grabbed her hand and squeezed it.

Delilah's entire body went taut at the girl's touch. Then her cheeks warmed.

"Slow down," Briar said, voice even. She flicked a look over her shoulder before settling back on Delilah. "I . . . might have an idea. But I need you to do something for me."

Mouth having gone entirely dry, Delilah just raised her eyebrows.

"Do something that'll get everyone's attention," Briar said. "Some kind of distraction. I should only be a few minutes."

"Are you going to kill someone?" Kieran squeaked.

Briar scoffed. "What is it with you two thinking I'm going to blindly murder people? No, obviously not. Now think of something—I'll be right back."

While Briar ducked into the crowd, quickly disappearing from view, Kieran and Delilah exchanged a look, Kieran's face entirely drained of color while Delilah's eyebrows threatened to scrape her hairline. When Delilah glanced at the crowd, she didn't see Briar anywhere.

"Got any ideas?" Kieran managed.

"One," Delilah offered. "But I can't guarantee it'll work."

"I don't like where this is going—"

"Everyone!" Delilah called out at the top of her lungs. The crowd quieted a bit, glancing over their shoulders as Delilah took a few steps back, heels clicking on the cobblestone. She spread her arms out wide as she announced, "Welcome to the Dawnsummer Festival and its opening event here at the Library of Curses! On behalf of the library, I have a very special treat for you."

Delilah held up her hands, creating a shower of green sparks. "A magic show!"

Kieran managed to go even whiter than before.

A low rumble went through the crowd as people exchanged looks and raised their eyebrows. While their expressions didn't exactly scream *excitement,* they still focused on her. Delilah breathed deeply and took stock of the scents on the air, quickly determining that very few, if any, of these people were witches.

Perfect.

Delilah untied the green ribbon from her hair, letting her curls fall freely down her back. Her eyes began to glow faintly as she channeled magic into the ribbon, the scent of cinnamon sugar perfuming the air. The end began to rise, seemingly of its own accord, dancing as if in the breeze.

With a deep breath, Delilah began to spin.

Generally, she didn't consider herself much of a dancer— though not because she hadn't learned how. As a child, Ruby had told her that witches could try a lot of different ways to channel their magic before they found the one that fit best, and Delilah had been intent on picking something lovely and graceful—something very different from how she considered herself. She'd learned quickly that her body simply didn't want to bend and leap like the other girls in her ballet classes, much to her disappointment. Instead, she decided to try other forms of dance before ultimately deciding baking was more her speed.

She had, however, become decent at ribbon twirling.

As Delilah did her best to smile widely, her ribbon left a trail of sparks in the air, popping like fireworks above her head and raining down around her. The little flecks of light merged and shifted into the shape of flowers and vines that twisted on the wind. As the breeze caught more of the flecks, Delilah felt the crowd squarely focused on her, their eyes darting between the sparks with wonder in their expressions.

Softly, Delilah smirked.

After a minute or so, she spotted Briar emerging from the crowd. Briar parted her lips as if she was going to mouth something to Delilah, but froze. After a moment, Delilah realized it was because Briar was watching her dance, her eyes skating over Delilah's twirling form as if she were a piece of fine art.

Beside Briar, Kieran cleared his throat, and his sister seemed to refocus as if she'd been stuck in a trance. She quickly shook her head and flashed Delilah a thumbs-up.

Delilah spun on her toe, shooting off one more spiral of sparks from her ribbon before landing in a curtsy before the crowd, bowing her head.

The crowd burst into applause while Delilah straightened, smiling at them and waving.

"Eleven a.m. tour!" a booming voice suddenly cut through the din. "If you have tickets for the eleven a.m. tour, please come to the front doors!"

Briar gestured to Delilah to join them, mouthing, "That's us."

With one last smile to the crowd, Delilah followed after Briar and her brother to the doors.

CHAPTER ELEVEN

Rule #15: Sometimes the kinder the smile,
the darker the heart.

"You didn't hurt anyone, right?"

Briar snorted at her brother's whispered question as she stepped over the threshold into the library, having just passed her ticket to the witch at the door. "Only emotionally."

As if on cue, someone at the door cried, "What the hell? They were just in my pocket, I swear!"

Briar's eyes glinted as she grinned.

As the three of them stepped into the Library of Curses, Delilah instantly picked out a dizzying array of magic scents lingering in the air—a pleasant mix of vanilla, honeysuckle, fresh coconut, and sea salt. Shelves hugged the walls, and huge spiral staircases led upward to layer upon layer of mezzanine levels packed with more bookshelves. Even from the ground floor, Delilah could see all the way to the soaring roof, which had to be at least twenty stories up. The banisters had been decorated with paper roses made of old book pages, and glowing, violet-tinged motes lit the shelves so people could get a better look. Along the sides of the walls were fenced-in platforms that made a soft *tick tick tick* noise as they rose to higher levels, taking groups of people up.

Witches hung around everywhere, dressed in traditional garb as they chatted with nonmagical visitors, all huddled together in their tour groups. Voices echoed through the wide, open spaces as the librarians showed people around, gesturing to weathered tomes and using their magic to levitate the books and pass them around from person to person. Others read aloud from scrolls, causing the words to lift off the pages and circle around their heads, drifting through the air like leaves caught in the breeze.

"Welcome to the Gellingham Library—or, as many of you know it, the Library of Curses," said Delilah's group's tour guide, a young witch with flaxen hair and tan skin, as she gestured to the floors and floors of mezzanines around them. She walked backward, somehow not bumping into anyone. It took Delilah a second to realize that she had a familiar—a small red cardinal—flying overhead, whose eyes she could see through to avoid obstacles.

"I'm going to be taking you through our collection of some of the oldest and most infamous curses in Celdwyn," the guide continued, "and telling you a little about their history."

Delilah raised her hand.

The tour guide coughed out a laugh. "Wow, don't usually get questions this fast—yes?"

"How are the curses organized?" Delilah asked.

"By type—for example, we have bad-luck curses on the lower

floors, then going up alphabetically, we have things like death curses, generational curses—"

"And which floor are the generational curses on?"

"The sixth floor," the tour guide said, some of the manufactured sweetness bleeding out of her tone, replaced by a twinge of annoyance. Still, the smile never left her face. "However, we'll be skipping the family curses today, so if you follow me, we can head for the eighth floor. . . ."

She kept talking, but Delilah immediately tuned her out. As the group strode forward, Delilah hung back, gesturing to the twins to join her. They kept a few feet between themselves and the rest of the tour group as Delilah lowered her voice to a whisper: "The second we get on one of those lifty things, we should sneak off at the sixth floor."

Kieran blinked. "You mean the elevators?"

"The—sure, what you said." She nodded toward the rest of the group. "Follow my lead."

Delilah and the twins rejoined the group, only half listening as the guide explained the history of cursewriting: when it started with glyphs etched into stone, moved on to paint on animal skin, and slowly evolved over the centuries to its current form as written scrolls or manuscripts before being outlawed by the Witches' Council. On another day, Delilah would have been fascinated by the discussion—specifically of the transition from using glyphs to modern language—but instead, she kept an eye on the people getting on and off the elevators on the sixth floor. The elevators paused briefly at each floor, and it would be easy to step off quietly.

Perfect.

It wasn't long before their group boarded, and Delilah managed to elbow her way through with the twins to the back, closest to the exit. As soon as the elevator began to ascend, machinery whirring, Delilah began counting the floors under her breath. Lucky for them, the tour guide was gesturing to the open space of the library, pointing out details of the architecture, so everyone had their backs facing Delilah and the twins.

As they paused on the sixth floor, Delilah glanced both ways before stepping off, pulling the twins with her.

They ducked behind the nearest bookshelf and held their breath.

The platform rose to the next floor.

"All right," Delilah whispered. Her heart was racing. *I can't believe that worked.* "Let's go search for 'P' and see what we can find. Remember, be quiet and act like you're supposed to be here."

The sixth floor of the library was larger than Delilah had expected, as if bigger on the inside than it appeared on the outside. Shelves upon shelves of books went back as far as she could see, while other shelves held carefully wrapped scrolls or even stones with symbols etched into their sides. Small golden signs indicated which letters were on which shelves, starting with "A" near where they stood. Nearby, a round desk housed three librarians. Two of them were flipping through books while one around Delilah's age stacked scrolls delicately on a rolling wooden cart. None of them glanced in their direction.

Delilah and the twins tiptoed through the stacks as silently as they could manage. Sweat pricked on the back of Delilah's neck. *Easy.*

It didn't take long for them to find the "P" section, and the three of them spread out across the shelves in search of Pelumbra. Delilah thumbed through old leather books containing volumes of curses. In the past, many witches had been prolific in their cursewriting, sometimes filling full grimoires with their work. Some had even written thousands of curses for the purpose of selling them to the highest bidder, allowing nonmagical people to purchase curses to be placed on their enemies by simply filling in the blanks with their names.

Delilah plucked one leatherbound book off the shelf, thumbing through to the table of contents. It didn't take long for her to realize that the curses were organized by the name of the witch who wrote them, not by the families they impacted. She closed the book in her hand with a *thump*. It exhaled a puff of dust into the air.

"Shit," she breathed. All of a sudden, her throat felt like it was about to close up.

Unless the curse was written by a fellow Pelumbra, it could be in any of these books or scrolls. Assuming it *was* even on the shelf.

This might be a little harder than she'd thought.

About to tell the twins what she'd discovered, Delilah found that Briar had disappeared from sight.

"Kieran!" she whispered.

He was busy gawking at a large piece of jade kept in a clear box on the opposite shelf. "Hmm?"

"Where did Briar go?"

"Oh, um . . ." Kieran glanced around, then moved a few steps down the aisle, eyes scanning for his twin. He pivoted sharply, starting to say, "She was just here—"

At that moment, Kieran crashed directly into someone, sending an armful of scrolls flying into the air.

"Oh—oh, no, I'm so sorry!" Kieran sputtered. "I didn't—"

The person he'd crashed into met his gaze wide-eyed and gaping. Delilah realized with a start that it was the younger librarian she'd spotted before, stacking scrolls on a cart. He was slim, with a mop of tight black curls. His skin was brown, and he had a smattering of dark freckles across the bridge of his nose. A traditional white witch's cloak hung from his shoulders, though it appeared to be a bit short for his long legs. A pair of round glasses slipped down his nose, looking as if they were about to fall.

At the sight of him, the words fizzled in Kieran's throat, turning into a squeak.

"What in the world are you doing here?" the librarian asked, blinking as if he couldn't believe what he was seeing. He pushed his glasses back into place. "This floor is only for librarians and licensed witches."

"Um." Kieran gulped. "We're, uh . . . looking for a bathroom?"

Delilah had to stop herself from groaning.

"Ash, who . . . ?" Another librarian appeared behind the boy, her eyebrows raised. "I don't remember checking either of your licenses."

"We, um . . . left them at home?" Delilah offered, her fake smile lopsided.

The woman's expression darkened. "If you're here with a tour, then you should know that straying from the group is grounds for being kicked out of the library. We can't let just anyone wander around here—there's very sensitive information in these stacks."

"What if I told you we were here on some very . . . delicate personal business?" Kieran asked. Delilah's head whipped around to look at him as he withdrew a slip of paper from his jacket. He revealed to the woman the top of the page, where a family crest with two raptors was printed. "Pelumbra-related business."

At that, the boy—Ash, based on what the woman had called him—sputtered in disbelief.

The woman reached out and casually took the paper from Kieran's hand, squinting at the crest. Delilah and Kieran held their breath.

She began to unfold it, and Kieran cut in, "Um—you don't need to—"

The woman's eyebrows rose. "This is a piece of stationery."

"Official stationery," Kieran argued. He'd begun to sweat along his hairline. "Straight from William Pelumbra himself."

"All right." The woman handed the paper back to Kieran and shook her head. "Sorry, kids. I'm going to have to escort you out."

"You don't understand!" Delilah cut in. "I'm here because of my Calling! If I don't find this specific curse—"

"Miss, please," the woman said. "I don't want to have to call security."

"Aniera!" a voice called. "We've got a straggler over here!"

"Let me *go,* you asshole!" Briar cried a few stacks away.

The librarian sighed as if this was shaping up to be the longest day of her life. "Ash, why don't you escort these folks and their friend out of the library?" She shot Delilah and Kieran a look and added to Ash, "Don't hesitate to use a knockout spell if necessary."

Delilah held up her hands. "Um—not needed! Promise." She shouted, "Briar, come on, we're leaving."

After a bit more cursing on Briar's end, Delilah and the twins allowed Ash to escort them down the spiral staircase in silence, his eyes following them as they went. Briar glared at everyone they passed, practically ready to bare her teeth at them, while her brother hung his head. Delilah's head swam, quickly rattling off her options. She could run—but they'd almost certainly catch her. Maybe try to fight and knock them out? Technically, it was three-on-three, although something told her Kieran's glass bones might shatter if he tried to punch someone. He'd been looking grayer with every attack, the shadows under his eyes deeper than ever. Plus, she doubted it would be subtle. *Shit, shit, shit.*

She had nothing. A minute later, Ash walked them to the door, following until they crossed the threshold. Delilah spun around, desperate to try once more to convince him how badly they needed this break.

"Best of luck," he said, heading inside. Delilah didn't even have a chance to respond.

Kieran, however, suddenly stiffened as Ash passed behind him. Before Delilah could ask, the doors to the library closed behind Ash with a bang.

"What was that?" Briar asked her brother, clearly having noticed as well.

"I'm not sure," Kieran said. He reached into his back pocket and found a slip of paper.

"But I have a feeling we can find out."

CHAPTER TWELVE

Rule #4: There are some fires that simply
won't go out.

*Meet me at the Red Pearl Teahouse in Shui City
tomorrow at noon. I have information about the
Pelumbras that might interest you.*
Bring your friends.

Delilah set the crumpled note down, frowning. "Where's Shui
City?"

Ariel looked up, eyes brightening. "You don't know Shui City?"
When Delilah shook her head, they added, "I grew up there—it's
a neighborhood on the western side of Gellingham."

The entire crew—Delilah, Kieran, Briar, Santiago, Ariel, and
Adelaide—sat at the dinner table aboard the aeroship. Plates of
peppercorn steak and broccoli with lemon zest and truffle oil
(Briar, predictably, heaped all her broccoli onto Kieran's plate) sat

in front of them. Kieran was passing around the note the young librarian had slipped him before vanishing into the library, tentatively picking at his food while everyone read it.

Delilah, meanwhile, still felt as if her entire body had been thrown off balance. She'd spent so much time trying to figure out her way into the library, just to blow it before they could find anything of use. What kind of cursebreaker was she if she couldn't even come up with a successful plan? If Briar hadn't thought to pickpocket the tickets, they wouldn't have even made it inside.

She wouldn't say it out loud—not when they might have a lead—but the acidic mix of guilt and embarrassment flooding her guts made her want to break down and cry.

"It's a unique neighborhood," Ariel explained, breaking Delilah out of her shame spiral. "It's all waterways instead of roads, so transportation is limited to bikes and gondolas. A lot of people moved there about thirty years ago when a magical blight killed most of the crops and started a famine in Celdwyn's neighboring country of Fenshi, and they named it Shui City to distinguish it from Gellingham. My family is still there."

"Oh," Delilah said, putting on a smile. Now wasn't the time to get in her own head about the library debacle. "That's great about your family. Are you planning to visit them?"

Ariel nearly choked on their water as they took a sip. They swallowed and cleared their throat, saying, "No. We're estranged."

Delilah's eyebrows rose. "I'm so sorry."

Ariel shook their head, waving it away. "Nothing to be sorry about. I'm much better off this way."

"Don't you miss them?" Kieran asked.

Ariel bit their lip for a moment. They looked to Santiago—Delilah had to assume he knew more of the story than anyone else. He shrugged and Ariel sighed.

"Sometimes. But . . ." Ariel ran a hand back through their hair. "One of the things you'll notice—or maybe already have noticed—about growing up and leaving home is that you start comparing your childhood to other people's. And the longer you spend away and the more people you talk to, the more you realize that your life before wasn't . . . healthy."

Briar nodded softly.

Ariel took a bite of their steak and swallowed it. "I left home because I knew that I wasn't happy there. I haven't gone back because I realized, in retrospect, *why* I wasn't happy." They waved their fork in the air. "*But.* I still remember every corner of Shui City by heart. If you need a guide, I'm happy to take you."

"You're not afraid of going back?" Briar asked.

Ariel shook their head. "Nah. Plus . . . now that you mention it . . . there are a few loose ends I didn't tie up before I left that might be good to attend to." They glanced at Santiago. "How do you feel about going to Shui City tomorrow?"

"I can't even begin to imagine what nonsense you have planned," Santiago said with a melodramatic sigh.

"That's the spirit." They looked to Adelaide. "How about you, Addie?"

She blinked, pursed her lips, and then went back to politely cutting her steak.

"Worth a try." Ariel said to Delilah and the twins, "I'll call and reserve us a gondola from Gellingham. Assuming you actually want to meet a total stranger at a teahouse based on nothing but a note. Could be a trap."

Kieran politely dabbed at his lip with his napkin. "I don't think so. Considering he said he has information about the Pelumbras, I would assume he doesn't know *we're* Pelumbras. And he wants to meet in a public place in the middle of the day."

"It's also our only lead beyond breaking back into the library," Briar muttered.

While the statement hadn't been aimed at her, it still made Delilah wince. *It's in the past now—nothing I can do about it but keep going and do better in the future.*

"We'll watch each other's backs," Delilah promised.

"All right, then," Ariel said with a nod. "We'll leave in the morning."

❧

Delilah, the twins, Ariel, and Santiago left the ship the next morning after breakfast. They took the first trolley into town and disembarked on the other side of Gellingham, past the library. The final stop sat beside the Gell River, a wide, gray-green stretch of water lined on both sides by willows with reedy branches that dipped down into the water. Sprays of tiny yellow flowers bloomed up and down them, and a buttery sweetness filled the air. The slow-moving surface of the water carried fallen blossoms downstream.

A single boat waited at the dock. It was wooden, about ten feet long, with four supports leading to a small pointed roof, as if it were a little house. Round paper lanterns hung from the roof, tassels fluttering in the breeze. The boatman stood at the back of the dock, an oar in his hand. He was broad-chested, handsome, with gold-toned tan skin and dark brown hair. He looked to be about Delilah's age, with a loose white shirt and close-fitting green pants.

"Ariel," he said upon seeing them. "It's been a while."

Their face brightened. "Ru—look at you! You're practically an adult."

"Don't tell my parents that," he said, chuckling. "They'll make me work more than I already do."

Ariel stepped onto the dock and hugged the boatman before saying, "Santi, Delilah, Kieran, Briar—this is Ru Shao. We grew up together in Shui City. He was my little brother's best friend."

Ru held up a hand. "Good to meet you all. Be careful to spread out so you don't rock the boat too much."

Santiago climbed into the boat first, careful to duck to avoid hitting his head on the low roof. Ariel followed, sitting in the back with him.

As they did, Delilah asked Kieran, "Did you know Ariel had a little brother?"

He shook his head. "They don't really talk about their family."

Delilah nodded and followed him onto the dock. Ru held out his hand to help everyone. Inside were benches wide enough for two people to sit. Kieran climbed in, then Delilah. Briar hesitated at the edge of the dock. Ru offered his hand, but she didn't take it.

Delilah held hers out. "Come on."

Briar set her jaw. At the edge of the dock, she carefully reached for Delilah's hand. She stepped into the boat with one foot, her eyes moving up Delilah's arm to her face. Heat warmed her cheeks for a moment as she stared into Delilah's eyes.

She tried to pull her foot in, and it snagged on a piece of rope.

Briar let out a yelp and tumbled. Delilah tightened her hand and pulled, yanking Briar toward her. The boat rocked, knocking them both back. Delilah's back hit the bench while Briar landed on top of her, gasping and blanched.

"Careful!" Ru shouted, stabilizing the boat against the dock. He peered into the boat. "Everyone good?"

Briar blinked, staring down at Delilah, who had unconsciously grabbed her with both arms, hugging her against her chest. Briar felt bony and small, the fall pushing her eye patch up her forehead so both eyes stared at Delilah, wild. For a heart-stopping second, Delilah couldn't take her eyes off Briar's lips. The feeling from the other night came back vividly, and Delilah went rigid. Color flushed both of their cheeks. Delilah's heart sputtered and raced.

For fuck's sake—pull yourself together, she mentally screamed at herself.

Delilah dropped her arms. Briar yelped and tumbled to the floor. She sprawled, groaning and cursing as she rubbed her elbow.

"Sorry! Are you okay?" Delilah asked, sitting up, eyes rounded.

Briar weakly held up a thumb. "Fine."

"Everyone in?" Ru asked. When everyone agreed, he said, "Then we're off."

Ru pushed off from the dock and guided them to the center of the river. It was slow-flowing, the breeze blowing tiny yellow flowers through the air. The waves lapped gently against the sides of the boat.

Briar pulled herself up and begrudgingly sat next to her brother, who was chuckling over her fall. Briar shot him a glare, and he coughed to cover it, still smiling.

Shui City came into view a few minutes later. The same willow-like trees lined the streets, tufts of long grass surrounding their bases. Stone walkways led to arched bridges over the waterways. Fish split in half down the middle hung from ropes tied between trees, drying into jerky in the sun. Children chased each other through the narrow alleyways between the two-story houses with thatched roofs and balconies that looked out at the water. More boats with lanterns hanging from their roofs floated by, and Ru waved to the other boatmen as he dipped his oar in the green water and pushed forward.

"What brings you back to Shui?" Ru asked Ariel. "Your parents made it sound like you were never coming back."

Ariel opened their eyes—they'd been smelling the blossoms in the air. "Tying up loose ends. Hopefully, I can pop in and out without their seeing me." They shot Ru a look. "You won't tell them, right?"

He shook his head. "Course not. Rory would kill me if I ratted you out."

As soon as Ru mentioned Rory, Ariel's smile faltered. *I wonder if that was their little brother's name,* Delilah thought.

Ariel quickly recovered, though. "Thanks, Ru."

He nodded, then asked, "Ariel mentioned on the phone that a few of you weren't tagging along to their parents' place. Where are you headed?"

Delilah hadn't realized that was where Ariel and Santiago were going. It was a bit of a surprise, considering what Ariel had said about their upbringing, but it didn't feel right to pry. *Maybe they're trying to make amends,* she thought.

"The three of us are going to the Red Pearl Teahouse," Kieran chimed in with a sweep of his hand, indicating his twin and Delilah.

Ru let out a low whistle. "Ah, you're in luck. It's up ahead."

Ru pulled the boat over and held it to the dock. Delilah stepped out first, followed by Kieran and Briar, who had begun to look a bit green. Kieran offered to help Briar off the boat, but she just scowled, stepping onto the dock carefully.

"We'll come pick you up at one o'clock," Ariel said.

"Try not to get kidnapped or hurt," Santiago added.

"We'll do our best," Delilah called ruefully, waving. "Good luck with your loose ends, Ariel!"

Ariel waved back while Santiago sighed and Ru pushed the boat away from the dock. The twins and Delilah gingerly made their way up the stairs onto the street, which was bustling with bikes that dinged and swerved around them. The walls of the buildings were decorated with a mix of old wooden signs in Fenshi and Celdwynian and new art painted in bright colors, depicting golden fish, flowers, and children with handfuls of balloons. A street vendor sold golden-sugar lollipops shaped like monkeys and dragons, as well as skewered candied strawberries and hawthorn fruits. Delilah bought a dragon pop, and when she licked it, it tasted like lavender.

"The teahouse is down this alley," Kieran said, pointing, as Delilah came away from the vendor. He checked his watch and said, "It's nearly noon. We should get going."

They found the Red Pearl Teahouse through an archway in the alley. The sign outside in Fenshi was intact, but the one reading COFFEE/TEA in Celdwynian was missing a few letters, their shadows still visible against the white wall. A short, twisted tree with cloudlike bundles of leaves sat in the entry, with little gold tags hanging from the branches. Beyond it were tables occupied by old couples sipping tea and younger people sitting alone, writing or sketching. Against the back wall were jars upon jars of different teas. Delilah and the twins sat at a table near the window, keeping their eyes peeled.

"I'm nervous," Kieran said, wiping his sweaty hands on his pants. "What if this is a trap?"

"Too late now," Briar muttered. She asked a passing waitress, "Can we get some milk oolong? Thanks." When Delilah and Kieran both shot her a look, she added, "If we're going to get attacked, we might as well enjoy some tea in the meantime."

The waitress had just returned with cups and a pot of oolong when a voice behind them said, "You're the ones from the library, right?"

The three turned to find the young librarian sliding into a seat beside Delilah, across from Kieran, his wildflower honey–colored eyes studying them as he settled in. He wore black pants, a blue button-down shirt, and a silver waistcoat the same color as his round glasses. Delilah inhaled and caught a subtle earthy and warm scent, like applewood smoke, that she had missed in the chaos back at the library: magic.

Kieran's entire demeanor changed in a second. His pale cheeks flushed, his bright eyes widened, and he straightened in his chair. "Oh! H-hi there. Good to see you again."

Delilah and Briar met each other's eyes, Delilah's wide, while Briar furrowed her brows and frowned.

The librarian nodded. "Good to see you as well. Not sure if you heard yesterday, but my name is Ash. I'm an apprentice librarian. I apologize for the unorthodox message, but I worried that talking to you about something this sensitive at the library might not be the best idea."

"Probably didn't help that they were about to call security to throw us out," Briar muttered.

Ash managed a weak laugh. "That was also a roadblock, true. At first, I thought you might be Pelumbras when you showed Aniera that stationery—it's not uncommon for members of the family to drop by. But then . . ." He trailed off, glancing at Kieran. "I don't mean this as an insult, but when I saw what you were wearing . . . well, the Pelumbras are the kind of wealthy that wouldn't be caught dead in worker's slacks. They're all quite ostentatious in how they dress. Velvet and tassels and such."

Kieran flushed again. Briar muffled a laugh against her knuckles, and Delilah elbowed her under the table to cut her off.

Ash cleared his throat. "But—I'm sorry, how rude of me. I haven't even asked your names."

"Kieran!" Kieran sputtered. Everyone turned to look at him as he quickly cleared his throat to cover up a crack in his voice. "I'm . . . I'm Kieran. Nice to meet you."

Delilah introduced herself as well. After a moment's pause, Delilah shot Briar a look. She stopped snickering at her brother and said, "Right, sorry. I'm Briar. Kieran's my twin, and Delilah's our friend."

"Nice to officially meet all of you," Ash said with a small nod. "If you don't mind my asking, what was your business at the library?" Looking at Delilah, he added, "You said it had to do with your Calling?"

While her eyebrows shot up and Briar narrowed her eyes, Kieran burst out, "We're trying to break a curse. And it's—uh—related to the Pelumbras."

Ash inhaled sharply. "Oh dear—did they put a curse on you?"

The twins' eyes met, and after a pause, together they said, "Yes."

For the first time, Ash's pleasant expression and formal aura disappeared as his mouth curled into a frown and he spat, "Bastards!"

Kieran's big smile drooped at the corners.

"It appears we are on the same page, then," Ash said, squaring his shoulders as he regained his composure. His eyes once more met theirs as he explained: "My full name is Ashmont Bartelle. The Pelumbras are the closest thing my family has to enemies."

Kieran turned fish-belly white.

"Kier?" Delilah asked. "You okay?"

"Um—of course! Yep. I'm doing amazing." He took a sip of his tea, hand faintly quivering. He lowered his cup and explained to the girls, "The Bartelles are another high-ranking family in northern Celdwyn. They're wealthy, like the Pelumbras, and w— *they* used to have several business partnerships. Before, um . . ."

"Before the Pelumbras got half my family killed a couple years ago," Ash said through his teeth. He took a breath, but his eyes still smoldered. "Because all of them are greedy, cruel people who will cut any corner to make an extra dollar. There's no such thing as a Pelumbra with a heart."

While Kieran went even paler, Briar lifted her tea and said, "Cheers to that."

Ash's forehead wrinkled for a second before he clicked his glass against hers. He asked, "What led to the two of you getting cursed by the Pelumbras?"

A bead of sweat trickled down Kieran's temple while Briar evenly explained: "We grew up in Havensbridge, the town at the base of the mountains where the Pelumbra estate is located. We're both witches and come from a poor family, so they invited us to their estate to give some of the younger generation practice doing combat magic against outsiders, offering us a place to stay in exchange. William Pelumbra got so annoyed that we were so much better at magic than his nieces and nephews that he taught us a lesson by putting a curse on us."

"How cruel," Ash said, his eyes shifting from Briar to Kieran as he added, "I'm so sorry."

"It's okay," Kieran said, rubbing the back of his neck sheepishly. "Not your fault."

While Ash was still transfixed by Kieran, Delilah—who couldn't help but be a little impressed by Briar's impromptu little story—nudged her and raised her eyebrows.

Briar whispered, so quietly Delilah could barely hear it, "One of us has to know how to lie on the spot."

Meanwhile, Ash cleared his throat, tearing his gaze from Kieran. "It seems the three of us have been wronged by them, then. My story's a bit different. When I was younger, the Pelumbras partnered with my family to build a coal mine over a seam that ran under our estate. While my family is wealthy, we didn't have the money to access the seam. The Pelumbras offered to pay for the construction in exchange for splitting the mine's profits. My family signed the deal and let them hire workers. Within a few months, the Bartelle-Pelumbra Valley Mine was ready to open."

Kieran shrank back into his seat.

"Until," Ash explained, "the day before mining was supposed to begin. The Pelumbras invited the Bartelles to tour the mine and show everyone what they'd built. My parents took me and my older sister. I was only ten, so I was practically vibrating with excitement when we descended into the tunnels. William Pelumbra brought a number of his relatives as well, as if it was some big party.

"We were midway through the tour when alarms started going off. My parents grabbed my sister and me as smoke started filling the tunnels. Someone screamed that there was a fire, and pure chaos erupted. The ceiling started caving in, and fire ignited the entire seam at once. The smoke made it impossible to breathe. My parents and I were able to get out through a vent, but we lost my sister because she"—his fingers curled back into fists—"she tried to go back and save one of the Pelumbras."

"I can't even imagine," Delilah whispered, at a loss for words.

Ash clenched his jaw "You want to know what gets me about it?" He met her eyes. "Not a single Pelumbra even got hurt. I remember running through the tunnels, and it was like the falling rocks and smoke *avoided* them. It was impossible—as if they couldn't be hurt. And to top it all off, the coal seam ran under our estate, and the fumes leaking out of the ground made our home uninhabitable. The mine is still burning to this day, and we've never found a way to put it out, so we can never go back."

"No wonder you hate the Pelumbras," Briar muttered.

Ash took a long drink from his cup before letting out a breath through his nose. "Since then, I've spent years trying to figure out what happened. We can't investigate the mine, since it's still burning, but a working theory is that the collapses and fire started because of faulty construction from the Pelumbras' cutting corners and being cheap about it. And considering what I saw down there, I can only assume there's some kind of blessing on the family—something that makes them lucky in impossible ways."

"How could a blessing do that?" Delilah asked. "I always thought magic like that wasn't that powerful—that it would just help you find lost objects or guess the winner in a betting game. Not have your entire family survive a freak mining accident."

Ash nodded. "Right—and that's why I've started to suspect that the Pelumbra blessing isn't normal. I haven't worked with curses for that long, but I know enough to think it's a geas."

Delilah's eyes widened with recognition while Briar frowned and asked, "Um—what's a geas?"

"It's a magical blessing with a condition, essentially," Ash explained. Delilah had heard of geasa from Theo, but more as a children's folktale than anything real. "In this case, I think the Pelumbras have a geas that acts as both a blessing and a curse: one member of the family bears the weight of the family curse so everyone else gets the benefits of the blessing. Depending on how nasty the curse is, it would explain why the Pelumbras are so lucky as a family—why their fortune has grown exponentially since they came into power, why they always win elections, why they never seem to die of anything other than old age. They sacrifice one of their own to benefit the whole family."

"Sounds about right," Briar said through her teeth. Fearing that the girl's grip might shatter her teacup, Delilah reached out and gently touched her wrist.

Briar's hand loosened.

Ash nodded, jaw clenched. "You sound like someone who wants revenge."

Briar cracked her neck. "Wouldn't be against it."

"In that case, I do have some good news." Ash put his palms flat on the table, his gaze sliding between the three others. "There's a Pelumbra vault, kept off-site in the library's restricted archive, that no one has touched in over a century. Exactly the sort of place you'd keep family trees, birth certificates . . . and maybe—just maybe—the written form of the geas. And if we had the written form, we could find a way to destroy their blessing forever and get the revenge we deserve for what they did to us."

"That's incredible!" Kieran said, his eyes lighting up for the first time since Ash had brought up his family. "What do we need to do to access the archive?"

"Well—it's a bit complex. The archives are restricted to the archivists, the owners of the vaults, and people with written permission from one of the library's trustees. But—that's part of why I wanted to speak to you. I suspect that if we have more than one testimony as to why we should be allowed to access the Pelumbra vault, we can convince one of the trustees I know. He's a bit insufferable, but he has a soft heart, especially for cursed people."

"Sounds reasonable to me—where would we find this trustee?" Delilah asked.

"I suppose you've probably heard of him," Ash said. "It's Klaus Hammond."

CHAPTER THIRTEEN

Rule #8: Anything can be a weapon if you think outside the box.

Delilah's world ground to a halt.

She'd never had any particular interest in meeting her father. Well, aside from some fantasies of berating him for abandoning her and her mother without so much as a birthday card for seventeen years. That might feel good. But she certainly hadn't thought about asking him for a *favor,* much less one that could decide whether or not she kept her magic and potentially saved her friends' lives.

This is gonna be a nightmare.

"He lives in Gellingham," Ash continued, clearly not noticing that Delilah had begun to spiral. "But he's been out of town for a couple of weeks on a . . . what was the term Aniera used . . . *spiritual retreat* with a group called the Moondew Coven. They're a huge nomadic group of witches that travels around Celdwyn and neighboring countries."

Delilah didn't hear much of the last of Ash's statement, as she was a bit busy seething. He paused and asked, "You okay, Delilah?"

"I guess since we're all sharing, I might as well." She squared her shoulders and let out a breath through her nose. "Klaus Hammond is my father. Never met him, but he is."

Ash reeled back. "What? How—do you know for sure it's him?"

"Believe me when I say my mother paints a very . . . colorful picture of the night of my conception," Delilah said, wincing as she remembered how many times Charlotte had told that story to friends and travelers at the pub. In retrospect, it was surprising no one had come looking for Delilah before Kieran. "It would be hard to make that up."

"Well—maybe that will make things even easier if it's Klaus's daughter asking for access to the vault." Ash nodded. "The Moondew witches will pass through in a week for one of their traveling-market stops in the Pinwhistle Forest. We should be able to track him down there, since it's just outside the city. I also don't know what sort of progress you've made on breaking your curse, but at the same time you might be able to ask the witches if they know of any panaceas for it. If, of course, you're interested. I can't force you to—"

"I'm interested," Kieran piped up. When Delilah raised her eyebrows, he amended, "Er, we're interested. Yes."

Delilah glanced at Briar, waiting for the girl to shoot her another *what's up with him?* look, but suddenly her face had gone pale. Her shoulders were tensed, her jaw working as she stared into her teacup.

"Briar?" Delilah asked, her voice barely more than a whisper.

She shook her head, not meeting Delilah's eyes. "It's nothing. Never mind."

Meanwhile, not having noticed the exchange, Ash aimed a small smile at Kieran. "Wonderful. Well, thank you for hearing me out and offering to help. I know trusting strangers isn't the most comforting prospect. But I think we can make this partnership work to our advantage."

"I'm really looking forward to being your partner," Kieran sputtered. He rubbed the back of his neck. "Or—um, I feel good about this."

Ash beamed. "I do too."

"Wonderful," Briar said dryly. She pointed to the clock and said, "We should head out. Ariel and Santiago should be back soon."

"She's right," Delilah said. Then, to Ash: "Should we plan on seeing you in a week and a half?"

He nodded. "You can count on it. I'll wait for you at the base of the eastern trail of the Pinwhistle Forest. It was good talking with you." He bit his lip and added, "You too, Kieran."

Kieran's smile was bigger than Delilah had ever seen.

"Nice job keeping your clothes on in there," Briar told her brother, clutching a tanghulu, one of the hawthorn-fruit-and-strawberry skewers they'd seen on sale outside the teahouse. She bit off a candied orb and, chewing, added, "Looked like it was a real struggle not to tear them off and let Ash take you then and there."

Kieran nearly spit out the crepe-like jianbing he'd bought himself while they sat on a bench on the street beside the Gell River, waiting for Ariel and Santiago to return. The three had spread out to get lunch after they said goodbye to Ash, who had to head back into the city for work. Delilah had just finished inhaling some pork buns.

Kieran blushed. "I—I wasn't *that* obvious."

Briar's eyelids hooded for a moment. Then she dropped her voice—sounding uncannily like her brother, and said, "Nooo, Ash, don't hate me for being a Pelumbra, you're so sexy, aha."

Delilah tried to stifle her mirth and wound up spitting out a staccato laugh before dissolving into giggles. Briar grinned, clearly proud of herself, while Kieran rolled his eyes.

"He's very attractive! Listen, I've been on an estate with no one but my relatives for most of my life. I never learned how to talk to good-looking guys without looking like a fool!"

"He was very cute, I'll give you that," Delilah offered.

"Eh," Briar said with a shrug. "If you're into that sort of thing. The *I want revenge on your whole family* thing lost him some points."

Kieran glared at her. "I don't think I asked for your opinion on romance, Miss Reads-Smut-under-the-Breakfast-Table."

Delilah gasped, grinning, while Briar's visible eye flickered with blue magic. "You promised you weren't going to tell anyone about that."

To Delilah, Kieran added, "There were some very scantily clad ladies on the cover."

Briar lurched forward and grabbed the lapels of his jacket. With impressive strength, she hauled him out of his seat. Her eyes flickered toward the river, and Kieran begged, "Not in the water—!"

Before Briar could toss him, though, they all paused at the sound of heavy footfalls on the walkway. A whistle cut through the burbling conversation of the road. Their heads snapped around to discover two figures darting toward them, one with an object stashed under their arm.

"Hey!" the figure in front cried. "Kieran! Delilah! Briar!"

"Ariel?" Kieran realized. "Santiago? What—"

"Stop them!" a man running behind them cried. There appeared to be three pursuers, dressed in black-and-red uniforms.

"Get behind me," Briar said, dropping Kieran. Her visible eye sparked blue, and light began to collect around her fingertips.

Kieran and Delilah exchanged glances before stepping back. Briar crouched for a moment to collect a handful of dirt, straightening just as Ariel and Santiago reached them.

"Go, go, go!" Ariel cried. The object under their arm appeared to be some kind of vase. "Ru's at the end of the road with the boat!"

"I'll catch up," Briar promised. Meeting Delilah's eyes directly, she said, "Go."

Delilah's heart fluttered for a fraction of a second. She shook her head, blushing with embarrassment at the brief betrayal in her chest, then started running along with the others.

"City guard," Ariel explained, not nearly as out of breath as Santiago, as they flashed Delilah a guilty smile. "Caught me stealing."

"A—menace," Santiago wheezed. "You're a—terrible menace— to society."

Townsfolk dodged out of their way as they barreled past. A man with a cart selling spun sugar in the shape of roses shrieked as Ariel nearly elbowed him into the river to move him out of the way. Santiago softly apologized as he ran by.

At Delilah's side, Kieran breathed heavily, lagging behind more with every step. *He's not strong enough for this,* she realized with a start. *Briar has drained him too much recently.*

"Hey!" Delilah called as she and Kieran began to trail behind. "We—we can't keep g—"

Something exploded behind them. Everyone skidded to a halt, spinning to see a huge dust cloud rising into the air. People ran out from inside covered in dust, coughing.

"Briar!" Delilah shrieked.

She had time to take four steps back toward the dust cloud when a small figure sprang out, landing on her feet as she completed a backflip. She spun in a graceful, leaping arc and threw two more handfuls of dust in the air.

Just as two of the city guardsmen emerged from the dust cloud, Briar flicked her wrists. The dust in the air ignited. Bursts of flame caught the guardsmen's clothes, and they cried out as they desperately patted out the fire.

Briar pivoted, panting, and took off sprinting toward Delilah and the others. As she passed Delilah, she asked, "What are you waiting for? Run!"

Delilah's heart sped up. Briar flew past her, and Delilah picked up again, sticking closer to Kieran. While he was still breathing heavily, the pause to catch his breath seemed to have been enough to keep him from collapsing.

As Ariel had promised, Ru waited in his gondola not far ahead.

Santiago helped steady the others as they quickly boarded. Ru pushed off from the dock with his oar and began to propel the boat down the river, where they'd come from this morning.

"Everyone okay?" Delilah asked.

Briar dusted some dirt off her shoulders. "Could use a shower. Don't exactly like improvising weapons. Certainly not dirt."

Kieran was still trying to catch his breath. He asked Ariel, "What—what is that?"

"Oh." They removed the object from under their arm, and Delilah realized with a start that it wasn't a vase but an urn. It was made of clay, and had a glossy red finish. "Right. This is Rory, my little brother."

"Perhaps not our smoothest timing," Santiago explained. "The house certainly seemed empty at first."

Ariel's mouth curved into a wicked grin. "You should have seen the look on Mǔqīn's face. She thought I was a ghost. Rory would have thought it was hilarious."

"I'm glad you got him," Ru said. He glanced over his shoulder, confirming that no one was following, and let out a sigh of relief. "He was always happiest with you. Even with your wild schemes."

"He always wanted to travel the world as a pilot," Ariel explained to Delilah and the others. "He wouldn't want to be sitting on a shelf in our parents' house. So"—they patted the urn— "I thought he could come with us."

"I see you're all unscathed as well," Santiago said, giving them each a once-over. "You weren't ambushed?"

"No ambush," Delilah confirmed. "A librarian's apprentice wants to help us."

"Not exactly true," Briar corrected. "He's obsessed with revenge against the Pelumbras. So we're on thin ice." She jabbed a thumb toward her brother. "Apparently he's into that, though."

"I'm sorry," Kieran said, burying his face in his hands and hanging his head. His breathing was still a bit too ragged for Delilah's comfort, and he was shaking a bit, but he seemed to be recovering. He added, voice muffled, "Do you ever see someone so attractive your brain stops working? And it's like you've been possessed by a demon that makes you do and say stupid things you'd never do otherwise?"

Unconsciously, Delilah's eyes wandered to Briar's mouth for the briefest second until she found Briar doing the same to her. They both snapped forward, tensing, cheeks flaring red and sweat breaking out on the back of Delilah's neck.

"Never," Briar snapped.

"Can't relate," Delilah agreed.

"Aw, how cute," Santiago chuckled. "Kieran has a self-destructive crush. What's his name?"

"There could be Shui City guards after us right now. Maybe we should focus on staying quiet and inconspicuous," Kieran argued.

"Nah," Ru said, scanning the riverside. "Looks like we lost them. Should be in the clear."

"You heard the man," Ariel said with a wide smile. "Tell us everything."

Kieran groaned while everyone else sat back in their seats, relief flooding over them in waves.

CHAPTER FOURTEEN

Rule #3: Old wisdom has it that the color of one's
magic is indicative of their personality: lush green for
stability and stubbornness, red for passion and rage,
purple for the aloof, yellow for the shrewd,
and palest blue for a haunted mind.
Current wisdom states that mileage may vary.

That night, back on the aeroship after everyone had eaten dinner, Delilah holed up in the study and added to her notes on the Pelumbras. She wrote down everything Ash had told them, circling the word *geas* over and over. She was lost in thought, doodling Cinnabar on the corner of a page, when the door opened and Briar came into the room.

"So this is where you're hiding," Briar said, flopping down on the couch nestled against the window. The moonlight poured in, casting a silver sheen on her skin. She sprawled out, closing her eyes and yawning. "What are you doing?"

"Just making notes for myself." Delilah closed the journal and watched Briar start picking at a loose seam on the couch. "Got all the dirt off?"

Briar snorted a laugh. "Yeah. Took a while, though."

"How did you do that, by the way?" Delilah asked, setting the book down beside her on an ornate end table. "Make that dust cloud into fire?"

Briar smiled. "Ledrith. It's, y'know, combat magic based on dance. It's kind of my specialty, like you and your baking."

"Oh, right. You mentioned that back in Dothering." Delilah blinked. "But ledrith is so . . ."

"Graceful?" Briar guessed. "And I'm not exactly dripping in grace, huh?"

Delilah flushed. "I wasn't going to put it like that."

"I like to put my own spin on it," she said, chuckling, seemingly unfazed by Delilah's accidental jab. "I could show you one of these days if you ever wanted to learn how to do some basic attacks. It's not hard."

"Really? Witches where I come from tend to be . . . really secretive when it comes to showing their techniques to other witches. They get nervous about their abilities being copied and losing their influence."

Briar blinked. "Why? That's stupid."

"I guess you didn't really grow up with the small-town witch culture, huh?" Delilah nodded. "If you'd be okay showing me, I'd love to learn."

"Absolutely." Briar swung her legs off the couch and stood up, gesturing for Delilah to follow her. "Come on. I can show you on the top deck."

"Right now?"

Briar shrugged. "Why not?"

Fair enough, Delilah thought. She followed Briar out of the sitting room and down the hallway, with its impressionist paintings and creaking hardwood floors. It felt as if they were on their own. Kieran had gone to bed early—Delilah tried not to notice how tired the day's excitement had left him, but it was obvious in the bruises under his eyes. She heard Santiago and Ariel laughing as they played a game of cards at the dining room table. She hadn't seen Adelaide since they'd returned, but Delilah suspected she was probably straightening up in the kitchen or reading.

Delilah and Briar climbed the stairs to the top deck. Night had brought a chill to the air, the last of the cold before summer fully took hold of Celdwyn. Briar rolled her shoulders back and shucked her oversize sweater off her shoulders, revealing a black tank top and the freckled, pale skin of her arms and chest. She turned, framed from behind by the trees of the airfield, the other aeroships, and the stars glittering in the sky.

Delilah's heart thumped.

"Do you want to change out of that dress?" Briar asked, gesturing to the calf-length green frock Delilah had on.

Delilah shook her head. "I'll be fine. Just don't light it on fire."

"No promises." Briar came to her side and said, "You want to start with your feet apart, weight distributed evenly between them. Square your shoulders. Bend your knees."

"So militant," Delilah said with a laugh, doing her best to follow Briar's instructions.

She scoffed. "Not even. If I were being militant"—she came around behind Delilah, then suddenly kicked her feet apart and reached up, pulling Delilah's shoulders back without hesitation—"I'd do something like that."

Delilah tried to throw an elbow out to connect with Briar's sternum, but Briar caught it with an open fist. "Nice try, kitchen witch."

"You're such an ass," Delilah grumbled.

"I'm being *helpful,*" Briar argued. She came to stand within Delilah's view, but not so close they could touch each other. Inexplicably, Delilah still felt where Briar had grabbed her shoulders, the skin warm, tingling as if she had shot a tiny spark of electricity into Delilah's nerves.

"The hardest magic," Briar began, stepping into the same pose, "is making something out of nothing. That's why I used the dirt earlier—it's easier to channel magic into an object as opposed to just using raw magic. You can, if you're powerful enough, but it's better to start with something." She reached into her pocket and pulled out a couple small stones, tossing one to Delilah. "Hold that between your palms."

Delilah did. Both Briar's eyes began to glow blue as she explained: "Now start pushing magic toward it and follow what I do."

Delilah nodded. She took a breath and mentally pulled from the reserve of magic that resided in her chest, channeling it down her arms and into her fingers, eyes glowing green.

Briar pulled her hands apart. The stone levitated between her palms, sparking with blue energy. She planted one foot in front of her, then brought the other around as she turned, moving the ball of light around with her. With a sudden rush of movement, she spun, launching off her planted foot and hurling the sparking ball of light up into the air. The rock inside it exploded with the magic, raining down on the two of them in a shower of blue sparks.

Delilah bit her lip and took a breath before attempting to copy the movement. She wasn't nearly as graceful, and when she tried to pivot off her solid foot, she stumbled a bit, but it didn't stop her from launching her ball of magic into the air. It was much smaller than Briar's, and didn't burst with nearly the same amount of pomp, but still, the explosion set off a shower of green sparks like fireflies in the darkness.

"Not bad," Briar said. "Has anyone ever told you that you've probably got more raw power than most witches?"

Delilah shook her head. "No. I always thought I was pretty average."

Briar shook her head, grinning. "Nah. I'll tell you what— whoever told you that only said it because they knew you were stronger than them."

Delilah thought back to all her lessons back in Kitfield, all the times Ruby told her she would make a good witch for another town. Of course she wouldn't let on that Delilah was more powerful than she was—why would she?

"Huh." Delilah met Briar's eyes. "Does that intimidate you?"

Briar sputtered a laugh. "You'll have to do a lot more than produce that skimpy magic ball to intimidate me, Delilah."

Delilah's ears turned pink. It was so strange, hearing Briar casually saying her name like that, laughing and smiling as if they hadn't despised each other a few weeks ago.

Or maybe that wasn't it. Maybe it never had been loathing that kept them at arm's length.

"Okay, fine," Delilah said, rolling her eyes. "Show me again."

They spent the next hour or so practicing, Delilah eventually caving and changing into a thin shirt and pants after she tripped on her dress a few too many times, much to Briar's smirking delight. She typically hated wearing anything masculine—she'd spent a good amount of her childhood being made fun of for her height, often being asked if she was secretly a boy—but she didn't even think of it now, standing beside Briar, who didn't seem to care in the slightest about how people presented themselves.

By the time they finally stopped, Delilah had a fine sheen of sweat on her forehead and curls stuck to the back of her neck. She sat on one of the deck chairs while Briar grabbed them both water from the kitchen.

"Thanks," Delilah said, taking the water glass from Briar's hand. She tapped it against Briar's. "Cheers."

"You're pretty good," Briar said, taking a seat beside her. They both stared up at the stars, catching their breath. "I bet that if you ever got sick of baking, you'd have a strong future with ledrith."

Delilah shot her a small smile. "That means a lot."

Briar shrugged. "Just being honest."

The two sat in silence for a moment, taking in the vastness of the sky. Delilah found her thoughts drifting back to earlier that afternoon and their conversation with Ash.

She bit her lip. "Briar? Can I ask you something?"

Briar's eyebrows rose. "Maybe. What do you want to know?"

"Earlier, at the teahouse, Ash mentioned panaceas, and you seemed . . . less than excited about the prospect." Delilah softened her voice. "What is a panacea?"

Once again, Briar winced. She shook her head and said,

"Panaceas—they're sort of . . . magical cure-alls. The idea is that they can remove any curse or other dark magic from a person. They're either very, very rare or fictional. But a lot of people go looking for them, hoping for a workaround that will break their curse if they're out of options."

"That seems like a good thing," Delilah said.

Briar shook her head. "No. No, it's really not."

Delilah stared at her, head cocked, waiting for an explanation, but suddenly Briar's eyes looked hollow. It was as if her body had shut off and the only thing still working was behind her eyes.

"I . . . I take it you have a reason not to trust stuff like that," Delilah guessed. "You don't have to talk about it if you don't want to."

Briar quieted, pulling her knees in closer. She ran a finger over the top of her arm, tracing one of the more obvious scars that cut across her skin. It was pale pink, skin puckered and uneven. Delilah had noticed that one before but wasn't about to start asking where each mark came from—she'd assumed it was a consequence of growing up in the woods.

"If I tell you," Briar started, meeting Delilah's eyes, "you have to promise not to look at me the way you did when Ariel told you about their brother, or Ash and the mine fire."

Delilah's eyebrows shot up. "What?"

"When you pity someone," Briar said, "you get this look on your face like you're hurt."

Delilah frowned. "That's sympathy, Briar."

Briar shook her head. "I don't care what you call it. Just don't do it, okay?"

"Okay," Delilah agreed, quiet. "I won't."

Briar squeezed her eyes shut and took a breath.

"When Kieran and I were born, my mother decided the best way to give him a longer life was to send me away," Briar said, staring intently at her scar, careful to avoid Delilah's eyes. "The Pelumbras told her it wouldn't help, but she insisted. Ultimately, it turned out she didn't send me away because of that—it was because she was disgusted by me. She didn't want to acknowledge that I was hers.

"My parents asked a bunch of different family members if they'd take me." Her voice sounded hollow. "No one wanted a cursed baby they had to hide away somewhere. They'd nearly given up when Wrenlin contacted them and offered to take me. She was only nineteen, and it had been less than a year since the curse had killed her brothers. She'd cut ties with the family and moved to Gabriel's Edge to get away from them. She hated them because they'd essentially let her brothers die in front of her. And my mother was so desperate to get rid of me, she agreed to turn me over to a teen hermit in the woods."

Delilah nodded, desperately trying to keep her face set. "Your mother sounds terrible."

"I don't know. I'm not sure I blame her. From what I heard, when I was born, I . . ." She considered her words. "I didn't look right. Not like a normal baby should. Not like Kieran did."

Delilah pressed her lips together. She couldn't imagine what Briar meant. "What compelled Wrenlin to take you?"

Briar scowled. "She'd made some promise to her brothers that she was going to break the curse one way or another. So when I was born, she decided the only way to honor her brothers was to take me and kill the thing that killed them. She took me in specifically to figure out a way to fix me."

"Never a great angle to approach parenting from," Delilah mused.

Briar rolled her eyes, nodding. "She was so wrapped up in the fact that I was cursed that she just . . . forgot I was also human." She rubbed her eyes. "My whole childhood was one theory about the curse or another. Eventually, she decided there was no way to break it and the only hope was to use a panacea."

She flinched, squeezing her eyes shut before she added, "Wrenlin didn't have a lot of money. My parents sent her funds to take care of me, and she blew nearly all of them on fake panaceas. Every week, there was something new, some salve to rub on my chest or a potion that made me throw up for three days straight. And I took it, because I was a little kid, and I didn't know any better.

"And there was this one time when I was . . . seven, maybe. I'd just come down from an attack, and she was wiping dirt off my face. She told me that one day I wouldn't have to feel that kind of pain. Without thinking, I told her that the attacks don't hurt me." Briar hugged herself, staring down at her knees. "Because they usually don't. Maybe at first but—after it starts, it feels . . . amazing. Like I can do anything. And it's terrible to admit that I enjoy it when I know it hurts Kieran so much, but when I was a little kid, I didn't understand that. I just told her the truth.

"She lost it. She told me that I deserved to be cursed. After that, the fake panaceas she tried were . . . invasive. She chose things that she knew would hurt me, and if I told her it hurt, she would remind me how terrible I was for enjoying how the curse made me feel. That this was how I could atone." Briar took a shaking breath, pressing her finger into her scar, hard. "This one was the worst. She pinned me down and cut open my arm to put this bundle of herbs she bought off some witch into the wound, saying it would suck the curse out of my blood. After, it got infected, and I got sick. It took me weeks to get back to normal."

Delilah pressed her fist to her lips. She hadn't realized how deeply she'd tensed until she moved it away, her muscles aching. She asked, "Did you . . . did you ever tell anyone?"

Briar nodded. "Once. Every year my father, William, would visit to check on me. When I was little, it was the most exciting thing in the world. I'd stand there at the window, so happy that my dad was going to come visit."

She bit down on the inside of her cheek. Her eyes started to shine. "He always smiled when he saw me. He'd pick me up and hug me and tell me he loved me. I thought he was the best person in the world. And after this"—she pointed to the scar—"when he came to visit, I told him what Wrenlin had done. I was sure he would finally see that he needed to take me home, even if I was cursed."

A tear slipped down Briar's cheek, and she rubbed it away with her fist. "He saw it and he just . . . didn't even react. He ran his fingers through my hair and kissed my forehead and said that Wrenlin was doing what she had to so I could be fixed." She exhaled a shaking breath as tears tightened the back of her throat. "And he left me there. He left me with her. He didn't even care."

She choked on a sob, and Delilah crawled to her side. She reached out to hug her, then hesitated.

Briar sniffled, shaking her head. "You don't have to touch me."

"No—that's not—" Delilah blinked tears out her eyes. "Can I? Is that okay?"

Briar nodded, tears dripping down her chin.

Delilah reached out and pulled the other girl closer, tucking her against her chest. The bare skin on her arms was dappled with goosebumps. Briar closed her eyes and tried to steady herself, taking slow breaths through her nose and wrapping her hands around the fabric of Delilah's shirt.

Briar rubbed the tears on her cheek off on her shoulder and muttered, "You made the face. I told you not to make that face."

"I don't pity you, Briar," Delilah whispered against the girl's peach-fuzz hair. "I don't."

"You should," Briar muttered. "I deserve it."

Delilah tightened her grasp. "What happened to you isn't your fault. You were a child. Wrenlin and your father and everyone else—*they* failed *you*. You aren't a problem that needs to be fixed."

"Aren't I?" Briar said, not opening her eyes. "That's the whole reason we're here. So you can try to fix me."

"You aren't your curse," Delilah said. "Just like I'm not mine."

"Sometimes it seems like that's all anyone ever sees," Briar whispered. She opened her eyes and looked up at Delilah. "Sorry. I didn't mean—I didn't mean to . . . cut myself up and spill my guts all over you."

Delilah sputtered a laugh, rubbing away the dampness on her own cheeks. "You have such a way with words." She rubbed her thumb in a circle over Briar's arm. "And I asked, didn't I? Thank you for telling me. I . . . I understand a lot more now."

"And if we go to this market with Ash, you won't make me try any panaceas?" Briar asked.

Delilah shook her head. "No. I'd never make you do something that hurt you."

"Even if it was the secret to breaking the curse?" Briar asked. "Even if it meant you'd lose your magic?"

Delilah shook her head. "You're the only one who can make choices about things like that. I can't tell you what to do."

Briar managed a small smile. "Damn right."

"There you go." Delilah let go of her and pulled away, rubbing her upper arms. "I need to go inside or I'm going to freeze, but . . . thanks for trusting me."

Briar nodded. "Yeah. I'll . . . be inside in a bit. I just need a minute."

"I'll make tea for us," Delilah said brightly.

Briar looked the other way to try to conceal the smile she was fighting. "Thank you, Delilah."

As Delilah stood and headed toward the stairs, she paused to press a hand against her chest, momentarily overtaken by the feeling of warmth inside.

She descended the stairs.

CHAPTER FIFTEEN

Rule #13: Be prepared: the past has an annoying habit
of coming back.

As the next week passed, Delilah and the others waited for their chance to find Klaus Hammond with the Moondew Coven. Delilah busied herself researching geasa at a few of Gellingham's local bookstores in an attempt to distract from the complex ball of emotions that surrounded meeting her father. She had no love for Klaus, but there was a part of her, deep down, that was curious about him. Still, she did her best to shove that down in favor of learning the ins and outs of geasa.

It turned out they were extremely uncommon in the present but had been much more common around the time when the Witches' Council took power. They were typically used by powerful witches trying to get revenge on other powerful witches—knowing that the complex bond between blessing and curse made it harder to remove. Delilah jotted that down, writing a note underneath that said *Witch from another prominent family?*

When Delilah asked Kieran whether the Pelumbras had had partnerships with other wealthy families besides the one they had with the Bartelles, he couldn't think of any. Historically, they relied largely on themselves.

"It's easier to trust family," Kieran said with a shrug. "Not that we always get along—we definitely don't—but family always comes first."

Delilah added another note to the page: *Cast by one Pelumbra on another?*

That seemed like a long shot.

Meanwhile, Kieran got in touch with Ash. A few times, the four of them met up in Gellingham to lay out their plan of attack and, after that, just chat.

Or—some of them did, anyway. Delilah and Briar found themselves with front-row seats to the Kieran and Ash show, a thrilling spectacle with a lot of gentle hand touching and laughing way too hard at each other's jokes, which weren't funny. Ash would pull a book from his bag to show Kieran a passage, and they'd sit there smiling and chuckling to themselves while Delilah and Briar wrinkled their noses. It was like they forgot they weren't the only two people on the planet, which was impressive, because Briar was growing more and more obvious about pretending to gag herself.

The day before the coven was due to stop outside town, Ash excused himself from their table to grab them coffee, and Briar finally broke.

"So, uh," she said, palming her cheek and languidly staring across the table at her brother, "have you and Ash fucked yet or what?"

Kieran's jaw dropped. "Briar!"

She cocked an eyebrow. "Is that a no?"

Kieran frowned, eyebrows bent together. He looked at Delilah, wide-eyed, waiting for her to defend him.

Delilah simply examined her nails. "If you haven't, you ought to."

"You two are unbelievable," Kieran snapped. He fretted with the paper in front of him to busy his hands, shaking his head. "I don't even know what you're talking about. Ash and I are just friends."

Briar and Delilah both squinted at him.

"What?" he asked.

Briar cleared her throat and put a hand on Delilah's arm. In an eerily accurate imitation of her brother's voice, she said, "Oh, Ash, you're *so funny.*"

Delilah dropped her voice an octave, putting her hand over Briar's. "Not as funny as you, Kieran. I could listen to you talk all day long."

"Stop it," Kieran said.

"I'd rather you shut me up," Briar continued in Kieran's voice, fluttering her eyelashes and shimmying her shoulders. "Let's go kiss in the stacks. The smell of books makes me *so hot.*"

"*Kieran,* you're so bad," Delilah said, biting her lip.

Briar swooned theatrically. "Spank me with a cursed tome."

"Please," Kieran begged, face burning red. He pressed his hands into his cheeks. "He's gonna come back and—damn it, I will *literally* pay you to stop."

"Admit you like him and we might," Briar said with a devilish grin.

"Fine!" Kieran threw his hands in the air. "I like Ash! A lot!" He buried his face back in his hands. "Are you happy?"

"Extremely," Briar chuckled.

"I might be a little happier if he didn't indiscriminately loathe every Pelumbra's guts," Delilah said, softening her voice in case anyone walking by happened to be listening. She leaned across the table and whispered, "I'm not trying to criticize your taste, but are you sure you want to be with someone who's made a revenge pact against your family?"

Kieran exhaled, shrugging. "Every relationship has hurdles, right?" When he saw the girls' expressions, he added, "Look, I already wanted to distance myself from the Pelumbra name. Why not give it up completely? Ash doesn't have to know."

"I'm the last person who would ever tell you to maintain ties to the Pelumbras," Briar said, "but like it or not, that's who we are. We have their curse, after all. You can't just pretend to be someone else and hope he never finds out."

"She's right," Delilah said. "If he doesn't accept you for who you are, you shouldn't try to change for him."

"I'm changing for *me*, not just him," Kieran argued. "The original Kieran Pelumbra is gone. I'm my own person. My own person who isn't associated with my past. Or with the people who hurt him."

"You're playing with fire," Delilah warned.

"It'll be fine," Kieran swore. He noticed something over Delilah's shoulder and added, "Now pretend we weren't talking about this—he's back."

"Coffee?" Ash said a moment later, setting a mug down in front of Kieran.

"Yes, please," he said, beaming.

Delilah and Briar exchanged a look but didn't say anything else.

❦

The next day, a summer storm began to collect in the southern corner of the sky, bringing with it heavy air tinged with a breath of cold. Delilah met Briar and Kieran by the gangway, a bag of supplies slung over her shoulder.

"You ready?" she asked.

"Ash is going to meet us at the trailhead," Kieran said with a grin. When Delilah and Briar both rolled their eyes, he added, "Please behave yourselves."

"No promises," Briar muttered in Delilah's ear.

Santiago caught them just before they headed out and passed out food wrapped in beeswax cloth. He and Ariel were planning on making a supply run that morning, leaving them to their own devices. They thanked him for the snacks and headed out to catch the trolley.

They took it about half a mile down the road, where they got off at a stop that was nothing but a small sign up against the tracks. Another sign farther up a dirt path welcomed visitors to the Pinwhistle Forest. The trees were massive and climbed high into the sky, pines with broad branches and bark that smelled faintly of peat and vanilla. Sunlight mottled the trail, and silvery ferns sprouted up beside it.

Ash stood beneath the welcome sign, dressed in a checkered button-down shirt tucked into tan pants, and thick hiking boots, a walking stick in his hand.

"You made it!" He nodded up the trail. "It's just up this way. Shouldn't take us more than an hour."

"Great," Kieran said, beaming. He fell into step beside Ash. "I've never gone hiking. Have I told you that? Maybe I told you that."

They started off, seemingly unaware of Briar and Delilah behind them.

"Love makes you dumb, huh?" Briar said.

Delilah nodded. "Seems like it. Come on."

The four of them trekked up the trail, sweat breaking on Delilah's forehead. Kieran quickly found himself gasping for breath, sweat dripping from his brow. He'd recently developed a phlegmy rattle in his lungs, and he stopped to cough a few times and dab his brow. Still, he kept a decent pace, so Ash hung back with him while Delilah and Briar took the lead. The forest bloomed with every shade of green, deer darting through the trees and birdsong clear on the breeze. They passed a few witches on their way down, clearly having hit the market at sunrise to get the best goods. Some carried bags rattling with jars full of ingredients to brew potions, while others had armfuls of flowers that smelled of a sweet enchantment that made Delilah's stomach flutter.

They made it about halfway up the trail before Delilah stopped them. Kieran desperately tried to catch his breath, while Briar tilted her head softly to the side.

"I've been able to smell magic on this trail since we got here," Delilah explained. She pointed into the trees. "But suddenly it veers off this way. I think that if other witches have already taken this trail, they turned here."

"I suppose that would make sense," Ash said, gently thumbing his chin as he considered it. Kieran watched him as if he were the sun rising over the mountains after a long, cold night. "I know they like to set up the market so it's a bit harder for nonmagical people to find. Perhaps we should follow this witches' trail."

"Seems like a very good way to get lost in the woods," Briar grumbled.

"I agree with Ash," Kieran said, rubbing his forehead with the back of his hand to stop a droplet of sweat. "I think we should follow the trail."

Delilah bit her lip. "Listen, I'm not a bloodhound. I can't promise I can actually follow this."

"I'm sure we can follow other things—footprints and what-not," Ash said, stepping in front with his hiking stick and pointing to a few boot marks in the dirt. "See? We'll be fine."

Kieran nodded and jogged to stand beside him while Briar and Delilah, brows furrowed, exchanged a look.

"I suppose we can try?" Delilah offered.

"Fine," Briar grumbled. "Into the woods."

At first, it was easy enough. The witches who had forged the path in front of them hadn't been trying to cover their tracks, by any means, leaving broken branches and plenty of prints in their wake. However, as the sun continued to cross the sky, the four of them only got deeper and deeper into the woods, no longer able to see the Gellingham skyline in the distance.

Just after noon, Briar asked, "Delilah, can you still smell magic?"

Delilah paused, inhaling. She caught the familiar scent of Briar and Kieran's curse, with the subtle smell of Ash's magic under it, but nothing else. Clearly, the look on her face as she realized she'd lost the other magic scent told enough of the story. Briar cursed under her breath.

"We could retrace our steps," Delilah offered. "Head back to the main trail and try again."

"Maybe we missed a turn somewhere," Ash guessed. He reached out and touched one of the trees, muttering, "We could try going north. I suspect they'll hold the market farther from the city—"

"If we keep wandering around, we're only going to get more lost," Briar pointed out. "We should turn back. This is pointless."

"We can't just give up on finding Klaus," Kieran pointed out.

Briar met his gaze. "You've been gasping for breath for the last mile. If we don't turn back now, you're going to be too exhausted to keep going."

Kieran's cheeks flushed, and Ash looked at him—really looked at him—for the first time, a small frown creeping down his face. Kieran tried desperately to wipe the sweat from his face, shaking his head.

"Sorry," Ash said. "I—I didn't realize you were tired."

"It's not that—it's the curse," Kieran explained, averting his eyes from Ash's softened gaze. "It makes it so I'm not quite as . . . strong as most."

"Maybe we should rest for a bit," Delilah offered. "Discuss our options and see how we feel after lunch."

"I would appreciate that," Kieran said, his voice still almost too quiet to hear.

The four of them found a small clearing for lunch, all trying to cover up how often they looked at Kieran, trying to tell whether or not he was okay. His face stayed red—from discomfort or exertion, Delilah wasn't sure—and he didn't talk much as he ate the sandwich Santiago had prepared for him.

At the very least, Santiago had once again pulled off a wonderful lunch—he'd packed Delilah a sandwich with rapini, mozzarella, sharp provolone, and tomato jam on a sesame seed roll. She was just about to take the last bite when she inhaled and caught the subtle scent of magic in the air—sandalwood mixed with the softest floral edge.

"A witch is coming," she breathed.

Briar instantly stood, magic rippling in electric bursts around her fingertips. She started to say, "If it's Regen again—"

But then a voice rang out: "Briar? Is that you?"

A tense beat froze everyone in place for a moment.

Then Briar's eyes widened.

"Laven?"

Out of the trees stepped a short, slim man, dressed in a patched cloak, a bent, pointed hat, and scuffed boots. He had feminine features that Delilah briefly misread as meaning he was around their age; at second glance, she saw evidence of crow's-feet and faint forehead lines in his tan skin and knew he was more likely in his mid-thirties. He used a long stick to pick his way through the undergrowth, stepping silently through the ferns.

"This is quite a surprise," he said, removing his hat to brush a hand through his thick black hair. He had a high voice, lilting and soft. "I never thought I'd see you so close to a big city." His eyes flitted to Delilah and the others, grinning. "And you made friends."

Delilah raised an eyebrow, and Briar shrugged. "It was against my will, but they're not so bad." She held a hand out toward the man and explained: "Everyone, this is Laven Alvarez. He's a traveling witch who took me in for a bit after I ran away from Gabriel's Edge. He's the one who taught me how to summon a familiar."

He whistled and a small kestrel swooped down from the sky, landing on his shoulder. Delilah almost couldn't believe he was real and not from a storybook, what with the outfit, the familiar, and the general aura of a practitioner from a long-forgotten era of witchcraft.

He reached out, and the bird nuzzled his fingers. "Sera was the one who spotted you. I couldn't believe it. Half because you ran away from me so suddenly I worried you had died, and half because the Briar I know would never get lost in the woods."

Briar frowned, hooking a thumb to the others. "Blame them. For the lost bit, I mean. The running away . . ." She shrugged. "Sorry. I hate goodbyes."

Laven smiled pleasantly. "I understand. I had a feeling it was going to happen sooner rather than later." He looked at the others. "Lovely to meet you. I assume you're looking for the market?"

They all nodded, and Delilah asked, "Do you know how to get there?"

Laven nodded, pointing to the kestrel on his shoulder. "Sera can lead us back. I've recently joined the Moondew Coven, so I'm heading in that direction as well. It'll take about a half hour."

"Sounds good to me," Briar said. She glanced at her brother. "Does that work for you?"

Kieran nodded. "Half an hour of walking—that I can do."

"Good." Briar looked back to Laven and explained, "Oh, by the way, this is my twin, Kieran. And these are our friends, Ash and Delilah. Delilah's on her Calling, trying to break our curse."

Laven's eyebrows shot up. "That's quite a big task for a Calling."

"You're telling me," Delilah said, stuffing the last of the beeswax wrap from her sandwich back in her bag. "Well—shall we head out?"

Everyone nodded, and Laven nudged Sera on his shoulder. The bird took off with a flap of her wings, gliding through the trees in front of them. While Ash and Kieran hung back a bit, walking at a slower pace, Briar and Delilah joined Laven.

"You never mentioned you had a traveling companion before you joined us, Briar," Delilah said, shooting a glance at Laven.

"I caught her trying to steal from me," Laven said with a chuckle, his stick softly *clack-clack-clack*ing against the rocks as he guided them northeast, uphill and away from Gellingham. "I was camping north of Eldagenny, in the west. Imagine my surprise when I thought a fox had gotten into my pack and instead discovered her pocketing my jerky."

Briar rolled her eyes. "I had only just run away. I didn't have any money, and I'd run out of food."

"I felt bad for the poor thing," Laven said. "Asked her if she wanted to come with me to the next town and wound up traveling around most of western Celdwyn with her."

"It was about two months," Briar clarified. "And then, ah . . . I felt like I could make it on my own. So I left."

Delilah nodded, trying not to let it show how much the idea of Briar wandering through the woods, starving and alone, got to her. It occurred to her that she still barely knew anything about Briar's past, and she was annoyed with herself for not asking.

"I'm glad you were able to help," Delilah told Laven.

Laven shrugged. "It's a difficult life for a witch without a town or a coven—I know that from experience. It was the least I could do." His eyes moved between Briar and Delilah, and he nodded as he told Briar, "It's comforting to know you're not alone."

"It's, ah . . ." Briar trailed off, sneaking a peek at Delilah before quickly refocusing on the path ahead. "It's definitely . . . different."

Delilah bit her lip to stop herself from smiling and looked ahead as well.

The rest of the journey through the forest was filled with easy conversation as Briar and Laven caught up. He didn't seem to hold any resentment over Briar's abandoning him. He seemed like the sort of man who took everything in stride, unruffled by Briar's gruffness or Delilah's questions about the market and what might be there. Delilah quickly understood why Briar had stuck with him for so long: nothing seemed to faze him.

Soon, the trees around them began to thin, and they reached the summit. A myriad of magic smells instantly hit Delilah— everything from herbaceous to floral to spicy, as if she'd stepped into a world-class kitchen. Instead of stalls, like those at the farmers market back in Kitfield, colorful caravan wagons made up the Moondew Coven's market, with different goods set up outside them on fancy rugs or hung on clotheslines. Wonder sparked in Delilah's chest, lighting up her eyes and bringing a smile to her face.

"It hasn't really gotten going yet," Laven explained as Kieran and Ash caught up with them. "This is just the beginning of the festivities. Most of the finest goods won't even come out until later, when the moon is out." He shrugged. "Old witch superstition: the best time to buy is midnight."

"You said you've been traveling with the Moondew witches for a bit, right?" Delilah asked. When Laven nodded, she briefly bit her lip and paused before asking, "I . . . I was wondering if you know where Klaus Hammond is. I need to speak with him."

Laven's eyes widened. "Klaus? Are you hoping he might help with your Calling?"

"Sort of." Delilah debated telling him, then admitted, "He's my father."

Laven blinked and fell silent for a moment but didn't react with the shock that usually followed Delilah's revealing her parentage. "You know, I did think you looked a bit familiar. It's uncanny, actually—you have his face."

Delilah's eyes hooded. "Not the first time I've heard that."

"Ah—I see there's perhaps some tension there." Laven withheld a laugh. "Klaus has been straying from the group during the day and mostly just sleeping here. I suspect he'd be traveling alone if he weren't the type to get lonely and bored so easily. He'll likely be back around sunset."

"What's he doing?" Briar asked. "Wandering around in the woods for fun?"

Laven shrugged. "He hasn't told us. He's taking a hiatus from his typical cursebreaking jobs, but beyond that, we aren't sure what he's been up to. When I asked, he changed the subject and pretended it had never come up."

"Sounds like most of the interactions I've had with him at the library," Ash said, sighing. He touched Kieran's wrist softly and said, "Would you like to look at the market? It's really something."

Kieran's eyes lit up. "I'd love to." To Delilah, he said, "I'm sure there's plenty we can do to pass the time while we wait for Klaus to get back."

Delilah inhaled the scent of magic again and grinned.

"Let's take a look."

Delilah, Kieran, and Ash spent the rest of the afternoon excitedly exploring the market, Briar lagging behind and keeping to herself, as she tended to in crowds. As they explored the rows and rows of stalls, music bubbled up from performers in a sort of central square circled by the wagons. People with wild makeup on stilts threw powder in the air that came to life in rainbow plumes of smoke, twisting into shapes ranging from cats to seaside scenes. The magic sparked wonder in Delilah's chest. As the powder sank to the ground, it perfumed the air with the smell of caramel.

When Ash reminded Kieran about asking around for panaceas, Briar began to bristle, and Delilah quickly made an excuse for them to split up. Kieran blushed at the idea of being left alone with Ash, but Ash agreed that it would be better to head in different directions to cover more ground. They went their separate ways as the sun was beginning to sink, the sunset a pink-and-orange blush across the tree line.

"Thanks for that," Briar said, rubbing the back of her neck as she exhaled. "I . . . I don't think I would have been able to keep it together if we talked about that stuff much more."

"Don't worry about it," Delilah said, hooking a thumb back to point at herself and beaming. "I've got your back."

Briar quickly turned her face away, flushed, and muttered under her breath, "You're so embarrassing sometimes."

Delilah just laughed. "Don't pretend you don't like it."

Briar rolled her eyes, but she couldn't stop the corner of her mouth from quirking up in a smile.

They headed on, Delilah leading the way. They passed a band playing upbeat music accented by horns, an upright bass, and a tambourine. A crowd of people, split into pairs, glided across the grass, far more skilled dancers than Delilah had ever seen.

"The musicians must be witches," Briar said, seeing how Delilah was staring. "If you start dancing to their music, you'll know the steps even if you've never practiced them before."

A wicked grin crossed Delilah's face. She *loved* this sort of thing. Occasionally, witches traveling through Kitfield would perform songs like this in the town square at festivals, and Delilah would force her mother or friends to take to the floor with her. There was little she enjoyed more than getting lost in a song.

She turned to Briar, holding out a hand. "Join me?"

Briar looked as if she might vomit. "In front of all these people?"

"You said it yourself: anyone can dance to this."

Delilah reached out and grabbed her hand, yanking her forward despite a yelp of protest. Delilah muscled Briar into the correct stance, their fingers interlocked on one side and pressed to the hip on the other. Briar's skin was hot to the touch. The feel of it instantly brought back the feeling of Briar's lips on hers, the way her hands had gripped Delilah's dress.

Delilah's stomach fluttered, and she nearly winced.

She's just a friend, Delilah chided herself. *And this is nothing but simple fun. Don't overcomplicate it.*

Delilah pushed the images of their kiss from her mind and took the first steps. Just as Briar had said, Delilah knew exactly what to do as if she'd been practicing for years. They glided into the crowd, feet jumping almost of their own accord, twirling each other around. Delilah's heart thrummed. The beat picked up, and both of Delilah's hands went to Briar's waist. Briar's visible eye widened before Delilah lifted her into the air, spinning her around and placing her softly back on the ground.

Briar whispered, *"Wow."*

"Not so bad, right?" Delilah laughed.

Briar took a breath. "Not at all."

The song ended, and everyone in the crowd began to clap. Delilah curtseyed theatrically while grinning at Briar, who scoffed and shook her head.

After Briar refused another dance, the two of them decided to grab dinner. They found a wagon selling kebabs and sat down on the grass outside the market. Lights turned on, and darkness overtook the woods around them. Clouds began to roll in thicker, blocking out all but a sliver of the full moon.

Through a mouth full of kebab, Briar asked, "Hey, Delilah? Can I ask you something?"

Delilah looked up from her skewer. "Sure."

Briar bit her lip, eyes falling to the grass at her feet. Softly, she asked, "Have you ever seen the written form of your family's curse?"

Delilah *hmm*ed softly, shaking her head. "No—I don't think anyone in my family has. But as soon as your curse is broken and I pass my Calling, my first stop is going to be the Library of Curses. Then, hopefully, I can find it."

Briar ripped up a few blades of grass and fiddled with them between her fingers. "Do you think there could be . . . exceptions?"

"Exceptions?" Delilah took a sip of water from the canteen she'd brought along. "What do you mean?"

"Like, do you think"—her cheeks flushed pink—"maybe . . . certain people might be immune to it?"

The color drained from Delilah's face.

Shit.

"No," she said firmly, mind swimming. Her stomach was in the process of tying itself in knots, the kebab she'd just eaten threatening to reverse course. *Please, please tell me this isn't what I think it is.*

When Briar's brow wrinkled, Delilah shook her head, inwardly cursing.

"Look, I . . . there was a time when I really was convinced there could be." Delilah bit the inside of her cheek, not allowing herself to look at Briar as she spoke. "When I was still with Theo, I thought that maybe, *just maybe,* our love was different. If it was bigger, realer, truer, then maybe the curse couldn't touch it. I let myself live in that fantasy for months, until it came crashing down around me."

Delilah took a breath to steady herself as the back of her throat burned with threatening tears. "So no. There are no exceptions."

Even if I'd give everything to find one.

Briar was silent for a moment. She hadn't reacted so much as gone cold. Delilah wished she could read the expression on her face, but it was just . . . blank. Like she'd left her body to sit there like a statue.

Briar whispered, "Theo was a boy, right?"

"Yeah. Why?"

"Has your mom only ever been with men? What about your grandmothers?"

"I'm pretty sure they've only ever been interested in men," Delilah said. She wrinkled her nose and turned so she was facing Briar, tilting her head to the side. "What does that have to do with anything?"

Briar looked pointedly in the other direction, crossing her arms and frowning. "Nothing."

"Nothing?" Delilah repeated with a cocked eyebrow.

"It's just that . . ." Briar wrapped her arms around herself tighter, hiding her cheek against her shoulder. Her voice came out muffled and quiet. "In the past, sometimes people didn't consider that a woman could love another wo—"

"Delilah!" a voice called. "Briar!"

"Damn it," Briar grumbled under her breath. She whipped around. *"What?"*

Kieran and Ash stopped in their approach. Kieran was dressed in a new shirt with the top buttons undone, his hair held back with a shining piece of twine. Ash had bought a new pair of small ruby earrings that glinted in his earlobes. Both of them smelled strongly of magic, and their faces were warm and grinning.

The boys exchanged a look before Kieran asked, "Is now a bad time?"

Delilah shook her head, even though her mind was absolutely racing. *What had Briar been about to say?* "Er—it's fine, really. What's going on?"

"Laven told us that Klaus is back," Ash explained. He pointed to a green wagon at the edge of the market with a single light on inside. "He's in there if we want to talk to him."

Delilah's stomach clenched. She'd been so distracted with everyone else she hadn't even had a chance to process the fact that her father was here, in the flesh. Seventeen years of speculation about him had made him seem more like a legend than a person—it was hard to imagine he was just across a clearing.

To think, she could finally tell him in person where he could shove it.

Not right now, she reminded herself. *This is purely business. I'm meeting him to help the twins, not berate him.*

That can wait for after the curse is broken.

"Would it be okay if I spoke to him alone?" Delilah asked. When Ash raised his eyebrows, Delilah added, "Just at first. I've . . . I've never actually met him."

"Of course," Ash said, nodding. To Briar, he said, "Laven also said to tell you that he's constructing a bonfire, if you want to check that out."

"Better than sitting here in the dark," Briar grumbled. She stood and offered Delilah a hand, helping her up. Her hand lingered in Delilah's grasp for a beat too long before she let go, averted her eyes, and said, "Good luck with your dad."

"Thanks." Delilah flashed her a smile. "Maybe . . . maybe we can talk about your theory a bit more when I get back?"

"O-oh, right. Sure. Of course. Talk to you soon." Briar went to her brother's side. "Come on. Let's go."

CHAPTER SIXTEEN

Rule #20: Stay away from mushrooms.

Klaus's traveling wagon was somewhat apart from the others. A small string of twinkling lights framed the wooden door, as if he were a performer in a show and this was his dressing room. Delilah glanced over her shoulder at the still-bustling market before approaching the door, poised to knock.

She paused for a moment. Frankly, she could barely believe it. She was about to meet her father. The man who stepped into Charlotte Bea's life for a single night and changed it forever. The one who had never so much as tried to help her, or his daughter, break their curse. The one who spent his days lounging in luxury as one of the best-known witches in Celdwyn while Charlotte struggled to find someone to teach Delilah magic.

Delilah ground her teeth. *I'm not here for me. I'm here for Briar and Kieran.*

She exhaled and knocked on the door.

"Come in!" a booming voice came from inside. "Door's open!"

He's just a man, Delilah reminded herself. *Technically, yes, he's my father, but he's also a normal, typical m*—

Delilah's thoughts cut off the second she opened the wagon door.

The place was a mess. Expensive clothes were strewn about, hanging over the small stove in the corner, draped over the sink, and all over the floor. While Delilah smelled Klaus's magic—somewhat rosy and bold, like fresh currants—it wasn't the prominent scent in the small living space. No, that was a combination of whiskey and body odor.

The man himself sat splayed across a bed nestled into the back half of the wagon. The sheets were in a tangle, Klaus half covered by them. When Delilah stepped inside, he sat up with a yawn. He wore a loose white shirt with puffed sleeves, strings hanging down from the neckline, where it opened to a hairy, tanned chest. Delilah withheld a gag.

"You're quite tall," he said as Delilah ducked inside, slurring the words a bit.

"Thanks for that," Delilah snapped.

Klaus narrowed his eyes at her for a moment, and Delilah couldn't help but wince—she *did* look like him. He had the same thick, curly hair, wide eyes, and distinct nose that she did. His hair was beginning to gray at the temples. Delilah was used to seeing his picture in the newspaper with his hair neatly slicked back, but now it hung over his eyes, grown out and untamed atop his head. Clearly, this was not the camera-ready Klaus Hammond the general public might expect.

His brown eyes narrowed a bit before he inhaled and nearly lost hold of the glass of liquor he had clenched in his fist.

"I'll be damned," he muttered. "Delilah?"

"You know my name. That's—a start, I guess." She pointed to a chair across from him, beside the stovetop. "Can I sit?"

Instead of responding, he simply stared at her, stubble-shadowed jaw agape. After a moment, he stood, though he had to stoop somewhat, due to the low ceiling and his impressive height.

"I can't believe this," he said, setting his drink down unsteadily on the counter. "After all this time. I've always wondered if—when—this day would come." He squinted at her, as if she were a spirit that he could barely see in front of him. "Seventeen years and I still remember the scent of the Bea family curse. And there's also"—he inhaled softly—"there's another curse—not yours, though. But the smell of it is clinging to you. It must be from that girl I saw you dancing with."

Delilah jerked back. "You saw that?"

"On my way back in. It was a bit of a spectacle. It's rare to see two people look at each other like that." Klaus smiled a bit to himself. "How long have you been together?"

"*Together?*" Delilah repeated. She shook her head. "W-we're just friends."

"Is that so?" He sounded doubtful, and it made Delilah suddenly feel like a bug under a microscope. Thankfully, he dropped it. "Nonetheless, it's evident to me that the curse on that girl is very strong. Is that why you're here? To ask me to break her curse? Or the one on your family? That's why everyone comes to me, you know."

Delilah stood there for a moment, stunned.

He was so . . . *arrogant.* She'd expected something a little more along the lines of *how nice to finally meet you,* at very least. Maybe a question about how she was doing, or what her mother was up to? Maybe even some kind of apology, even a flippant one?

But certainly not *this.*

She opened and closed her mouth as rage began to simmer within her. Klaus swirled his drink around, not taking his eyes off her, as if waiting for her to sheepishly admit he'd read her correctly.

Even after what she'd told herself about not getting angry, Delilah couldn't stop herself.

"No!" she spat. "Of course not! You think—ugh, why would I ever ask *you* for help? You didn't even bother to break the curse on my mom when you met her, let alone the same one that wound up on *me,* your *daughter*! The whole point of my Calling is to break Briar's curse myself. Why would I ask some drunken fool like you to do it for me?"

Delilah didn't realize how much her voice had risen until she met Klaus's eyes and found them staring back at her, all evidence of excitement gone. She exhaled, looked out the window, and crossed her arms.

"You don't think very highly of me, do you, Delilah?" Klaus said, taking his drink in his hand. He took a sizable pull from the glass before putting it down and refilling it.

"Why would I?" Delilah asked, regaining composure over her tone. She gestured at their surroundings. "You're not even breaking curses anymore. Hell, you're the one who sent Kieran to me in the first place! You're the whole reason I'm in this mess."

"Kieran?" Klaus tilted his head to the side. "I'm not familiar with that name."

"Kieran Pelumbra? He found you in a bar in Gellingham a while ago and told you he needed to break a family curse? You sent him to Kitfield on my birthday so he could hijack my Calling? Any of this ringing a bell?"

"Not particularly," he admitted. "But a Pelumbra family curse . . . now that would really be something."

"Of course, why would you remember?" Delilah repeated, laughing mirthlessly. *What an asshole.* She looked around at the floor and kicked a dirty undershirt out of her way. "What are you even doing out here anyway? Aside from shirking your duties?"

"I'm taking a hiatus from my work," Klaus explained with a shrug. "It's healthy. You'll understand someday when you're older."

Delilah raised her eyebrows but didn't say anything.

"If you must know, I've been searching for something in the woods." He stumbled back, thankfully landing on his bed, before tapping his nose. "Perhaps you smelled it on the way up here. I believe there's a magic vein beneath the ground here somewhere."

"A what?" Delilah asked.

"You know how witches came to be, yes? The old stories?" When Delilah just looked at him blankly, he explained: "All over the world, there are veins of magic running through the ground— not unlike precious stones or minerals. Collecting magic from these veins is what gave the first witch her abilities, and since then, others across the world have been able to absorb magic from these veins. These days, of course, they've nearly all dried up, but I suspect there's one still lingering around here."

Delilah blinked. "So. You're wandering around the woods looking for some underground magic that may or may not be real?"

He pointed to her and grinned. "Exactly."

"That's . . . really something." Delilah shook her head. She couldn't care less about what this man did with his free time. Better yet, maybe if he spent more time in the woods, he would get eaten by a bear or something. "Listen, I could sit here all day and discuss the past and your work or—whatever. But that's not why I'm here. My friend Ash told me you're a trustee of the Library of Curses and you might be able to give us written permission to access the archive."

"Ah." He wagged a finger at her. "There it is. I had a feeling you weren't just here to meet your father."

"You're only a father in the biological sense," Delilah snapped.

"I suppose that's true." He tapped his chin as he stared at the ceiling, then continued: "Well. A letter—what exactly do you want to access in the archive?"

"There's a Pelumbra vault," Delilah explained. "I need to get in to help break the curse on my friends." She thought of the twins' faces and felt her shoulders fall. "Please. They mean a lot to me."

Klaus's face softened for a moment.

"The Pelumbras," he repeated. "That's quite an ask. I wouldn't want to make an enemy of one of Celdwyn's most powerful families."

"Please," Delilah repeated. "This isn't some trivial thing. There are lives at stake."

As Klaus stroked his chin, deep in thought, Delilah felt as if she might combust from the amount of pressure building in her chest. However, just as he was opening his mouth to speak, there was another knock on the door.

"Yes?" he called.

"Is Delilah in there?" came Ash's voice. "Something happened!"

Delilah went to the door and opened it. "Ash? What's going on?"

The library apprentice's eyes were wide, his brown skin slicked with sweat. "Something is going on with Kieran, and Briar disappeared into the woods. Laven is helping Kieran, but I—"

"Shit," Delilah cursed. "They must be having an attack." Delilah spun on her father. "I'm not done here, but I have to help my friends. Just—please think about it."

She took off running with Ash before Klaus had a chance to respond.

❦

Delilah found Kieran lying beside the bonfire Laven had started, three witches crowded around him. Laven was in the middle of checking his pulse. Kieran, meanwhile, was passed out with his eyes closed, his skin even more pallid and translucent than normal, the blue veins beneath visible.

"He seems stable," Laven said, meeting Delilah's eyes as she and Ash came to a halt beside him. "I can try to paint some protection runes on him if you think it would help."

Delilah shrugged. "I don't think it would hurt to try."

"What happened?" Ash asked, looking between the various witches. "One second he was fine, and then—his blue eye started glowing—"

Delilah felt a pang in her chest as she remembered the first time she'd seen the twins have an attack—how much the worry and anxiety had eaten her up from the inside. She touched Ash's arm softly. "It's part of his and Briar's curse," she explained. "This happens when she's draining his magic. He . . . should be okay." She tried to recall how long it had been since they'd had an attack. Four days, maybe? *That's barely any time at all.*

Shit.

Ash knelt at Kieran's side. He reached out, then pulled back, as if nervous that his touch might break him.

"Did you see where Briar went?" Delilah asked Laven, who was removing a small pot of ink and a brush from a bag on his hip. Delilah had heard of witches who mainly cast their magic through drawn or painted runes, but she'd rarely seen the process in action.

Laven pointed into the woods. "She ran that way. I suspect we don't need to worry about her as much as her brother."

Delilah's eyebrows shot up. "B-but she's out there in the woods! There could be mountain lions or wolves or—"

"She'll be fine, I promise you," Laven said, suddenly more serious than Delilah had heard him. For a second, a shadowed look passed over his eyes. He shook his head, refocusing on Kieran as he began to paint symbols on the exposed skin of his arms.

A few moments later, a droplet of water hit Delilah's arm, and the low rumble of thunder sounded in the distance. Laven looked up at the cloudy sky and cursed.

"No market tonight, I suppose," he muttered under his breath. To Ash and Delilah, he said, "You're welcome to stay in my wagon while you wait for Kieran to wake up and for Briar to come back. I'll bunk with one of the other witches for the night."

"That's very generous of you," Ash said. He looked up as the rain began to come down more, a droplet landing on his cheek and tracing down his skin. "Let's move him."

❧

With Laven's help, Delilah and Ash were able to carry Kieran to a caravan wagon near the center of the market. This one was decorated with golden flower details painted over the dark purple exterior. Inside was much like Klaus's accommodations, but there was a second bed in a loft above the first.

"Some of you will have to share beds, unfortunately," Laven said.

"You can share with Kieran," Delilah told Ash after they laid Kieran down on the lower bed. When Ash's face immediately heated, Delilah added, "You okay with that?"

"I—I would want to ask his permission first," Ash said. "It would be improper to assume. I'd rather wait until he wakes up."

Delilah nodded, impressed. She appreciated Ash's chivalry. "Fair enough. Y'know, you're a good guy, Ash."

"I—I try." He took a seat in a chair across from Kieran's bed.

Laven stepped in after them. Delilah took a chair beside Ash while the older witch sat beside Kieran to continue painting his runes. Outside, the rain began to come down hard, sliding down the arched windows of the wagon in heavy streams.

"Quite a storm," Laven muttered.

Ash saw the way Delilah had begun to chew her bottom lip and asked, "You're worried about Briar?"

Delilah nodded. "I know she can take care of herself. Hell, she's probably the most powerful thing in that forest by a long shot, but . . ." She glanced out the window into the rain, watching as witches ran to collect the items from their market stalls, feet splashing through growing puddles in the grass. "Maybe I should go after her."

"I wouldn't," Laven said, voice low.

"Why not?" Delilah demanded, a little harsher than she intended.

Laven paused for a moment, paintbrush hovering over Kieran's skin. Delilah could tell he was trying to think of the proper way to say whatever he was thinking. Then he exhaled a sigh.

"I made the mistake of following her once when we were traveling together. She'd told me not to, and when I found her . . ." He winced. "Well, she didn't forgive me after that. I suspect it's a big part of why she ran."

"You make it sound as if she's hiding something," Ash said.

Laven shook his head. "Everyone has parts of themselves they choose not to show others. She doesn't want to get hurt more than she already has been, so she hides. I understand that now." His eyes fell on Delilah. "That's why I'd suggest you leave her be. If you push her"—he shrugged—"she'll be gone before you know it."

Delilah scowled, crossing her arms. On the one hand, Laven knew Briar—maybe better than Delilah did—and she'd up and left him without even saying goodbye. But at the same time, she couldn't imagine how it would feel to be stuck in a rainstorm in the dark with no one coming after you. The thought made her muscles tense, and she couldn't stop shimmying her leg or chewing her lip.

Still, Delilah decided to drop it. "Fine. Understood."

Laven paused as if he was debating saying something else on the topic, but stopped himself. Instead, he said, "I see why she likes you."

Delilah's eyebrows rose. "What do you mean?"

Laven chuckled. "You're as stalwart as she is."

"It is impressive," Ash agreed. "The difference between how Briar speaks to you compared to how she speaks to everyone else—she really cares for you."

Delilah scoffed. "Oh, come on. She's just as much of a pain in the ass to me."

Laven shook his head. "No, he's right. It is different. I suspect she's quite . . . fond of you."

Delilah felt a blush threatening. She quickly pointed to a deck of cards sitting on the table and deflected: "Well, regardless, it seems like we've got a while until Kieran wakes up. Anyone up for a round of Curses and Blessings? I can beat almost anyone."

Laven and Ash both raised their eyebrows, clearly seeing through Delilah's attempt to change the subject. Ash, specifically, looked as if he might say something, his lips parted and rain still speckling the lenses of his glasses.

Finally, he shook his head and said, "You know what? Curses and Blessings sounds lovely."

Delilah breathed a sigh of relief and grabbed the cards.

That night, as the darkness grew thicker and the rain continued to fall, Kieran remained unconscious. Occasionally, he would let out a wheezing cough, but aside from that, he didn't stir. After a few hours of playing cards and chatting, Laven had left to stay in a friend's wagon while Ash fell asleep upright in his chair.

Delilah remained awake as all the lights in the other wagons went out for the night. She stared at her father's, debating whether to try to speak to him again. He was probably passed out by now, considering how much whiskey she'd seen him drink.

For a fraction of a second, she found herself thinking of how she couldn't wait to complain to Briar about what an ass Klaus had been—and frowned.

Ash snored softly in the chair beside her. Kieran's chest rose and fell softly in the bed, his eyelashes quivering as he dreamed. Outside, thunder rumbled, and a lightning strike cut across the sky.

Delilah's heart ached as she remembered what Laven had said: *She doesn't want to get hurt more than she already has been, so she hides.*

She doesn't have to, Delilah had wanted to say. *Not from me.*

She absently picked at a loose thread on her dress. She couldn't just let Briar sit out there in the rain and the dark alone. If it was her out there, she'd want someone to come for her. And whatever it was that Briar wanted to hide, it didn't matter as much as her safety.

Delilah stood, looked around, and spotted a heavy cloak hanging from a hook on the wall. It was wool—perfect for keeping the rain out. She snagged it and fitted it around her shoulders, flipping the hood up to cover her hair.

"I'll be back," she promised Kieran's sleeping form, "with your sister."

Silently, she crept out into the rain.

After a cursory look around the encampment, Delilah headed for the woods. Lightning slashed across the sky once more, thunder echoing in her ears. She reached up and held the hood in place over her eyes as wind whipped past her, spraying her with cold rain.

Her boots squelched in the mud while she pushed herself forward into the trees. The branches above creaked in the wind, creating a low, collective groan. She inhaled, trying to catch the scent of rot that always clung to Briar, only to discover that the perfume of the rain and the wet earth covered anything she'd typically be able to smell.

After about twenty minutes of pushing deeper and deeper into the woods, Delilah began to worry that she'd have nothing to track. The faint lights from the caravan behind her had faded, and now all she could see around her was trees. Her heart began to beat a little faster. The thunder continued to rumble, the intervals between blasts becoming shorter.

Just as she was beginning to lose hope, she came across a bramble shivering in the wind, its thorns long and thin. Caught on the edge of one of them was a scrap of fabric—black, just like the coat Briar had been wearing.

Delilah reached out and grabbed it, rubbing the damp fabric between her fingers. She summoned green light to her fingertips and illuminated the ground in front of her, eyes shining in the dark like a cat's.

There, in the mud, was a faint but visible set of boot prints. Delilah's heart leapt.

Pocketing the scrap of fabric, she kept going for another fifty feet or so, pushing through the skinny branches blocking her way, before discovering something disturbing. There, at the base of a tree, were more scraps of cloth, these torn and bloodstained. Delilah gasped as she caught the scent of Briar's curse on them—it was definitely her blood.

"No," Delilah whispered, bending down to touch the ruined shirt. "No, no, no—"

A boom of thunder made her jump as lightning flashed overhead.

"Briar!" Delilah cried out. She straightened, desperately searching for boot prints. The rain battered against her face and soaked through her skirt and socks.

She caught sight of another boot print nearby and ran, only to discover the boots themselves abandoned beneath a soaring pine. Delilah picked one up—it was just as mangled as the other clothes. A jagged slice through the toe revealed a muddy sole.

Delilah's heart slammed against her ribs, her breath barely more than short gasps. *I'm too late.*

"Briar!" she cried out again, voice catching as terror clawed its way into her throat.

Before she could finish the thought, something rustled in the trees to her side. Delilah froze, clutching the clothing scraps to her chest. A branch broke as something moved. Something big.

A massive shadow loomed against the pines.

Delilah's hands shook. She held her breath, chest aching,

desperately praying it didn't know she was there. She didn't dare move, muscles taut as they held her stock-still in place.

Lightning split the sky and, for a moment, lit up the space between Delilah and the creature. She saw the edge of a muzzle full of jagged teeth. Something hung out of its mouth—something limp.

A ghostly blue ember glowed on the other side of the creature's head, and the scent of rot rose from it.

"Briar!" Delilah shrieked.

The creature straightened, then let out a muffled yelp and leapt in the other direction. There was no subtlety to its escape—it tore branches from the trees and crushed them underfoot as it ran.

It's got her in its mouth, Delilah thought, nearly slipping in the mud as she pushed off to pursue it. *But if her eye is open—that means she's still alive!*

Delilah ran as she never had before. She vaulted over roots and logs, barely noticing as twigs scraped her skin, leaving hairline cuts across her cheeks and exposed arms. Magic flared at her fingertips. She scooped up stones only to spin and launch them in the creature's direction, making it dive out of the way as the stones exploded in a shower of sparks.

"Give her back!" Delilah snarled.

Just as Delilah was beginning to catch up, the creature suddenly launched itself forward. She didn't have time to notice why until her foot hit the edge of a ridge. With a shriek, she hit the muddy slope, tumbling head over heels through mire and underbrush.

Her body finally came to a stop at the bottom of a ravine,

mud caking every part of her. Blood from scrapes began to drip down her face and arms while her bones and muscles ached from the impact. Her arms trembled as she struggled to pull herself up, groaning at the dull pain seeping into her skin.

Delilah wiped grime out of her eyes. For a moment, she thought she'd somehow fallen into a portal to a different world.

All around her were massive, multicolored mushrooms that stood at least eight feet tall, while most towered twenty feet in the air. The gills glowed with bioluminescent light, as did white spots atop the mushroom caps. The light they cast was dull pink, and the air shimmered around them.

When Delilah inhaled, she instantly recognized the smell: it was the earthen undercurrent that always accompanied a witch's magic. Shakily, she stood, reaching out a hand toward the shimmering air. Dust collected on her fingertips. When she examined it more closely, she realized what she was looking at: spores.

Her head spun. Softly, she began to hear whispering. Not specific words, just quiet mutterings that rose through her thoughts like smoke.

Delilah swayed a bit, squinting. She could barely remember what she'd come there for. What had she been doing? Running, but why?

Something up ahead moved, but Delilah barely noticed. She was instead inching closer to the nearest mushroom, the whispering in her head growing louder. If she got a tiny bit closer, she might be able to understand what they were saying.

A low, guttural sound snapped Delilah out of her trance. She blinked, regaining focus just in time to lay eyes on a creature the likes of which she had definitely never seen.

This was different from the monster she'd been chasing. That had been spindly, with bones jutting out of it and long, willowy limbs. This creature was nearly a bear, except for the strange gossamer sails across its back. They twitched as it pulled its lips back from its teeth, growling. Delilah realized with a start that the sails were strange, malformed insect wings that burst from the bear's back like a fungus. Its eyes glowed pink, the fur around its neck matted with moss.

Delilah took a step back. As the bear snarled, the wings twitched uselessly on its back. It had around ten of them, all slightly different shapes and sizes.

"I won't hurt you," Delilah promised, backing up inch by inch toward the slippery ridge. "Just let me go."

She backed into something. Her head twisted around just in time to discover she'd bumped into another mushroom. Spores rained down on her.

Instantly, her head began to swim, as it had before. In front of her, the bear suddenly morphed into two bears, then four, all stalking forward with saliva-slick teeth.

All the strength left Delilah's knees at once, and she sank to the ground. Her vision darkened at the edges.

In a blinking second, the bear lunged for Delilah. A guttural snarl ripped from its throat. Delilah weakly held up her arms, closing her eyes.

But the impact never came. Instead, there was a loud thump as something landed in front of her with a low, animal cry. Delilah cracked open an eye just enough to see a large figure standing between her and the strange bear.

The creature stood on four legs, claws sinking into the mud.

It had a lupine muzzle that led up to a ghost-white face with one glowing blue light in place of an eye set far back in its socket. In addition to pointed ears like a wolf's, it had massive horns made up of intertwined, twisting pieces of bone that ended in sharp points. A coat of feathers started at the back of its head, working its way down its back and onto its arms. The spine was arched; vertebrae burst free from the skin, spiked and coated in blood. Its legs were almost reptilian, with midnight-black scales running down from the hips to the talons at the end of its toes. A long, scaled tail ended in a tuft of feathers.

When Delilah gasped, the creature stood back on its hind legs, head swiveling toward her.

Delilah's heart puttered to a halt.

As a girl, she'd heard stories of monsters, beasts twisted by dark magic that hid out in the shadows where witches didn't go. Her mother used to say if she didn't go to bed or eat her vegetables, something would creep out of the night and steal her away.

Looking at the creature in front of her, she knew with certainty it was fully capable of dragging her into the dark.

The bear stood where the creature had swatted it and let out a bellowing roar. Spittle flew from its massive teeth. The creature tore its gaze from Delilah, a growl rumbling in its throat; the feathers on its head stood on end as it charged once more at the bear, slicing long claws into its side. One of the bear's misshapen wings flew off, landing in the mud, still twitching slightly.

Delilah gasped, only to breathe in more of the spores. The sound of whispers in her head grew stronger, drowning out the noise of the fight in front of her. Her eyelids grew heavy, and her vision blurred. Between long, shaking blinks, Delilah saw the creature bite down on the bear's neck, making it bellow.

"Help," she whispered, so faint she could barely hear her own voice. "Help me."

Her eyes fluttered closed, and her body slumped, unconscious.

CHAPTER SEVENTEEN

Rule #18: The monster is never the monster.

The first thing Delilah noticed when she awoke was how bruised that fall down the ravine had left her and, in turn, how incredibly hard and uncomfortable the ground was.

"Ow," she moaned, reaching up to rub her bleary eyes. She heard a sudden burst of movement near her and blinked awake to see a shadow fleeing her side.

She sat up with a start. She was lying near the mouth of a cave, a fire crackling a few feet from her in a makeshift pit. It spit sparks, the wood clearly damp. Someone had removed Laven's stolen cloak from her and stuck it under her head as a pillow. Her dress and boots were still muddy, but it seemed the rain had washed much of the mud off her exposed skin.

Delilah rubbed her nose; when she pulled her hand away, she found some of the shimmering residue from the mushroom forest on her fingers. Her heart rate picked up as everything came back to her in a rush—the strange, twisted bear and its fight with that monster.

The one that had caught Briar.

The one that had . . . saved her?

Delilah opened her mouth to call out but stopped as her nose began to tingle. The next moment, she let out a kitten-like sneeze against the inside of her elbow. It left a shimmering residue on her skin. She groaned, muttering, "Ugh, gross."

The sound of soft laughter outside the cave made her head jerk up.

"Hello?" she called. Her fingers skittered across the floor as she reached for a stone, magic rushing to her fingers. "Who's there?"

For a moment, there was silence. Delilah rose to her feet, the stone floating in her hand as she prepared to throw it at anyone who approached.

Finally, whoever had laughed let out a heavy sigh.

"It's me, dumbass," a familiar voice called.

"Briar?" Delilah jumped, a grin breaking across her face. "Briar! You're okay!"

She took a few strides before Briar called, "Stay back!"

Delilah paused, suddenly remembering the bloodstained scraps of cloth she'd found in the woods. She didn't know the whole story, but it had looked as if Briar had lost her shirt and pants. Delilah grabbed her cloak off the ground and went to the mouth of the cave.

"I'm serious!" Briar snapped, voice growing shakier and more high-pitched as Delilah approached. "Delilah, don't—"

Delilah poked her head outside, keeping her eyes closed. She held out the cloak, trying not to laugh. "Here. You can wear this. I won't look, I swear."

"I— Oh. Thanks." Briar took the cloak as Delilah kept her eyes closed, chuckling.

Fabric fluttered in the air as Briar drew the cloak around herself. She asked, "Why are you laughing?"

"I never thought you'd be the type to care about modesty," Delilah replied. She heard Briar clip the neck broach that held the cloak together and, assuming she was now decent, opened her eyes. She started to say, "How did you lose all your—?"

A scream burst from her throat before she could stop it.

A clawed hand clapped over her mouth, stifling the sound, as Briar snapped, "I told you not to look!"

It took a few solid seconds of staring for Delilah to realize what she was looking at. The person standing in front of her was Briar, definitely, but it was as if she'd stolen some of the features from the monster in the woods. Spiraling bone horns poked out above her eyebrows, and her mouth and nose were contorted into something resembling a snout. Feathers covered her head, crawling down her neck and disappearing into the cloak. Her fingers ended in long, pointed claws, and patches of black scales coated her forearms and legs. A scaled, feather-topped tail was wrapped around her left leg, twitching slightly.

Briar's face flared bright red, the blush rushing up into the tips of her now-pointed ears.

Delilah reached up and removed Briar's hand from her mouth, her jaw going slack. She blinked. Her brain swam, unable to explain what she was seeing.

"What *happened* to you?" she finally asked. After a second, she gasped and jolted, a thought occurring to her. Frantically, she pulled the sleeves of her dress back, checking to see if her arms were still normal or if scales had appeared on her too.

Briar's forehead wrinkled. "What—what are you doing?"

"Those mushroom spores did this, didn't they?" Delilah asked, frantically running her hands over the back of her neck to check for feathers. When she didn't find anything, she grabbed Briar by the shoulders and said, "Listen, we'll figure this out, okay? I'm sure there's a way to get you back to normal." Her voice rose. "Why aren't you *panicking*? We have to do something!"

Briar stared into her eyes, brow furrowed. Whatever had happened to Briar had stretched her legs, so she was now nearly the same height as Delilah. She opened and closed her mouth, a soft hum sneaking out. "You . . . you don't know what's going on?"

"No—but I have a strong theory, and that's a good start!" Delilah said, holding out her palm and hitting her fist against it. "Maybe—if I'm immune to the mushroom spores—I can reverse-engineer a cure—"

"You're so dumb," Briar marveled.

Delilah froze, frowning. "Why would you say that? I'm trying to help you!"

"Think with your brain, idiot!" Briar gestured to herself. "*I'm* the monster, Delilah! That thing you were chasing? That was me! The thing that fought that bear? Also me!"

Delilah froze, eyes wide. Slowly, the gears in her brain began to click into place. She remembered all the times Briar had run off when she and Kieran were having attacks, when she'd made them promise to never come into her room without her permission, the ripped clothes on the deck—

"B-but"—Delilah shook her head—"there was so much blood!"

"Yes, well." Briar cringed. "It's not a . . . pretty transformation, exactly. If I resist, my body sort of . . . breaks itself into shape. So. Blood. Like I said, not pretty."

"But I saw—there was something in its mouth—"

"My mouth," Briar corrected flatly.

"But it looked like a *body* hanging out of the side!" Delilah snapped. "I—I thought you were getting dragged off into the woods to be eaten!"

"Oh. That was probably . . ." She opened her mouth to reveal jagged teeth as she stuck out what Delilah realized was a sizable blue tongue, like a skink's.

Delilah's eyes rounded like twin dinner plates. Finally, she was too stunned to speak.

Briar noticed and pulled her tongue back into her mouth, turning pink again. She cleared her throat and looked at the ground. "Right. Anyway. Do you want to talk inside, maybe?" She trailed off, frowning. "Assuming you're . . . willing to. I—I can go—"

"No!" Delilah shook her head. "No, don't go. I'm fine, I swear. Just"—she shook her head—"surprised."

Briar scoffed. "No kidding." She turned and headed back into the cave, the firelight making her twisted shadow longer along the rock wall.

Delilah glanced over her shoulder at the woods. It was pitch-dark, clearly still night, but the rain had finally stopped. She sighed shakily and went inside. Briar had taken a seat on the ground and seemed to be trying to find the best way to hide her body within the cloak. Delilah took a breath and sat down next to her.

Briar furrowed her brows, staring at her.

"What?" Delilah asked.

"You're"—Briar pursed her lips—"you're not . . . afraid of me?"

"Not right now, no." Delilah's eyebrows rose. "Should I be? I mean"—Delilah gestured to Briar's mouth—"you could do some damage with those. I have to say, they're impressive."

Briar fought back a smile, which, admittedly, did have a sinister effect, what with the massive fangs and sharpened incisors. "You won't be seeing that weird bear anytime soon."

"Oh! Oh, the bear!" Delilah sat up straighter, holding her hands out at her sides. "You took down a *bear*? Wait—I need you to explain from the beginning. What exactly happened?"

Briar turned and stared into the fire. Delilah wasn't sure if she was aware of it, but the edge of her tail flicked back and forth across the cave floor like a hunting cat's. She tried not to stare at it and failed miserably.

"While you were talking to Klaus, I noticed Kieran's eye starting to glow," Briar explained. "I immediately took off running. I mean"—she gestured to herself—"maybe not the best way to show up to a gathering of powerful witches, right? I was so concerned with getting there that I didn't have time to save any of my clothes." She frowned. "Which is deeply unfortunate. I loved those boots."

"So whenever you siphon magic, you change into that big . . . um . . . creature?"

"You can say 'monster.'"

"But it's you," Delilah argued. "And you're not a monster. Not in my mind anyway. You'd have to, I dunno, snatch up some townsfolk and eat them alive for me to think of you as a monster."

"Very low bar," Briar muttered. She rubbed the back of her neck and sighed. "Anyway, yes. Technically, I can turn into this whenever I want—which was useful when my father kept sending his men for me after I ran away from Wrenlin's. But I can't stop it when we're having an attack. Something about being exposed to that much magic at once . . . triggers it."

"Does Kieran know?" Delilah asked.

Briar shook her head. "No. If he didn't already think I was a monster for sucking his magic out, can you imagine what he'd think if he saw me like this?"

"It's because of the curse, not anything you did," Delilah pointed out. "He knows you're not hurting him on purpose. He'd understand."

"Understand this?" Briar gestured to herself, half-curled beneath the curtain of Laven's cloak. "How would he? Who looks at literal, *physical* proof that someone is a monster and thinks, *Oh, I bet she's probably a good person once you get past the fangs.*" She squeezed her eyes shut. "Wrenlin always said the reason I got this half of the curse is because I was born wicked. Kieran's the good twin, and I'm . . . not."

Her words felt like a fist around Delilah's heart. *If I ever see Wrenlin again, I'm going to finish what Briar started with the cleaver.*

"That's bullshit," Delilah snapped. "You're not inherently bad, and your curse isn't somehow proof that you are. Plus"—she pointed to Briar's face—"you *are* a good person, regardless."

Briar wrapped her arms tighter around herself, hiding the lower half of her face in her arms. Voice muffled, she said, "I appreciate the sentiment, but—I know how this goes. You're in shock right now, so you haven't had time to realize how bad—h-how *disgusting*—this is." She winced, catching a glimpse of the scales on her arms. "Even when I'm normal again, you'll be thinking of this. I'll always be the monster that pretends to be Briar, because now you know what I really am."

Her breath caught, and she looked away, shaking.

Delilah's throat began to tighten. The smell of the curse was even worse now than it usually was, mingling the scent of decay with the woodsmoke from the fire. She cursed her stomach for lurching at it.

Shaking off the burning in her nostrils, Delilah scooted closer to Briar and pulled her into a hug.

"What—?" Briar started to protest.

Delilah buried her face in the feathers on Briar's neck. "You don't get to assume you know how I feel, okay? I care about *you*, not this. And, okay, yeah, it might take me a little time to get used to the idea that you can turn into a magical creature and kill bears or whatever, but I will. Because—because I lo—"

She choked, catching herself.

"Delilah?" Briar asked.

"I—I," Delilah stuttered. *Was I about to say—? No, no way. It's just that I'm all worked up.* "Never mind. Just—know that this doesn't change anything for me. And if you don't want anyone else to know, I'll keep it a secret."

With a breath, Briar's shoulders sank. It was as if Delilah had finally given her permission to relax, and the moment she did, she realized how tightly she had wound herself. She melted into Delilah's grasp, wrapping her arms around her and pressing her cheek against Delilah's.

Warmth spread across Delilah's skin where they touched. Briar's heart, hammering in her chest, began to slow; she breathed in the smell of Delilah's hair, even with clumps of mud drying between her curls. The feathers on Briar's neck tickled Delilah's skin, and Delilah felt the protruding vertebrae of Briar's spine through the cloak.

"Thank you," Briar breathed.

Delilah pulled back enough to look Briar in the face. "Your secret's safe with me. Oh—and thanks for saving me from that bear. That was really brave."

Briar didn't move, her eyes closed. Into Delilah's neck, she whispered, "That thing didn't have a chance against me." She paused, eyebrows pressing together. "The . . . wing growths were weird, though. Never seen anything like them before. Or the mushrooms."

"Me neither." Delilah hummed to herself softly in thought. "Klaus mentioned something about a magic vein running underground around this area, and that whole place smelled like magic. I wonder . . ." She sat back, letting Briar go and crossing her arms. "I'll talk to him when we get back. If you don't mind my asking— how long does it usually take for you to turn back after an attack?"

"That's . . . sort of the problem." Briar held up her scaled arms. "This weird in-between thing—it usually lasts only half an hour or so. But it's been almost two hours since I brought you here and started changing back. This attack was strange, though—it was like something was stopping me from absorbing Kieran's magic, and now I've been stuck like this way longer than normal."

Delilah's mouth formed a soft *oh.* "I think Laven might have done that. He painted some runes on Kieran to try to protect him. Maybe that stopped you from siphoning the magic correctly."

Briar let out a low growl. "Damn it, Laven." She let herself fall back, spine pressed against the rock, holding her fingers up in front of her face. "When I brought you back here, I was sure I'd be normal again by the time you woke up. So much for that plan."

"We'll just wait it out here," Delilah suggested. "Plus, Kieran and Ash have that whole wagon to themselves. Maybe they'll finally move past arm touching."

A lopsided smile broke across Briar's face, which Delilah noticed had mostly reverted to normal, though her teeth were still jagged. "I'm so thrilled this horrible night could help my brother get some action."

Delilah laughed, covering her mouth with her hand. Briar raised an eyebrow at her, and she explained: "Sorry, it's just—your tongue is too big for your mouth and it's giving you a lisp."

Briar turned beet red.

"It's cute," Delilah said, giggling.

"It's *not*," Briar groaned, throwing her arms over her face. "I'm going to kill Laven."

While she had her face covered, Delilah snuck a better look at her, assessing the way she had mud caked all over her bare feet and her knobby knees poked out from under the cloak. Her tail flicked softly against the cave floor next to Delilah.

Without thinking, Delilah touched it.

It suddenly tensed, the feathers peeling back at the tip to reveal a hooked barb that pointed in Delilah's direction.

"Whoa!" she cried.

"It's venomous," Briar warned. "I wouldn't try that again if I were you."

"Venomoush," Delilah repeated, mimicking Briar's lisp.

It had seemed impossible to make Briar turn any redder, but that somehow did it, much to Delilah's cackling delight.

"I hate you," Briar moaned. "More than anything."

Delilah lay down on the cave floor next to her, grinning. "No you don't."

While Briar's arms were still mostly obscuring her face, Delilah caught the tiniest edge of a smile.

"Fine," Briar conceded. "I don't. But don't push it." She revealed her glowing eye. "I'm very dangerous."

"Dangeroush," Delilah repeated.

Briar groaned loudly while Delilah broke into hysterics, her laughter echoing through the cave in a delighted cacophony.

Delilah hadn't realized she'd fallen asleep on the cave floor until the sound of echoing voices roused her from a dream. Sleepiness kept her eyelids heavy, and she wrinkled her nose with frustration at the sudden intrusion, wrapping her arms tighter around the weight pressed against her.

She felt the soft flutter of breath against her throat. In her sleep-heavy brain, nothing about that struck her as unusual.

Until a familiar voice called out, "Delilah! Briar!"

Delilah's eyes creaked open, and it dawned on her that the warm shape she'd unconsciously wrapped herself around in sleep was, in fact, Briar, curled into a small ball, her head nestled gently beneath Delilah's chin.

Briar's eyes opened, and for a second, the two girls just stared at each other.

The moment realization hit them, they shot up, Briar knocking her head into Delilah's chin and Delilah cursing colorfully. Both now bright red, Briar hurriedly pulled the cloak around herself while Delilah swiftly disentangled their legs and scooted away.

"Ow," Briar groaned, rubbing the top of her head. To Delilah's relief, the feathers were gone, as was any other evidence of what she had seen last night.

"Delilah! Briar!"

The girls turned their attention to the sound. At the mouth of the cave stood Kieran, sweat slick across his forehead and his curly blond hair pulled off his face. Ash appeared after cresting the small hill that led up to the cave, and behind him was Laven, his walking stick in hand and his familiar on his shoulder.

"You're okay!" Kieran cried. He ran forward and fell to his knees in front of them, wrapping Delilah and Briar in a fierce hug with each arm. "I was so worried."

Delilah hugged him back while Briar hesitated for a moment before doing so as well.

"We got a little lost," Delilah explained as Kieran pulled back. "I'm so sorry we worried you."

"I told you I could find them," came another voice.

Delilah straightened to find none other than Klaus Hammond standing beside Laven with a wide grin on his face.

"We've been out looking since before the sun rose," Ash explained, joining them inside. "Kieran wasn't going to rest until he found you."

"So much for them getting alone time," Briar muttered so only Delilah could hear.

Delilah bit back a laugh and said, "Thanks for finding us, Kier."

"It was mostly—" Kieran started to say.

"I was the one who did the tracking," Klaus explained, hands on his hips. "What kind of father would I be if I let my daughter get lost in the woods without helping?"

"Kieran offered to pay him," Laven explained, unfazed.

"That tracks," Delilah muttered. She rose to her feet, dusting dried mud off her skirts. "Well—thank you for finding us. It'll certainly make the trip back easier."

"What led you out here in the dead of night anyway?" Ash asked. "It can't be safe in these woods in the dark."

"I—I got lost," Briar lied. "And Delilah found me. Decided to camp here for the night—for safety, of course."

"She fought off a bear," Delilah cut in before she could stop herself.

All the men raised their eyebrows.

"With—with my magic," Briar clarified, blushing.

"How impressive," Klaus said.

"Actually, it was a very weird situation," Delilah said. She met Klaus's eyes. "There's a massive mushroom forest not far from the Moondew camp. The whole place reeks of magic—and the bear Briar fought had a bunch of strange growths on it. Do you think that could be because of the magic vein you're looking for?"

Klaus's eyes widened. Suddenly, he too came to stand beside them in the cave. "Absolutely. Strange changes in the environment are the first sign that you're close."

"I suppose you're in luck, then," Delilah said. She snuck a glance at Briar before she added, "You know . . . I think we could show you where that is. In exchange for that letter allowing us to access the library archive."

Kieran's and Briar's eyebrows shot up, Kieran wide-eyed while a wicked grin appeared on Briar's face.

"Only seems fair," Laven agreed. Seeing as he was notably shorter than Klaus, he had to reach to pat the other man on the shoulder. "What do you say, Klaus?"

Klaus's eyes darted from Laven to Delilah and Kieran. After a moment, he nodded. "Fair enough. I'll write that up as soon as we return."

"In the meantime, we should get going," Laven said. "We'll need the extra daylight if you all want to get back to Gellingham before nightfall."

"Yes—let's get going," Kieran said. He smiled at Delilah and his sister again. "I'm so happy you found each other. It would have been terrible to be trapped out here alone."

"Yeah," said Delilah. She felt warmth in her chest as she snuck a glance at Briar, with her slim arms and freckles and dirt beneath her fingernails. "I'm glad we found each other too."

CHAPTER EIGHTEEN

Rule #25: Aside from the solution described in a curse itself, the best way around one is a loophole. It's just a matter of being brave enough to find one.

Back at the encampment, Delilah and Briar were able to change into new clothes—and get Briar some shoes—before they showed Klaus the route to the mushroom forest. Delilah warned him about the spores and to keep an eye out for strange animals. At the sight of the mushrooms at the bottom of the ravine, he was as wide-eyed as a child who'd been set loose in a sweets shop.

Just as he'd promised, back at his wagon, he wrote them a letter to access the archive.

While the others started packing their things for the hike to the trailhead, Klaus asked Delilah if he could speak to her alone.

"You know," he said, once they'd come to stand a bit farther from Laven's wagon, "you strike me as a very impressive young witch, Delilah. Your abilities seem to have been honed quite masterfully."

She set her jaw. *No thanks to you.* "I was lucky to have a good teacher who took me in. It's pretty taboo for a village witch to teach someone who isn't their blood. But I assume you know that."

Klaus bit his lip. "Well, one way or another. Your mother must be proud of you."

"I hope so." Delilah kicked softly at the grass. The thought of her mother softened her expression. *I wonder what she'd think if she knew I finally met him.* Charlotte had never seemed to hold any ill will against Klaus, even if Delilah fully thought he deserved it.

But after a long pause, Delilah added, "She talks about you sometimes."

Klaus's eyebrows shot up. "Ah. That's . . . a bit of a surprise. I would have thought she'd be settled down with someone else by now. Charlotte's a lovely woman."

"That's not really possible for us," Delilah muttered. When Klaus cocked his head, she explained: "Our curse makes it so the Bea women—all of us—are cursed to never find true love. The moment someone falls for us, they lose all their memories of us."

"Oh my. That's unfortunate." Klaus's eyes slid to Laven's wagon, where Briar was currently taking items from Kieran's pack and transferring them to hers. He asked, "Are you positive that's what it is?"

Delilah had to hold in a cutting laugh. "No Bea woman has ever been married or in any sort of long-term relationship for generations. Not that they haven't tried, but it's never panned out."

"How interesting," Klaus mused, stroking his chin. "Perhaps . . . if we should run into each other again, you can tell me a bit more about this curse. I suspect that it doesn't function quite as you think it does."

Delilah froze. For the second time, she felt a warm little tickle in her chest. A tiny fragment of something larger, something that terrified her to consider. Still small enough to snuff out.

But large enough to catch fire too.

"What do you mean?" Delilah asked, lowering her voice. She didn't dare do anything until she heard him actually say what she was thinking.

"Delilah!" Kieran called from across the field. At his side, Briar struggled to hoist her overburdened pack over her slim shoulders while Kieran smiled sunnily. It appeared he wasn't carrying anything. "We're ready to go!"

"One second!" Delilah pivoted back to Klaus. "Seriously— what do you mean? Do you think there's some kind of . . . ?"

"Exception," Klaus hummed. Delilah's entire body tensed at the word. Little did Klaus know how the spark in her chest suddenly flared, threatening to burst into flame. "Could be. Or not."

"What kind of exception?" Delilah's heart had started to pound. She could feel it in her hands and her throat, so loud the blood in her ears drowned out all other sounds. The logical half of her begged for her to shut her mouth and pretend she hadn't heard him, but the other half . . .

Delilah's eyes betrayed her, landing on Briar. Her slim build, the way she stood with her hands on her hips. The backpack she carried was comically large compared to her small frame, but it didn't seem to bug her. She was too busy rolling her eyes at her brother to notice, a small smile on her face.

Her smile. Slightly crooked teeth, a little bit lopsided. Lips pale pink like the inside of a seashell. She didn't used to smile like that, but recently, something had changed.

When Delilah looked back at Klaus, he had a hand over his heart and was fighting back a smirk.

"Who knows?" Klaus said, slipping the hand in his pocket. He glanced between the girls, nodding. "Perhaps it's something to experiment with."

Delilah's face reddened. "E-experiment? What do you mean?"

Klaus chuckled. "Oh—nothing. Just thinking out loud. Now you should get going—don't want to keep your friends waiting. Best of luck at the archive."

Delilah opened her mouth to coax him into telling her more, but that was the moment when Kieran shouted her name again, and Briar and Ash both chimed in to tell her to join them. She waved them off and called, "Coming!"

She turned back to her father. "Look, um . . . thanks. For your help. It was good to meet you, I guess."

"You as well, Delilah." He reached out and patted her shoulder in what might have been endearing if it weren't so forced. "Safe travels."

She wished the same for him, and set off toward her friends, mind abuzz with what he'd said.

Perhaps it's something to experiment with.

The trip back to Gellingham was uneventful. Everyone was tired from the night before, but thankfully, Laven volunteered to help them find the main trail so they didn't have to stumble through the woods any more than they already had. When they arrived at the trailhead, Laven said goodbye, taking special care to tell Briar he was happy she'd found such good travel companions.

Ash bid Delilah and the twins farewell once they made it down the trail. After a moment's pause, he leaned in and gave Kieran a hug.

"I'll see you tomorrow," he said hurriedly to Kieran. Delilah could have sworn his face seemed a bit sweaty and hot. "Klaus's letter technically only gets you and your cursebreaker into the archive, so I'll wait outside for you. We can discuss whatever you find then."

"R-right," Kieran stammered. "Thanks for coming, Ash."

"Anytime." He nodded to Delilah and Briar. "See you tomorrow."

As soon as Ash had departed, Briar elbowed Kieran in the ribs, snickering.

"Ouch!" he yelped. "What?"

"Please tell me you've admitted you're into each other," Briar said.

Kieran's voice caught. "I—no, of course not."

Briar and Delilah exchanged a look, sighing in defeat.

On the path back to the airfield, tall grasses tickled their ankles, the tiny blinking lights of fireflies glowing among the blades. The chirping of crickets floated in the warm air. The sunset had just started to cast its blush across the sky when the aeroship came into view.

"It would be a bad idea," Kieran admitted after a few minutes, during which Delilah had forgotten what they'd been talking about. "We need him to help us right now, and if he knew I was a Pelumbra . . . I don't think he'd be okay with it."

Briar shrugged. "I dunno. Sometimes people surprise you."

Delilah smiled as they walked on.

That night, back on the ship, after everyone had gone to bed, Delilah snuck down to the kitchen. It had been so long since she'd baked anything that she'd started to feel strangely antsy about it.

Truthfully, ever since she'd heard the word, she'd been on edge: *exception.*

She retrieved flour, sugar, and lemons from the pantry, leaving them in a pile with eggs and butter from the icebox. She put on a record featuring a velvet-voiced man warbling love songs, turning it down low enough that it wouldn't keep Briar awake if she could indeed hear it through the vents.

She measured out the flour, combining it with butter and sugar in a sky-blue mixing bowl. She summoned magic from the well in her chest as she combined them, so the end of her mixing spoon glowed faintly with energy. She pictured a sword that could cut through the layers of choking vines around her thoughts— something that might help her achieve a bit more clarity when it came to her situation.

She'd told Briar: *I can't be close to anyone in that way.*

Her heart squeezed, and the magic in her hands sputtered for a moment, scorching the edge of her dough. She cursed, dropping the spoon and letting the magic recede up her arms, shaking her head.

She shouldn't even be entertaining this thought. What was the point when all she could do was get hurt?

Theo's face returned to her mind's eye. The day everything had fallen apart had started off perfectly: it was a beautiful day in Kitfield, the flowers still blooming in late summer and the trees shading the cobblestone walkways around town. Delilah and Theo had spent the night before at the beach, discussing all the things they wanted to do together when his Calling was over: travel the world, become famous cursebreakers, live in the big city—everything Delilah had spent her childhood daydreaming about.

She'd shown up at the cottage he was renting, delighted to start their day. The sun was shining, the sky was blue, and she got to meet up with the boy she was falling in love with.

But when he opened the door at her knock, his expression had been blank. At the sight of her, Delilah noticed the tiniest flash of gray magic across his eyes. Not the color of *his* magic. His had always been a warm shade of burgundy. This was something else.

"Hi," he'd said, forehead wrinkled. "Can I . . . help you with something?"

Delilah's heart had clenched as the word *no, no, no* echoed in her mind like a broken record. Bile rose in her throat. The world beneath her feet cracked like ice atop a frozen pond.

"Theo?" she'd breathed.

Please. Please remember me.

"Theodore," he'd corrected. "Not many people call me Theo these days."

The ice beneath Delilah's feet had shattered.

Pulling herself from the memory, she winced, tears threatening. She hadn't cried over Theo in a long time. For the last six months or so, his memory had stopped feeling quite so sharp when it resurfaced. While at the beginning, it had cut like a shard of glass each time she held it in her hands, time had ground down the jagged edges.

It still hurt, though. Probably always would.

So what would make her relationship with Briar any different? Sure, Briar had admitted she was attracted to Delilah back when they'd shared that drunken kiss, but that didn't mean it was anything more than that. And yes, since then things had been easy between them. Delilah woke every morning excited to see her, and every time she earned one of Briar's elusive smiles, her heart swelled, but—

It didn't matter how Delilah felt about it. It hadn't with Theo, and it wouldn't with Briar. Her curse would still cut her out of Briar's memories if she did return those feelings.

Unless . . .

Unless.

Delilah sliced a knife through one of the lemons. As she began to juice it, a droplet slid over her skin, stinging a scrape on her palm from her fall last night.

She thought of how she'd woken up to find Briar tucked into the outline of her body, and how she'd so desperately wanted to hold her. She'd spent the night trapped in nightmares of waking to find Briar gone, too afraid to stay with her secret out in the open. It had scared Delilah so much that even her sleeping form found itself grasping for her.

Maybe it was too late to put out this spark.

Delilah finished mixing her filling, pouring it over the short-bread crust as soon as it came out of the oven. With her hands empty, she wrapped her arms around herself, feeling hollow.

You'll only make it worse if you hope, she reminded herself.

She leaned back against the counter, tilting her head up to look at the grate over the vent that led to Briar's room. She imagined her now, slumbering in that massive bed, and how it would feel to fall asleep to the sound of her breathing.

Maybe, Delilah thought, sending out a silent prayer, *she's worth it.*

CHAPTER NINETEEN

Rule #10: If you love something, let it go.

The next day, Delilah, Ash, and the twins set out for the archive.

Delilah was a mess. She'd barely slept, dark circles bold beneath her gray eyes. Most of the night, she'd tossed and turned in bed, feeling as if she was being torn in half by her thoughts. The magic lemon bars she'd made hadn't helped clear her mind at all; in fact, she was pretty sure they'd made her more anxious, probably due to how she was feeling when she made them.

What she knew was this: if she gave in to her feelings—which at this point were nearly impossible to hide—and Briar wasn't an exception, her heart would break all over again.

But if she did and she was . . .

From her spot on the trolley bench beside Delilah, Briar glanced in her direction, as if hearing her thoughts. "You okay?"

Delilah immediately straightened and cleared her throat.

"What, me? Of course. I'm fine. Just, uh . . . a little nervous about the archive is all."

Briar knocked her knee against Delilah's. "We'll be all right. If nothing else, we're good at thinking on our feet, right?"

We. Our.

"Fuck," Delilah breathed, the word barely audible.

"What was that?" Briar asked.

Did I say that out loud? Damn. "Nothing."

On the bench across from them, Delilah caught Kieran and Ash exchanging a look, but they didn't say anything.

Ten minutes later, they arrived at their stop and walked a few blocks to the archive building. The outside was significantly less exciting than the towering, ivy-covered library: the archive was dome shaped and squat. It didn't appear to have any windows, which wasn't a surprise—Delilah didn't know much about curse preservation, but Theo had talked about how sunlight could bleach pages, so it made sense to keep them under artificial lights.

"Well," Ash said, glancing at them. He hooked a thumb toward one of the two old pine trees that stood like sentinels outside the front door. "I'll wait out here for you in the shade. Best of luck."

He reached out for Kieran, then hesitated. He settled on giving him a pat on the shoulder. Kieran blushed.

Under her breath, Briar muttered, "Unbelievable."

Delilah scoffed and nudged her toward the door.

There was no guard there, which was a relief after the fiasco at the library. When Delilah and the twins stepped inside, they found a dank, dark space. Before them stood a front desk that was currently empty, and rows and rows of shelves behind that. The smell of old paper and leather lingered in the air, and the only lights were floating pale blue orbs that bobbed like boats on water. Compared to the bustle of the library, the archive was deathly quiet.

The three stood in silence for a moment before Briar loudly questioned, "So do we just walk in or . . . ?"

"Sorry!" came a masculine voice. A figure popped up from behind the desk. He wore the same kind of traditional witch's robe as Ash had when they met; his dark hair was shaved on the sides and woven into locs on top. His skin and eyes were both warm shades of deep brown.

At the sight of him, Delilah's heart stopped.

Not noticing, he continued: "My apologies—it's been a slow morning, so I thought I had time to catalog a few things. How can I help?"

Briar's eyebrows rose at the sight of color draining from Delilah's face. Delilah, however, barely registered the look. It was as if the world around her had gone blurry, leaving only the boy behind the desk. Her broken-glass memories of him seemed to sharpen all over again, stabbing into Delilah all at once. The days spent together in the woods, the nights cuddled by a fire on the beach, the whispered promises of a future together in Gellingham—it was nearly enough to make her knees buckle.

Before she could stop herself, she breathed, "Theo?"

Briar's head snapped to Delilah, eyes widened in horror. *"Theo?"*

Kieran whispered to his sister, barely loudly enough for Delilah to hear, "Do we know him? I think I missed something."

Theo, meanwhile, just blinked. "Oh, um, sorry—have we met? There's something familiar about your face, but I can't place it."

Delilah's throat tightened. She could feel her hands starting to shake. She'd never been the type to be overwhelmed by her emotions, but now all she could do was stand there. Tears formed in her eyes.

I can't do this. Not again.

"You remember us, don't you?" came Briar's voice at Delilah's side. Delilah suddenly felt Briar's hand on her back, steadying her. Her touch was warm, even through the fabric of Delilah's shirt. The feeling was enough to yank Delilah out of her spiral, if only a little.

Her breathing evened.

With a brief look sideways at Delilah, Briar added, "We met back in Kitfield. At the pub? I'm Briar—I think my friend Delilah and I beat you at darts a couple times. You'd had a bit to drink, though. Don't blame you if you forgot."

"Oh." Theo chuckled. He tapped his palm to his forehead. "Kitfield! Of course. That makes sense. You'll have to forgive me—I was a bit of a mess on my Calling. Sometimes I feel like I barely remember any of it. Good to see you both again, I suppose. What brings you in?"

Briar said, "We were hoping you could show us the Pelumbra vault."

Delilah's throat had gone completely dry, her words with it. She pulled the letter out of her pocket and laid it flat on the desk, doing her best not to shake.

"Klaus Hammond gave us permission to access the archive," Kieran explained, gesturing to the letter. Vaguely, she realized she was going to owe the twins one hell of a favor for covering for her.

At the mention of Klaus's name, Delilah thought that if Theo had been drinking anything, he would have spat it out. She recalled that she had once told him that Klaus was her father, and Theo had been just as shocked as he was now. Before knowing about Klaus's parental abandonment, Theo had been a big fan of his. Delilah supposed that, in forgetting about her, he'd likely forgotten that too.

Theo reached for the letter. Grabbing a magnifying glass at his side, he held it over the Hammond family seal, and his dark eyes widened. He mouthed Klaus's name, amazement coloring his tone.

"I'm impressed that you found him. I've worked here for a year, and I've never gotten to meet him," Theo said. As he read the letter, he mouthed the word *wow.* "What I wouldn't give to pick his brain on cursebreaking. A letter like this is quite an honor— must be a very important Calling."

"Does that mean you can show us the Pelumbra vault?" Kieran asked.

Theo replied, "With *the* Klaus Hammond's blessing? Of course—I'll take you back to it. Follow me."

The three followed Theo into the labyrinthine stacks. Old books and scrolls sat behind panes of glass set into the shelves. Though the glass was foggy with age, Delilah made out leather-bound grimoires flanked by ancient vellum scrolls and even small pamphlets stitched with twine to hold the pages together. Some of them glowed faintly, while others gave off the scent of sulfur and charcoal. The lights mostly didn't touch them, leaving them half obscured by shadow.

Of course Theo works in a place like this, Delilah thought. *He always said he would.*

Trailing a bit behind Kieran and Theo, Briar nudged Delilah.

"If it's too much," Briar said, "Kieran and I can handle this. You don't have to stay."

Delilah immediately shook her head. "No. No, I—I'm okay. I swear."

I am definitely not okay.

Briar raised a quizzical eyebrow at that but didn't press. Instead, she reached out, gave Delilah's hand a squeeze, and kept walking.

At her touch, Delilah's stomach fluttered.

It took them a few minutes of weaving through the shelves to reach the back of the archive, where a soaring wall of vaults stood. All the vaults had different doors, crafted from varied metals and in different shapes and sizes. Some were rusted, their hinges sealed shut from years of disuse. Others had clearly been installed more recently, metal locks polished enough that Delilah could see the blur of her reflection in them even in the dim light.

Theo led them to a particularly small vault just below eye level. It was small enough that Delilah wasn't sure she'd be able to put two hands into it at the same time. It was unremarkable, the little door dusty enough that it was hard to read the letters across the front that spelled out PELUMBRA.

For the first time since they'd entered the archive, Delilah's mind finally snapped away from Theo. Instead, her heartbeat sped up as she said, "It's . . . tiny."

Much too tiny for something as significant as the Pelumbra family curse.

Shit, shit, shit.

A muscle in Briar's jaw twitched. "This is it? Are you sure

there isn't—I dunno—a bigger one? The Pelumbras aren't exactly known for their subtlety."

"There's no lock either," Kieran observed. His voice sounded strained. "Is this maybe, um, a different Pelumbra family? I'm talking about the ones in, oh, every part of the government, most large businesses in Gellingham—"

Theo cut him off. "This is the only Pelumbra vault we have. But you're right about it missing a physical lock. There's a spell engraved in the metal. I was under the impression that no one can turn the handle unless they're directly descended from the witch who made the door. But considering that Klaus Hammond gave you permission to access it, I assume you have another way of opening it."

Kieran gulped.

At that moment, a bell chimed from the far side of the room where they'd come in. They all paused for a moment before it rang again twice in staccato bursts.

Theo called, "I'm coming! Just a second." He told Kieran, "I'll be right back—but please don't take anything out of the vault without my supervision. Nothing inside is supposed to be accessed without an archivist present."

Kieran started to promise he'd wait, but Theo was already taking off for the front desk.

As he disappeared into the stacks, Briar leaned in close to her brother and whispered, "What are you waiting for? Open it."

"What? Why me?" Kieran snapped back. Sweat had begun to bead on his brow, despite the dank cold of the archive. "You're a Pelumbra too!"

"It's not like it's gonna bite you," Briar pointed out. She paused, rubbing her chin. "Or—it *probably* won't. I guess you never know in a place like this."

"Very reassuring, Briar—thank you." Kieran exhaled through his nose, squeezing his eyes shut. "I really hope this is worth it."

He reached out, long fingers hesitating in the air in front of the handle. He winced before muttering another curse and grabbing hold of it. A beat of tense silence passed between the three as he tightened his grip. A faint, silver light glowed from between Kieran's fingers as he twisted the handle.

The vault popped open with a small exhalation of dust.

"It worked," Kieran breathed. His eyes lit up, and he glanced back at Delilah and Briar. "It worked! And it didn't even, I dunno, explode o-or—"

Just then, a voice from the front of the room rang out, "I *said* those children don't have permission to access the vault, regardless of what they told you. Now bring them to me before I remove them myself."

A chill climbed Delilah's spine. She knew that voice—she'd heard it back in Dothering and Gabriel's Edge, surrounded by the cloud of citrusy, sharp magic. The one that had snarled Briar's name with disdain as he hunted her.

Regen Pelumbra.

"Shit," Briar cursed while her brother managed to turn an even paler shade than normal. "We have to get out of here."

"How?" Delilah asked, craning her neck to peek through the stacks. The archive was dark enough that it was hard to make out the figure standing in front of the desk. Still, even from a distance, it was clear from the way he was shifting on his feet that he was growing impatient.

And he just happened to be directly in the pathway to the front door.

Delilah swore under her breath. "There's no way around him."

"He's got us cornered!" Kieran squeaked.

Briar's expression hardened. For a second, Delilah thought she saw the flare of pale blue light in her visible eye.

"Kieran, grab whatever's in the vault," Briar said, her tone leaving no room for argument. While he nodded and got closer to reach inside, Briar closed the space between herself and Delilah and stood on her toes to whisper in her ear: "Skirt the edge of the archive and make sure Kieran is following you." Something gently nudged Delilah's calf, and when she looked down, she nearly jumped at the sight of Briar's barb-tipped tail. "I have an idea."

"A-are you going to . . ." Delilah bent her fingers and used her hands to imitate a set of fanged jaws biting down.

Briar's forehead wrinkled. "What?"

Delilah lowered her voice even more, whispering behind her hand. "Are you gonna . . . eat him?"

"The fuck? No." She pointed to the barb, the tuft of feathers surrounding it obscuring it from view. "I told you it's venomous, right? I'm going to stab and paralyze him so he can't follow us."

"Oh. Wow." Delilah blinked. "You're sort of amazing, you know that?"

Briar turned bright red. "What? Shut up. Get out of here."

Heart beating a little faster than she would have liked, Delilah reached out for Kieran's free wrist as he finally managed to get his fingers around whatever was in the vault and wrench it out.

"Come on," she told him while Briar turned to make a beeline for Regen. "Follow me."

"Where—?" Kieran started to question, eyes briefly darting sideways to follow his sister.

Delilah tugged his wrist. "Don't worry about her. Let's go."

Kieran didn't have time to protest as Delilah all but yanked his arm out of the socket, pulling him toward the far edge of the room. He made a few sputtering sounds as he stumbled after her but quickly shut up when she shot him a sharp look and made a faint *shush* sound.

The two crept around the shelves as Regen's voice rose louder and louder. Theo was shushing him, asking him to keep his voice down or he'd call security. For a second, a part of Delilah wanted to step in and defend the boy, an old protective urge pulling at her.

Keep the twins safe, she reminded herself. *They're what matter, not my old heartbreak.*

"Do you have any idea how much funding the Pelumbras donate to this place every year?" Regen demanded. He didn't notice the shadow creeping up from his side. "Probably your full salary twenty times over—"

He cut off with a sharp gasp.

Theo yelped.

"Run!" Delilah shouted to Kieran.

He did as he was told, bolting toward the door on Delilah's heels. She glanced over her shoulder in time to catch a glimpse of Regen swaying before dropping to the floor like a deadweight. His face was bent in a snarl, eyes rage-bright and teeth locked. The scent of simmering citrus magic tainted the air.

Theo stared in horror as Briar sidestepped around him, her tail vanishing into thin air. She caught Delilah's eyes, nodding, and ran.

"You—wait!" Theo shouted. He threw a finger out at Kieran, who was clutching what he'd taken from the vault—a small jeweled box—to his chest. "Drop that!" As he shouted, some of the glass on the shelves rattled and cracked.

Kieran squeaked.

Without looking back, Delilah grabbed his slim wrist and yanked him toward the door. Theo shouted again, and Delilah barely caught a flash of light out of the corner of her eye. Suddenly, an alarm began to blare.

When the light cleared, Briar was on Delilah's heels. "Theo's taken care of—let's go. I hear guards coming."

"Did you—?" Delilah started to ask in horror.

"Knocked out," Briar clarified. "I'm not that bad—after all, it's not like he broke your heart on purpose." She considered the statement. "Though, if he had, I *definitely* would have made it hurt."

Delilah's skin warmed.

The three bounded up to the door, Delilah all but dragging Kieran behind her. Blood rushing in her ears, Delilah thrust her shoulder into it. It flew open.

Only to reveal an iridescent blue magic barrier between them and the outside.

"Shit!" Briar said. She threw herself at it and bounced back as if it were made of rubber. She punched it for good measure but to no avail. She bared her teeth, trying again. "Come on, come on!"

From outside, Ash's voice called, "Delilah? Kieran?"

"Ash!" Delilah called. "Help!"

To his credit, Ash didn't miss a beat. He sprinted from his post under the pine tree and immediately scanned the door, looking for some kind of flaw in the barrier. Then he snapped his fingers, his face lighting up.

"Librarians on duty always carry pouches of hawthorn sawdust just in case!" he cried. "The archivist should have some on their belt too. Quickly—you can throw a handful at the barrier to cancel out the magic!"

"Got it!" Delilah told Briar, "Cover me."

The sound of footsteps storming in from the wings grew louder as Delilah shot across the room. She found Theo lying on the ground, his eyes closed. If she didn't know better, the soft rise and fall of his chest would have made her think he was asleep.

She knelt down beside him, brushing a loc from his forehead. He looked older than the last time she'd seen him—less like a boy and more like a man. A hint of stubble dusted his jaw, and his features had sharpened a bit. In a strange way, Delilah found it comforting. This wasn't the Theo who had broken her heart. He was different now.

"I'm sorry," she whispered. She reached for the belt around his robe, hunting for a pouch. Much to her relief, she found one hanging off his left hip. As she began untying it, she added, "I really can't be around you without making your life harder, can I?"

Softly, he stirred. Just as Delilah yanked the hawthorn dust pouch from his belt, his eyes opened.

Then, ever so gently, a look of recognition passed over his face.

"Bea?" he breathed. "Is that you?"

She froze.

No way.

"I've missed you." He held up a shaking hand as if he was going to stroke her cheek. Instantly, Delilah's eyes welled with tears. She knew that voice, that tone, that nickname. The one she'd longed to hear again—the one that she'd told herself she'd hear again one day when she broke her curse.

But now it felt oddly . . . hollow. In her fantasies, he'd say her name and she'd be overwhelmed by the need to kiss him and hold him close as she used to. Everything would be as it had been, her broken heart finally mended.

It occurred to her, quite suddenly, that she had absolutely no desire to be in his arms.

Just then, as it had months before, a grayish light suddenly flickered in his eyes. The look of recognition vanished. A familiar ache returned to Delilah's chest—but not the kind that hurt so much as hung heavy between her ribs.

Theo blinked, disoriented. "What's . . . what's going on?"

"Nothing you need to worry about," Delilah told him. She gently wiped the tears that had escaped away. "And, ah . . . I missed you too, Theo."

She shot him one final watery smile before jumping to her feet and running to the door.

"Stop right there!" one of the guards spilling into the room called.

But Delilah was already reaching into the pouch and launching hawthorn dust at the barrier. On contact, the barrier melted in a shimmer of light.

The twins ran through, then Delilah. She slammed the door behind her.

Ash said, "Okay, listen—I'll block this door as long as I can to give you a head start. Take the alleyway down to Argent Street and go up six blocks. Then get on the trolley heading north. It's a little out of the way, but no one will expect you to take that line out of here, since it's away from the central stops. And once you're out of the city proper, leave and don't come back. If a Pelumbra saw you, there'll be city guards looking for you everywhere. They're all in the Pelumbras' pockets, and they won't stop until they find you."

Kieran's forehead wrinkled. "But—what about you? I—I don't want to just leave you—"

Ash cut him off by taking his hand and gently squeezing it. "I'll be fine. Once you're out of the city, call me on the line I gave you. Maybe . . . maybe I'll come find you."

Kieran's eyes started to shine.

"Kieran, come on," Delilah said, nodding down the block. "We gotta go."

Kieran hesitated for a moment before he suddenly leaned forward and pressed a kiss to Ash's lips. Ash froze for a moment before kissing back, his fingers laced tightly with Kieran's. Kieran pulled away, touching his forehead to Ash's as he let a hand gently trail down the back of his neck.

"Thank you," Kieran told Ash as he stepped away. "For everything."

Releasing Ash's hand, Kieran nodded to the girls, and the three of them sprinted for the street.

CHAPTER TWENTY

Rule #16: If you're looking for blight in a family tree,
start at its roots.

"I mean, all things considered," Briar offered, "that could have gone a lot worse."

Kieran, meanwhile, sat with his head nestled in his folded arms on the dining table back on the aeroship. The engine beneath them was whirling as the ship rose into the clouds—Ariel had been quick to get them off the ground the moment they'd made it back to the ship after escaping the archive and hopping off the trolley. They were flying the ship as high as they could without risking damage to the balloons or wings, hoping that would keep them out of range of any vessels that might be tailing them.

And while Ariel was fighting to keep them out of danger, Kieran was, predictably, moping. "What if I never see him again?" He sighed, voice muffled by his arms.

"Maybe it's for the best," Briar said with a shrug.

Briar and Delilah sat across from him, Briar holding the box he'd nabbed from the vault. It was small, carved out of elegant dark wood and decorated with filigree. There was a latch on it that appeared to be rusted shut, though Briar currently had a steak knife she was attempting to pry it open with.

Tongue between her teeth while she focused, she added, "Better this than dealing with his inevitable rejection upon figuring out you're a Pelumbra."

Kieran lifted his head just enough to glare at her. "You don't know that."

"Be realistic, Kier."

"He likes me! And I like him! Maybe it's that simple." Kieran finally straightened, crossing his arms as he set his jaw and shot Briar a look. "Besides, I think you're projecting."

Briar's face pinkened. *"Projecting—?"*

Before she could finish, though, she suddenly managed to slide the steak knife beneath the box's latch, popping it open with a click. The trio's eyes all snapped to the box, its lid having opened a crack, though not enough to show what was inside. Carefully, Briar set down the knife.

"Finally." She flipped open the lid and reached inside. "Now we can read this stupid curse and figure out how to . . ."

She trailed off as she lifted a pinkie-size paper scroll from inside, tied with a silver bow. Tugging one end of the bow, she let the ribbon drop back into the box before she unrolled the scroll. As she did, her eyebrows bent together, mouth in a tight frown. She turned it over once, mouthing the word *where* . . . ? to herself.

"You have *got* to be kidding me," she snapped. She swore

loudly, her eyes flashing blue while the lights above them flickered. She threw the scroll down on the table, pressing her palms hard against her eyes. "There's no way. After all that, after *everything*—"

"What is it?" Kieran asked.

Delilah picked up the scroll gingerly, holding it up to the light. It was blank.

She flipped it over, confirming her suspicion. "There's . . . nothing here. It's just a blank piece of paper."

"No!" Briar shouted. She slammed her fist against the table, rattling the vase of flowers Santiago had painstakingly glued down in case of turbulence. *"Damn it!"*

"B-but—it can't be blank." Kieran took the paper from Delilah's hand, turning it over and over on the table. His fingers started to shake. "It . . . it can't."

Delilah's mind swam. There had to be some kind of explanation, *something* they had to be missing. Because if there wasn't, that would mean . . .

That they were back to square one. With no leads left for the twins.

And it was only a matter of time until she lost them both.

"No." Delilah stood up, grabbing the box. She turned it upside down, shaking it, as the spark in her chest began to blaze. "The damn box was rusted shut, there's no way someone put a blank scroll in a magic vault for no reason. We have to be missing some—"

The sounds of footsteps cut her off, and Delilah looked up to find Adelaide standing in the doorway, a duster hanging limp at her side.

"Adelaide, hey! You—you've worked for the Pelumbras for a long time," Delilah started. She held the box and scroll out toward her. "Have you seen this before? Maybe know something about the world's most infuriating blank scroll?"

Adelaide, meanwhile, stood frozen, her dark brown eyes rounded like twin moons. Her hands began to shake. The duster dropped from her hand and clattered to the floor.

"Adelaide?" Kieran asked. "Are you . . . ?"

In a burst of movement that Delilah wasn't expecting, Adelaide stole the box from her hand. Her lips parted, but no sound came out, despite the strain in her throat.

Tears pricked in her eyes. Her slim thumb traced the filigree on the edge of the box.

Kieran started to say her name again when suddenly her eyes flared with fiery magic. The scent of it came off her in waves, the ends of her white-blond hair lifting slightly and trembling in the air.

"What—?" Briar started to ask.

That was the moment the box caught fire.

Delilah and the twins all yelped as white-hot flames tinged with blue flared brightly against Adelaide's palms. She didn't move, eyebrows bent inward and fingers tightening around the box as it crumbled to ash in her hands. Almost as fast as they'd appeared, the flames shrank, the box nothing but dying charcoal smeared across Adelaide's palms.

And in the center of them sat a tiny golden spyglass dusted with ash.

As the light faded from her eyes, Adelaide thrust the spyglass toward Delilah.

Delilah, meanwhile, was too dumbfounded to speak. After a moment's hesitation, she took the spyglass, holding it tenderly, like a baby bird whose bones might snap beneath her fingers. The metal was cold. The only evidence that it had ever been consumed by flame was the ash that marred the lens.

Adelaide's eyes went to the table where the scroll sat, her expression stern.

"What," Briar said, still wide-eyed and staring at Adelaide, "the *hell* was that?"

"I've never seen . . ." Kieran blinked. "Adelaide, how . . . ?"

"Hold on," Delilah said. She gently rubbed the glass clean on her skirt before snagging the scroll off the table. "I have an idea."

She held the spyglass up to her eye, pointing it down toward the scroll. Much to her surprise, the glass blocked out all the light, leaving nothing but a black void staring back at her through the lens. Frowning, she shifted it to the paper and hovered over it.

After a moment, the spyglass lens cleared to reveal curling, golden text scrawled across the scroll.

Delilah nearly dropped it. "It's here! It's—!" She cut off, squinting. "It's . . . huh."

"What?" Briar demanded, jumping to her feet. "Is it our curse?"

Delilah read the text over twice more, her heart beginning to race. No, this wasn't Briar and Kieran's curse. This was something else entirely.

"It's not yours," Delilah breathed, slowly letting the spyglass fall. "It's Adelaide's."

❧

While Delilah read the text aloud, Kieran copied down Adelaide's curse: " 'A secret known, not yours to tell, lock loose lips, bid voice farewell. You shall not speak through word or sign until the day Pelumbra blood forgives you for your crime.' "

"Crime?" Briar repeated. "What crime?"

Kieran shrugged. "I don't know. No one back home ever mentioned Adelaide's having done anything wrong."

Adelaide, meanwhile, had taken a seat at the table, her hands folded in front of her as she stared hard at them. If Delilah had to guess from the shine of her eyes, she was trying to stop herself from crying.

"Maybe that was on purpose," Delilah said. Taking up the paper on which Kieran had copied the curse, she read it over again, nodding. "This rhyme feels a bit juvenile, so I have to assume it was written pretty quickly. Someone wanted to keep Adelaide quiet on short notice."

Delilah rubbed her chin and added, "But this last line—*until the day Pelumbra blood forgives you for your crime*—that seems like a really simple solution."

"Wait—are you saying all I have to do is forgive Adelaide and that'll break it?" Kieran asked.

Delilah shrugged. "I mean, you're a Pelumbra, right? So . . . I don't see why not."

Adelaide's eyes widened and darted to Kieran, pleading.

"You really think it's that easy?" he asked. When Delilah shrugged, he turned to Adelaide and said, "Well, if that's all it takes . . . Adelaide, I—I forgive you."

Delilah hadn't been expecting much. Despite the fact that the answer was written down right in front of her, she still found herself gasping as a faint silver glow began to shine from Adelaide's skin. The lingering scent of her curse, buried under Kieran and Briar's, suddenly began to dissipate in favor of the warm, smoky scent of her magic.

Adelaide inhaled sharply, a hand flying to her throat. She clutched it for a moment, gasping for air.

"Adelaide?" Kieran asked worriedly, standing from the table so his chair let out a shriek against the hardwood. "Are you okay—?"

He cut off as her eyes rose to meet his, a grin warming her typically placid expression. She coughed out a sob, then ran to his side, throwing her arms around him. Kieran's eyebrows shot up as she wept into his shoulder.

Likely because, for the first time, there was a whisper of a voice behind her sobs.

"You did it," Adelaide said. Her voice was soft, rich and low and faintly accented in the lilting way that many people raised in northern Celdwyn spoke. She pulled back, keeping one hand on his shoulder as she gazed at the girls, tears spilling down her cheeks.

"You set me free."

❧

It took a while for Adelaide to collect herself, during which time Ariel and Santiago joined them. Ariel said they were slowly headed east, where the mountains rose into the clouds, offering them a bit more cover in case Regen tried to chase them from Gellingham. Santiago had made a stew for dinner, which Adelaide picked at while she sat huddled beneath a blanket, her eyes red from crying and her face puffy. She gently thanked Santiago, which nearly set her off again.

"I'm sorry," she said as she swallowed a mouthful of stew. "It's . . . it's been so long. I thought I was doomed to never breathe a word for the rest of my life. It's . . . overwhelming just to be able to say thank you."

"If you don't mind my asking," Kieran said, setting his spoon down for a moment, "what exactly happened that led to your curse? No one back home ever mentioned that it had to do with the Pelumbras."

Adelaide's expression darkened. She rubbed her thumb in circles atop her other hand, her long eyelashes fluttering as she blinked away a fresh bout of tears. After a long pause, she exhaled and said, "It's a long story." Meeting Kieran's eyes, she added, "Are you . . . willing to hear me out?"

He nodded.

Adelaide sighed. "It was a long time ago. I was nineteen, living at the Pelumbra estate. I don't think anyone ever told you this, but . . . I'm something like your great-aunt. Just a couple generations removed."

For a moment, everyone went quiet. Kieran's lips parted, his eyes huge, while his sister went ghostly white. Delilah's gaze shifted between the three of them, and after a second, Adelaide's words made sense. Based on what Delilah had seen of the other Pelumbras, many of them—Kieran included—were light-skinned and had flaxen hair. Adelaide was no exception. She and Kieran even shared a few features Delilah had never noticed before— namely, the same long, straight nose and pointed chin. Now that she thought about it, they could pass as cousins.

"You're a *Pelumbra*?" Briar said, incredulous. She ran a hand across her ginger buzz cut. "But—from what Kieran's told me, they were treating you like a servant. Like *dirt*. I thought it was just . . ."

She didn't have to say the last part.

I thought it was just me.

She trailed off. Gently, Adelaide reached out, putting her hand over Briar's.

"You're far from the only member of our family they've thrown aside in favor of their own selfish interests," she said gently, meeting Briar's eyes. She reached out her other hand and took Kieran's, squeezing it as she said, "I need you both to know I tried my absolute damndest to save you from that fate. Just as I tried to save every other set of twins in this family for two hundred years. But . . . there's only so much a silent maid can do against the most powerful magic family in Celdwyn."

"Hold on—two *hundred* years?" Ariel repeated, aghast. "I mean, I realized you haven't aged in a long time but not *that* long."

"I suppose you can't make fun of me for being the oldest on the ship anymore," Santiago whispered to them.

"Two hundred and nineteen, to be exact," Adelaide said. She shrugged, gesturing to her youthful face, nary a wrinkle to be seen. "Not that you'd know it from looking at me. I suppose I owe it to the curse for saving me from shriveling into an immortal husk."

"I've never heard of a curse that could do that," Delilah murmured. "That's wildly powerful magic."

"Indeed." Adelaide let out a breath, then pulled her hands away from the twins'. "For generations, I've served the Pelumbras, hoping one of them would offer me forgiveness. Endless days and nights tending to their needs and not once did they even consider—" She cut off, steadying herself as she stopped her voice from rising anymore. "I was sure that it would be easy. Just wait for the next generation to come of age, and they'd forget the hatred their parents had for me. But until now . . . it never happened."

Before anyone could ask, Adelaide continued: "When I was nineteen, I was living on the estate with my mother, Annabel, and my father, Edward. I was engaged to be married to a Bartelle boy, hoping that I could do what my mother had for the Pelumbras: bring magic to their bloodline."

"The Pelumbras weren't witches before your mother?" Delilah asked.

Adelaide nodded. "She was the first. Back then, witches were just beginning to be absorbed into society after millennia of subjugation. Village witches were a new fixture, and wealthy families were looking for a way to get a leg up on other wealthy families. My father, Edward Pelumbra, had the bright idea to marry a witch after he met my mother at a traveling market.

"In exchange for the cushy lifestyle the Pelumbras could offer her, my mother—a skilled writer—wrote Edward a blessing as a wedding present. It's the same blessing that is still on the Pelumbras today: it gives them supernatural luck. It's the reason they've been able to become such a prominent part of Celdwyn's upper society and get away with so many shady dealings."

"It's like Ash was saying about the mine," Delilah said to the twins. "How during the cave-in, somehow no Pelumbras were hurt while a bunch of Bartelles died. He was right about the blessing."

"Does that apply to our curse?" Briar asked. She'd already wolfed down her entire bowl of soup, a smudge of broth still on the corner of her mouth. "Because Ash thought we might have a geas, is that it?"

Adelaide's eyes darkened. "It . . . it all comes back to what I did."

There was a beat of silence before Adelaide continued: "My mother had been married to Edward for almost twenty-five years and was as faithful as can be. But Edward—he was never satisfied with a single lover. Especially one like my mother, who became very sick after having me and never fully recovered. There had been rumors in the family for ages that he was having an affair, but I refused to believe them. Edward was my father, the head of the Pelumbra family. Why would he neglect his duties as a husband and a father with someone else when he loved us so much?

"But one night, I was in the estate's library when I overheard my father speaking with someone. When I went to investigate, I found him talking to a woman named Pearl, who was the village witch of Havensbridge. It turned out he'd been having one of his many affairs with her, but she'd accidentally fallen pregnant with his twins. I overheard them discussing what to do about it, and Pearl insisted that he find a way to get rid of my mother so the two of them could be married and their twins raised as the Pelumbra heirs.

"I was so hurt that my father would betray my mother like

that that I instantly ran to tell her. But as I tried to flee the library, Pearl caught me. In a panic, she cursed me into silence to keep me from telling my mother. Trouble was, my mother had come looking for me to discuss wedding plans."

"What did she do?" Delilah asked.

Adelaide grimaced. "I think she realized that her relationship with my father was doomed. He'd moved on—he was starting a new family with a new witch. My mother was sick, as I mentioned, and knew she didn't have much time left regardless. So she did two things.

"First, she returned to the blessing that she'd given my father as a wedding present. She was . . . angry. Rightfully so. But that doesn't excuse the fact that she chose to target Edward and Pearl's unborn twins." Adelaide inhaled, squeezing her eyes shut. "They were the first to bear your curse."

The twins exchanged a look. Briar asked, "So Kieran and I got screwed over because your asshole dad cheated on your mom?"

Adelaide winced. "Well . . . yes. She couldn't take back the blessing, so instead, she made it a geas by adding a condition to it: your curse. And for me . . ." Adelaide held out her arm, then pointed to the spyglass that had been hidden in the box. "Point that here."

Delilah's eyebrows rose in question, but she did as she was told. After a moment, the darkness in the glass faded, to reveal curling script written on the inside of Adelaide's wrist: *You shall not die silent.*

Delilah read it aloud and said, "Is that . . . a blessing?"

Adelaide nodded. "Because she wasn't of Pelumbra blood, my

mother couldn't break my curse, so she thought she could help by giving me a blessing—turning my curse into a geas as well. But all it did was make me functionally immortal while I remained unable to speak."

"What happened after all that?" Delilah pushed.

"Well . . . my mother passed away not long after. The magic it took to create two powerful geasa depleted her of what little life she had left. That paired with the heartbreak . . . it took her away from me." Adelaide's eyes began to shine again. "After she died, my father said that the Bartelles didn't want me to marry into their family anymore because I was mute. Without my mother or my betrothal . . . all I had left was my life at the estate. So for years and years and years I worked, hoping that one day my father's new family would forgive me. But as time went on, I faded further and further into the background until I just . . . gave up."

Kieran reached out, placing his hand over Adelaide's. "I'm so sorry, Adelaide."

"Backing up a bit," Delilah chimed in. She was still stuck on something Adelaide had mentioned before. "You said your mother is the one who wrote Kieran and Briar's curse. Do you know what it says? And how to break it?"

Adelaide bit her lip. "I . . . no. Not exactly."

Everyone's shoulders deflated.

"But I do know where it is." Adelaide nudged Kieran and asked, "You know the old wing at the estate?"

He nodded. "Sure. Where Father's study is, behind the ballroom."

"It's there," she explained. "Scratched into the foundation of the estate itself. My mother carved it into the stone with her own hand where she'd written the blessing years before."

"So wait." Delilah tapped her chin with her finger as her brain worked. "All we have to do is go to the Pelumbra estate and find it, right? And then we can figure out how to break it?"

"Easier said than done," Ariel said, looking up from their stew. "The Pelumbras have a ridiculous number of guards around. They aren't going to let us stroll back in. The second they see our faces, we're done for."

Kieran rubbed his chin. "Maybe . . . maybe we don't have to show our faces."

Everyone turned to him, eyebrows raised.

He explained: "Every year, the Pelumbras host a masquerade ball for all the notable families in Celdwyn. It's the biggest party we throw all year, and the estate is packed. Granted, I was never allowed to go—the curse and all—but I did my best to spy on it. The only reason I got away with it was because the estate security team were so focused on the party, they didn't have time to monitor me."

Delilah's eyes widened. "Kieran, that's perfect! When do they host the ball?"

"On the summer solstice," Kieran explained.

"That's three days from now!" Briar exclaimed. She turned to Ariel. "Do you think you can get us to the estate that fast?"

Ariel nodded. "We'll have to make a stop for fuel and supplies, but we certainly have a fighting chance."

"It's settled, then," Delilah said. She stood up, putting her hands on the table. "We infiltrate the ball, sneak into the estate, and find the curse. All in favor?"

Everyone said, "Aye."

"Well, then." Ariel stood. "I guess we'd best start heading north."

And north they went.

CHAPTER TWENTY-ONE

Rule #2: Take care not to let tangles in the head
knot the strings of the heart.

Soon after Adelaide finished her story, Ariel retreated to the cockpit to start the journey to the Pelumbra estate. The engine whirred nonstop; the wings beat with a creaking fervor that never slowed. The temperature inside the ship rose over the next few hours, just as it had when they'd raced to get to Gellingham. Delilah began to worry that the engine might overheat and burst into flames.

Dressed in her lightest pajamas, she lay in bed that night, staring at the ceiling. Sweat wet her brow though she was lying on top of her blankets, and her nightshirt stuck to her damp back. She'd flipped her pillow so many times there was no longer a cold side, much to her chagrin.

And to top it all off, her brain had decided to fixate on Theo again.

In all the chaos of breaking Adelaide's curse and their retreat from Gellingham, Delilah had barely had a chance to process having seen her ex. As much as it had hurt to see his familiar face again, it hadn't been exactly what she'd anticipated. Of course she'd wanted him to remember her, to say her name as he had before. But when he did . . .

It didn't feel like before. Not like when she'd been in love with him.

But more important than the realization that her flame for Theo seemed to have gone out was the fact that, for a moment there, he *had* known her. The recognition had been there as he whispered her name.

How could he remember me, even if it was only a few seconds?

She didn't have any answers. Her first thought had been that the hawthorn dust might have done something, but she'd always heard hawthorn had no impact on curses.

Despite her lingering resentment toward her father, part of her wished she could pick up the phone and call Klaus to ask if he'd ever heard of a curse losing power like that. He might even have seen it in all his days of cursebreaking.

And maybe he could tell her whether or not it was a sign that maybe, just maybe, something about her curse was changing.

Delilah used her sleep shirt to dab at the sweat on her neck. At this rate, the heat paired with her racing thoughts would keep her awake all night. With a groan, she sat up, swung her legs around, and headed toward the kitchen to get some ice and a cold cloth.

The hall was silent as she headed out to the deck. Kieran's door was closed—he had gone to bed early. It wasn't the first time. Ever since his last attack in the forest, he'd been sleeping a few extra hours each night, no longer joining the others for breakfast at the usual time.

Delilah told herself it was general exhaustion, but she knew that wasn't true.

She had only made it a few steps onto the deck when she caught the sound of voices. She paused, glancing sideways to find Adelaide standing against the edge of the deck, hands resting on the banister. At her side was Briar, slumped forward with her chin atop her hands as she stared out at the night sky. Delilah froze, taking a single step back toward her cabin.

Still, she lingered.

"Were they all like me?" Briar asked Adelaide, not looking at her. "The . . . other cursed twins? Did they also turn into, um . . ."

Adelaide nodded. "Every one. They were born halfway between their human and cursed forms, just as you were. I acted as midwife for nearly all of them—you included. Only a few members of the family are privy to exactly what the curse entails for the twin in your position, so they called on me each time to assist with the births."

"So was Kieran born first or was I?"

"Kieran was first. About five minutes before you."

"Well, that explains why my mother wanted me dead. I can imagine it would be quite a horror show to deliver a nice, healthy baby only to follow it up with a twisted monster." Briar wrinkled her nose. "I do hate that he's the older one, though. I always hoped I was the elder sibling."

Adelaide chuckled. "I won't tell him if you don't. Plus, you were far from a twisted monster. You had a shock of red hair and the cutest little horn buds. So well-behaved too—Kieran was jaundiced and colicky from the start. You mostly liked to sit in my arms and stare out the windows at the mountains. You were so . . . sweet. And happy."

Briar all but barked a laugh. "Guess that didn't last long."

Adelaide went quiet. As they talked, Delilah tucked herself around the corner behind some crates to fully obscure herself from view. She wasn't typically the sort to eavesdrop, but something about the way Adelaide's eyes shimmered made her want to stay and listen. Whatever she had to say, she'd been thinking it for a long, long time.

Adelaide exhaled through her nose. "You know, I tried to take you away once. Your father had decided to send you to Wrenlin, and I was absolutely crushed. I'd been taking care of you since you were born, and it felt like I'd be losing my own child. So I wrapped you up in a blanket and tried to sneak out in the middle of the night."

Briar's eyebrows shot up. "You did?"

"I almost got you out too. But your father caught me before I could leave the estate. He took you from me and locked me in a room for days until he could send you off to Wrenlin." Adelaide's eyes welled with tears, and two escaped, sliding down her cheeks. "I'd spent nearly two centuries with my curse, but that day, I tried so hard to scream that my curse-locked jawbone cracked. Losing you and knowing I couldn't protect you from our family . . . it was the worst day of my life. Worse than when I was cursed. And I'm so, so sorry I couldn't protect you."

Her voice cracked on the final words. She hung her head as tears dribbled off her chin, turned silver by the moonlight.

Briar was quiet for a long beat. She shuffled her hands in front of her and shifted on her feet, clearly unsure of what to say. Delilah nearly stepped out then, wanting to do something to comfort Adelaide, but stopped herself. *It's not my place.*

"It's not your fault," Briar finally said. She rubbed at her own eyes, sniffling. "You tried. That's more than anyone else did for me back then. Plus, that was the past. These days, even with the curse, I'm . . . happy. More than I think I've ever been."

Adelaide dried her eyes and cleared her throat. Gently, she whispered, "You have no idea how good that is to hear. After Wrenlin took you, I spent years wondering if I'd ever get to see your smile again." She let out a watery chuckle. "I'm glad I've gotten to."

There was a brief pause before Adelaide added, "I suspect some of that is Delilah's doing, is it not?"

Briar flushed. Delilah's pulse fluttered in her throat, stomach suddenly weightless. Half of her begged to slip away and let the two have the privacy they deserved. But the other half—the one that had been thinking about Briar nonstop since the woods— won out.

Briar coughed and cleared her throat. "I—um—I guess you could say that."

Adelaide's face warmed. "You two have gotten quite close."

Briar sighed. Her fingers skated across the banister, absently tracing shapes in the wood. "That's one way to put it, yeah. How could I not? I mean, come on—she's funny an-and whip-smart and so damn beautiful it makes me feel like I'm melting from the inside out."

Heat rose from Delilah's chest, radiating out like a tiny sun. Absently, she pressed a hand over it, feeling her speeding heart beneath her fingertips.

She thinks I'm beautiful?

Then a shadow passed over Briar's face. "But a girl like her isn't ever going to love a monster like me. Not when there are people like that Theo guy falling for her. She deserves someone like that, not. . . ." She looked down at her hands, sighing. Her shoulders tensed, and she drew her chin closer to her chest. "Not like me."

Delilah's heart felt as if it were made of lead, growing heavier with each word. Briar couldn't truly believe that, could she?

Adelaide reached out and put a hand on Briar's shoulder. Briar shot her a questioning look, then Adelaide gave her shoulder a pat.

"You know what I've learned these past two hundred years?"

Briar cocked her head.

"People most regret the moments they stayed silent," she admitted. She pushed her hair out of her face as it blew in the breeze, setting her gaze squarely on Briar. "Delilah can't read your mind. And you can't know what she'll say until you tell her the truth."

Briar said, words dripping with sarcasm, "Right, I'm sure if I tell her about my"—she choked on the word, eventually spitting out—"*feelings,* she won't doubt me at all after what she's been through. Great plan, Adelaide."

Delilah's heartbeat slammed like a trapped animal against her ribs.

If she has feelings for me, does that mean . . . ?

To her credit, Adelaide just laughed. "Say what you will, but I've spent two centuries watching people fall in love. What you and Delilah have? Something tells me it's worth the risk."

"But what if it's not?" Briar winced as soon as the words were out, as if she hadn't meant to let them slip free. Her forehead wrinkled, and she rubbed her temples. "If I tell her, I might ruin everything. And if I do—who's to say it will even matter? This whole Pelumbra estate infiltration is a long shot. If we get there and we can't get past the guards to find the curse . . . or if we can't break it in time . . ."

Briar trailed off.

"Does she know?" Adelaide asked softly. "What will happen to you?"

Briar shook her head. "No. I didn't tell her. I . . . couldn't."

The brightness in Delilah's eyes flickered out. *What . . . will happen?*

Adelaide's expression darkened. Softy, she reached out and offered Briar a little side hug. After a long beat of hesitation, Briar hugged her back.

"I suppose you have a lot to think about," Adelaide said, rubbing Briar's forearm. "But I'm here. Maybe seventeen years too late, but I'm here."

Briar nodded softly. "Thank you, Adelaide."

"Of course. Now I should be getting to bed." Adelaide pulled away, reaching out to brush an eyelash off Briar's cheek before she squared her shoulders. For once, Briar didn't recoil from being touched. "And so should you. Just . . . sleep on what I said, all right?"

Briar snorted. "What are you, my mother?"

Adelaide chuckled, but there was a note of something tight and pained beneath it. "If only I could have been so lucky. Good night, Briar."

"Night."

The two went their separate ways, leaving Delilah to sit behind her stack of crates with damp eyes and an aching heart.

And after a few long minutes, she made up her mind.

If she doesn't believe I can love her, she thought, *I'll just have to prove her wrong.*

🌿

As the sun set the next day and everyone gathered for dinner, Ariel came into the dining room and announced that they would need to stop overnight.

"What?" Briar demanded. "Why?"

"We're low on fuel, and I need to replace the cooling fluid," Ariel explained. They fanned themself. "I don't know if you've noticed, but it's a little past cozy in here."

Delilah nodded—even after she'd finally fallen asleep last night, she'd woken up more than once in a puddle of sweat. The only relief this day had been standing on the deck in the fresh air, but at the speed they were going, the wind was bad enough to twist Delilah's curls into knots in seconds flat. Other than that, she'd spent most of the day looking for excuses to stick her head in the icebox, much to Santiago's annoyance.

"And that will take all night?" Delilah clarified.

Ariel shook their head. "No, but by the time we get to the nearest town, it'll be after-hours for any sort of aeroship maintenance shops. Best we hang out for a night and leave in the morning. With the pace we've been keeping, we should still make it to the estate on time."

"Can you at least pick a town where I can buy some good ingredients?" Santiago asked. He pointed to the burrata, tomatoes, basil, and crusty baguette he'd placed on the table. "Gellingham's burrata put every other one I've tried to shame, and I fear these children will mutiny if I don't keep up the quality dishes." He eyed Briar. "Except that one—she seems happy to eat any slab of meat I put in front of her, so long as there isn't anything green touching it."

Briar rolled her eyes and crossed her arms. "You're welcome."

"I can't promise you any good cheese," Ariel said, "but we're stopping in Wyvern Springs. Which, if it wasn't apparent from the name, has a hot spring."

"Oh! I've read about that place," Delilah said, eyes bright. "Some people swear the water has healing properties."

"Might be nice," Kieran mused. He gently touched his face, his faint smile fading. Recently, his cheeks had increasingly hollowed out, and the dark thumbprints beneath his eyes stood out starkly against his pale skin.

Delilah's chest tightened.

She didn't want to say it out loud, but it was beginning to feel like they were running out of time.

"Hmm . . . now that I think about it, perhaps it isn't the best idea to get off the ship," Santiago said, gesturing to Delilah and the twins with a piece of bread. "If anyone has followed us from Gellingham, we need to be able to make a quick escape. We can't do that if you're off frolicking in the hot springs."

"I actually don't think Briar is physically capable of frolicking," Kieran pointed out.

She kicked him under the table, making him snicker behind his hand.

"Regardless, I agree," Ariel said. "Assuming this all works out, we'll turn the ship around and celebrate *after* we finish breaking the curse."

"So . . . we should just stay on the ship?" Delilah clarified.

Ariel nodded. "Yep. We should be touching down in an hour."

Delilah did her best to smile and nod, the picture of perfect obedience, until the adults had turned and left the room. Her eyes flicked to Briar, who was picking the tomato and basil off a piece of bread topped with burrata.

She had an idea.

CHAPTER TWENTY-TWO

Rule #23: Watch out for tricks of the light.

The airfield where Ariel had landed was small, with only one other aeroship. The field was at the foot of a tall, jagged peak, one of many looming around them. These were the Slicetooths, Delilah knew, the most dangerous mountains in Celdwyn and by far the biggest. Their peaks were snowcapped even at the tail end of spring. Thick fir and spruce forest made for a beautiful verdant coat that was broken up only by burn scars from wildfires and sharp, rocky drop-offs curtained by waterfalls. The crisp air smelled like rain, vanilla, and pine.

As the ship grew silent that night, Delilah tiptoed from her room across the hall. Glancing in both directions, she tapped a fist against Briar's door.

After a few heart-pounding moments, Briar opened it. She had on a loose tank top and men's undershorts. Yawning, she scrubbed a hand over her buzzed hair.

"Hey."

"Hey." Delilah's face lit up. She bit her lip to try to contain her smile, hoping her blush wasn't too obvious in the low light. "I know Ariel said not to leave the ship, but I was looking at some maps of the area in the study, and there's a footpath that leads from this airfield directly to one of the pools at Wyvern Springs. It's technically closed right now, so . . ."

Briar's eyebrows rose. "You want to break into a hot spring?"

"It's perfect, right?" Delilah's eyes glittered. "We'll get the whole place to ourselves. And we can be in and out before anyone here notices we're gone."

"Do you wanna wake up Kieran too?"

"I was thinking maybe just the two of us?"

"You— Oh. Sure." Briar blinked in surprise, beaming. A smile like that from her was such a rare thing it made Delilah's heart squeeze in her chest, her pulse picking up and turning her blood effervescent. With her cheeks warm and her expression open, it was all Delilah could do to stop herself from swooning.

Briar hooked a thumb toward her room. "I'll change into swim clothes and meet you downstairs."

Beaming, Delilah jogged back to her own room to change. Her swimsuit was a one-piece: tight blue-and-white shorts that went to her mid-thigh and a cap-sleeve top. She snagged a towel from her bathroom and quickly snuck back out of the room, tiptoeing across the deck and down the stairs to the gangway.

She paused for a moment as the soft sound of voices floated down the hallway from the study. Keeping on her toes, Delilah crept a little closer.

To her surprise, it was Kieran's voice. When she leaned to peer into the room, she found him curled up on the couch with his legs under him, the ship's phone held to his ear as he twisted the cord around his finger. He was grinning, his expression warm.

"I'm glad you weren't freaked out when I . . . kissed you," he whispered into the receiver. He grinned, blushing. "I . . . I really didn't know if you felt the same way but . . . I just felt like I had to go for it."

Must be Ash, Delilah realized. Kieran really was head over heels.

The faint sound of footsteps behind her was the only warning Delilah got before Briar appeared at her side and whispered, "So do you think he's going to start giggling and kicking his feet next or . . . ?"

Delilah tamped down the urge to yelp and steadied herself. "You have *got* to say something before you just pop out of the ether."

"But then I wouldn't get to see the look on your face every time I scare you." Briar grinned, nodding toward the exit. "Come on."

Delilah melodramatically rolled her eyes before turning to follow on Briar's heels. Kieran's voice faded as they crept along the corridor, past the old paintings of dead Pelumbras nailed to the walls. Even though Adelaide, Ariel, and Santiago were most certainly asleep, with little risk of waking up, Delilah's heart thumped furiously in her chest, blood rushing in her ears.

Briar held the gangway door open, trying and failing to withhold a laugh when Delilah bumped her hip hard against the doorknob by accident and held in a curse. Mouthing more and more colorful curses, Delilah gently smacked Briar on the shoulder while she snorted, her attempts at not laughing only making it worse. Delilah, not doing much better, whispered for her to be quiet, while Briar retorted the same thing back in a bad impression of Delilah's slight southern Celdwynian accent. That earned Briar an elbow in the ribs.

Still poorly holding in laughter and shushing each other, they snuck down the gangway, towels thrown over their shoulders, and headed for the path to the hot spring.

The trail took them into the woods, the path lined with strings of lights yoked from tree to tree. They cast a yellow glow on the thick underbrush, which was damp from recent rain. Beads of dew glittered like tiny jewels on the ferns and the tips of pine needles. The air was cool and crisp, near silent aside from the hoots of owls in the trees and the rustling of tiny animals in the underbrush.

It was barely any time before the trees opened up to a clearing surrounding the hot spring. There, nestled in the mountainside, were five rocky pools scattered across a couple of acres of flower-lined paths and a lodge, where a few lights flickered—probably guests getting ready for bed now that the pools were technically closed. Well lights were wedged into the rock rims around the pools, but they'd been turned off for the night, leaving only the moon and the distant glow of the lodge to illuminate the still water.

"Delilah, over here," Briar whispered, pointing to the nearest pool.

It was partially obscured by trees, perfect to keep away any prying eyes from the lodge. Briar draped her towel over a tree branch before wading in. The water was dark, the steam rising up from it turning silvery in the moonlight. Briar sank down into the water, floating on her back with her arms out. Her long eyelashes fluttered as she exhaled a breath and closed her eyes.

Delilah's heart raced.

Leaving her own towel on a branch, Delilah stepped into the spring. It was warm but not so hot that she'd need to get out soon. Slowly, she came to Briar's side and lay back in the water so her head was next to Briar's but their legs floated in opposite directions. Above them, the stars glittered in the vast, unclouded sky.

For a long while, they simply gazed up in silence.

Just say it, Delilah berated herself. *This is the perfect moment. Just open your mouth and—*

Briar broke the silence before Delilah could. "Hey, Delilah?"

"Hmm?"

"There's something I've been thinking about," she said. She swallowed thickly, opening her eyes to again gaze at the sky. Her lips moved, but no sounds came out for a moment. She winced, trying to find the words.

Delilah's pulse quickened.

"When my family talks about our curse," Briar began, "they mostly focus on the dying twin. They know exactly what will happen: when Kieran runs out of magic for me to take, he'll die. But they don't know what will happen to me."

Delilah turned her head to get a better look at Briar. It seemed like there might be the faint shine of tears in her eyes.

"Kieran dying was always the palatable part to the Pelumbras. He'd be their perfect martyr, and the family would go on.

But me?" She winced. "If Kieran dies, there's no turning back for me. I'll become the monster you saw in the woods, and I'll never change back. My mind will still be there, trapped in that body until I die."

Delilah tensed, starting to say, "Briar—"

She cut in, "In the past, when one twin has died and the other transforms permanently, the Pelumbras offer the living twin a choice: to die at their hand or to stay imprisoned at the estate. There's a cell deep in the mansion where the twin can live out their days as a monster, hidden from prying eyes. But . . . from what Adelaide told me, none have ever chosen that option."

Delilah's breath caught. Her body suddenly felt heavier, as if the weight of Briar's words might drag her underwater in an instant.

"I don't know if I would either," Briar whispered.

Instantly, Delilah was on her feet, water rippling around her. While Briar straightened as well, Delilah's eyes began to burn. Briar barely had time to fully stand before Delilah threw her arms around her, squeezing.

Briar started, "What are you—?"

"I'm not letting you go," Delilah growled into Briar's short hair. Her eyes shone with pale fire in the moonlight. "No matter what happens with the curse, all right? I don't care if you're trapped in your other form—I'm not letting the Pelumbras touch you. Never again. I'll burn their whole estate to the ground if I have to."

"Delilah—"

"I'm serious." Delilah pulled back, hands on Briar's shoulders.

She squeezed them. "I am going to put every fiber of my being into ending this curse, but if I can't? I'm not going to lose you."

Briar's eyes began to shine. For once, though, she didn't try to hide the emotion on her face.

So quietly Delilah could barely hear her, Briar whispered, "Don't do this."

Delilah blinked. "I don't under—"

"Don't act like you might feel the same way about me that I do about you."

The world around Delilah came to a screeching halt. Her pulse sped up, thrumming in her chest and in her throat. Even with her feet now squarely resting on the bottom of the hot spring, it felt as if the world had been wrenched out from underneath her. She could barely remember how to breathe.

"How . . . do you feel about me?"

Briar's expression twisted as she pressed her lips into a line and stared firmly in the other direction. She hugged herself tightly, her shoulders tensed as if she were preparing for a blow.

Finally, she opened her eyes and softly whispered, "Like I'm falling in love with you."

For a single, out-of-body second, it occurred to Delilah how many times she'd imagined hearing those words. How she'd sat in her classes with Ruby, staring out the cottage window, fantasizing about the day she would break her curse and be swept off her feet and pulled into an embrace by someone she loved. Even when she knew she wasn't allowed to think like that, every so often she would let her mind wander to an impossible future where someone could illuminate the darkness that held her heart.

An exception.

Briar chanced a glance at her. "You don't have to—"

She cut off as Delilah pulled her into a kiss.

This one was nothing like the first kiss they'd shared on the ship. That one had been angry, all pressure and teeth. This one was gentle, Delilah softly cupping Briar's cheek against her palm as she let her other hand slide down Briar's spine and into the water.

For a moment, Briar was tense, as if too shocked to process what was happening. Then, though, she melted into Delilah's arms. She pressed their bodies close, sparking a flare of warmth that made Delilah hum against Briar's lips. Briar's hands found the soft edges of Delilah's waist, one dipping into the water to trace her tailbone while the other rose to her shoulder blades. Delilah could feel the other girl's heartbeat hammering against her ribs, heat leaching from skin to skin like ink across paper. Steam from the spring surrounded them, shining droplets collecting on the edges of their eyelashes.

Delilah had spent so long envisioning this moment, even when she'd mentally kicked herself for doing it. She'd imagined what Briar would feel like against her, how she'd touch her like something precious. Night after night, she'd lie awake on the ship telling herself not to let her heart overpower her head, trying to build the wall around her heart higher and higher.

Briar pulled away, face flushed and breath heavy. Her lips parted as if she was going to say something, then closed.

Her head tilted toward the shining moon, and silver flashed over her eyes.

The flash, the blank expression—

Delilah's stomach dropped like a lead weight.

No, no, NO.

Briar blinked, seeming to snap back into focus. "Delilah? Are you okay?"

Delilah was frozen. Memories of the day Theo forgot burned in her mind. Even with Briar staring up at her in question, all Delilah could think of was the cracks in the foundation she'd built up so purposefully since she had learned about her curse.

Her stomach twisted, and she suddenly felt sick. Her skin took on a waxy, ashen sheen as the color drained from her.

What am I doing? Why would there be an exception?

It's going to happen again.

Even if it was Briar. Briar, who was somehow both blunt and sharp at the same time, honest to a fault and beautiful like lightning cutting across the night sky. A girl, a monster—something else entirely. Something that made Delilah's heart race and the skin down her spine tingle as if it had been touched by a cool breeze on a summer's day.

She was falling—hell, maybe she had already fallen—for Briar. The exact thing she'd promised herself she'd never do again.

Briar took a step back, the light leaving her eyes. "Oh."

Delilah's eyes welled with tears. She felt as if she'd been torn in half, desperate to reach out, to say that she was just in her head, but she couldn't. Her hands had begun to shake, bile crawling up her throat. The tears dribbled down her cheeks, and the shame hit her like a slap. She'd never wished so desperately that she could be like any other person, who could simply hand their heart to someone else.

Bea women aren't like everyone else, her mother had told her once. *We don't get to love like they do.*

Even though she wanted this so, so bad. To hoist Briar onto the lip of the spring and kiss her until her lips bruised—to walk her back to the ship and tuck in beside her in bed, falling asleep to the sound of her breath. To watch the way the moonlight pooled over the sharp planes of her cheekbones and illuminated her trembling eyelashes. To wake up in the morning and tell her the dreams she had every night about a future together, curse broken, two hedge witches in a cottage at the edge of the woods, where they'd make their home. A familiar of her own summoned to curl up with Cinnabar on cool nights while Briar wove her fingers into Delilah's hair and whispered her name.

A life that wasn't possible for her. She'd been stupid to tell herself it was. Even if Briar still remembered her now, she wouldn't for long. Delilah blinked, more fat tears rolling down her cheeks.

It was only a matter of time before she lost her.

"I'm sorry," she whispered. She squeezed her eyes shut, bringing her fists up to press into them as her shoulders trembled. "I'm so, so sorry."

Briar winced, and it felt like a dagger between Delilah's ribs. In a second, Briar's face morphed into the familiar scowl that Delilah knew so well from the day they'd met, the anger behind her eyes the only life in her.

Shoving past Delilah, Briar stepped out of the spring, snagged her towel off the tree, and rushed toward the path in silence.

Delilah waited until she was sure Briar was gone to fully burst into tears.

She bowed her head as sobs clawed their way free from her

throat. Her body shook, chest aching like someone had taken a spoon and carved out her heart from between her ribs. She sank into the water, but she could barely feel the warmth anymore. Her skin had gone cold, throat thick and burning.

I'm a fool.

It was all she could do to keep from wailing.

As another wave of sobs shook free from her chest, the sound of crunching gravel made her freeze.

Delilah sniffled, glancing up. "Briar?"

But she never got to see the person's face, because the next moment, they were holding a glowing hand out toward her, the scent of peppery magic heavy around them.

The last thing Delilah heard was the sharp ringing of a bell before she fell unconscious.

CHAPTER TWENTY-THREE

Rule #5: Some secrets have teeth.

When Delilah awoke, she was sitting in a wingback chair—still in her swim clothes—with a fur rug beneath her feet and a cozy fire roaring in front of her. After a moment of blinking herself back into consciousness, she realized she was in a log building with large arched windows. The air smelled like woodsmoke, whiskey, and aftershave.

In a panic, she jumped to her feet, a towel that had been wrapped around her shoulders sliding to the floor. She swung her head left and right, only to find a gangly, pale man staring at her from where he stood in front of the exit.

"Oh no," he muttered. Clearing his throat shakily, he called out, "Um, boss? She's awake."

Delilah immediately stepped into a ledrith stance that Briar had taught her, magic sparking at her fingertips. "Who the *hell* are you, and what am I doing—?"

"Delilah, hold on."

She paused at the sound of the voice. Pivoting on her heel, she spun in time to come face-to-face with none other than Klaus Hammond, wearing what may well be the most ridiculous suit Delilah had ever seen. The whole thing was covered in live roses growing out of the white fabric. The scent of them perfumed the air, as if Klaus had washed the suit in rose oil before putting it on. His hair was slicked back, highlighting his graying temples and his trimmed salt-and-pepper beard.

"Klaus?" she said. She blinked in disbelief. "What is going on? Why am I in a log cabin, and who is *that?*"

"Oh." Klaus hooked a thumb to the man by the door. "That's Henrick, my assistant. I sent him to go get you." He paused, shooting Henrick a stern glare as he added, "Granted, knocking you out wasn't really what I meant when I said to make sure you came without conflict."

"Sorry," Henrick said, his large ears turning pink. Now that Delilah had a good look at him, he appeared to be barely out of his teens, still gangly and knobby. "I panicked."

"What, is this your first day on the job or something?" Delilah demanded.

Henrick swallowed, the prominent lump in his throat bobbing. "Y-yes, actually. I cannot stress enough how poorly I handled this, and I apolog—"

"Okay, okay, it's fine. Just . . . don't go around knocking people out like that. Folks will get the wrong idea." Delilah turned to her father. "Anyway. That doesn't answer my question of where I am and also how in the world you found me."

"You're in the Wyvern Springs Lodge," Klaus explained. He

crossed the room and took a seat in a second wingback chair adjacent to the one Delilah had woken up in. He folded his hands in his lap. "I followed your ship here from Gellingham after I heard you'd stolen something from the archive. There's something urgent I need to speak with you about."

There was a pause while Delilah waited for her father to continue, but instead, he just sat there for a moment. Then, shooting a look sideways, he said, "Henrick, that was your cue to leave."

"Oh! Right. Sorry, sir." He opened the door, offering Delilah a nod. "Lovely to meet you, Miss Bea."

He stepped out, shutting the door behind him.

"You might want to train him a little more before you ask him to stalk and kidnap someone again," Delilah suggested.

Klaus scoffed. "I'll add it to my to-do list. Now let me cut to the chase."

He reached around to the other side of his chair and took a large leather tome from where it sat on an end table. He cracked it open and, licking his finger, flipped around a number of pages before finding what he was looking for. Book face-up in his hands, he leaned to close the distance between them and passed it to Delilah. "Give that a look."

Delilah eyed him but did as she was told. She frowned as she picked through the cursive script, written in golden ink on a crumbling old page.

It read:

> *Here on out, a curse will weave*
> *Between the branches of the family Bea.*
> *Each mother a daughter, and a daughter a mother,*

> *But no longer shall ever a lover*
> *Be tied in affection to one or the other.*
> *Should true love creep in,*
> *Let it be skimmed*
> *From his memories held within,*
> *For never again will a man's heart beat for she,*
> *Unless love is proclaimed in truth beneath the*
>   *silverwood tree*
> *To those wretched women Bea.*

Delilah's jaw dropped. There was a ringing in her ears and a feeling of unreality as she stared at the words. She realized after a moment that she'd forgotten to blink, to breathe.

"Is this . . . my curse? How in the world did you find it?"

Klaus smoothed his hair. His rich brown eyes went to the fire, his expression more subdued than Delilah had seen it. He rubbed a thumb over his knee, bouncing it slightly.

Was he *nervous*?

"After we spoke in the forest, I got to thinking about . . . what you said." He closed his eyes, exhaling a sigh. "How I was only a father in the biological sense. I knew that was the case, but hearing you say it made me feel . . . a bit sad, I suppose."

Delilah finally tore her eyes from the flowery script, pinning her gaze on him. "A *bit sad*? That's it?" She paused for a beat. "Hold on. Did you find this curse, track me down, and have your lackey knock me out and kidnap me just to try and *apologize*?"

"Exactly." Klaus pulled at his collar. "I made a few mistakes in my youth, Delilah."

"Understatement of the century," she grumbled.

Klaus pressed his lips together. The fire crackled behind him, spitting sparks up the chimney. The room smelled faintly of smoldering embers. "I also found you because I need to tell you something. About me. And—our family."

"Please tell me it's not another curse."

"Goodness, no. If there was a curse on the Hammonds, I would have broken it decades ago." Klaus continued, unfazed: "No—you see, the Hammonds have been witches for a very long time. Some have even argued we might be some of the first, descended from the earliest magic practitioner, who gained her powers by harvesting magic from a vein beneath the ground. You'll recall that, back in the woods, I was searching for one such vein. Did I ever tell you why?"

Delilah shook her head but didn't speak.

Klaus sighed heavily. "I've been in the cursebreaking business since I was fifteen. Fame found me early in life. But before that . . . I was just a boy growing up in northern Celdwyn with his family." He gestured to the room around him. "Here, in fact. At these springs."

Delilah said, "Wait—really?"

"Our ancestors were the caretakers of this spring for generations." Klaus stood, going to a bookshelf on the far wall. He pulled down a small box, then brought it to Delilah. He opened it to reveal a number of tiny, inch-long glass vials with corks in the tops. They all appeared to be empty.

"This is what I've built my career on," he said, gesturing to the interior of the box. "Do you know what these are?"

Delilah shook her head.

"They used to contain water from the springs," Klaus explained, picking up a vial and twisting it around in his fingers. He tossed it in the air and caught it. "You see, Delilah, that first magic vein that gave witches their powers? It was here, beneath our feet. And the magic made the water from these springs into a panacea."

Delilah's eyebrows shot up.

"It was an old family secret," he said. "Every generation, we passed the knowledge down again. When I was young, I realized that letting the spring sit back there unused made no sense. Its water could remove any curse! So I set out with this box full of vials containing the water and broke my first ten curses."

"So you never were some . . . prodigy," Delilah realized, knitting her brows. "You didn't actually know how to break all those curses."

"Well, some of them I did," Klaus said. "Some curses are so easy to break you simply need to read the written form to know. But the tougher ones"—he set the vial back in the box, then set the box down on an end table—"I handed off one of these, and everything resolved itself. I simply made the formerly cursed people promise they'd never reveal my secret."

You're a fraud, Delilah wanted to say. Her cheeks burned, and the back of her throat tightened. *You're not a master cursebreaker. You're just a guy with a magic spring.*

"Problem is," Klaus continued, closing the box and sitting back in his chair, "I got too cocky. I had a legacy to uphold. So I used every single drop of enchanted water from the spring."

Delilah blinked. "It's . . . gone?"

Klaus nodded. "Since then, I've been getting by on my reputation. Which is why I've been looking for another magic vein—with the hope that I can use it to create more panacea without my career being yanked out from under me."

Delilah's shoulders sank. "Then why are you telling me this?"

Klaus shrugged. "Because I want to try to explain why I did what I did. When I met your mother, I smelled the curse on her. But I had to be strategic with the Wyvern's water and . . . I never thought I'd see Charlotte again. Much less have a daughter with her."

"But you could have come back," Delilah pointed out. "You've known about me for seventeen years, and not *once* did I get even a letter from you, much less a panacea. I guess I wasn't important enough to waste that kind of resource on, right?"

Klaus set his jaw, heaving another sigh. "Well, I am certainly not without my flaws. Were it not for my incredibly good looks, and my natural charisma, and my—"

Delilah cleared her throat pointedly.

"Mm. Sorry." Klaus squared his shoulders. "But! That doesn't mean I can't make up for my mistakes. After all"—he gestured to the book—"I pulled quite a few strings to get that. Had everyone at the Library of Curses looking for it day and night in the hope that it was somewhere in the stacks."

Delilah set her jaw, her skin feeling too hot and too tight.

"Read the final three lines again," Klaus instructed.

Delilah blinked. She tried to swallow, but her mouth had gone dry. Softly, she let her finger find the second-to-last line, the golden letters glittering in the firelight.

" 'For never again will a man's heart beat for she,' " she read.

The realization hit Delilah like an electric shock. She read the curse over again until her vision fogged with tears. She pressed her knuckles to her lips and ran her fingers over the letters.

In the past, Briar had said, *sometimes people didn't consider that a woman could love another wo—*

Another woman.

" 'A man's heart,' " Delilah whispered. Briar was right all along. "The curse only impacts men."

Klaus nodded.

"I can't believe this." Delilah rubbed tears away, rereading the curse over and over. The paper was so brittle, it was beginning to break free of the binding, coming loose in Delilah's hand. She gave it a faint tug so she could hold it up and examine the page in the light. "But . . . does that mean that a girl could break it?"

"Not break," Klaus corrected. "Weaken, maybe. But breaking it seems limited to a specific location—beneath a silverwood tree."

Delilah's mind sparked with the image of Theo's recognition back at the archive. "Weaken? What do you mean?"

"Sometimes, because of a physical curse aging or because of some outside influence, like a loophole in a curse, it can start to lose its power. It won't function quite right—that's one of the best indicators that a curse is close to breaking."

A loophole. An exception.

Delilah's breath caught.

"And considering how you looked at that girl back at the Moondew camp," Klaus went on, "it seems like you don't need to worry about the curse. Problem solved."

Delilah blinked, her mind wrenched away momentarily from thoughts of Theo's flicker of memory. Unsure if she'd heard him correctly, she asked, "What?"

"Consider the written curse my apology," Klaus said. "Now we're even."

"Even?" she repeated. She stood, coughing out a humorless laugh as she gently folded her curse and held it between her fingers. "You haven't done anything, Klaus. The curse isn't broken. Even if it doesn't impact women, that only helps me, not my mom. You just pulled a few strings at the library because, for perhaps the first time in your life, you felt a twinge of guilt for abandoning your child. That's not an apology. That's an attempt to ease your guilty conscience."

Delilah shoved the book into his hands.

"Take that back with you to the Library of Curses," she told him. "And while you're there, see if they can find you a dictionary with an explanation of what an apology actually is. In the meantime, I have to go try to fix my own mistake."

While she turned her back on him and made her way toward the exit, Klaus called out, "Delilah! Come on now, there's no need to be upset—"

But she was already out the door, slamming it behind her.

By the time Delilah got back to the ship, it was dead silent. Kieran was no longer in the study, and he'd turned all the lights down when he'd gone to bed. While she'd been painstaking in her efforts to be quiet the last time, Delilah now bounded up the stairs two at a time, heart slamming. She threw open the door to the deck and sprinted across it, shouldering her way into the hallway to her, Briar, and Kieran's rooms.

She started rapping on Briar's door before she'd even fully come to a stop. She kept going, even when she didn't get an immediate response.

After a few moments, though, a small ball of light slid out from under the door. Instantly, Delilah recognized Cinnabar before he'd even taken his cat form. As the ball shifted, though, the orange tomcat glared at her, tail swishing.

He opened his mouth wide as if he were yawning but kept it open.

From inside his throat, Briar's sleepy voice came, "Whoever this is, go to sleep. It's the middle of the night."

"It's me," Delilah said. For a moment, she debated whether or not she needed to speak closer to Cinnabar's mouth, as if it were a phone receiver, but decided against it in favor of knocking on the door again and breathlessly adding, "Briar, I have to talk to you. It's really important."

"Have you considered that maybe I don't want to talk to *you*? After you kissed me and then decided *eh, Briar's not worth my time* after I poured my heart out to you? I mean, *fuck,* Delilah."

"I know." Delilah cringed. It didn't help that she was staring into the mouth of a cat with particularly sharp teeth. "I was being really, really stupid. But please just hear me out."

Cinnabar's face didn't give anything away, nor did Briar's silence. Delilah shifted from foot to foot as the familiar slowly closed his mouth, instead glaring at Delilah with his ears half swiveled back.

"Look, I'm sorry," Delilah whispered to the cat. "I'm only human. We can't all be constructs made of pure magic, okay?"

Cinnabar shot her a look that said, *Clearly.*

Just then the door opened a crack.

Briar's blue eye appeared. "You'd better have a damn good apology, Bea."

"I'm sorry," Delilah said. She flinched. "About tonight. I started thinking about my curse a-and couldn't stop these racing thoughts that I might lose you—"

"You acted like I'd somehow contracted a deadly disease mid-kiss."

"I know." Delilah's shoulders wilted. "And it was so, so stupid of me. Especially because it turns out that you were right all along."

That, for what it was worth, caught Briar's attention immediately.

"Right about what?"

Delilah pulled the piece of paper she'd torn out of Klaus's book and passed it to her. "About there being an exception. Read this."

Hesitantly, Briar opened the door the rest of the way, taking the paper from between Delilah's fingers. She flattened it out with her thumb, her eyes darting as she read it. "Is this . . . ?"

Delilah nodded. "My curse."

"How did you find it?"

"Long story—I can tell you later." She reached over to point at the second-to-last line. "See that?"

Briar wrinkled her nose. "Terrible poem, frankly."

"Well, yes, but—" Delilah's eyes widened. "You were right. There *are* exceptions. In fact, anyone who isn't a man is an exception. I'm just the first Bea to ever fall for one."

Briar didn't speak for a moment, too stunned to formulate words. The low glow of the lamps cast a pale radiance around her skin, her cheeks rosy and thick lips parted, eyes big and glowing and wild.

Delilah remembered the picture she'd seen the day they'd met, with Briar as a child standing beside her aunt, that empty look in her eyes. The kind only a long, ceaseless period of sadness could put there.

They weren't empty anymore.

Delilah reached out and brushed her thumb against Briar's bottom lip. This close, Delilah saw all the tiny scars on her skin, on her forehead, and the larger one through her eyebrow. The way her throat wavered when her breath hitched, and the gentle divot at the base of her neck. The blush suffused through her cheeks, turning the tip of her nose pink.

"I care about you, Briar." Delilah reached across the doorway to gently take hold of her hand. "More than I've ever cared about anyone like this. Maybe more than I'll ever care about anyone for the rest of my life. I tried so, so hard not to—because I was scared that if I let myself fall for you, I was going to get hurt like I did with Theo. But . . . you were right. All along. And I was a fool not to believe you."

This time, Briar closed the distance between them, pulling Delilah down by her still-damp swim shirt and pressing her lips to hers. Briar held her as if she needed an anchor. Delilah felt the flutter of her pulse in her throat and her chest, like the rush of beating bird wings.

Briar pulled back, still clutching Delilah's shirt. "Come inside."

"Oh, I don't need your cat to invite me in with that weird mouth-speaker spell?"

Briar rolled her eyes, snapping her fingers so Cinnabar vanished with a *poof.* "Thin ice, Delilah."

"Would it make it better if I told you that you were right one more time?"

Briar considered it. "Probably wouldn't hurt."

"You were right."

Briar bit back a smile. "Thank you, I know."

Briar took Delilah's hand and led her inside, shutting the door behind her. Delilah realized that she hadn't seen the room since Briar moved in. New heavy curtains covered the windows, and the floor was spotless. Her bed was artfully made, with the pillows stacked like at a fancy inn.

Once the door was closed, Briar's eyes brightened. She pulled Delilah back into a kiss, smiling against it. Delilah's heartbeat took off in a frenzy. They backed up, kissing their way to the bed until Delilah sat back on it, smiling. Briar pulled herself up beside her, her blush having turned her pink from her throat to her ears.

When Briar's fingers met Delilah's back, her skin lit up, every nerve sparking and alive. Briar fell back against her duvet, and Delilah straddled her. Briar slipped her tongue between Delilah's parted lips. For a moment, it felt as if gravity was gone and she'd become weightless, held down only where Briar's hands warmed her skin.

Delilah pulled away for a moment, reaching behind her to grab a fistful of her swim shirt and shuck it off over her head. Briar was still staring wide-eyed when Delilah met her lips again. Briar broke the kiss, her hand pressed to Delilah's bare shoulder.

"Wait," Briar said. Her eyes wandered up and down Delilah's body, and for a moment Delilah flushed with embarrassment. She became acutely aware of the asymmetry of her breasts, how the paunch of her stomach stuck out, and how thick her arms looked compared to Briar's. She wasn't generally self-conscious of her appearance, but she'd also never been looked at with the moony-eyed wonder in Briar's gaze.

She reached for her shirt, but Briar said, "Er—no. Don't."

"Was that too fast?" Delilah asked, face hot.

"No, no—not at all. I just . . . Hold on."

Briar lifted herself up enough to grab a handful of her tank top, sliding it off and dropping it beside the bed. Delilah had always known Briar was knobby in the elbows and knees, but seeing her like this made it clear she was slim all the way through. She was softer in the stomach than Delilah had expected, and her narrow hip bones disappeared into the waistband of her shorts.

"Now we're even," Briar explained, breathless.

Delilah smiled, one hand reaching down to cup Briar's hip, thumb tracing the bone.

"No one has ever, um"—Briar averted her eyes, blushing—"seen me like this."

Delilah shook her head. "Me neither."

Briar's eyebrows rose at that, and Delilah had to assume she must have thought she and Theo had been intimate. They'd kissed, sure, but Delilah hadn't felt ready to do more than that.

To her credit, Briar didn't press. Instead, she chanced a look at Delilah, trying to bite back her grin. "I like you. A lot."

The insecurity that had momentarily frozen Delilah melted away. She leaned down and kissed the space where Briar's neck curved into her shoulder. She whispered, "I like *you* a lot too."

Taking her time, Delilah let her hands move across Briar's bare skin, kissing her languidly. For once, it didn't feel as if they needed to rush. Briar touched Delilah as if she were made of fine silk, stopping to appreciate each freckle and mark on her skin. Delilah felt no urgency, no threat looming over them, just the solid, safe feeling of being held by someone she knew would never intentionally hurt her.

After some time, she pulled back and fell into the pillows beside Briar, breathless and grinning. Briar too struggled to catch her breath, seemingly on the verge of giggling. *That's a first,* Delilah thought.

She leaned over and kissed Briar's neck once more before asking, "Can I sleep in here?"

"Sure," Briar said, her eyes closed as she beamed. She opened the blue one to look at Delilah and said, "I'm so glad you found your curse."

Delilah kissed her forehead, holding her close.

"Me too."

Delilah slept soundly until just past three in the morning, when heaving, pained breathing woke her.

Her eyes peeled open. While it was still dark, there was an

eerie blue light brightening half the room. Briar sat at the edge of the bed on the other side, her back hunched and arms wrapped around herself, fingers digging into her upper arms. The vertebrae of her spine were visible, surfacing and sinking with her labored breathing.

"Briar?" Delilah asked, her mouth cottony with sleep. "You okay?"

"It's happening," Briar rasped, voice thick and gruff as if she'd been screaming. "I'm—I'm having another attack."

"Right now?" Delilah crawled closer to her. "Can I do anything?"

"Listen to me," Briar begged, hunching deeper into herself. Her breath came out in a hiss, lungs tight with pain. "You should go. You don't want to see me like this."

"No, I—" Delilah reached out, touching her bare shoulder. It was sticky with sweat, hot and feverish. Delilah gasped. "Wow, you're burning up. Does this always happen?"

Briar winced at her touch, then swung her head around. Delilah gasped.

Both Briar's eyes burned brightly with blue light, so strong it lit up her ashen, sweat-soaked skin and made shadows dance around the room. For the first time in a while, Delilah was hit with the stench of the twins' curse, so strong her eyes watered and her stomach clenched.

"Delilah," Briar repeated, white fangs shining behind her quivering lips. "Please."

Delilah studied her for a moment. She was shaking, biting back a whimper. She shuddered as feathers pushed through her scalp, slick with blood that ran down the back of her neck and dripped onto the bedspread. Two bumps had appeared above her eyebrows, and the skin began to tear, weeping crimson.

Even with Briar's glowing irises and jagged fangs, what struck Delilah the most was the fear in her eyes.

"It's okay." Delilah stroked Briar's trembling shoulder. She squeezed it gently. "You've always been by yourself when this has happened, right? Let me stay. I don't want you to have to be alone again."

Briar's glowing eyes shone. When she blinked, two fat tears rolled down her cheeks.

Voice shaking, she whispered, "I don't want to scare you away."

"You won't." Delilah reached out to her. "I promise. Maybe— maybe you can squeeze my hand if that'll help?"

Then, ever so quietly, Briar took it and whispered, "Thank you."

Delilah elected to avert her eyes as Briar let the attack take hold of her. Briar cursed faintly under her breath, voice growing more gravelly and less human as the seconds ticked by. Her grip tightened around Delilah's fingers, shaking faintly. Her skin was hot, cooling only when smooth scales emerged from beneath it. Still, Delilah didn't let go of Briar's hand.

She waited until Briar was silent to look back.

Slumped with half her body on the bed was the creature from the woods, lupine snout buried in the sheets while she caught her breath. In the far back of Delilah's mind, she had almost convinced herself that what Briar had said couldn't be true—that the strange in-between stage Delilah had seen was the most monstrous she could be. But to see it this close, to smell the rot on her skin and the stink of blood in the air, was nearly enough to churn Delilah's stomach. Her heartbeat quickened.

When Briar opened her eyes, though, the twist in Delilah's guts loosened.

Even with the horns, the midnight-black scales running up her arms and legs, and the wicked talons decorating each of her digits, her eyes were the same. One blue, one brown, still human where they shone in the faint moonlight. Still shining with that same fear.

I'll always be the monster that pretends to be Briar, because now you know what I really am, she thought.

No. That wasn't true.

As carefully as she could, Delilah reached out and cupped Briar's hollow cheek. The bone was sharp underneath her papery skin. Slowly, Delilah ran her fingers down Briar's jaw, then she leaned forward and pressed a kiss to Briar's sweaty forehead between the twisting bones that made up her horns.

"You okay?"

Faintly, Briar nodded.

"Good." Delilah hesitated for a moment as the increasingly skeletal image of Kieran flashed through her mind. "Do you . . . think Kieran's okay? Should I go check on him?"

Briar's eyes went to her bedroom door, and her pointed ears drooped. Delilah hadn't realized they moved—there was something strangely cute about it. Still, Briar didn't move from Delilah's side, glancing back at her with shining eyes.

"Or . . . I could stay here and check on him a bit later?"

Briar nodded, and Delilah decided Kieran could wait for at least a little while. Delilah flopped back against the pillows and, after a moment, Briar slowly curled up beside her, careful to avoid jabbing Delilah with her horns. Delilah wrapped an arm around her, and for a moment, she swore she could smell the faintest aroma of jasmine beneath the stink of the curse.

"Thank you. For trusting me."

And while Briar couldn't say anything in return, the feeling of her muscles finally relaxing against Delilah's touch was more than enough.

CHAPTER TWENTY-FOUR

Rule #26: Take time to appreciate the scenery.

The next morning, Delilah awoke with her arms around Briar, who'd returned to her normal self sometime in the night. While she'd fully intended to check up on Kieran last night, she'd fallen asleep before she could. The familiar sound of the engine thrummed through the air, and it occurred to Delilah that they must have taken off again. For a second, her brain struggled to fit the pieces together as the night came back to her—the hot spring, Klaus's confession, her curse, kissing Briar, the attack—

It was enough that she almost wanted to close her eyes and get some extra sleep to make up for it. Before she could, though, the rumble of her stomach let her know she should probably get breakfast.

As gently as she could, Delilah unwound herself from Briar, who let out a soft sigh in her sleep. Delilah imagined that last night's attack took a lot out of her. Witnessing it had only proved Delilah's suspicion that Briar suffered through them just as much as—if not more than—Kieran did.

I'll let her sleep, Delilah decided. *She probably needs it.*

Delilah resolved to bring Briar breakfast if she wasn't up in an hour or so, then slid out of the bed and tiptoed across the floor to go back to her own room and put on real clothes.

Once she was dressed, she made her way downstairs. Ariel and Adelaide were at the table, set with a spread of delicious-looking food, chatting while Santiago sipped his coffee. It was still such a nice surprise to hear Adelaide's voice, especially when she sounded so excited as she regaled Ariel with tales of how terrible it was to work for the Pelumbras year after year.

"Oh good, at least one of you decided to wake up," Santiago said as Delilah came to take the seat beside him. "The food was getting cold."

"Long night," Delilah offered.

"Trouble sleeping?" Adelaide asked.

Delilah pursed her lips. "Something like that."

"Doesn't explain why the twins are taking so long. Do you think Kieran is finally sick of my cooking?" Santiago asked. He scooped scrambled eggs onto his plate, adding hot sauce from a bottle he kept in his pocket. From what Delilah had seen, he had an extremely impressive collection of hot sauces. "No. Impossible. I'm far too talented for that."

Footsteps creaked on the stairs, and the next moment Kieran appeared. Instantly, Delilah froze.

He was even paler than usual, his hair entirely lifeless, the shadows under his eyes dark. His cheeks were shallow, sunken, as if the bones of his skull were visible. His blue eye had barely any light at all, and when he found everyone looking at him, he forced a smile, chapped lips cracking as he did.

He shuffled to a chair and slowly sat down, leaning heavily on the table.

"Before you say anything, I know." He slapped a pancake down onto the plate in front of him, then let out a weak cough into his elbow, wincing. "If everyone could refrain from pointing out anything negative about my appearance, that would be great. Because if you do, I'll cry."

"You want more sugar cubes for your coffee?" Santiago offered.

Kieran nodded. "Yes, please."

Santiago got up to grab more sugar while Delilah scooted her chair over to wrap her arms around Kieran. Guilt tangled her stomach in knots—she knew she should have checked on him last night. He leaned into her, forehead in her shoulder, moaning.

"Dying is terrible," he muttered, voice trembling.

"I know," Delilah said, rubbing her hand in a circle around his back. "I know. I'm so sorry, Kier."

"I just . . ." His breath was shaking. On the verge of tears, he pulled back to look at her. "Before I left home, I had no idea what was out here. I wasted my entire life trapped on the estate. It's not fair I only got to be happy at the very end."

"Kieran," Delilah whispered, eyes softening.

"Kid," Ariel said, pointing their fork at him, "you'd best not talk like that. Not when we're here, all right? We gave up everything to come with you."

"Ariel is right," Santiago said, setting a plate of sugar cubes down in front of Kieran. "We're not giving up on you. So you can't give up on yourself."

"I don't want to give up," Kieran said, shaking his head. He closed his eyes, tears slipping down his cheeks. "I really, really don't. But I don't know how many more attacks I'll be able to make it through."

Everyone went quiet.

Then the stairs above them creaked.

Yawning and rubbing the back of her neck, Briar came around the corner. She wore crisp blue pants and a black shirt with blue-and-white flowers tucked into the waist. Her usual muddy boots were replaced with saddle shoes that looked as though they'd never been worn. It was the first time Delilah had seen her in an outfit where every part was form-fitting. Her heart skipped a beat.

"Well," Santiago said, holding his hand out to Briar. "Look at this. She cleans up nice."

Briar frowned. "I'm going to change."

"No!" Delilah snapped. Everyone looked at her, and she blushed. "You look . . . really nice."

"You do," Kieran agreed. Briar's face blanched when she saw him, and he instantly grimaced. "Well, a lot nicer than me, obviously."

She didn't move, her eyes only growing wider and shimmering.

"I'm okay," he promised, putting on a smile. "I just need to shower. A-and finish breakfast. I'll be okay."

"I'm sorry," Briar said, shaking her head. She pointed her gaze to the stairs. "I'm so sorry. I—I'll eat in my room. I shouldn't've—"

Delilah hopped up from her chair, going to Briar's side and catching her wrist before she could flee the scene. Briar looked askance at her.

"Hey," Delilah said, meeting her eyes. "Slow down. You didn't do anything on purpose. It's okay. No one blames you."

"She's right," Kieran said. "And it'll make me feel worse if you run away."

"Plenty of food to go around," Santiago added, gesturing to his spread.

"You know it hurts Santi's feelings when people don't compliment his cooking to his face," Ariel added.

"We miss you when you don't join us," Adelaide agreed.

Briar's eyes flitted between everyone at the table. Her arm was tense in Delilah's grasp.

"Come on," Delilah said.

Briar shot her a questioning look before finally mumbling something like a yes. Delilah grinned and pulled her over to the chair beside hers.

"Thank you," Delilah whispered as they sat down.

Briar swallowed thickly. "Only for you."

And even as anxiety over Kieran's condition burned in the back of Delilah's mind, her heart fluttered.

That afternoon, Delilah went out onto the deck and rested her arms on the edge, looking down at the tree-covered hills below. Ariel had the ship flying as fast as it could, and they expected they'd make it to the base of the Slicetooth Mountains by tomorrow night. Delilah bent down and put her chin on her hands, taking a long breath.

"Hi."

Delilah's gaze rose to find Kieran coming to stand beside her, staring wistfully out at the pines and the distant snowcapped mountains. His shoulder-length curls were lank, cheeks pallid. As he leaned against the railing, Delilah couldn't help but notice he seemed to be catching his breath. His slim fingers drummed against the railing, bony and pale. She did her best not to stare.

"Hey. I'm just taking in the scenery," Delilah explained, turning her gaze back to the tree line. "Trying to . . . clear my head. Been thinking a little too much for my own good."

"About what?" Kieran's face screwed up in a frown. "Oh, goodness, I hope it's not me."

"For your information, it's you *and* Briar."

"Right. I suppose that makes sense." Kieran cleared his throat. "I, ah, couldn't help but overhear some . . . *words* last night."

Delilah's gaze snapped to meet his. Had he overheard their conversation before the attack overtook Briar? Could he have figured out her secret? If he had, did that mean—?

But before her thoughts could spiral further, he added, "I hope the two of you worked out whatever you were apologizing for. Maybe I misheard, but I could have sworn I heard Briar say you kissed her."

Delilah blinked. *He must have heard us when we were talking in the hallway.*

"I guess that would be something of a surprise, considering . . .

everything." Delilah tucked her hair behind her ear, failing to contain a little smile.

His eyebrows shot up. "Wait, so—you did? Kiss her, I mean?"

Until that moment, Delilah hadn't thought about how she'd feel telling others about her and Briar's relationship. She'd spent too much of her life feeling that she had to hide her attractions, lest she be pitied for her curse. To admit she'd let her feelings get the best of her would have made a younger version of her cringe.

Now, though, she attempted her best casual shrug. "Might have managed it once or twice."

"Seriously?" The disbelief in his voice made it sound less like a question than a lighthearted accusation.

Delilah nodded. "To make a long story short, it turns out my curse only makes it so *men* can't fall in love with me. And Briar figured that out sooner than I did."

Kieran's eyes widened. "So she finally admitted she's in love with you?"

Delilah froze, blinking. "Did she tell you that?"

"You're kidding, right?" Kieran snickered. He failed to hide his smile as he palmed his cheek. "She didn't have to say anything. We've all been thinking it."

"We?" Delilah repeated in horror.

Kieran snorted a laugh. "Delilah, come on. Briar hasn't taken her eyes off you since the day you met. And when you're not around, you're all she talks about. Santiago and Ariel have had a bet going about how long it would take you to notice. Ash and I almost started one too, but he insisted it wasn't our business, even if it was obvious."

"Are you serious?" Delilah blinked, putting her hands on her hips while she gawked at him. "You people are terrible."

Kieran shrugged. "In our defense, we're rooting for you."

"Rooting for who?"

The two turned to find Briar behind them, hands tucked in her pockets while she cocked an accusatory eyebrow. The faint way she wrinkled her nose almost made Delilah laugh—she had a habit of looking much more serious than she was.

Kieran, however, didn't hesitate. "You and Delilah. Since I hear you two finally figured out how kissing works. I guess those smutty novels finally came in handy."

"*Rich* coming from you," Briar snapped back.

"I kissed Ash before you kissed Delilah."

Briar scoffed. "I kissed Delilah before you even *met* Ash."

"What? When?"

"In the kitchen before we landed in Gellingham. You interrupted us."

"No way." Kieran shot Delilah a look. "Is that true?"

Before the dumbstruck Delilah could offer a response, footsteps approached. "Hey! Here you all are," came Ariel's voice. They, along with Santiago and Adelaide, joined Delilah and the twins at the railing, while Briar and Kieran turned a near-identical shade of pink. The sight was nearly enough to make Delilah burst out laughing.

"We were looking for you," Adelaide explained, gently folding her hands in front of her. Her white-blond hair was swept back into a bun at the nape of her neck, and the sun hit her face in such a way that it warmed both her gaze and her grin.

"I expected that you'd be stress-baking by now, Delilah," Santiago ribbed.

Delilah shrugged. "There's still time."

Ariel, meanwhile, just laughed. They pulled a small cloth packet from their pocket, wrapped in twine. "Well, anyway, I'm glad we found you three. I was in the control room and kept thinking how beautiful the scenery is up here, and I figured I might . . . let some of Rory's ashes go."

"The north is lovely," Kieran agreed. "Properly picturesque for that."

Briar stepped back. "I can, um—go—"

"Nah—come on." Ariel slung an arm around Briar's shoulders. "I want you *all* here."

She tensed for a second before steadying herself. "Oh. Ah . . . all right, then."

Ariel removed their arm. They wet the tip of their finger against their lips and held it up to test the direction of the wind. Then they unfolded the cloth and tossed a plume of ash into the air. The wind whipped it up so it spun before it dissipated, fading into the sky.

Santiago and Delilah each wrapped an arm around Ariel as they tucked the cloth back in their pocket.

"You know," Ariel said, "as much as it pains me that we're going *back* to the Pelumbra estate, I'm glad it's with all of you."

"Thank you for all your help," Kieran said, leaning gently against Delilah while his eyes followed the path that Rory's ashes had made in the wind. "I never would have made it this far without the five of you. I'd probably still be trapped in my room at the estate waiting for the inevitable."

Briar offered her brother a soft look. "Maybe it isn't so inevitable." She gently reached over and threaded her fingers through Delilah's and squeezed.

Delilah's heart fluttered. *Maybe,* she thought, *just maybe, Briar was right.*

The six of them stood in silence, watching the clouds coast by.

CHAPTER TWENTY-FIVE

Rule #11: Know when to play the part and when to throw away the script.

That evening, as the sun was beginning to set, Ariel landed the ship in a clearing half a mile from the Pelumbra estate. They'd elected to avoid the main line of air traffic, all heading toward the estate—Kieran explained that the ships filling the skies would mostly belong to other Pelumbras returning home and to upper-crust families on their way to mingle with Celdwyn's most influential family. Instead, Ariel had decided to circle in, hoping to avoid anyone who might recognize the stolen ship.

The ship came to a halt in a tiny meadow beside a mountain lake that was completely invisible from the air. If Ariel hadn't known the area so well, they'd never have found it. Once the ship was quiet, the engine cooling and the wings stationary, Delilah headed to the gangway door.

Kieran was already waiting, leaning against the wall for support with his arms crossed. He wore a silver tie to match the blue-and-white color scheme of his suit. His curls were tucked in a bun at the back of his head, the short parts wrangled into place with bobby pins. Delilah had lent him some of her makeup to add a bit more color to his cheeks and conceal the shadows under his eyes, and it had worked wonders. The silver mask he wore, decorated with swirling, vinelike designs, helped as well.

His eyes rose to meet her, and he smiled. "Hey—I like the dress. I'm glad there was something in the back of Briar's closet that fit you."

Delilah scoffed, smoothing down the flowing emerald-green skirt. The dress was floor length, with a sweetheart neckline and gossamer sleeves that hung past her hands and ended at a point like the curved petal of a calla lily. Her hair was done up in a bun with one curl hanging on each side of her face, framing the golden vulpine mask she wore.

"I'm just lucky you decided to grab one of every size in formal wear before you met her. Otherwise, I'd be shit out of luck."

Behind her, someone inhaled a sharp breath.

Delilah turned to find Briar staring at her, wide-eyed, from the bottom of the stairs. Her suit was inky black, the shirt underneath crimson. The top three buttons of the shirt were undone, revealing the curve of her throat and a sliver of her collarbone. She wore a black mask with catlike eye holes and a pointed nose.

The sight of her made Delilah's pulse thrum and her skin warm. "You okay?" Delilah asked.

Briar seemed to snap out of whatever trance she was in, clearing her throat and blushing under her mask. "I, um—yeah. Obviously. You just . . . look . . . nice."

While Delilah's expression melted into a soft smile, Kieran

whispered, "That might be the highest compliment she's ever given."

Delilah told her, "You look nice too."

Briar's face went even redder. "Ah, come on."

Before Delilah could try to drive her point home, however, Ariel's voice called out, "Look at you all! Cleaned up so nicely and everything."

They emerged from the cockpit beaming, Santiago and Adelaide on their heels. While Ariel and Santiago had on their usual clothes, Adelaide wore a simple powder-blue gown with an elegant high neckline and ruffled sleeves. She held a white mask in her hand, smiling gently at the three of them.

"You're not coming?" Kieran asked Ariel and Santiago.

Ariel shook their head, scoffing. "Hell, no."

"What they mean to say," Santiago quickly corrected, "is that someone needs to stay behind to make sure the ship is ready to go if anything happens. Ariel and I aren't too keen to risk being spotted by our former employer—to whom, by the way, this ship actually belongs—so . . . we're happy to stick around here."

"I'll be joining you, though," Adelaide said. She swept to Kieran's side and offered her arm, which he took. "I can show you to the wing where the curse is kept. Hopefully sneaking away will be simple with all the hubbub of the ball."

"And we trust Adelaide to keep an eye on you," Santiago added. "In case anything goes wrong, that is. She's a witch with over two hundred years of experience, after all."

Adelaide chuckled. "You flatter me."

Delilah cocked an accusatory eyebrow. "You know, it almost sounds as if you're worried about us, Santi."

He scoffed. "Well, maybe a bit. Despite my best efforts, you've all grown on me. Like a particularly precocious fungus."

"Aw," Delilah managed.

"He does care," Kieran echoed, chuckling.

"That goes for you too," Ariel said, pointing a finger specifically at Briar. "Don't think your antisocial little games have worked on us. We still want you back in one piece."

Briar coughed out a note of surprise, then cleared her throat, averting her eyes. "Oh, um. Thanks?" She shook her head. "Look, this touchy-feely shit isn't really my style. Can we just get this over with?"

Delilah offered Ariel a smile. "I think that's code for *The feeling is mutual.*"

Looping her arm through Briar's, she added, "We're off, then. See you all on the other side."

With that, Delilah, the twins, and Adelaide headed for the gangway.

Under the cover of the falling darkness, the four were able to make their way through the woods and arrive at the entryway to the Pelumbra estate without any fuss. The estate was sprawling—more like a compound, with multiple houses built within the same fenced perimeter. Connecting them were paths lined with lampposts, which were lit with unnatural magic that cast a pale silver glow across the cobblestones. Groups of witches in masks and finery chatted and laughed as Delilah and the others wandered up the path to a building that towered over the others.

Surrounded by trees, it was a castle-like mansion with multiple turrets and windows lit with pale golden light. A long driveway looped around the front, where candy-colored cars idled while more witches stepped out of them. Most wore the latest fashions, but a few seemed to wear more traditional robes.

Kieran pointed toward the mansion. "That's where we're headed."

Adelaide added, "We should be able to slip into the private wing through the back of the ballroom. But we'll need to keep up appearances until we can get inside. Try to keep your heads down."

Delilah swallowed a lump of trepidation in her throat. The four barely seemed to breathe as they closed the distance to the mansion. The cold mountain air bit at their exposed skin, even though the sun had been warm in the afternoon. Even in summer, the cold sank its claws deep into the jagged mountains.

It was easy enough for them to slip inside with the crowd—they were well-enough dressed to blend in but not so flashy that they stood out. As they stepped through the massive double doors, a foyer opened into a high-ceilinged room. More guests passed their coats and bags to servers who looked a lot closer to Delilah and the others in age than anyone else there. The walls were decorated in yellow-and-white fleur-de-lis wallpaper and portraits of people in old witch's robes. Delilah smelled a blend of what had to be at least fifty types of magic. She'd never been in a room with so many other spellcasters before.

"This way," Adelaide said. "Come on."

She brought them down a hallway to the edge of a mezzanine.

There they found the ballroom. Its soaring ceiling gave way to a huge space full of tables covered in pale-pink linens and topped with extravagant bouquets of multicolored roses. At the center of the room was a champagne tower made of crystal cups precariously placed. The walls were mostly windows, looking out at a huge garden full of topiaries that stretched back into the woods. Glowing enchanted orbs hung over the paths outside, brightening the way in pastel-pink light.

Just as they went to the stairs to descend, a butler cleared his throat and stepped into their path.

"Pardon me," he said in a creaky voice. "Might I ask your names? I want to make sure you're seated at the correct table."

Just as their eyes widened, a familiar voice behind them said, "They're with me."

Delilah spun to find a towering figure standing behind her, dressed in a fine eggplant-colored suit with a black mask over his eyes. Even with it, though, his nose—Delilah's nose, in fact—was unmistakable.

"Klaus?" Delilah whispered.

He shot her a winning smile and, to the butler, said, "I can show them to the Hammond table."

The butler studied them for another moment. Meanwhile, Kieran looked about ready to hyperventilate at the cursebreaker's sudden appearance. Briar shot Delilah a look while Adelaide studied Klaus with her lips pressed together.

"Ah, of course. Thank you, Mr. Hammond." The butler stepped aside, holding his arm out toward the stairs. "Go right ahead."

"Come on," Klaus said, nodding to Delilah and the others. "Follow me."

❧

"What in the world are *you* doing here?"

Try as she might, Delilah couldn't keep the annoyed edge out of her voice. Mostly because she hadn't forgiven Klaus for his poor attempt at an apology back at the hot spring, but also because this was the most anxious she'd been since she'd left Kitfield.

"I always attend the Pelumbras' balls," he replied as he settled into his seat. A different member of the staff had led Delilah, Klaus, Adelaide, Kieran, and Briar to a table near the edge of the room, which was empty aside from a single name plate with Klaus's name on it. "Well, not always. I haven't exactly gotten along with the Pelumbras in the past. But something told me that you'd be here, so I figured it might be nice to accept their invitation this time around."

"I thought I made my feelings very clear at the hot spring."

"You did," Klaus said. He unrolled the napkin beside his plate before setting it in his lap. "Which is the other reason I'm here. I gave it some thought, and it occurred to me that perhaps I didn't come at apologizing from the right angle."

Delilah scoffed. "You think?"

"I understand why you might be angry," Klaus said, "but all I want is to prove to you that I am sorry—"

"Bullshit."

"Keep your voices down," Adelaide cut in. Her eyes shifted

from Klaus to Delilah. "The last thing we need is to attract attention."

Delilah and her father both quieted, Delilah glaring at him as if he were a stain on her blouse.

Not long after, the waitstaff brought out the first course. To the Pelumbras' credit, the food was amazing: flaky golden crust over bite-size pieces of beef and roasted sweet potatoes in a buttery sauce, followed by salmon dripping in a sweet and tangy reduction. All the while, waitstaff brought around refills of champagne, which Delilah turned down each time. She needed to be on her toes.

Klaus, however, was quick to excuse himself in an attempt to get whiskey.

When he was gone, Adelaide leaned in and gestured for Delilah and the twins to do the same. "Once the dancing starts, we should have enough cover to sneak through that door over there," she said, gesturing to a white door with a gold handle near the one that appeared to lead to the kitchen. "It'll be locked, but I still have my key from when I was a maid here. It lets me through every door."

Kieran's eyebrows shot up. "They gave you a master key?"

Adelaide scoffed. "Well, when you need someone to clean the rooms that contain all your dirty secrets, giving it to the silent maid is really the only thing that makes sense."

As Kieran started to reply, Delilah noticed that Briar had gone pale, her uncovered eye staring pointedly at the table nearest them. Delilah followed the girl's gaze to a couple who appeared to be her mother's age. The wife had long red hair streaked with gray, while the husband had curly blond hair cropped near his ears. Half the woman's face was covered by a white mask, and she appeared to be skinny to the point of gauntness. Her fingers shook slightly as she reached for her glass of red wine. Her husband was broad-shouldered and slim, his brow furrowed behind his golden mask as he cut into a thick piece of beef.

Delilah shot Briar a questioning look.

Briar gulped. "Those are my parents."

"Oh." Delilah inhaled sharply. "Shit."

"I'm not sure they'd be able to recognize me even without the mask on," Briar breathed. "The last time my father visited Wrenlin was . . . three years ago? And my mother probably hasn't seen me since the day I was born."

"Hey." Delilah reached across the table and gently placed her hand over Briar's, meeting her visible eye. "They don't matter, okay? Family isn't family if they don't even have the decency to treat you like a human being. Those are just two people who happened to bring you into this world. Sometimes it starts and stops with that."

Briar blinked. She slowly pulled her gaze from them, shifting to meet Delilah's. She paused for a moment, words seeming to hang on her lips. But just as she was about to say them, she closed her eyes and nodded softly. "Yeah. You're right."

It wasn't long before Klaus returned with his drink. The waitstaff brought out a small dessert of creamy chocolate and raspberry gelato, and soon after, the music's tempo began to pick up. A few couples rose from their tables and took to the dance floor. They were doing a slow waltz, and based on their impeccable timing,

Delilah assumed the musicians had to be playing a song like the one at the Moondew Coven's market.

"Come on," Adelaide said. She pointed to the floor as more and more people left their tables. "Let's join them. They'll turn down the lights soon, but we need to blend in until then."

Adelaide held a hand out to Kieran, who paused for a moment before taking it. She nodded for Briar and Delilah to do the same. Briar's shoulders tensed for a moment as she cast another look toward her parents' table.

"It's okay," Delilah said. "We'll avoid them."

Briar rose and slipped her hand into Delilah's. Just as they moved to follow Adelaide's lead, Klaus cut in.

"Delilah," he started. "Wait, please. Can I speak to you for a moment?"

"Now really isn't a good time," she snapped back.

"It'll only take a moment—"

"First you have to prove to me you mean it," Delilah growled. She tightened her hand around Briar's. "Maybe then I'll consider talking to you. But until then, I'm a little busy trying to save my friends."

She led Briar to the floor, leaving her father alone at his table.

"You okay?" Briar asked.

Delilah nodded. "I will be."

The moment they'd gotten to the dance floor, Delilah and Briar's feet had instantly slipped into a natural rhythm, Delilah stepping back while Briar stepped forward, and they glided around an arc in time with the other dancers. It had taken a song or two for Briar to loosen up, but now she moved with ease.

Delilah straightened as the song changed to something slower. She pulled Briar closer as a few of the people around them changed partners, casually tapping each other on the shoulder and stepping in.

Still, it was a bit of a surprise when someone appeared behind Briar and tapped her on the shoulder.

"May I cut in?" a familiar voice asked.

Both girls glanced up to find a boy with rich, dark skin and thick black curls. His mask was navy blue, with a long pointed nose and intricate swirling details painted on in silver. The smell of his magic—applewood smoke—was unmistakable.

"Ash?" Delilah asked quietly. "What are you doing here?"

Before he could answer, the lights around them dimmed to darkness, the orbs that had been bobbing in the air all slowly floating to the staircase. A couple stood at the midway point, suddenly lit up by the soft golden light. It was Briar and Kieran's parents, standing a healthy distance away from each other. Their father's eyes glowed gold as he pressed his fingers to his throat, casting a spell to amplify his voice.

"Welcome, my friends, to our estate," he said. "I'm William Pelumbra, the current head of the Pelumbra family. I want to extend a welcome to all of you here—some of the most powerful and influential witches in Celdwyn—for a night of feasting and revelry. The Pelumbras have long been called one of the most fortunate families in Celdwyn, and tonight we celebrate the continued success of our family and our associates."

"Parasites," Ash snarled under his breath.

"Please let our staff know if there's anything they can do to ensure the best night possible," William continued, gesturing to a line of waitstaff at the edge of the room, most holding plates of finger food or drinks. "Remember, no request is too large on Pelumbra grounds. Now enjoy your evening, and long live the Pelumbras!"

The crowd echoed his final words and burst into applause while Ash's jaw tightened to the point that Delilah feared his teeth might shatter.

While the dimmed lights slowly floated back out onto the dance floor, the crowd resumed their dancing. Their expressions were bright as the music shifted to something more upbeat, featuring a violin and a piano. Ash, meanwhile, was trying to steady himself, shoulders nearly shaking with rage.

"I came looking for Kieran," he finally managed, swallowing down the terseness in his demeanor. "I had a feeling you all would be here. I . . . need to speak to him. Ever since he told me how he felt back in Gellingham, I—I've needed to say it back. In person. I can't let him disappear into the ether without his knowing I feel the same."

"That's, uh, nice and all, but how did you even manage to find us in here?" Briar muttered.

Ash gestured to Delilah. "There aren't many six-foot-tall girls with curly hair wandering around the Pelumbra estate."

Delilah flushed. "Fair enough, I suppose. But Ash, this isn't exactly the best timing. Maybe it can wait until—"

Ash, however, seemed to have tuned her out as his eyes fell on a head of blond hair a few feet away. He instantly began to push through the crowd, eyes bright.

"Shit," Briar cursed.

Delilah and Briar followed behind him, Delilah trying to get his attention again, but it was no use. Wading through the crowd, the three of them found Adelaide and Kieran standing near the edge of the dance floor. Both stared wide-eyed as another blond boy—maybe a few years younger than Kieran—clapped a hand on his shoulder. He had rosy cheeks and a gangly frame that indicated he'd likely just had a growth spurt.

"Your parents made it seem like you wouldn't be here!" the boy said brightly. "I'm so glad you made it! I've missed having you around the estate—it's been so boring since you left."

"Kieran?" Ash interrupted.

Kieran turned to look at him, his face draining of color. "Ash? I-is that you? What are you doing here?"

"Looking for you. I need to tell you—"

"Oh, hello!" the lanky boy said, holding out a hand to Ash. "I don't think I've met you before. I'm Wickton Pelumbra, Kieran's cousin."

Beside Delilah, Briar whispered, "Oh, fuck."

The light in Ash's eyes instantly winked out, and he went stock-still. "Cousin?"

"Don't see the resemblance?" Wickton threw an arm around Kieran's shoulders, pulling him into a side hug and grinning toothily. "Our dads are siblings. If it weren't for the fact that mine's younger, he'd probably be the head of the family. But William's all right too, I guess."

Ash's eyes bored into Kieran's. "Your father . . . is William Pelumbra?"

Delilah, under her breath, whispered, *"No."*

"Um—" Kieran went even redder. "I—well—technically, I'm—ah . . ."

Ash stepped away from him, eyebrows furrowed as he shook his head. "You lied to me. You—you *used* me."

"No, Ash, it's not like that!" Kieran said, taking a few steps to follow him. "Truly, I didn't mean to hurt you. I just wanted to be someone else. Someone worthy of a life where the ultimate victory wasn't dying to keep the Pelumbras afloat. A person worthy of being with someone like you."

Ash's face heated as his frown etched deeper into his face. "Don't say that."

Kieran started, "Ash—"

"I should have known you were too good to be true," Ash muttered. He shook his head, breaths shaky. "I was completely honest with you. I *trusted* you."

"I was honest about—" Kieran cut off, averting his gaze. "I was honest about how I felt about you."

"Great. Well. I suppose at least there's that." Ash turned his gaze sharply to the floor. He spat, "You're just as bad as the rest of your awful family, you lying, manipulative bastard. Screw you, Kieran."

All around them, couples paused in their dancing, eyes falling on the little group. Wickton looked positively gobsmacked, while Kieran's eyes shone with tears. Murmurs of his name began to float through the space; people turned to look at each other, wrinkling their foreheads. Delilah, Briar, and Adelaide glanced around in horror.

Adelaide grabbed each of the twins' wrists. "We're getting out of here."

Before either of them could say anything, an explosive *crash* echoed through the space.

Everyone in the ballroom whipped around as the glasses stacked into a champagne tower at the center of the room rained down to the floor, sparkling wine splashing in all directions as the glasses exploded into shards. Guests screamed and jumped out of the way until the final glass had toppled, revealing a man standing behind the table.

Klaus held up his hands. "Goodness, I guess that's why they told us not to touch!"

He shot Delilah a quick wink.

"Let's go," Delilah urged Adelaide and the twins. "Now!"

With that, they spun, fleeing through the gaping crowd.

CHAPTER TWENTY-SIX

Rule #1: Love conquers all.

Escaping from the ballroom floor was a blur, and Delilah could barely wrap her head around it as Adelaide waved them through the door into the locked wing of the mansion.

"We're not going to have much time," Adelaide said. "As much as Klaus's distraction helped, it won't be long before Pelumbra security comes after us."

"What can we do?" Delilah asked, breathless. Beside her, Briar was looking over her shoulder at the door while her brother blanched, not daring to speak a word.

Adelaide reached into her dress pockets and withdrew a few bracelets woven out of golden thread. She passed one to each of them, explaining, "I wove these before we left. They should silence your steps and blur you from the view of anyone pursuing us. Follow my lead, and we might be able to make it before guards are swarming this place."

Delilah slipped the bracelet around her wrist and watched as the hue of her skin faded to match her surroundings, like a chameleon against a tree branch. When she glanced at Briar, she discovered that the bracelet had done the same for her—she wasn't completely invisible, but it would require a double take to pinpoint her.

Adelaide gestured down the hall. "This way."

They followed her in tense silence. The hallway was much darker than the rest of the mansion had been so far, with dusty stone floors and walls covered in fading crimson wallpaper that looked to be at least triple Delilah's age. The smell of must and aged paper hung in the air, adding a heaviness to it. The only light came from flickering bulbs on the walls, barely half of which appeared to be working.

They rounded a corner just as the sound of a door bursting open exploded through the air. Adelaide hurriedly waved them into a dark closet and shut the door behind them. They hid in the shadowed enclave, Delilah with her back against the wall and Briar against her chest.

Carefully, Adelaide opened the door a crack as the sound of footsteps stormed past them, flashes of people in uniform appearing in the visible sliver of space. Delilah's heart hammered in her ears, and she tried her best to hold her breath.

"Check all the doors," a familiar husky voice said. Delilah's arm hair stood on end at the sound of it, sweat pricking on her brow.

Regen Pelumbra.

He added, "They're crafty, and Briar specifically is a danger to anyone who gets close. Watch out for her."

Delilah wasn't positive, but it looked as if Briar smiled at that.

"When I say so," Adelaide whispered, pointing at the door, "cut left and run. Then we'll—"

Just then, the door flew open.

The four of them went as still as corpses. Standing on the other side was a man in black, an emblem of a two-headed raptor sewn onto his breast pocket. He had a sharp jaw and seemed to be grinding his teeth.

Delilah's breath caught.

He stepped back, eyes going back to the hallway. "Clear!"

Stepping away, he left the door ajar, and as the sound of his boots faded down the hall, the four of them exhaled the breaths they'd been holding.

"You," Briar told Adelaide, gently rubbing the woven bracelet, "are a very impressive witch."

"Give it two hundred years—you may beat me yet." Adelaide straightened. "The curse is kept down this way. Stay quiet."

The guards appeared to have mostly dispersed. As the four picked their way down another musty hallway, the only one they ran into was too busy examining a side room full of books to notice them creeping by. Briar stuck close to Delilah while Kieran trailed a bit behind. As they kept going, Delilah couldn't help but notice his pace slowing, his breath growing faster and more ragged as he tried to keep up.

"Slow down," Delilah whispered to Adelaide. "Kieran—"

"I'm fine," he choked, face slick with sweat. With the low light, it was impossible to pinpoint, but his eyes seemed to glint with unshed tears. He wheezed, knees looking on the verge of giving out. "I can do this. I can."

Delilah and Briar exchanged a look. After a quick nod, they went to either side of him, letting his arms drape over their shoulders.

"Lean on us," Delilah told him. "We'll get there together."

After a second, Kieran nodded gratefully, then relaxed some of his weight against each of them.

As quickly as they could, the girls kept pace with Adelaide until they reached a large wooden door that stood at the base of a spiral staircase. What little light there had been in the previous hallway had mostly faded out, making it almost impossible to see.

Adelaide fished her key out of her pocket, jammed it in the lock, and twisted.

"It's in here," she explained. She glanced over her shoulder at them. "Ready?"

The trio nodded and together said, "Ready."

Adelaide shouldered the door open, revealing a darkened basement space. When she flipped on the lights, Delilah discovered that the floor was made of stone, as were the walls. There were no windows, meaning the only light came from a few ancient sconces that flickered as if they might go out at any moment. Sturdy stone support columns rose from the floor to the ceiling. Otherwise, the space was completely empty.

Adelaide pointed to a pillar in the center of the room. "There. It's on that pillar."

The four approached it gingerly. The air felt stagnant, as if no one had entered the room in decades. The closer they got, the more apparent the carving on the pillar became.

"It's here," Briar breathed. "I . . . almost can't believe it."

Delilah came to a stop in front of it, squinting softly. The words were written in an ancient curling font, making it almost inscrutable.

"'Only when the curse-bound Pelumbra is seen for what they are,'" Delilah read, doing her best to make out the text as it wrapped around the pillar. She squinted. "Sorry, it's kind of hard to parse. There's a letter here that almost looks like an L, and then . . . ah . . . 'in spite of it will the twin blessing and curse dissolve together.' In spite of what?"

"That's no business of yours, Miss Bea."

Delilah spun around with a gasp. Standing in the doorway they'd come through was the man in the golden mask, his blond curls shining in the light. He'd removed his mask, revealing a face that shared a few features with his children.

William Pelumbra.

"Father," Kieran breathed.

William stepped inside, and only then did Delilah realize he was flanked on either side by more familiar faces. On his left was Kieran and Briar's mother, her skin as white as chalk, while on his right was Regen, stern-faced and glaring.

And behind them, a group of black-clad guards.

"I need you to step away from the pillar," William said. His voice was thunderous and baritone—much deeper than his son's. He didn't need an amplifying spell to make Delilah tense at its volume. "We can do this peacefully."

"Do what?" Delilah retorted. "Prepare for the death of your children? What kind of parent would condemn their kids to that fate?"

William's lip twitched. "You must be Klaus's daughter. Explains his stunt back in the ballroom."

The woman beside William cleared her throat. "You know, Delilah, we've always had a cordial relationship with your family. No need to jeopardize that now. Why don't you let us care for our children and you can return to your father? No harm done."

"Is that a threat, Camille?" Adelaide snapped. She took a protective step between the twins and their parents. "Because I'm not going to let you lay a finger on them."

Both parents gasped.

"You can *speak*?" Camille squeaked.

"Indeed." Adelaide's eyes flashed red-orange as magic began to spark at her fingertips. "And the moment I leave this place, I'm going to tell the world all the terrible things this family has done."

"Don't be too hasty, Adelaide," Regen taunted with a smirk. He gestured behind him. "We have something you all might be interested in."

With a nod, a couple guards stepped forward, shoving two figures ahead of them. Delilah gasped as their faces hit the sconce light, skin bruised and hair mussed.

Ariel and Santiago.

"It's pretty easy to spot that ship you stole if you're looking for it," Regen said to Kieran. "We've known you were here from the moment you stepped inside."

"Then why let us get this far?" Delilah shot back.

"Because we needed a place away from prying eyes to do this," William said. He gestured to Ariel and Santiago, who appeared to only be half conscious. "Let me offer you a deal. Adelaide,

Delilah—we'll let you walk out of here unscathed with these two. You just need to leave our children to us."

Briar's visible eye widened, landing on Delilah in terror. For a sinking second, Delilah realized what she was thinking.

That Delilah was going to abandon her.

"Like hell," Delilah spat.

Regen's lip twitched. "But you don't even know the alternative yet. If you don't surrender the twins to us, your friends die."

The guards holding Ariel and Santiago withdrew knives from their pockets and held them up to their throats.

"And then," Regen added, "we kill you."

"These are *children*," Adelaide snarled, gesturing to them. "You'd allow your own son and daughter to suffer *and* murder their friend?"

"She knows too much," Camille muttered quietly.

"You're really willing to risk your life for twins who are doomed to die?" William asked Delilah. To her surprise, he seemed . . . sincere. As if he truly couldn't believe what he was hearing.

"Of course I am," Delilah said, fingers clenching into fists. "Because I'm not a monster."

"That's a shame," William said. He nodded to his guards. "Restrain them."

The crowd of guards surged forward like a dark sea around the Pelumbra adults. The smell of magic immediately overwhelmed Delilah's senses. Guards' eyes glowed, some stepping into ledrith poses.

Delilah glanced at the twins.

Not today.

In a flash, she slid into the ledrith pose Briar had taught her, a bolt of green light shooting from her palm and manifesting into a thorned vine that whipped around a guard's throat. She pivoted, firing another at the guard behind him.

At her side, Adelaide's eyes burned red. Her fingers moved as if she was weaving the air, and Delilah realized that a sparkling gold thread appeared wherever they moved. Adelaide slung a braided spike of it at another guard, and it shifted into a lightning bolt in midair. It struck the guard in the chest, sending her to the ground in convulsions.

Delilah slid fluidly from move to move, shocks of magic slicing through the air. One hit a guard in the eyes, instantly blinding him, while another punched into a different guard's head and sent him sprawling on the ground, unconscious.

Regen shoved the guard holding Ariel out of his way, eyes bright yellow-green. Delilah had to leap out of the way as he stamped a foot against the stone floor and a wave of quaking magic shot through it toward her. She barely had time to dodge before he shot off another and another, making her duck and jump in some kind of twisted dance meant to keep her moving until she dropped dead.

In her desperate attempts to escape Regen, she nearly missed as a guard came at her from the side. He reached for her, fingers clawing. Delilah's hand shot up and wrapped around his wrist, sending an electric current up his arm until he screamed and stumbled back, hitting the ground with a heavy thump.

Another guard grabbed for her hair, snagging a handful of curls. Delilah yelped. Her hand waved wildly, searching for her attacker's skin to try to jolt him with magic.

Just then, a poison barb at the tip of a feathered tail stabbed into the guard's neck. He stiffened before falling to the floor, blood leaking from the puncture wound as the poison instantly paralyzed him.

Briar stood over where Delilah had fallen, teeth sharpened into fangs. "Don't touch her!"

A couple of guards tripped backward in horror at the sight of her. Her fingernails had lengthened to claws, midnight-blue scales lining her forearms. She hissed between her fangs, blue tongue flicking out as her glowing eyes burned. The light of them caught on tufts of bloody feathers that had begun to push free from her scalp.

"*Briar?*" Kieran cried, his eyes round. He turned to Delilah, asking, "What is happening? Is that a spell?"

"Long story," Delilah mouthed back.

Stepping from between the retreating guards, Camille Pelumbra met her daughter's eyes, a silver blade in her hand. "I should have tucked a dagger between your ribs the moment you were born," she snarled.

While Delilah's incandescent rage made the attack sloppy, she hurled a powerful strike in Camille's direction, a roar escaping her lips. Thick vines wrapped around the woman's throat so tightly her eyes began to pop out as they choked her. Blood ran from each puncture mark on her throat, creating a gruesome collar that dripped down into the neckline of her dress.

"Do not," Delilah growled, "*ever* speak to her like that again."

Briar's expression softened, and her cheeks warmed.

The scent of burning hair plus a cacophony of screams made Delilah and Briar spin. In front of the pillar, blocking Kieran from harm, was Adelaide. A woven pair of gloves burned up her forearms, the skin barely even flushed from the heat. She hurled fireballs at another advancing guard, then one at Regen as he struggled to reach her.

"Can you imagine what two hundred years of rage feels like?" she roared in William's direction, the tips of her hair beginning to lift of their own volition. "Because you're about to find out."

But before she could hurl another fireball, a pained whimper behind her made everyone freeze.

Kieran's knees buckled as his eye began to glow ghostly blue. Adelaide barely had time to catch him before he fell.

"Kieran!" Delilah cried.

Just then, Briar hit the floor with a wince. The hiss of agonized breath through her teeth sucked all the sound out of the room. Her body trembled, every muscle tensed. Her blue eye was brighter than Delilah had ever seen it, wisps of blue light leaking out and illuminating her cheeks. She muffled a groan as her finger scratched at the floor, claws lengthening. There was a sickening, wet crunch as something in her spine snapped. She wailed, voice choked by tears.

"They're having an attack," William breathed. To the guards, he shouted, "Get back into the hall! Don't get close to Briar, or that creature will rip your throat out."

Kieran's skin was an oxygen-starved shade of bluish pale, Adelaide the only thing keeping him standing. His lips were chapped, cracking, and wet with blood. His breath sounded rheumy and ragged, like something was leaking into his lungs, drowning him from the inside. Briefly, his eyes met Delilah's before they rolled back into his head, leaving nothing but the bloodshot whites visible.

He slumped, and Adelaide had to guide him to the floor before he slid out of her grasp. He gagged and choked as he clawed at his throat. Foamy red spittle leaked from the corner of his mouth, dribbling down his neck.

"No!" Delilah cried, starting to run to him.

Adelaide, however, held up a hand to stop her.

"Delilah," she said, meeting the other witch's eyes. "Listen to me. We're out of time."

"No!" Delilah cried. She pointed to the pillar. "W-we have to destroy that! We have to—"

Adelaide's searing gaze burned into hers, drawing her attention back. "Delilah, listen to me. There might still be a way to save them. I need you to tell Briar how you feel about her, as honestly as you can. Don't leave anything out."

Eyes shining, Delilah argued, "Kieran's *dying*, Adelaide! There's no time—"

"Please, Delilah." Adelaide's eyes welled with tears. "Just try. For them."

Delilah's astonishment lasted only a moment as Briar let out a pained cry, the guards shrinking back in horror before turning to flee. In the firelight, Delilah saw more oily black feathers push free from Briar's head, slick with blood.

Delilah sprinted to her side, landing in a crouch in front of her. Briar gasped for breath, her skin practically boiling as it scrunched and pulled into new positions. Her chest heaved, her ribs looking too large for her body, like a cage expanding from the inside.

Delilah had to force herself not to look away, no matter how desperately she wished she could block out the image of Briar's body being torn apart and reshaped into something new.

"I'm sorry," Briar choked, tears streaking down her cheeks as her teeth lengthened into jagged spikes. "You have to get out of here before I . . . I . . ."

"Briar," Delilah said, tears filling her eyes. She shook her head as they streamed down her cheeks. "Stay with me, okay? Just for a while longer."

Briar winced as a bone in her face snapped, pushing her nose out farther. Still, she held Delilah's gaze.

"I can't lose you," Delilah sobbed, fingers tightening around Briar's face. Tears blurred her vision, her heart galloping through her ears as she shook her head. "Please don't leave me."

"I don't want to," Briar said, tears streaming down her face. "I'm sorry. I'm sorry."

Delilah choked on a sob. She ran a hand back across Briar's face, over the feathers on her shoulders. Her skin was feverishly hot and sticky with sweat, pulled taut over bones that didn't quite fit. The shape of her went blurry through the tears in Delilah's eyes, and it was all she could do not to grab her as tightly as she could, as if that would stop Briar as she knew her from slipping through her fingers.

Briar, who had made her feel like no one else ever had. Who she'd spend the rest of her life with if she could, in their little cabin in the woods. Who haunted every one of Delilah's dreams, asleep and awake, always filling her chest with warmth the moment she stepped through the door. Who made her laugh and cry in equal measure, who was always so genuinely herself without any hesitation or care for what others thought. Who Delilah would give anything to keep.

Shaking, Delilah pressed her forehead against Briar's, pulling her closer. "I won't let you go," Delilah told her. "I can't. Because I love you, Briar."

She leaned forward, closed her eyes, and kissed her.

For a moment, the world around them ground to a halt. Delilah held Briar close, her feathers brushing Delilah's cheeks. Then, behind her closed eyes, Delilah saw light. When they opened, she expected to see fire raining down on them.

Instead, Briar's skin glowed silver.

She held up a hand and watched as the claws sank back into her skin. Her eyes widened as the tiny shoots of light brightened every inch of her, shining like a beacon. Her horns melted into a shower of pale sparks, as did the feathers poking through her skin. The spikes along her back vanished like dust.

Just then, the ground beneath them began to shake. Delilah barely had time to brace herself as she realized where the tremor was coming from: the curse-carved pillar in the center of the room. Massive cracks shot up the stone. Adelaide had to grab on to Kieran's unconscious body as pieces began to fall, barely able to get him out of the way before the entire thing crumbled.

As the dust cleared, Briar let out a choked breath and something rose from her lips. Whatever it was, it looked . . . alive. It was black on the outside but glowing from within, a strange, oily mote that hung weightlessly, like a soap bubble. It floated between Briar and Delilah's faces, the familiar smell of undergrowth and rot coming off it. It rose into the air, and the girls followed it up as beams of light broke through.

The next moment, it exploded into starlight.

Briar blinked as the light in her skin faded. Her previously brown eye had become blue, matching the other with its soft glow. Her small smile grew until it was an ear-to-ear grin, tears streaming down her cheeks.

"No way," Delilah whispered.

"Of course," Briar said, breathless. "'When the curse-bound Pelumbra is seen for what they are and *loved* in spite of it will the twin blessing and curse dissolve together.'" She gazed into Delilah's eyes. "You did it."

Delilah sputtered a laughing sob. "I did it."

Briar tackled her in a hug, knocking Delilah back onto the stone floor. She kissed her fiercely, arms tight around her. Delilah reached up, cupping her face, happy tears streaming down Briar's cheeks and into Delilah's palm. Delilah wrapped her arms tightly around Briar, pulling away to bury her face in the space between her neck and shoulder.

Suddenly, a shrill voice drew them back to reality.

"You *horrid* little creature!"

Delilah and Briar glanced up to find Camille glaring at them a few feet away, her red-painted lips pulled back to reveal pearly white teeth. She stood over Kieran's collapsed form, tears streaming from her eyes.

That was the moment Delilah realized he still wasn't moving.

"Look what you've done!" Camille screamed. She knelt down and put a hand on Kieran's cheek, mascara-stained tears dripping from her chin onto his shirt collar. Her body shook with a sob as she clutched at his curls. "You've killed my son! My only son!"

"Kieran?" Delilah leapt to her feet, taking a few steps toward him. The joy that had been burning so brightly in her chest was instantly replaced with creeping, icy dread. The cold grabbed her tighter and tighter as her eyes flicked from Kieran's still chest to his lifeless pallor. Tears welled in her eyes. "No. No, no, no—he can't be gone. We broke the curse, w-we—"

Just then, a sharp gasp rattled Kieran's chest, and his eyelids fluttered.

He flew up into a sitting position, nearly knocking into his mother's chin. He began to cough violently, shoulders shaking. After a moment of gasping, he spat out a blackish lump that landed on the stone floor in front of him.

After a second, it dissolved into silver light.

Delilah watched in awe as color returned to his skin, washing away the dark circles under his eyes—both of which were a warm shade of brown. His hair lost its lankness, turning from dishwater blond to vibrant gold like his father's. His cheeks and bony limbs began to fill out. He reached up and wiped his mouth, where a smear of blood and saliva had leaked down his cheek, before turning his gaze on his mother once more.

He growled, voice stronger than Delilah had ever heard it, "Get away from me."

Camille skittered back, eyes round.

"Kieran!" Delilah and Briar both cried at once.

He smiled at them, and for once, it didn't seem to pain him to do so.

"Kier?" Camille asked, eyes pleading. Her body trembled. "Oh no, my sweet boy, don't you see? Th-this isn't right. You, your sister—your curse was your duty to the family."

He shook his head. "I left that family." He gestured to Delilah and the others. "And I have a new one. One that cares *who* I am, not whether or not I 'get' to die to keep other people happy."

"You're a Pelumbra," William spat, coming to stand beside his wife. He placed a meaty hand on her shoulder. "Whether you like it or not."

"You're right," Kieran said. "But I'm my own person. I can acknowledge where I came from without being defined by it."

"Oh, *quiet,* you," William snarled. His hands worked in and out of fists as he let his gaze move between his twins. Delilah smelled his magic, acrid and sharp, beginning to perfume the air. "You never did know when to stop waxing poetic and just *shut up.*"

William's eyes fell on Delilah, and his lips pulled back from his teeth.

"And *you*. You did this." His hand rose, golden magic sparking off his fingers. He jabbed one in Delilah's direction, eyes burning with fury. "You poisoned my children's minds against their own family. Who do you think you are, upending *centuries* of blood, sweat, and tears that his family has sacrificed? I'll cleave your head from that pretty little neck!"

Delilah threw her hands up, but before William could attack, a bright burst of light blinded everyone in the room. Camille let out another shrill scream.

When Delilah's vision blinked back into focus, her father stood in the doorway, his hair mussed and his eggplant suit rumpled. His nose was bent at an awkward angle, and a trickle of blood leaked from it.

"Let's not get carried away there, Willy."

"Klaus," William growled. "I thought I had security handle you."

Klaus gestured to his bleeding nose. "Indeed, which is why I intend to send the medical bill for this directly to your accountant. Tell me, William, how will it look when I tell the press that you injured me and threatened to kill my daughter? I can't imagine that the Pelumbra reputation will remain intact."

"No one cares what happens to your bastard child. You certainly haven't cared until now," William spat. "Anyway, who would believe you over me?"

At that moment, Adelaide stepped between the twins and their parents, flames leaping from her fingers. "You're putting a lot of stock in your reputation, William. Especially when it was built on a blessing that no longer exists."

"She is correct," another voice chimed in. "Your gift is gone, no?"

Santiago staggered to his feet where the guards had dropped him before they fled down the hall. He ran his hands through his hair, slicking it back so a cut on his forehead smeared. He cleared his throat, then spit a spatter of blood and saliva onto the floor.

"You're not even a witch anymore," William snarled. "What can you do to me?"

Without another moment's hesitation, Santiago threw a left hook into his chin. William stumbled back, cursing, while Santiago rubbed his knuckles. Camille backed away, hands over her mouth.

"I don't need magic to make you pay for what you've done," Santiago warned. "Now you're going to let us go, or you're not going to leave this place with your face in the same arrangement."

"Well done, Santi," Ariel groaned from the ground, offering a weak thumbs-up. "Give me five minutes and I'll plant one on the other side of his face."

William set his jaw. He glanced around the room, seeming to mentally count the number of people who stood against him and Ariel. Guards lay scattered across the floor, knocked out or moaning, while the rest had fled. Near William's feet, Regen lay paralyzed, his eyes darting back and forth wildly as his shoulder twitched slightly.

"You're outnumbered, my friend," Klaus warned.

After a long, pregnant pause, William finally spoke. "Fine," he said. "Get *out*. All of you. And never come back."

"You"—Camille wept, eyes once again pinned to Delilah and Briar—"are wicked."

"Runs in the family," Briar shot back.

"Come on," Delilah said to her companions, tightening her hand on Briar's. "Let's go home."

EPILOGUE

The sleepy town of Kitfield was the perfect reprieve after an adventure.

Delilah Bea's adventure, specifically.

The day she came home from her Calling, her mother and all the villagers met her in the town square. She'd arrived on the path from the nearby airfield, as many travelers did, only to find herself engulfed in hugs by a crowd of people who'd raised her. They all demanded to know how she'd broken the Pelumbra curse, asking what clever scheme she'd used. They only went quiet when Briar caught up to her and Delilah took her hand.

"Everyone," Delilah announced, gesturing to the other girl, "allow me to introduce Briar Pelumbra." She tried and failed to contain the besotted grin that had begun to creep across her face. "I'm quite in love with her, if I may say so myself."

Briar rolled her eyes. "You're such a sap." Then, quieter: "Feeling's mutual."

"But how—?" someone started to ask.

"Give them space," Charlotte said, stepping in beside her

daughter. "Delilah's barely been back a minute. I'm sure she'll tell us the whole story over a pint at the pub. In the meantime, we're going home so I can have a proper chat with Briar. It's not every day my daughter brings home a new member of the family."

At the sound of that, Briar's expression warmed.

Later, they'd say the party that ensued lasted days. Delilah and Briar managed to outdrink every man in town as the raspberry ale flowed and they recounted their love story. After the first day, she brought her crewmates and reintroduced her family and friends to Kieran. When Charlotte raised an eyebrow at him, Delilah quickly interjected that he wasn't a terrible person, despite hijacking her Calling. She also introduced Kitfield to Ariel and Santiago, who suddenly seemed much closer than they'd ever been before, and finally, to Adelaide, who greeted them all with warmth and joy. The first three nights at the Landsmeet were considered some of the wildest the pub had ever seen. Delilah swung the Pelumbra twins around the dance floor while Santiago taught Ariel how to foxtrot.

The only night that rivaled it was when a mysterious stranger crashed the party, taking down his hood to reveal none other than Ashmont Bartelle.

Kieran choked on a sip of pinot noir. "Ash?"

Delilah looked up from an arm-wrestling match Briar had goaded her into. Ash stood at the pub's threshold, looking out of sorts.

"Is this an assassination plot?" Briar asked.

Ash came to stand by their table. He asked Kieran, "Can I . . . talk to you?"

"What are you doing here?" Kieran asked.

Ash swallowed a lump in his throat. "I asked all over the north to see if anyone knew where you were going. Klaus told me you were heading this direction. I just . . . want to talk."

Kieran furrowed his brows. "I thought we were done."

"Well, I—I did some thinking," Ash said, rubbing the back of his neck. He swallowed, glancing at Delilah, and explained: "I realize now that I was so caught up in my own revenge plot that when I found out who you were, I didn't see you as the Kieran I knew. I couldn't think past it, even though I should have known you weren't lying to hurt me."

"I understand why you were angry," Kieran offered. "It was wrong of me to lie to you. Especially for so long."

"I get why you did, though. I was so . . . vengeful." Ash took a breath. "But my sister wouldn't want that for me. She gave her life trying to save your family members. I . . . I shouldn't blame you for that."

"Well, the blessing is destroyed," Kieran offered. "The Pelumbras are just a normal family now."

"And their business ventures are all starting to collapse," Briar pointed out. "Turns out that without supernatural luck to keep them going, the shoddy decisions they made don't exactly hold up to scrutiny. Not to mention Klaus Hammond's publicly admonishing them. They're under investigation by at least ten different organizations now."

"I don't care about the Pelumbras anymore," Ash said. He reached out and touched Kieran's cheek. "I care about *you*. And I hope you can forgive me for what I said."

Kieran's eyes shone. "Do you forgive me for lying?"

"Isn't that obvious?" Ash asked. "Yes."

Kieran managed a small laugh. He stood and said, "Then yes. I forgive you."

"I want to do better for you," Ash explained. He slipped his hand into Kieran's. "And I was hoping you'd take me back."

Kieran grinned, and the next moment, he pulled Ash against him and kissed him. Briar gagged and looked the other way while Delilah rolled her eyes, biting back a smile.

From the dance floor, Ariel shouted, "Get it, Kieran!"

Kieran turned pink in the cheeks and flipped them off.

They all spent the rest of the evening sitting around the table, catching each other up on their adventures. When the night ended, Ash went back with Kieran, Ariel, Santiago, and Adelaide to the ship, while Delilah and Briar went to Charlotte's cottage. Charlotte made them drink a gallon of water each before they passed out in a heap on Delilah's bed.

For the next few days, Delilah took Briar and the others to all the places she loved most, from the beach at the edge of town to the Sunflower Bakery on Wisteria Street, where they tried the lemon bars. Santiago liked them. Briar complained they were too sour, but Delilah argued she just had bad taste.

On the sixth night of their stay, Kieran, Ash, Ariel, Adelaide, and Santiago headed out for Gellingham. Delilah had promised they'd be in touch, though she was unsure when she'd follow them.

What she did know, though, is that she *would* follow them back to the city. She'd spent the nights since she'd been back planning it out: the apartment she wanted to rent, the car she was going to save up for. Gellingham drew her back for more than one reason: not only did she still need to pick up her official witch's license from the Council there, but she also intended to open her own cursebreaking business.

As she and Briar watched their friends board the ship, Briar turned to her and said, "Any chance you might be free this evening?"

Delilah cocked an eyebrow. "I could certainly be persuaded. Why?"

"Would you still go with me if I said it was a surprise?"

"I might be able to pencil it in." Delilah beamed. "Lead the way."

Before long, Briar had led Delilah to the edge of town, where the forest met Silverside Lake. The moon hung heavy in the sky, and the placid water was a mirror image of the cloudless night. Delilah and Briar took a seat beneath a massive willow tree, peering up through the branches as the stars began to poke through the twilight, shining brightly.

After sitting in comfortable silence for a bit, Briar said, "I spent a while talking to your mom this morning." She reached out, wrapping an arm around Delilah and leaning her head against her shoulder. "She told me these willows are kind of rare. Only grow in this specific region."

"Is that your surprise?" Delilah chuckled. "Tree facts?"

Briar scoffed. "No, obviously. Now, *as I was saying,* these aren't regular willows. Do you know what they're called?"

Delilah shook her head.

"Silverwood trees," Briar explained. "They used to grow all over Celdwyn, but because their wood is an unusually great magic conductor, only a few are left."

"Silverwood," Delilah repeated, the word rolling over her tongue. She wrinkled her brow. "Why does that sound familiar?"

Briar reached into her pocket and withdrew a piece of parchment. Delilah recognized it immediately.

It was the written form of her curse.

"I stole this from your bag this morning after your mom told me that," Briar explained, passing it back to her. "As soon as she said it, I realized there might be a way for me to repay you for breaking my curse."

Briar knelt in front of Delilah. Delilah's eyebrows rose, and she leaned back on her hands, elbows locked and chin tilted up. Briar smirked, then held up her hands, eyes pointed toward the curtain-like branches of the willow.

As the scent of Briar's magic—sweet and rich like jasmine—perfumed the cool night air, tiny motes of blue light rose from her fingers like bubbles. They glided into the willow branches and stuck to the leaves like string lights. Delilah laughed with delight as the glow grew brighter, illuminating the entire meadow in soft blue.

Briar slowly dropped her hands, meeting Delilah's gaze. Then she stood, offering Delilah a hand to help her up.

Delilah took it. Briar pulled her up, clasping her warm palm with both hands. Briar took a deep breath, as if trying to steady herself.

"What is this?" Delilah asked.

" 'For never again will a man's heart beat for she,' " Briar recited, " 'Unless love is proclaimed in truth beneath the silverwood tree.' "

Delilah's heart did a somersault.

"I-I've never been the best with words," Briar said, blue eyes shining in the magic light. Her smile grew as she said it, cheeks round and full and pink. "But when I'm with you, it's like all the anger I felt for so long is just . . . gone. You make me feel weightless. I wish I could go back in time and tell that little girl in Gabriel's Edge that the hell I went through with my family and my curse are worth it, because they brought me to you."

Delilah's breath caught in her throat, and tears welled in her eyes.

"I love you, Delilah Bea," Briar said, a small laugh tingeing her words. "And more than that, you've made me love being alive for the first time in seventeen years. I can't even begin to describe how much that means to me after everything I've been through. So I'll just have to say it again and again and again for the rest of my life so it's never, ever forgotten: *I love you.* And that's the truth."

The moment the words left Briar's lips, a strange sensation came over Delilah, warming every inch of her until—she realized with a start—her skin had begun to glow ever so faintly. Light leaked out from her pores, and suddenly she was overwhelmed with the smell she'd recognized on her mother for so long: the musty old-paper scent of their curse. A breath escaped her lips, hanging in the space in front of her like an exhalation in winter.

But this—it was dark, alive, twisting. It shone gold for a moment as Delilah reached out for it, the light dappled across her palm. It burst the next moment, showering cool sparks across her skin.

When she inhaled again, it was as if a weight she'd never

noticed before had been removed from her chest, and fresh air rushed in unfettered.

Tears dripped from Delilah's eyes as the last of the light escaped her skin. She turned her hands over in front of her, shaking, and coughed out a hysterical laugh. "You . . . you broke my curse."

She threw her arms around Briar and hugged her like she'd never let go. Briar buried her face in Delilah's shoulder, smiling so wide it had to make her cheeks ache. Delilah kissed her, holding her so tightly it nearly cracked her back. She cupped her face in her hands, pressing her forehead to Briar's, laughing and crying all at once.

Briar shrugged, fighting back her smile. "Eh, well, y'know. I figured I owed you one."

"You are *insufferable*," Delilah laughed. Suddenly, a realization hit her, and she gasped. "Wait—we have to go find my mom and tell her! Come on."

Delilah grabbed Briar's hand and took off in a sprint toward her mother's cottage. Briar yelped as she stumbled to try to catch up, sputtering a laugh. Behind her, the magic motes peeled off the tree branches, following after Briar like fireflies. They lit the way as the girls ran through the long grass, the breeze ruffling their hair and clothes.

When the cottage came into view, Charlotte was standing outside, her cheeks streaked with drying tears. At the sight of her daughter bounding in her direction, she broke into a grin. She balled up the skirt of her long dress in her fists and ran to meet the girls halfway.

"Mom!" Delilah called. "Mom, Briar broke our—!"

Charlotte threw her arms around Delilah, cutting her off with the force of her hug. Immediately, she broke down in sobs, her shoulders shaking.

"It's over," Charlotte said, arms tight around her daughter's rib cage. Her voice was muffled from where she'd buried her face in Delilah's collar. "We're free, baby. We're finally *free.*"

For a long minute, the Bea women simply held each other and cried. Briar glanced away, as if considering leaving them for some privacy. Charlotte quickly let go of Delilah with one arm and swooped Briar in with it. Briar yelped, tense for a moment before she relaxed into the group hug.

"Thank you," Charlotte told her. "Oh, Briar, *thank you.*"

Briar blushed, shrugging. "Anytime."

"Let's go in," Delilah said, pulling away and beaming. "I think this celebration calls for one of my chocolate-raspberry tortes, don't you think?"

With a grin and a nod, the three women went inside, hands clasped together. For the rest of the night, music floated from the open windows as they danced around the kitchen. Delilah dabbed chocolate on Briar's nose, and Briar filched raspberries behind Delilah's back. The scents of sugar, chocolate, and magic painted the night air, joining the pale motes that had stuck themselves to the cottage wall's creeping ivy.

Their celebration crept into the wee hours of the morning, until the rosy blush of dawn lit up the sky—the first sunrise to mark the start of the rest of their lives.

Free, together.

Kieran Pelumbra's spellbinding adventures are just beginning. Don't miss . . .

Extraordinary Quests for Amateur Witches

Coming Fall 2025!

ACKNOWLEDGMENTS

To say that great tragedy produces great art is perhaps something of an overstatement, but the sentiment, I think, holds true for this book. During the lockdown of 2020, I started writing this book purely for myself. I had no plan—just a vague idea of a sapphic romance where a young witch pursues her dreams of practicing magic and falls in love with a monster girl. What it wound up becoming, though, was my comfort project. Even when the world felt like a hopeless place, I had this story to fall back on. There was something incredibly healing about telling a love story featuring characters who have experienced trauma but are still able to love and be loved in the fairy-tale way they deserve. It gave me a lot of hope in those dark days, and I hope it does the same for all of the readers who've picked this up and decided to give it a try. Thank you, truly, for your support. 🩶

All of that in mind, I have so many people to thank for making this book of my heart a reality. First, my incredible, talented, showstopping agent: Erica Bauman—thank you for rolling with me over these last five years and three books. Publishing can feel like a battle sometimes, and I'm so lucky to have you fighting by my side. Also, you get pretty much all my dumb pop culture references, and that in and of itself deserves a round of applause.

To my editor, Hannah Hill: from the moment we had that first

Zoom call about this project, I knew you were the ideal person to help me shape it into what it is now. Your insight and enthusiasm have vastly improved not only this story but my writing, too. I am so grateful you decided to take a chance on my queer fairy tale and help it blossom into something I'm truly proud of.

And, to the rest of the team at Delacorte Press: I am blown away by your support and hard work on this book. Special shout-out to the folks involved with the cover design: art director Liz Dresner, designer Ray Shappell, and jacket artist Dani Pendergast. Getting those first color sketches made me cry happy tears in a Trader Joe's, much to the horror of everyone else in the cheese section—I couldn't have asked for better people to bring Briar and Delilah to life.

Next, to my critique partners, Alex and Ally, for your continued friendship and feedback three books in. Thank you for always rising to the challenge and helping me be the best writer I can.

I would be remiss not to mention the booksellers, librarians, teachers, reviewers, and other members of the book community who help put my stories in readers' hands. A special shout-out to librarians in particular—this book was inspired by my time in libraries, and I know firsthand how hard it can be to be a librarian, especially with the pandemic, book banning, and widespread boycotts against LGBTQ+ programming. Keep on fighting the good fight—the world is made a better place by your hard work.

To both my found and biological families: your love, support, and excitement are the best part of my life. Be it in Boston, Salt Lake, Los Angeles, Portland, or New York, I know I always have my people behind me. Specifically, thank you to my dad, who is an infinitely better father than anyone in this book, and to my mom for inspiring the one and only Charlotte Bea. And my cat, Squid, who I immortalized in the form of Cinnabar (as he deserves).

Finally, to Forrest and Jesaia, to whom this book is dedicated: thanks for playing along with all my deranged pretend games when we were kids. Thank god I learned to channel that energy into books so I don't have to chase Forrest around with a trowel for entertainment anymore. Anyway, thanks for letting me be your spare sibling—I love you both, forever and always.

ABOUT THE AUTHOR

KAYLA COTTINGHAM (they/she) is a *New York Times* bestselling author of queer speculative fiction, including *My Dearest Darkest,* *This Delicious Death,* and *Practical Rules for Cursed Witches.* Originally from Salt Lake City, Kayla now lives in Boston, where they love hiking in the woods, playing RPGs, and snuggling on the couch with their ridiculously large black cat/familiar, Squid.

kaylacottingham.com